My good friend
Mike
Hope you enjoy
William Simon
God Bless America

Three Sixty Five

William Simon

ISBN: 1456310119
ISBN-13: 9781456310110

This Novel is dedicated to my wife and best friend Joyce, my son Scott, my daughters Denise and Elizabeth, to Lulu my dog and to everyone who made the sacrifice to protect our country, and promote freedom around the world by serving in our Armed Forces. Special thanks to Bob Lund who appears on the cover of this novel.

INTRODUCTION

In November of 1965 I enlisted in the Army. After two months of basic training at Fort Knox Kentucky and another two months of training at Fort Dix New Jersey, I received orders to report to an Artillery unit near Pleiku in the Republic of South Vietnam. I was barely eighteen.

A Chicago south-sider, the second eldest of six kids, I was naïve, and had no experience with life's challenges, wonders or tragedies. I'd never been out of the city, never seen mountains, oceans, or any of the wonders nature had to offer. I'd never been to a wedding, been in love or known a woman. Never done or experienced even simple things like sleeping in a motel or eating at a fancy restaurant. A fancy restaurant to us was eating at White Castle. Most of all, I'd never seen death; all this would change.

This novel is fictional, the stories, incidents and characters in the stories are based on my personal experiences and the experiences related to me by other Vietnam Vets. It is a story of men, young men, and what men will do to retain sanity when everything around them borders on absurdity.

All Vets are changed forever.

Chapter One

"Loss of Innocence"

Friday May 3rd 1966. "As of oh-nine-hundred today, Pleiku has been removed from the 'Off Limits' roster," Captain Solomon pauses, looks across the faces of the men assembled in front of him, then continues, "Your Platoon Sergeants have permission to issue passes to anyone not on the duty roster," again he pauses, wondering if turning these men loose on the unsuspecting city of Pleiku will end up turning more of the citizens into Viet Cong.

"Many areas of the city remain posted as 'Off Limits' to American personnel and under no circumstances is anyone to violate those restrictions." Solomon tilts his head so First Sergeant Neuman can whisper something in his ear.

"Anyone who misses the truck *back* to the hill is going to be in a world of shit. The QC will arrest anybody found in the city after 2200 hours." QC are Vietnamese military police. They've replaced civilian law enforcement and they have the reputation of being corrupt and brutal.

"...and remember, VD is not to be taken lightly. Use your head and use a damn rubber." Solomon scans the faces of the men assembled in front of him, scowling as he does, then abruptly says, "*Dismissed!*" He turns and disappears through the door of the orderly room.

An almost child-like giddy excitement filters through the assembly. Fishe is near ecstatic when he says, "Simon, you know what this means, don't ya?"

"Yeah, whoever keeps their nose buried up Sergeant Bennett's ass is going to get a pass every week."

"*Pinetti!*" Everyone chimes in perfect harmony.

"No, baby, that's not what it means, it means we'll be gettin' some Pooh-say!" Fishe immediately starts doing the Motown Cool-Jerk dance routine he does in moments of elation.

"Yeah, baby, we'll be gettin' some of that slant-eyed poontang."

Saturday morning I exchange all my MPC - military pay currency - for Piasters fully expecting to spend every dime of it on alcohol and sex. Back in the hooch Jim Fishe is strapping his forty-five to his leg. We're not supposed to carry weapons into town, but watching him go through the machinations of concealing the weapon, I decide it isn't such a bad idea.

"Damn it, I should have gotten a side arm when I had the chance." I remove my bayonet and scabbard from my harness thinking I may be over reacting, but damned if I'm gonna get caught naked with nothing to put in my hand but my dick. I reach around and slip it under my belt, then tuck my shirt in over it. An hour later we're in the back of a deuce-and-a-half heading for Pleiku.

"Baby, I'm getting' laid at least four times!" Smitty is in one of his nervous states of excitement. He's bouncing around the back of the deuce-and-a-half like a Mexican jumping bean.

Coleman smiles, shakes his head a little and says, "Yeah, but you best be wearin' a swimmin' suit, baby, 'cause they got types of clap over here nobody's ever heard of, which is why I ain't never dipped the wick without one."

"Man, when'd you ever have the chance to get laid?" I ask, wondering how Coleman has had enough time or opportunity to climb between the legs of anything that isn't inanimate or dead. He's been hopping back and forth between fire bases ever since he's been in country.

"I had me one sweet little French half-breed on the road to Kontum at a gook car-wash." Coleman has his hand rubbing the side of his face mentally visualizing the experience.

"Carwash! What the hell are you talkin' about?"

"Yeah, man, they had a hooch set up on the side of the road near a little creek. They'd wash your Jeep for two bucks. While they washed the Jeep, the Mama-San had a couple of girls inside to take care of cleaning your pipes."

"More, more, tell me more?" Smitty asks nervously.

"Well, I hit the government house outside of Pleiku two times on supply runs. Least those broads are checked by medics once a week."

"Maybe we should just go there." Turner suggests.

Coleman says, "Yeah, that's where I'm going. At least there you feel a little more secure, there are always a couple hundred GIs hangin' around."

I don't have to think very long, "Hell, then I'm goin' too." It's decided, everyone is going, everyone but Farmly.

Farmly, with an indignant look of disdain, asks, "Doesn't anyone want to check out the town? Hell, not everyone wants to hump some twelve-year-old Vietnamese girl."

I wouldn't mind checking the town, intrigued with the prospect of looking around a foreign city, but since the only sex I'd ever had was with *Rosie Palm,* the prospect of getting laid preempts all other curiosities.

Coleman seals the deal when he adds, "By hitting the government house first you won't be as likely to screw some whore in an alley and get your throat cut."

At that, an icy chill courses through everyone's veins. All eyes fix on Coleman, everyone with the same mental image flashing in their minds. Sheesh, talk about raining on a parade.

The Deuce-and-a-half drops us off in the middle of the downtown business district. The streets are alive with activity. There are GIs all over the place. Small shops and bars line the streets, the bars displaying makeshift signs with very recognizable names, names like, Texas Bar, Chicago Club, and Club Hollywood.

"So how do we get to this snatch factory you been talkin' about?" Fishe asks Coleman.

Coleman points to a scooter like vehicle with a passenger cage on the back known to everyone as a Lambretta. It's the local taxi service. "It'll probably cost us a buck a piece."

Coleman and Varant negotiate our passage with the driver.

"How much you take us to number one whorehouse?" Coleman asks.

The driver, obviously not intimidated by Coleman's six-foot black looming stature looks at us and says, "Two dolla, you, you, you," He points at each one of us in turn.

"No way, man, *one dollar,*" Coleman argues indignantly.

"Two Dolla each," the driver scowls, looking as if we just strangled his little sister.

"Ten dollar you take all of us," Varant has his arm out and circling his hand to indicate he has to take all six of us.

"Okay, ten dolla."

We squeeze into the back. Four of us would have been a tight fit, but we manage.

It's a fifteen-minute ride. Not because it's so far from the city, but because the damned Lambretta is so slow.

The whorehouse resides within a fenced compound with QC and MPs posted at the gate. We pay the driver and make our way up to the main building. It's a long single-story building reminiscent of a cheap motel. Drab and dreary looking from the exterior, it would have been a good set to use as the Bates Motel. The right half of the structure houses a bar; the left half is a series of ten small rooms spaced five or six feet apart. Outside the bar several GIs are in the process of negotiating favors with some girl.

Inside, the bar is packed wall to wall with GIs and forty or fifty girls. It isn't even noon and most of the guys are already shit-faced. The girls are all over the place. We manage to find a table, park our butts and in the short span of five minutes two girls appear and begin marketing their wares. Their initial targets are Varant and Smitty. The girls, dressed in provocative silk dresses slit up the sides, wrap their arms around the necks of their prey, plop down on their laps and begin wriggling. The waitress, an old woman not likely to receive any offers, takes our order for a round of beers.

"You like?" The girl on Varant's lap is busy moving her bottom in a rotating motion presumably to get him aroused.

"Yeah, baby, I like, you chop-chop?"

"No chop-chop, just boom-boom."

"Where girls who chop-chop?" Varant stretches his neck and looks around the bar like he is trying to find the other girls.

"No girl here chop-chop, only boom-boom!" Her disdain is obvious.

I'm mystified. "What the hell is he talkin' about?" I look at Coleman hoping he will decipher the gibberish. I've only been in country a month and am not familiar with all the local colloquialisms.

"Boom-boom is pussy. Chop-chop is a..."

"...Blowjob," I finish the sentence for him.

Smitty is already walking out with one of the girls; Varant follows him ten minutes later.

My eyes wander around the room trying to take in all the activity. The smoke is thick but it doesn't hamper my inspection. There are no officers, only enlisted men, nobody above the rank of Staff Sergeant. The place reminds me more of a barn than a saloon. I inspect each girl not sure whether I'm sizing them up in general or just looking for one that will catch my eye. All of the girls are small, ninety pounds tops, with long jet-black hair, most of them looking more like girls than women. I'd guess their ages at fifteen or sixteen tops, but it's hard to tell. On an average, they're pretty plain looking even with the extraordinarily bad job of make-up application that seems common to all of them. Many have buck-teeth reminiscent of those exaggerated caricatures of the *Evil Japanese* I'd seen in old *Life* magazines. Though, most of them are plain looking, none of them are ugly and a few could almost be considered attractive. A couple of the more attractive ones appear to be half-breeds, part round-eye, part Asian. It's unlikely they have American fathers because we haven't been here that long. So, if I had to guess, it'd be French fathers. Since these are by far the most attractive girls, consequently they are also in the greatest demand and lead some schmo out of the bar about every ten minutes. Though they are the most desirable, I decide to opt for one that isn't getting quite so much action. The thought of following a couple dozen drunken GIs into the saddle is not exactly lighting the fires of eroticism.

Varant and Smitty return in about five minutes. There is no gibing about the obvious shortness of their encounter. We all know we're just as likely to end up doing the same thing. Turner is the next to go. A tiny girl with no noticeable breasts, sits on his lap, doesn't say anything, just starts blowing in his ear and thirty seconds later they get up and leave.

"Lee?" I lean over to get his attention. He seems totally fixated on all the activity.

"Huh, what?"

"We gonna get laid, buddy?"

"No, not me. I've got a fiancée back home and I worry dat I might get some disease. Den dey keep me here till dey cure me."

I look at Lee Lindlay, a big Swede farmer from Minnesota. There's nothing urban about him. I can't say he's simple, he just doesn't clutter up his mind with all the tripe the rest of us allow to complicate our lives. *Is he really planning on staying celibate for a whole entire year?* I, on the other hand, have no qualms about what I'm going to do.

"Shit, man, I've only gotten laid once in my whole life," I lie. "Hell, I might get my ass blown off next week, I'm gonna get all the pussy I can get." By the time I start my second beer everyone is back at the table.

"God damn! Man, that was some good pussy!" Fishe is ecstatic, grinning from ear to ear. "I'm goin' again."

"Me too," Smitty says as he gets out of his chair. He's obviously picked out his next victim and is moving off in her direction.

"What about you two?" Varant asks.

I look at Lee as I respond. "Lee here is thinking about becoming a priest. I on the other hand am going to go screw the hell out of one of these girls."

Two more girls approach the table. One plops on my lap and the other on Lindlay's. Lee puts his arm around her and cracks his huge *Dumb Swede* grin. I'm no better. I try sliding my hand up her thigh and almost make it to home base when she clamps her thighs together. "You no get sample unless you buy."

"Okay, how much?"

"I number one girl, you pay five hundred pee."

"Five Hundred! I thought we pay only two hundred?"

"Two hundred for number ten girl, I number one."

"I give three hundred."

"No way, GI, you pay four hundred."

"Okay, I pay four hundred, but you boom-boom long time."

"Her knees unclamp and my hand makes it to the *Promised Land.* I have a huge boner and know if I keep doing what I'm doing there won't be any need for me to go to a room with her. I get up, guiding her as I rise and she leads me out of the bar. She's wearing a silky sparkling dress cut just above the knees with slits in the side. She is small, less than five feet, with hair that hangs straight down to the middle of her back. The dress is snug and accentuates her bottom making it look bigger than it is. We enter one of the small rooms. The room is about eight-by-nine and a bed takes up most of the space. Being totally unfamiliar with protocol I grab her and try to kiss her, but she pulls away.

"No kiss!"

"What do you mean 'No Kiss'?"

"Kissing only for my number one boy."

Christ, I think, she's saving her kisses for her number one boy but giving her pussy to anyone who'll divvy up four or five bucks. In a way

I'm glad I don't get to kiss her. Who knows what she's had in her mouth over the past few hours?

She kneels down in front of me and undoes my trousers. My fatigue pants fall to the floor and she pulls down my olive drab boxers. I think she is going to give me a blowjob, but she takes my already throbbing penis in her hand and starts moving it around inspecting it. She stretches the skin back and looks all around. *She's checking me for VD sores.*

"You okay. Come, you boom-boom." She pulls her dress up above her hips - I already know she isn't wearing underwear - lays back and pulls her knees up against her shoulders.

I move to the edge of the bed standing with my pants around my ankles and her hand guides me into her...she has little pubic hair. As I enter I have to fight the urge to ejaculate. I don't think I'm going to last more than a few seconds, so, after I am totally embedded, I just stop. I move in and out slowly, pausing frequently to keep from losing it. She must sense what I'm doing because she starts moving her bottom in a small rotating motion.

Damn it, I think. *I'm not gonna last much longer.* I start pumping in a more rapid fashion and she stops the hip movements. I'm trying to keep from blowing prematurely; still, I can feel the volcano getting ready to erupt so I move even faster. Just as I am ready to shoot, I stop and freeze. I grab her hips to keep her from moving.

"You finne," she says and tries to pull away.

"No, no. I no finne!"

"YOU FINNE!"

There's danger of not being able to complete my mission. She presumes when I stopped, it was because I finished.

"No, I no Finne!" I start pumping again all the while she's protesting vehemently.

"You boom-boom two times." She says glaring at me.

"No way." I'm really going now. There is going to be no stopping this time. Four or five more pushes and it's over. I shudder and laugh as I ejaculate.

She pulls away, bitching and moaning in Vietnamese; gets off the bed and goes to a small pan of water in the corner. With her dress still pulled up above her hips, she squats over the pan and splashes water up on her pussy in a half-assed attempt to wash. She makes a quick wipe, rinses out the rag, and comes over to wipe off my best friend.

"You boom-boom two times, you number ten." She's really angry. She's convinced I nailed her twice.

"I only boom-boom once," I reiterate. "Here, I give you seven hundred pee, okay?" I look at her sulking face and hold out the money.

No sense in pissing her off. I don't want her blacklisting me among the other girls.

"Okay." She takes the money and her demeanor changes instantly.

Back in the bar she sits on my lap for a while but leaves when I refuse to buy her Pleiku tea. Pleiku tea is really just colored water, but they charge you two bucks for it. Varant and Fishe are on their third trip. A girl is sitting on Turner's lap and massaging his crotch vigorously. Coleman is standing in the corner negotiating with another girl. Lindlay, God bless him, is still holding out. We hang around another hour then leave and head back to Pleiku. This time we get the Lambretta ride for a buck a piece.

We split up in Pleiku. Turner, Lindlay and I walk around and agree to meet the others at Club Hollywood around five. That leaves us a couple of hours to explore the city. The streets are lined with sidewalk vendors and it becomes instantly clear most of the wares the vendors are selling come from a well-supplied black market pipeline. I can buy Sterno tablets, probably the ones that should have be in our C rations, five for a buck. The street vendors have most everything. Many of the items are clearly marked U.S. Army and I wonder why no one seems to care. I see army issue pocketknives, American cigarettes, American whiskey, C rations and army issue medical supplies. Between all the barkers, the variety of shops, the kids trying to pick your pockets, the bars and the hookers, it'll be a miracle if any of the GIs here make it back to base with any cash at all.

We work our way up and down the streets looking in shops and bartering with street vendors, though we rarely have any intention of buying.

We watch, amazed, as a Vietnamese woman, dressed in the standard black silk pajama pants, white blouse, and coolie hat, stops near the curb, reaches down, pulls up her right pant leg and starts taking a piss right there in front of everybody. She jogs her hip a little to the right and the stream of urine shoots out in that direction. We watch mesmerized by the spectacle.

"Jesus, are you shittin' me?" Turner can't believe the woman is pissing right in the middle of the street in front of hundreds of people.

Being young and of little experience I comment, "Jeez, I didn't think women could piss standing up."

After exploring for another hour or so we decide to stop and eat at a local restaurant. The restaurant is drab and appears to be used more by locals than Americans. We order what we think is beef, but Turner, the prick, tells us half-way through the meal it is probably rat or dog. When Turner drops the bomb about the meat, I immediately feel like retching. Lindley on the other hand is somewhat forlorn and appears to be enjoying it.

"You're not really considering eating that, are you?"

Lindlay looks at me, then hesitantly pushes the plate away. "Sort of reminds me of bear meat."

I know I am going to spend the rest of the night trying to wash the taste out of my mouth. We leave to join up with the others.

The inside of Club Hollywood is packed. Up on the stage, there are three good looking girls dressed in silky tight dresses singing in very bad English; the tables are mostly occupied by GIs trying to live this day as if it were their last. There are at least two girls at every table either sitting in some GIs lap or standing with a GIs arm encircling their waist.

We order beer. It isn't cold, but it isn't warm either, a nice change. We spot Coleman, Jim, Farmly and Varant at a table in the middle of the floor and join them.

"Most of these broads are just here to hustle you," Coleman says.

"Whata'ya mean?" Turner asks.

"They just come around, sit on your lap, rub you here and there and try to get you to buy Pleiku Tea. If you won't buy it they leave. Rarely do you find one that will screw."

"I gotta take a piss." Rising from my chair I look around trying to spot the John.

"Me too." Jim pushes his chair away as he gets up to follow me.

We work our way through the crowd to the bathroom. The only thing in the room is a sink with badly rusted fixtures and a large tiled square reminiscent of the slab at the bottom of a shower stall. It's about four feet square and has a four or five inch hole in the middle. The smell of urine in the room is overpowering. Four guys are standing there pissing on the slab, the urine draining down the hole. Two of them repack their equipment and leave. Fishe and I stand at the slab and begin urinating.

While I stand there pissing, I comment, "Man, good thing you don't have to take a crap. Hell, there's no toilet in here."

One of the other guys enlightens us as he buttons up. "They don't have toilets here, only toilet I've seen was in a hotel in Saigon."

"So how do they take a shit?"

"They just squat over the hole and let fly. When they're done they wash it down with a half-bucket of water."

"Damn."

Back at the table we find Lindlay and Varant are gone. Farmly is half-bombed and his normal pompous aristocratic edge seems to have vanished. He's smiling and playing stink-finger with one of the girls.

"You should have come to the whorehouse with us."

"You're right, god damn it! I should have. I'm just about ready to go join Varant and Lindlay."

"What do ya mean? Where'd they go?" I'm not looking at Farmly, but at the girl who is openly allowing Farmly to fondle her. She has about seven empty "Pleiku tea" shot glasses sitting in front of her.

"They went next door. Varant says the gangway next to this place leads to *Blowjob Alley*. I guess Lindlay doesn't think a blow job is really cheating." Farmly goes back to nuzzling the girl's neck while his hand is still firmly imbedded between her legs.

"Where's Turner and Coleman?"

"I think they're out there dancing with some broads, but they may have gone with Varant and Lindlay." Farmly points in the direction of a six by six dance floor.

Outside, next to the club, is a gangway leading back to a couple of three story buildings. The second building back has a small overhang protecting a row of lawn chairs set up beneath it. All of the chairs are occupied by girls, none of which are dressed like the girls at the whorehouse or in the bar. They are all wearing black silk pajama pants and white blouses that are commonly seen on most of the women over here. A black guy is negotiating with one of the girls for a blowjob and we try walking past them into the building. One of the girls blocks the door.

"GI want boom-boom?" She asks.

"No, we look for friends," Fishe tells her.

"No go in unless you pay for girl." She continues blocking our entrance.

"How much you chop-chop?" Fishe asks.

She says, "Girl chop-chop five dollar," Her attitude relaxing a little.

"Okay, you chop-chop five dollar." Jim hands her five hundred piasters.

She turns to me and asks, "You boom-boom?"

The thought of getting a blowjob is very appealing. I've never been orally stimulated, but heard all the stories. In high school there was a girl called *Blow-Job Betty,* getting her to blow you was a right of passage into the *In Crowd.* I never made it.

"No boom-boom, chop-chop." I say like a pro.

"What girl you want?" She waves her arm at the girls sitting on the porch.

Slowly, I eye each one, mentally evaluating their looks. It shouldn't matter all that much, but I look anyway. These girls are not nearly as nice looking as the girls in the bar and plainer than the girls at the whorehouse. I find one girl who looks to be middle age, maybe twenty or thirty. When she smiles at me I notice none of her teeth are black, a definite plus. Something common among many Vietnamese is the chewing of something called Beetel-nut. I think it gives them a buzz. Unfortunately, it eventually turns their teeth black. The Vietnamese we have working around the hill chew it constantly.

"You chop-chop five dollars?" I ask.

"Okay." When she stands up, I am surprised to see she is quite buxom. I follow her into the room. Unlike the whorehouse, there is only one room here. About eight beds are in the room; each bed has a small curtain about five feet high surrounding it. You can look right over the top of the curtain and see everything going on - assuming you'd want to. Moaning and gagging and talking can be heard emanating from several of the beds.

"Lindlay?" I pause and wait for a response, "You better be using a rubber." I can hear him laugh, but he doesn't respond.

The girl pulls the curtain back on an empty bed and encourages me to sit on the edge. She undoes my trousers and kneels down in front of me. She inspects my best friend who jumps to attention when she touches it. She bends forward and starts to administer the treatment. When she puts her mouth on it, it takes my breath away. She moves her head in a rhythm back and forth and I can feel her tongue. She stops every thirty seconds or so and pumps me violently with her hand. She looks up at me and says, "You boom-boom now?" It's clear she really doesn't like doing this.

"No, you chop-chop."

After a while, the novelty wears off and it doesn't seem all that fantastic. It actually is numbing and not nearly as pleasurable as I had imagined. I realize there's just no feeling like being inside a tight wet pussy!

"You boom-boom now?" She looks up while administering the hand treatment.

"Okay, okay, we boom-boom." I didn't have to say it twice. I pull out a raincoat and try to slip it on. She takes it from me and does it herself. She pulls off her black pajama pants and climbs up on my lap. When I enter her I know a blowjob is a nice novelty, but this is where my dick really wants to be. She rocks her hips back and forth as I open her blouse. I pull her left breast out of her bra and catch my breath. It's fantastic. It's perfectly shaped with a ski-slope upward curvature. I can't resist; I bend over and nuzzle it. I expect her to stop me, but she doesn't. After a few seconds I reach over and pull her other breast from its restraint. It comes out and flops all the way down to her waist. I stop and pull back: This thing is tubular. It's like a big fat hose and literally hangs down to her waist. My eyes keep looking back and forth at the two breasts… they're like Jekyll and Hyde.

"What the hell happened to that?"

She looks at me and cracks a smile. "This for GI, she points at the left breast, this for baby." She lifts up the right breast like it's a dead snake.

"Jesus Christ, lady, that's the most bizarre looking pair of tits I've ever seen!" My mind quickly recalls images from preteen browsing of National Geographic.

"Man, I hope she don't point that thing at you, it's liable to go off!"

I look up and see Smitty looking in over the curtain.

"Hey, ya mind, how about a little privacy?" We haven't re-started the screwing, but I'm still in and still up.

"Hey, guys! Come 'ere and take a look at the broad Simon's with," Smitty yells.

"Hey, you no watch. Go 'way. Go boom-boom girl." My companion echoes my plea for privacy.

"You gonna screw that girl or you gonna just sit there?" Fishe and Varant are now leering in over the curtain next to Smitty.

"What the hell happened to her tit?" Varant's eyes are bulging in disbelief as he notices her deformity.

"She must be a big Mama San with boucou kids." Coleman adds.

"Come on, you want me to show you how to screw her or are you gonna show us what kind of man you are?" Coleman eggs me on.

I grab her hips and start lifting and dropping her. After a few repetitions, she begins to pick up the pace.

"Yeah, baby, that's how you do it," Fishe chants.

We begin to move a little faster. The crowd around the bed has grown. Now there are a couple of marines.

"Si...mon, Si...mon, Si...mon." They begin to chant.

I'm hypnotized by the crowd of onlookers; I begin to move with the chant. The girl also seems to be enjoying it. As they chant faster, we move faster. Their pace quickens as does ours.

"Si...mon, Si...mon! Si...mon!"

We flail around like two animals. The muscles in my neck protrude; my calf muscles tighten like steel cables. The sweat pours off me. My partner sweats profusely. Her "Jekyl" breast bounces erotically, the family udder is flying around like an eel.

"Come on Army, give it to her!" One of the marines is leering at us like an eleven-year-old that has just seen his first Playboy.

"Oh, yeah," I groan. "Oh, yeah, it's comin', it's com...ing*!*"

I grab her hips and pull her down hard. I don't want to risk popping out at this crucial moment. My eyes roll, I quiver and shake, and my head jerks back as I ejaculate.

"Yeeaaaahhhh!" Everyone cheers wildly. The girl keeps rotating her hips and every time she does I jerk violently. She hops off, pulls off the rubber and starts to blow me again. It's fantastic. The guys go nuts when she does and start throwing money at her.

"You number one baby," they shout at her.

She still wipes me off even though I've been given the oral laving.

Some of the guys say things like, "Man, you really gave it to her...She loved every minute of it," etc, etc. I knew she probably enjoyed being the center of attention, but doubted I pleasured her in any way.

At least my encounter with *Jekyll* and *Hyde* provided the only topic of conversation on the ride back to the hill.

Sunday morning we get to sleep in for a change. I'm out of bed at about nine-thirty. The barracks resounds with the moans and groans of hung over GIs paying the price for being incapable of exercising restraint. As I head out to the shower, I hear Fishe's reel-to-reel tape recorder blasting Mitch Ryder and the Detroit wheels, his favorite tape.

After lunch a few of us get up a game of Hearts.

"Hearts is okay, but you white boys need to learn a real man's game," Coleman says as he rearranges his cards.

"Yeah, what's that?" Fishe asks.

"Bid Whist," Coleman says as he plays the nine of spades.

"What's so different about Whist?" I play a two of spades.

"Damn it!" Lindlay gets stuck with the dreaded Queen of spades.

"Whist is a thinkin' man's game, you gots to name your poison when you play. You say you're gonna take three tricks and you take two or four you lose, man. So it's much more skillful."

"Oh, it's like pinochle." I look at Coleman for confirmation.

"Naw, man, it ain't like no pinochle...well maybe a little. I'll teach you." Coleman rubs the stubble on his chin. He doesn't shave everyday and never shaves with a razor. His chin and jaw are spoiled with a rash of *bumps* that make it impossible for him to use a razor. He uses some chemical concoction that reeks of sulfur. He spreads this crap over his beard and it essentially dissolves the whiskers. After it sets for a while, he scrapes it off with a Popsicle stick. He says, it burned like hell at first but his face has become desensitized to it.

He doesn't socialize much with the other blacks around the hill and it's weird hearing him call them nigger, often saying things like, "Say, nigger, whatcha been doin'?" It's odd hearing the word nigger being used as something other than an insult. Most everyone has taken to Coleman, everyone but Pinetti. He's tryin' too hard to be a *good ole boy* and I don't think having a black for a friend increases your chances of being accepted.

Sergeant Bennett's hunched-over frame pushes through the screen door and ambles over to our game.

"Boys, I hate to spoil your day off, but there's a little war going on over here." We impatiently wait for him to drop the bomb and tell us what he wants.

"We'll be needin' ten men to accompany Lt. McGehee up a hill near the Cambodian border."

"Who's Lt. McGehee?" Fishe doesn't bother looking up.

"He's a fire control officer from Charlie Battery. He's gonna be the forward observer for some hush-hush fire mission."

"What kind of fire mission and why would McGehee need a squad, don't they just fly 'em up in a plane or chopper?"

You could tell Bennett wasn't prepared for questions, let alone ones that actually made sense. "Well, seems we've got a sniper's nest on top of a mountain that looks down on the Ho Chi Minh trail. Intelligence says there's been a hell of a lot of VC traffic lately and we're gonna send McGehee up there so we can nail 'em."

"So what's he need a squad for?" Coleman reiterates Fishe's question.

"Well, the mountain is a ways west of Kontum. We can't fly anyone up there because it will give away the position and the chopper pilot's say there's no good place to land. So we'll fly ya'all over to Kontum and truck ya to the mountain. From there it's about a three hour hump up the mountain. Pretty heavy jungle up there, so the humpin' ain't gonna be easy."

"What the hell Sarge, we just got back from Cu Chi. How come we gotta go?"

"...and you boys did a mighty fine job over there. Capt. Solomon gives the orders; we just follow 'em. You'll be leavin' in about an hour, so get your gear together." Bennett starts to turn away, pauses, then turns back and says, "You boys best be wary around McGehee." Dumbfounded, we just watch as he ambles his way out of the hooch.

"What the fuck you suppose he meant by that?" Jim says staring at the door with a blank look on his face. "How the fuck would I know." I'm already stuffing my backpack.

The chopper flies directly into the northern sky. The sun is hanging in the west like a blazing marker. At Kontum we load into a couple of three-quarter ton trucks and head west accompanied by two APCs from the 25th Infantry. Lt. McGehee is up front with the driver. Fishe, Coleman, Lindlay, Townsend, and I are in the back. Sergeant Keelerhall, Thompson, Rocco, Ramirez and Smitty are in the other truck.

It's about eighteen hundred hours when we reach the base of the mountain. The ride has been gruesome, dirt roads all the way. We're gagging and covered with dust.

"Okay, let's put on the paint." Keelerhall starts passing around camouflage grease sticks. We buddy up and paint each others face. Amazingly, I still remember from basic that the object isn't just to cover up the skin, but to break up the lines of the facial features.

Keelerhall gathers us around him, and in a very quiet tone he gives the order, "Okay, lock and load. Coleman you got point. No one fires unless a gook is picking your nose, got it?" We nod.

Keelerhall looks each of us in the eye, "Listen, we're less than a click from the border. There's VC all over the goddamn place. If we start shootin' up the place, there ain't nobody around here to help us. We just want to slip our way up to the sniper's nest and not bring any attention to ourselves. Coleman, head for that group of rocks up there. There's a small trail we'll be following. We're not in any hurry, so move it out slow."

Coleman moves out on point, I'm just behind Keelerhall, he follows Fishe, Lindlay follows me and McGehee is situated in the middle of the squad. McGehee has no insignia on his helmet, but his jungle fatigues have the black bar sewn into the collar.

The trail is barely a trail at all. It's grown over with heavy vegetation. I was going to douse myself with mosquito repellent before we moved out, but Keelerhall stopped me. "You can smell that crap a half-mile away. The odor'll give us away." So I didn't put it on...the mosquitoes will be eating good tonight.

Moving through the jungle is slow and tedious. We are constantly pushing things out of our face and every step is taken with one eye on the ground and one eye looking ahead. Booby traps are a constant threat and force us to move that much more slowly. Sometimes you can see ahead clearly, other times you have to keep close to the guy in front of you so you won't lose sight of him. The trail is steep and we're busting our asses moving uphill.

"How far to the nest?" Fishe asks.

Keelerhall holds up his arm with the halt signal. He turns to us and holds a finger up to his lips.

Just as we start to move out again, Coleman stops and holds up his arm. We freeze. He motions for us to take cover. We quietly move off the path and slip in under the vegetation. Coleman signals back to Keelerhall. He points two fingers at his eyes, then points to a spot some thirty yards ahead and to the right. We focus our attention in that direction. The sun is down and darkness is starting to envelop the mountain. In the fading light, we can only see the silhouette of a tree and just behind it is the glowing ember of a burning cigarette. We can just barely see him as the tree obscures most of his body. If we didn't see his arm going up to his mouth every time he takes a drag, we probably wouldn't be able to see him at all. We hold our ground for about ten minutes, but the smoker doesn't go away. He flicks the cigarette away and strikes a match to light another. As the impending darkness weans all the color out of the jungle, seeing him becomes all the more difficult.

Keelerhall decides we can't wait any longer. He points at Fishe, then points at me. He takes two fingers and makes like a little man walking, pulls out his bayonet and makes a slashing motion across his throat. You don't have to be Einstein to figure out what he wants us to do.

I want to say, *fuck me,* but think it instead. Fishe and I quietly drop our packs then start moving to the right very, very slowly. My eyes glued to the position of the smoker. Acid is pouring into my stomach and my hands are shaking like a leaf. Sweat is pouring off me. A large leaf cuts across my face, but I make no attempt to move it out of the way. We're ten yards right of the smoker. We see his arm come down and flip something away…he's still there. *A sentry,* I think, which means there are others around. We lie flat, motionless, both of us concealed under heavy foliage. I look at Fishe and we begin exchanging hand signals. We want to get as close as possible and charge from two sides, tackle him to the ground, keep him from firing his weapon, and cut his throat. Deep down, I have doubts about the likelihood of our success. Shit like that only happens in the movies. Alerting other VC in the area could have consequences too terrible to think about.

We separate every so slowly…Jim six yards to my left. We move as slow as is humanly possible. Moving every leaf, every blade of grass is an effort. My heart is pounding so heavily in my chest, I'm almost afraid the VC will hear it. I've already convinced myself, no matter what, I'm going to do it. I've run the scenario through my mind a dozen times. If we don't do it, the little bastard is going to kill us. His gunfire will bring his buddies and everyone will die.

We can see him now...black pajamas, no hat. AK-47 draped across his arms. He's leaning back against a tree looking in the opposite direction. We are eight feet away now. We've managed to get a good angle on him. I take my eyes off him for a second to glance at Jim. We crawl the last few feet slower than a snail moving across a sheet of sandpaper.

Fishe lays his rifle down, holds up one finger and mouths the word one. Then the second finger comes up; when the third finger comes up he bolts to his feet and lunges towards the VC. My lunge is a split second later. I want to scream, but don't. They're falling in my direction as I hit them and I have only one thought...*Grab that fucking gun!* I grab at the weapon with both hands. I see his finger pulling the trigger repeatedly. Miraculously, he doesn't have a round chambered! Jim and I are on top of him and the VC is squirming and thrashing like hell. Once I separate him from his weapon he stops resisting. Jim has the bayonet up to his throat, but hasn't done it. The VC sits up and holds up his hands. He starts to say something, but I nail him on the side of the head with the butt of the AK-47 and he keels over. It's an instinctive knee-jerk reaction…I'm afraid he's going to yell.

"Fuck, man, what should we do?" Jim whispers.

"We can't drag him with us. We're gonna have to do him."

"Shit, shit, shit." The VC is sitting up again, blood running down the side of his head. I can see the terrified look in his eyes. He knows what's going to happen. While trying to overcome our indecisiveness we fail to notice a second VC. He just appears out of the bush. All of a sudden he's just there, pushing his AK-47 into Jim's back, yelling some boing-boing shit that doesn't need any translation. The demeanor of the VC on the ground changes instantly. His look of fear replaced with a smug grin; he starts getting to his feet. *What the fuck should I do?* Before I can decide, Coleman flashes up out of the bushes behind VC number two. He buries his bayonet into the eye socket of the VC as he pulls him to the ground. Instantly, our gook is grabbing at the muzzle of the AK-47 trying to wrestle it out of my hands. Fishe grabs him from behind; I pull up my bayonet and stick it into his belly. He starts to yell but Fishe closes both hands over his mouth and pulls him to the ground. I pull the bayonet out and thrust it as hard as I can into his breastplate, into his heart. His eyes go wide; I look directly into them, my face only inches from his. He shivers and goes limp, his eyes still open. I spin around to find Coleman has pulled the bayonet out of the other VC's eye and has slashed it across his throat. There's blood everywhere. The three of us are covered with it. Jim is trying to wipe it from his face with his blood-covered hands. My fatigues are soaked with it. Coleman turns and waves up the rest of the squad.

"Holy fuck!" Lindlay whispers loudly.

"Gimme the gook's weapon," Keelerhall motions towards the AK-47. He takes it, slings it over his arm and says, "Take the other one." He nods towards Coleman. Thompson hands us our packs with a bewildered look of amazement on his face. He says, "Jesus, buddy, you sure you guys belong in our unit?"

We move out, quicker than before. It's dark, I'm numb and the dead VC's open eyes are burned into my memory. I can't get them out of my head. I keep thinking how quick it was. One second he was a living breathing human: then he was dead. Just like that, dead. Yesterday, I felt like a big man because I was screwing some girl in Pleiku. Today, I have the blood of another man soaking through my shirt. Is there guilt? I search my feelings. *Is this guilt I'm feeling? No,* I decide, it isn't guilt, it's fear. Remorse is not coursing through my veins fear is. Seeing how quickly and how easily life is taken, seeing how abruptly it ends, only makes me realize how easy it will be for someone to end mine. In my heart, I know I will never feel safe again. I know this as surely as I know that someday, no matter how I try to avoid it, I will end up dead.

We hump the rest of the way up the mountain and reach the sniper's nest around 2300 hours. I'm not the same person I was when I left Pleiku.

CHAPTER TWO

"SHELLS AND SMELLS"

We approach quietly. We are so quiet the only sound I can hear is my own shallow breathing and the rapid thumping of my heart. Keelerhall is on point, the rest of us are crouched and alert...waiting. Keelerhall surprises everyone by bringing two fingers to his mouth and breaking the eerie silence with a sharp loud whistle.

"Man, I hope this is the right fucking place," Fishe whispers in my ear.

"No shit," I mumble.

Then, from some unseen person, "Olive Oyl?"

"Popeye," Keelerhall responds with his half of the password. A dim red light shines from out of the darkness and Keelerhall moves towards the light; we follow, moving rapidly, no longer concerned about the noise.

The voice belongs to a Special Forces Staff Sergeant named McGrath who is chest deep in a sandbag-lined trench. We slide down into the trench and follow McGrath along the trench to the entrance of a bunker. The inside is illuminated with a lantern that glows a dim red light. Ponchos cover all of the bunker orifices to keep light from giving away the bunkers position.

"This is McGehee," Keelerhall motions towards the Lieutenant who hasn't spoken three words since we left Pleiku.

"Your men can sleep wherever they can find space...there's a couple of cots stacked over in the corner."

Most of us are gonna be sleeping on the floor.

"I'm gonna need some time with McGehee, post a couple of your guys out in the trench to relieve my men."

Our asses are draggin'. Getting up here was brutal. At times, the grade was thirty degrees or more through heavy jungle; once our adrenaline starts tapering off, most of us will crash like a beat up Chevy at a demolition derby. Hell, I could fall asleep standing up.

Keelerhall is smart; he knows his men. "Okay, Townsend, Thompson and Ramirez, get out there and relieve McGrath's men. There are no Americans wandering around up here, so if you hear something or see something, it ain't gonna be the 'Avon Lady'. Make sure you talk to the man you're relieving."

All three nod in acknowledgment.

McGrath breaks in, "Use your head, don't start firing at every noise you hear either. The VC have been as close as fifty or sixty meters but have never seen the bunker. We don't want to let them know we're here if we don't have to."

I strip off my blood soaked fatigue blouse to find the blood has soaked through my tee shirt and covers most of my torso, it's a disturbing reminder that just a short time ago I ended another man's life. I change into the other olive-drab Tee shirt from my pack. I use the napkins from a box of C rations and some water to try and wash the blood off my body. The emotional exhaustion is beginning to overwhelm me and I hit the cot with my pants and boots still on. I am just about to nod off when Keelerhall reminds us to clear our weapons. I pull the magazine, empty the chamber and then re-insert the magazine. A couple of seconds after my head hits the rack I'm out for the night.

My eye lids open even though my mind is doing everything it can to convince me I should still be sleeping. Something, a noise, some static, something, has stirred me from my deep slumber. I look at my watch... it's eight in the morning. It takes a few seconds for me to remember where I am. *Shit, it wasn't just a bad dream.*

The bunker is dug into the side of the mountain; about eighty percent of it is actually underground leaving just a small portion exposed. The exposed portion is well camouflaged making the bunker near undetectable, especially at night. The inside is about twenty feet by twenty. There is one entrance and two small openings, all covered with ponchos. There's a table with radio gear, maps and several manuals. There's also a small portable camping stove which I presume is used to make coffee and warm C rations. Static from the radio gear is what roused me.

McGrath is standing near the door, drinking coffee from a canteen cup. "So, K-hall says a couple of you guys had to do a little Lurp duty last night." Lurp is jargon for LRRP or Long Range Reconnaissance Patrol. Lurps operate much the same way the VC do, marching out into the jungle, sometimes for weeks, setting up ambushes, taking prisoners, trying to wreak as much havoc as is humanly possible. I also know that there isn't any way that I or any of my comrades qualify in any way shape or form as a Lurp. Especially, after having heard the stories that Lurps are extremely brutal and so efficient at what they do that they are feared by the VC.

"Yeah, we did what we had to do. Man, I was shittin' my pants. If it hadn't been for 'The Karate Kid,' Fishe and me'd be dead." The vivid mental image of the VC with Coleman's bayonet buried in his eye flashes through my mind.

"Karate Kid?" McGrath asks.

"Coleman...that's what we all call him. He's always doin' those karate exercises and breaking boards and shit like that. For a nig... I mean black man, he's pretty easy to respect."

"Yeah, well, only a fool wouldn't have been scared shitless." He turns to top off his coffee.

"No, it was more than that...we weren't ready...we fucked up. Instead of killing the gook, we grabbed him and froze. Neither one of us wanted to shove the knife in him. Pointing a rifle at someone a couple of hundred yards away and pulling the trigger is not like seeing the fear in their eyes or being so close you can smell his breath and tell what he had for lunch. In the end, he made it easy for us."

"How's that?"

"When you think, *This is it,* that you're gonna die, all of a sudden all those moral dilemmas don't seem to be rattling around your head anymore, all of a sudden, it isn't quite as hard to jam the bayonet in him."

"The next one will be easier." The tone in McGrath's voice told me he was no stranger to looking someone in the eye while putting an end to their life.

I pick up my fatigue blouse, "Shit!" The blood's dried and the shirt is stiff as a board. I wonder if the smell of blood might attract undesirable animals on our way down the hill. “Anywhere I can wash this?” I hold it up for McGrath.

“Just bury it. You can take one of my blouses. He opens a duffel bag, removes a shirt and tosses it in my direction. The shirt is devoid of markings. No name tag, no patches, no insignia.

“How long you guys been up here?” I ask, wondering how they are able to operate without eventually being detected.

“We’ve been here thirty days. We’ll probably move again in a week or so, maybe sooner.”

“Again?” I look up from buttoning the shirt.

“Yeah, we pull up stakes and move to a new location every five or six weeks. There’s tons of VC activity around here. Fortunately, they rarely get this high up the hill. Probably because it’s such a pain in the ass humping around up here, and I’m sure it’s got to interfere with their back and forth movements across the border.”

Outside the bunker I find the sun is bright and have to shadow my eyes with my hand. Coleman, Fishe and Thompson are sitting on top of the bunker with Keelerhall. A small ladder gives access to the top. The area on top is considerably smaller than the size of the actual bunker since a large portion of it is dug into the side of the hill. Above us, camouflage netting hangs several feet over our heads concealing everything and making the complex near invisible to any aircraft flying over, not that there is any threat of the North Vietnamese air force flying over, but some ARVN plane might spot it and the ARVN forces are heavily infiltrated with VC.

Looking out from the top of the bunker presents a spectacular panoramic view of the mountains and the lush jungle that covers them. A strange looking weapon is firmly mounted to a heavy metal stand near the front edge of the bunker. The stand is quite elaborate with several gears and cranks obviously used to position the weapon.

“It’s a fifty caliber,” Coleman says.

“No shit? It’s not like any fifty-caliber I’ve ever seen.”

“It’s not.” McGrath climbs up behind me. “This was specially designed for this purpose. It’s a sniper weapon. We can pick a guy off nearly a mile away.”

A mile? Holy Shit!

“Here take a look.” McGrath is looking through a pair of oversized binoculars, about three times the size of regular glasses. “They’re ranging binoculars,” he says as he steps back to give me access.

I step up and look through the binoculars. I'm looking at a road with several trucks moving slowly southward. I pull back from the binoculars and look...*shit...I can barely make out the trucks.* I look back through the binoculars amazed by their ability to magnify things so distinctly.

"Okay, watch this." McGrath gives me a regular set of 20/50 binoculars and takes over at the ranging glasses. One of his men, Sergeant Fleming, opens up the breach of the weapon and loads a single fifty caliber round.

"We've already got the weapon zeroed in to several spots down on the road, we can put a round within a couple of inches of anything on a twenty yard stretch of that road with just a slight adjustment of the weapon."

"See the third truck back?"

I look through the binoculars. The third truck back is an old rickety beat up rail truck with a couple of VC riding in the back. I know they're VC only because they have AK-47s slung over their shoulders.

"Watch this...they won't even hear the shot. It drives 'em fuckin' crazy." He goes back to the binoculars and peers through them.

McGrath calls out some numbers and Fleming dials in the adjustments then peers through the scope of the weapon and at the appropriate moment pulls the trigger. The fifty reports with a loud *Thwam.*

Watching through the binoculars I can't quite make out the driver, but all of a sudden the truck starts swerving and runs off the road. Everyone in the small convoy scrambles off the road and begins shooting in all directions. I don't hear the shooting till a few seconds later. Obviously, the VC have no idea where the shot came from.

"Drives 'em fucking crazy," McGrath chuckles.

"The little bastards are going nuts," Fishe comments looking through the ranging glasses.

"Fortunately for us, from down there it's near impossible to tell where the shot came from," but if there are any VC around up here when we're shooting, it'll give away our position.

"How often do they come and go?" Keelerhall asks while he watches the sideshow through his binoculars.

"There's traffic going back and forth nearly all the time. Much of it is local traffic, but a lot of it is related to either supplying the VC or moving troops back and forth, it's rarely more than a couple of trucks. Most of the big convoys come through at night.

McGehee chimes in, "I'm here as a forward observer and to grade the effectiveness of the shoot."

Thompson looks at McGehee and says, "How accurate do you need to be? Hell, those shells are gigantic! I wouldn't want to be within a city block of one of those babies when it goes off."

"Well, there are other things that need to be evaluated. Maybe we just want to make sure were not blowing up our own guys. There are a lot more things going on in this war than you know about." McGehee just turns away and doesn't elaborate any further.

In the late afternoon Keelerhall and McGrath get us together and pass out assignments for the evening. Ramirez, Thompson and Rocco will go with Fleming to man a couple of holes dug fifty yards down the hill, situated left of our position. This makes them strategically placed for creating a cross-fire. Basically, they are foxholes with vegetation-covered lids. When it's closed it leaves a small slit so the occupants can see, but conceals the occupants from the probing eyes of a VC patrol. They're used as listening posts. The rest of us will take positions around the bunker.

"Nothing should happen till after dark, but be prepared," McGrath says.

"Hey Sarge, I just had a thought," I look at McGrath and McGehee.

"What's that?" McGrath asks.

"Isn't that road actually in Cambodia?"

Keelerhall puts his hand on my shoulder, "Look," he says, "those little bastards are shippin' supplies and ammo down that road to keep the VC supplied so they can continue to kill Americans. Do you really have a problem with us shooting at those convoys?"

"Hell, no, Sarge, I haven't got a problem with that. Hell, if it was up to me, I say we march on Hanoi tomorrow. I only mention it because I wonder whether or not it's okay to talk about this."

"Well, I guess we would all be a lot better off if we don't elaborate on anything we see here. Anybody got a problem with that?"

"No problem here," Lindlay says.

"Not me," Coleman shakes his head.

"Cambodia? Where the hell is that?" Fishe chimes in.

During our watch, I keep pondering the practicality of the whole trip. Something just doesn't make sense. Hell, there's easier ways to evaluate the 175s, something just isn't right. In any case, I know we'll find out the truth in a very short time. *Damn it, sometimes I waste way too much time trying to analyze shit like this.*

After our watch I go inside to grab some C rations. While I sit on top of the bunker eating I watch McGehee. He looks through the ranging binoculars, checks his map, looks at his watch and scribbles numbers in his little notebook. His shirt is open and I'm overwhelmed with the feeling something isn't quite right, that there's something odd.

Hey! McGehee isn't wearing any dog tags. McGehee, a man in his late twenties or early thirties, is kind of old for a Lieutenant.

Without looking up from my rations I offhandedly ask, "So, Lieutenant, where you from?"

McGehee lowers the binoculars and looks at me. I can tell he's a little wary about answering.

"Chicago suburbs," he raises the glasses back up.

"No shit, where at? I'm from Chicago and know a lot of people from the suburbs. Where'd you go to school?"

"Boston College." He doesn't bother looking at me or removing the glasses from his eyes.

"No, where'd you go to high school?"

I can see instantly he doesn't have an answer for my question.

"You're not really from our unit, are you?" I glance at Fishe who's suddenly become interested.

"You ask too many questions, *Private.*" McGehee's neck is getting red.

"How come you aren't wearing any dog tags? Hell, I don't think you're even in the army." I should be smart enough to keep my mouth shut, but I'm like a kid who discovers a secret and can't wait to tell everybody.

"Simon, you're a little too smart for your own good." McGehee is in my face. "You don't need to know anything about me. You don't need to say anything about me and you certainly will be better off if we end this discussion right now."

McGehee quickly disappears down into the bunker, probably to shag Keelerhall on me.

Fishe, laughing and with a look of bewilderment, asks, "What the hell was that all about? Fuckin' with an enlisted man is one thing, fuckin' with the brass is something else." Jim shakes his head.

"He ain't no brass, he's probably intelligence or CIA." Coleman says climbing up to join us.

"Whoa...baby! Why would you think that?" Fishe is obviously as surprised by Coleman's conclusion as I am.

"You hear stories, man, I hear things. Every time something a little shady goes down, there's always someone like McGehee around."

Coleman looks back over his shoulder to make sure no one is within earshot. "I knew he wasn't no army last night. Hell, man, think about it. How many Lieutenants you know would've let Keelerhall run the show without sayin' jack shit? No, I knew he was special cargo when we started humpin' up this mountain."

As the day wears on McGrath's crew crank up the fifty every hour or so and drop some poor slob down on the road. You'd think after a while they'd find an alternate route. The road, being in Cambodia, is supposedly sanctuary from bombing and shelling. Hell, standing orders say we aren't allowed to cross the border in pursuit of a retreating NVA force so this makes the Cambodian border an easy route to the south. The North Vietnamese can move men and supplies through Cambodia and Laos pretty much without resistance. It makes our purpose in Vietnam that much more difficult. Cutting off enemy supply lines is essential to winning any battle this is something even a moron like me understands.

As evening approaches, McGrath and McGehee are on the radio constantly. We linger around the bunker entrance hoping to overhear something that will shed some light on our activities.

"Shadow, Shadow, report your position, over." McGehee releases the button on the mike. The radio squawks and several indistinguishable words scratch out of the speaker.

McGrath makes a couple of adjustments to the radio and McGehee repeats his first message. "Shadow, Shadow, report your position, over."

This time the response is much clearer. "Sky Watch, this is Shadow, do you copy over?"

"Roger, Shadow, we copy. Report your position."

"Sky Watch, we are in position and waiting for the party to begin."

"Roger, Shadow, Sky Watch out."

McGehee hands the mike to McGrath and everybody with more than one stripe gathers around the table. McGehee and McGrath are pointing at a map and hushed conversations are taking place.

After several minutes Keelerhall emerges with Thompson on his heels. Keelerhall signals for us to gather around and we huddle up. We're anxious.

"Okay, the show is gonna start in about thirty minutes. I'm gonna take Thompson, Ramirez and Rocco and we're gonna man the pits. McGrath's men are goin' halfway down the mountain to meet up with an incoming patrol. There's a good chance they won't be alone. If they're not, our goal is to get the VC in a cross-fire between the pits and the bunker ...any questions?"

"Yeah, what the fuck is going on?" Fishe asks the question on all our minds.

"There's a VC convoy headed this way. We're going to shell the hell out of them and there's a platoon of men positioned to mop up. After the barrage they'll be retreating to this position from somewhere over there." He points to Cambodia. You three will take up defensive positions here." Keelerhall points at Fishe, Coleman and me. "There will be a lot of activity going on. Don't get anxious and start shooting at everything you hear, it could be us, got it?"

"Got it, Sarge," we reply in unison.

"Okay, the password is *snatch hair*, you challenge anybody you hear coming your way. If you don't get *snatch hair* for a reply, you shoot. Got it?" He looks back and forth at us as we acknowledge.

Fishe and I take positions at the far end of the north trench and Coleman and Lindlay take the south trench. The trenches are four and a half feet deep. I can see down the hill in front of the trench for about forty or fifty yards then the vegetation gets too thick to see any farther. I leave Fishe at our position and climb up to the top of the bunker. McGehee is there alone using the ranging binoculars. I pick up the 20/50s and stare down at the road. McGehee swings the ranging binoculars north. When I see him do this, I follow with my glasses. A few miles to the north is a big convoy headed south.

"I make out sixteen trucks," I say out loud.

McGehee responds, "That's what I've got, sixteen trucks."

McGrath climbs up with a map and the radio, McGehee moves aside and McGrath looks through the binoculars. He looks at the map, then his watch and back at the map. McGehee is mimicking his movements. McGehee picks up the mike to call in the fire mission.

"Smasher one-nine, Smasher one-nine, this is the Sky Watch, over."

The speaker on the radio immediately comes alive with a static filled response.

"Roger, Sky Watch, this is Smasher one-nine."

Smasher one-nine is the operations officer back at the hill. He'll be in the operations bunker, where the walls are covered with plastic coated maps busily being marked by two or three enlisted men. There are several radios, all set to different frequencies, situated on a long table the length of the room. These are accompanied by an array of field phones connecting operations to many of our fire bases and support units. When McGehee gives the coordinates for the fire mission either Lieutenant Louda or Duke will contact the appropriate battery.

"Smasher, we have a fire mission, over." McGehee releases the button on the mike and waits for the response.

"Roger, Sky Watch, fire mission, go ahead, over."

"Fire mission coordinates..." McGehee feeds the coordinates back to operations and we wait. Several seconds pass then McGehee gives the order, "Commence firing!"

I peer through the binoculars at the road and then I hear it, a high pitched scream overhead. I instinctively look but then turn my attention back to the road and the approaching trucks. The first explosion is at least a hundred yards past the road. I can see the shock wave pour out from the explosion, like a ripple in a pond. The second shell is closer, but still a miss. McGehee is back on the radio adjusting the fire. He calls in the adjustments and we wait. Once again, I hear the shells scream overhead, a split second later a series of eight successive detonations impact on the road making at least six of the trucks disappear. The rest of the trucks are trying to negotiate around the debris and craters left by the first barrage. Men are scrambling out of trucks and heading for the protection of the jungle.

Once again McGehee calls in adjustments and another deadly barrage screams overhead arcing towards the road below. More trucks are destroyed and I guess at least a hundred NVA are scrambling around in the jungle. Staring through the binoculars, I can see that many of the NVA appear to be engaged in a fire fight, exchanging fire with an unseen force from the depths of the jungle on the west side of the road.

The sun is near set; behind us, on the east face of the mountain, it is probably already dark. On this side the sun shines like an eerie spotlight while it slowly makes its departure below the horizon.

"There they are!" McGehee points, McGrath and I train our binoculars on the road where McGehee is pointing. I see a group of about fifteen men cross the road. They cross quickly, running, and disappear into the jungle at the bottom of the mountain.

"Smasher One-Nine, Smasher One-Nine, this is Sky Watch, do you copy over?"

"Roger, Sky Watch, we copy, over."

"I have a fire mission, fire mission Zebra, do you copy, over?" McGehee peers through the binoculars as McGrath and I continue to watch. This time he doesn't give any coordinates. The fire mission is preconceived, already set up. I see NVA emerging from the jungle west of the road. They'll be crossing the road in less than a minute. *In pursuit,* I think.

"Smasher One-Nine, commence firing, commence firing!"

"Roger, Sky Watch, commence firing, over."

Once again shells scream over our heads, this time disintegrating the road and jungle into clouds of fire and debris. Each explosion makes the ground tremble, even all the way up here. The explosions are loud, very loud. I'm glad I'm up here and not down there.

Wham! Wham! Wham! Wham! The shells detonate in groups of four. Twenty rounds hit a section of earth about the size of two football fields. As the smoke starts to clear I can see that not one round has fallen short of the road, all either hit the road or west of it. Two hundred yards of the road and a sizable section of jungle are gone, obliterated, vanished, like it was never there to start with.

McGehee, without lowering the binoculars, says, "It looked like about fifteen or twenty gooks crossed the road before the barrage hit."

"Simon, get your ass back down to your position." McGrath picks up a field phone to alert the pits.

"Our incoming patrol will be up here in thirty or forty minutes. It looks like about twenty or so gooks are in pursuit, maybe four or five minutes behind them."

McGrath cradles the phone as I climb down into the trench. Then he removes the sniper weapon and puts an M-60 in place, loads it and I know that it won't be long till it is put to good use.

I move over to Fishe, pick up my M-14 and make a cursory check of the weapon.

"Did you catch any of the show?" I ask.

"No. I can't see shit from here. What's going on?" Fishe asks without looking at me, he keeps staring down the slope in front of the trench while I fill him in on what's happened.

"Man, I sure would like to know what the fuck is going on." Jim mumbles with a noticeable level of agitation, a product of the anxiety of knowing what is about to happen.

Anxiety is not a limited commodity. I try to deal with it by rationalizing our situation out loud. "Look, we've got the advantage. We've got four

Special forces guys, Keelerhall and Thompson know what they're doin', and we have the high ground."

"How long you think we got?" Fishe is looking at me now.

"I don't know. Maybe another thirty minutes, maybe an hour."

Jim adds, "Shit, it took us four fucking hours to get up here."

"Yeah, but we traversed all the way around the mountain, in the dark, while tryin' to avoid Charlie so we weren't movin' very fast." I'm not really trying to reassure him, I'm just talking to keep us both from thinking. We grease each others face, check our weapons again and wait.

McGrath has either turned off the radio or turned down the volume. In either case, we can no longer hear the static. There is only silence. The sun is down now. Darkness is upon us like a heavy blanket. Slowly, the sounds of the jungle emerge from the darkness: Insects chattering, the occasional cry of a bird, other unrecognizable sounds and the ever-present hissing of mosquitoes.

I can no longer make out McGrath or McGehee's silhouette on top of the bunker. The bunker with its netting and camouflage melds into the jungle making it appear to be an integral piece of the landscape. If the trench didn't lead directly to the bunker door, I'd have difficulty finding it.

Crack! A single shot rings out in the distance. It is answered with a tcha, tcha, tcha, tcha burst from an automatic weapon. Then, crack, crack, crack, crack, the unmistakable sound of M-16s. Several more bursts from AK-47s, then silence. My eyes are getting more accustomed to the darkness and I can once again make out McGrath's shape on top of the bunker. He's staring through a night vision infrared scope.

Twenty minutes elapse; my palms are sweating and I can hear my heart beating. I peel off my flak jacket and remove my shirt, then put the flak jacket back on over my olive green tee shirt. Something is near, very near, somehow I'm able sense it. I peer into the jungle watching for some indication of movement when a muted whistle is heard to the left.

"Pussy?" McGrath calls from the top of the bunker.

Fishe and I tense up, everyone waiting for the response. McGrath is staring through the infrared scope.

"Snatch Hair," is the muted response that comes out of the jungle directly in front of us.

"Okay, move your asses," McGehee calls out.

A squad of men, silhouettes in the darkness, emerges from the jungle. They move quickly and quietly across the clearing to our position and slide down into the trenches. The first guy into the trench drags a prisoner whose hands are tied behind his back. He's dressed in what appears to be an NVA uniform, an officer I would guess, but it's hard to make out in the darkness. He's pulled into the bunker by a rope wrapped around his neck; the mysterious Lt. McGehee follows them. The rest of the men take up defensive positions in the trench. The guy next to me pulls the magazine from his M-16, checks to make sure it isn't empty and reinserts it.

"They're about five minutes behind us," he says without looking up.

From the bush out in front of our position a red light flashes and Fleming calls out, "Snatch Hair!"

McGrath flashes his red flashlight and they move in. The Green Berets emerge from the jungle, scramble across the clearing to the trench on the other side of the bunker.

I hear the muted ring of the field phone from the top of the bunker and McGrath passes the word…eighteen VC just passed the pits…they are less than a 60 yards from our position.

The first two emerge from the bush moving into the clearing. This alerts the VC and they pause for a moment then begin advancing very cautiously. They are crouched down and moving slowly, looking back and forth trying to discern something in the darkness. Then, as if appearing out of thin air, there are four more. They're spread out across the front of our position. Five more become visible. They are about twenty yards away, the grade makes their advance clumsy and then, as if responding to some magic signal, every one opens fire. Light from the muzzle flashes pierces the darkness like a strobe light. The incoming rounds hit the dirt in front of us and kick dirt up into my face. The flashes from their weapons eerily illuminate the VC and make them easy targets till they dive for the cover of the jungle. A short burst from an AK-47 gives up a position and I squeeze off four rounds from the M-14. I pull the magazine out and let it drop to the ground; insert a second magazine without taking my eyes away from my field of fire. The exchange of fire is still rapid and heavy from both positions: ours from the trenches and theirs from the concealment of the jungle.

"Down in the trenches!" McGrath yells out.

Then, *Boom! Boom! Boom! Boom!* It's the unmistakable blast of Claymore mines. The blasts come from the right and left and are directed in a thirty-degree diagonal path across the front of our position.

From down the hill the unmistakable sound of an M-60 rings out. Keelerhall and his men must be cutting off the retreating VC. They're driving the VC back in our direction. They emerge from the jungle shooting in both directions...they're being cut to pieces. One charges our position with his AK-47 blazing, all of a sudden he freezes, his weapon has jammed. I can't believe nobody's hit him. He starts screaming and runs directly at us. Before I can bring my rifle to bear, he jumps in the trench. Fishe is moving and has his thirty-eight out of his holster. The VC is wrestling with the guy next to me, I'm trying to spin around when Fishe pushes me out of the way. He puts the thirty-eight up to the back of the VC's neck and pulls the trigger. The VC drops his weapon and spins around, he has a hideous look on his face and he's clutching at his throat. Fishe pulls the trigger again, this time with the thirty-eight pressed up against the side of his head. The head snaps, first back and then to the side. Blood, brains and bone splatter as his head snaps forward and he falls to the ground in a lifeless heap.

Our attention returns to the field of fire. The M-60's are still popping off short bursts, but there doesn't seem to be any movement.

"Cease Fire! Cease Fire!" McGrath calls out. "Stay in your positions." "Anybody hit?" No one replies. McGrath climbs down from the bunker and moves along the trench. He and six of the recent arrivals climb out and begin to sweep the area. Twice they stop and fire a couple of shots into a prone body.

Fifteen minutes later McGrath emerges from the jungle with Keelerhall and the rest of our men. They must feel the area is secure because they're using flashlights and checking the area more thoroughly.

We split into shifts so we can grab some sleep. We sleep where we are. We just sit on the ground with our backs against the wall of the trench and nod off. I find it difficult, but manage to drift off once only to be rudely awakened to stand watch for two hours.

When morning comes a squad is assembled and sent out to sweep the area. The rest of us go to work burying the VC bodies, twenty-three in all. Actually, we just pile them into the bunker and start hacking the sandbags up with trenching tools. The VC never had a chance. Some had so many bullet holes in them you couldn't count 'em. A couple of torsos had been cut in half by the Claymores. We drag them, with their guts hanging out, and toss them into the bunker. McGrath has disassembled the fifty and the rest of the equipment and is packing it up. We're done in less than an hour.

McGrath takes a couple of grenades, and with the utmost care uses them to booby trap a case of C rations. He pulls the pins on the grenades and holds the lever arms in place with the box C rations. He holds the rations in place as Fleming and I pile dirt on top of it. We pack the dirt and keep covering till only a corner of the C ration case is conspicuously sticking out of the dirt. Once we feel confident it isn't going to blow up in our faces, we back away slowly from the booby trap.

McGrath takes the lead and we move out to the southeast. We'll be traversing our way around the mountain again, this time in the daylight.

A lot of the equipment is left behind, buried along with the VC bodies. The major stuff, sniper rifle, binoculars, weapons and ammunition are all being toted down the mountain. The group is not quite the size of a platoon, but much bigger than a squad, our total now at twenty-six. Couple this with all the equipment we're carrying and the fact that it's daylight; it won't be hard to find us.

"So who do you think that is?" I ask Townsend as we work our way through some heavy foliage.

"You mean the gook?"

It seems rather obvious to me, but rather than make a smart-ass comment, I reply, "Yeah, the gook."

"Well, it ain't Ho Chi Minh. Looks like some NVA Colonel or something. McGehee isn't talking. I heard Fishe ask, but all he got out of McGehee was, 'You don't need to know'."

"Great," I mumble sarcastically, "We hump our asses up and down this stinkin' hill, nearly get our asses blown off and we don't need to know! Man, that's bullshit." My agitation has caused me to start talking louder than I should be.

Townsend turns to me with his finger to lips. "Not so loud, not so loud." I nod in agreement. Nothing else crosses my lips.

After twenty minutes of some pretty brisk humping, we stop and rest. While resting we hear two sharp explosions coming from the general direction of the sniper's nest. I know it's the booby traps; so does everyone else. Everyone is dead still for fifteen or twenty seconds, then without a word being spoken we're up and moving, this time at a quicker more determined pace. It's evident whoever is responsible for setting off the grenades, is only fifteen or twenty minutes behind us: The only conclusion…VC. They may not be able to determine our route, but it won't be difficult to guess our destination.

We move fast, as fast as the terrain will allow. Going down is always faster than going up. We all know that the VC in pursuit will try to have people waiting for us at the bottom, probably at several different places. We could be caught between two forces, a grim prospect for sure.

Townsend yells, "Shit!" I turn to see his feet come out from under him and watch him slide down the hill about six feet. Fishe and I stop to help pull him up. A few more yards down the hill and we move into a clearing or at least an area where we can see everybody in the group.

McGrath and Keelerhall stop and discuss our situation. They decide to split the group into two squads, K-hall leading one, McGrath the other. McGrath has us gather around and he points to our location on the map. He then traces out two paths of descent, one for us another for him. Our objective is to make a more direct descent to the bottom of the mountain, then sweep around the base to the position McGrath's group will come off the mountain. It is unlikely a VC force will be coming down the mountain ahead of McGrath, so if the VC plan to intercept they'll need an ambush set up near the bottom. Having our squad sweep around the base of the mountain will cover McGrath's flank. This will put the ambush between McGrath and us. I'm no strategist and I don't feel comfortable splitting up our group, but the plan seems logical.

Coleman takes point and we make our descent over ground much steeper than the trail we followed coming up. Many times the grade gets so steep we are actually climbing down. We reach the base of the mountain in about forty minutes.

We're spent. Most of us are out of breath, our leg muscles are throbbing, our arms tired and weak. It feels like we've been toting boxes of lead bars. The jungle at the bottom is much denser than it was at the higher elevations. K-hall lets us catch our breath while he checks his map and compass.

"Okay, listen up. We're going to sweep around the mountain to meet with McGrath here." K-hall points to a spot on the map.

"We're right about here." He traces his finger back to a spot that looks like it is about a half-mile from the rendezvous point.

"We believe the VC will try to set up an ambush here and they'll have some people here to cut off McGrath's escape route." Again he points to the map. If the VC set up as we expect, they'll be between us and McGrath assuming we can move in behind them undetected.

"I figure we've got a fifteen or twenty minute jump on McGrath.

If we don't get there in time those guys could be fucked. Don't forget, they already have VC chasing 'em down this hill. We don't want McGrath's team to end up surrounded. Keep your eyes open, keep it quiet and watch me for signals. Move it out."

Coleman takes point. He doesn't have to be told, he just moves out ahead of us. I have to take the left flank and Thomson takes the right. We are moving at a good pace. *Too fast,* I think. Coleman is out about twenty yards in front of the squad. The vegetation is heavy and sometimes we lose sight of him. The sun seems hotter down here than it was back up at the bunker. If the sun shines through the treetops just right, I can detect steam rising from the ground. The broad leaves of the jungle plants are still covered with droplets of dew still waiting to evaporate. The only detectable sounds are the noises we make pushing plants and leaves aside as we move through the jungle. A bird takes flight from a treetop squawking as it flies away. We freeze and watch it disappear.

The jungle thins a little; I can see all the members of the squad. I figure we've done about a 120-degree swing around the base of the hill and are actually moving upgrade again. Coleman stops, his arm goes up and the squad drops to the ground. Coleman squatting and still facing away from us, slowly backs up taking care not to rustle any bushes or make any noise and makes his way back to us.

"Sarge...six VC about sixty or seventy yards in front of us facing north with their backs to us. There's gotta be more, but I don't see 'em. There's one machine gun with two VC and another couple with an RPG. There's two more dug in to the right of the machine gun. You know they've got to have a couple of guys watching their backs, but I haven't seen 'em."

Keelerhall immediately starts whispering instructions. "Okay, we spread out. Ramirez...Rocco...you're on each side of me. Lindlay, Simon, Fishe...left flank. He points at a fallen tree and indicates that will be our position. Coleman, Townsend, Thompson...right flank. Pick a spot with good cover." Keelerhall pauses for a second; then continues, "Look, there's two possible scenarios: We hold tight till they open up on McGrath. They should be so absorbed with McGrath it'll give us the element of surprise. The other possibility is if we hear firing and the gooks pull out. It'll mean McGrath has come down to the northeast so they'll try to reinforce or go east to try and cut him off. If we see 'em getting ready to pull out we take 'em. Then we can move through to reinforce McGrath. Odds are in our favor, they're not expecting us." Keelerhall looks each one of us directly in the eye and tries to detect any confusion or misunderstanding. He convinces himself we understand and he motions for us to move out.

Oozing our way through the jungle, we spread out, spacing ourselves ten to fifteen yards apart. We creep through the brush ever so slowly. It is humid and sweat bleeds out of every pore in my body. My eyes move back and forth between the three VC positions we can see; I'm more worried about positions we don't see. Fishe and I settle in behind the fallen tree and Lindlay slides into a small depression to the right. From behind the tree, we can see two of the VC positions. The machine gun and two VC are dug into a little trench and have a couple of logs stacked in front for cover. They've made a small canopy out of brush and leaves to conceal their position. Their backside is completely exposed. We have good shots at both of them. Two more are visible thirty yards to the left of the machine gun. One of these two is carrying the RPG.

"I'll take the RPG, you and Lindlay go for the machine gun." I whisper in Fishe's ear and point. Fishe crawls to the right to convey the message to Lindlay.

From behind the fallen tree we peer through a small space between the trunk and the ground. I lean over to Fishe, "Ya know K-hall didn't say what we'd do if nothing happened. What if McGrath doesn't run into the gooks?"

Fishe looks at me as if I'm crazy. "Sooner or later they gotta go somewhere, then we nail 'em." Fishe grabs my arm and stiffens.

One of the VC manning the machine gun stands up, he says something to his companion and starts walking directly towards us.

Fuck, has he seen something? I start to bring my rifle up but hesitate because he isn't carrying a weapon. He walks to a spot a mere five yards in front of us, just in front of the fallen tree. I know everyone has their eyes glued to this guy. All we can see from under the tree is his torso from the waist down. He turns around facing away from us, pulls down his pants and squats. I want to turn away but know if either one of us moves we'll give away our position...we're stuck watching. He starts taking a crap right in front of us.

Jeee..sus Christ! I scream in my mind. Man, does this bastard stink. God damn it!

The smell is gagging me. I look at Fishe; he hasn't moved but his eyes are closed and his face is contorted into a hideous squinching look.

The gook finishes, stands up, and pulls up his pants. *The bastard doesn't even wipe!* As he starts walking back towards his position, I look at Fishe, my mouth agape; my eyes open wide in an expression of disbelief.

The gook settles back into his position and as he gets down, his partner says something to him and whacks him on the shoulder. "Probably asked him why he didn't wipe," I whisper.

The wait isn't long. A solo rifle report rings out in the distance. It's answered by a short burst from an automatic rifle then some muffled yelling and multiple weapons firing. We can see the VC tense up preparing themselves for the oncoming Americans.

Out of the corner of my eye I see K-hall stand, throw a grenade, then get back down all in one movement.

Whump! The grenade detonates, taking out a screaming VC. I instantly start pumping out rounds from my M-14. The RPG man half stands, tries bringing the weapon around, but I hit him three times and he crashes to the ground. I zero in the sight of the M-14 on the machine gunners. They're already dead. I lay my rifle on top of the fallen tree looking for another target. Townsend and Thompson are firing repeated bursts at a position I can't see. K-hall and Coleman are up. They're running towards the defunct machine gun position, also firing towards the same unseen target. Once they reach the little pit, they must outflank the VC because three of them burst from the bushes running in our direction. Townsend and Thompson cut one down immediately. The other two run directly towards us unaware of our position almost tripping over Lindlay. Lee stands as they pass and starts firing. He hits one and we drop the other.

K-hall yells, "Let's go, let's go!" Splitting into two teams, we start running in the direction of the yelling and shooting. We leave an alley of twenty yards between us as we run. I can see people running towards us, they materialize out of the jungle almost mystically. The first two I identify are McGehee and his prisoner. Behind them are three more of McGrath's squad, then, the whole squad appears.

As they move past us, Keelerhall yells out, "Cover, Cover!" The team starts dropping behind whatever cover is available. I can see the VC now, they are also running. They run, pause to fire a burst, then start running again. As they move towards us, McGrath's men open up, giving the impression they've stopped to fight. Three VC split off left, three split off right, the rest advance, firing, trying to draw McGrath's fire while the others plan to outflank him.

We drop the three VC on the left before they can even fire a shot. As they drop, we hear the other three scream and know they have also been cut down. The main VC group realizes they are surrounded; they begin yelling and shooting in all directions. Between McGrath's position, us to his left and K-hall flanking the VC on the right, the VC have only two options: press forward or retreat. They begin withdrawing in a hurry, but we manage to hit a couple more of them before they disappear into the jungle.

K-hall springs up from his position and waves his arm frantically. No further encouragement is required and in an instant, we're up and running,

McGrath already has his squad moving. Miraculously, only Ramirez has taken a hit. The sleeve of his left arm is soaked with blood and Sgt. Fleming is tying a bandage around it as we move.

We double time to the east covering a mile in about fifteen minutes. McGrath finally stops grabs the hand set from the radio and depresses the button to broadcast.

"Devil, Devil, this is Shadow, do you copy, over?"

"Devil, Devil, this is Shadow, do you copy, over?" He releases the button on the mike and waits.

"Roger, Shadow, this is Devil, I copy over. What is your position Shadow, over?"

"Roger, Devil. Our ETA to checkpoint alpha is one zero minutes, do you copy, over?"

"Roger, Shadow, we copy, out."

We're double-timing again. The jungle has waned into bushes and brush leaving the trees behind us. We approach a clearing and there are rice paddies to the south. From just around the bend I hear the unmistakable sound of choppers. As we move into a clearing, there are six Hueys, rotors turning and some men spread out protecting them.

We break into a full run; as we near, a Captain runs up to meet McGehee. Some words are exchanged and the Captain motions for us to board. We pile in, anxious to get off the ground.

The chopper jerks off the ground, moves forward for a short distance, and then pulls around in a hard right banking maneuver, performing a one-eighty. As we head east into the sun, I look at everyone. We're drenched; sweat pouring off us. As our respiration returns to normal and the level of adrenaline in our blood wanes, we slump, drained, exhausted and emotionally spent. Then, out of the blue, for some unknown reason Fishe blurts out, “Man, can you believe the bastard didn’t even wipe?”

“Yeah and what about that smell?” I say, reaching up and holding my nose. Fishe and I break into a raucous fit of uncontrollable laughter that quickly infects the rest of the squad. There is only one guy on the chopper from McGrath’s squad and he looks at us like we’re nuts. He has no idea what we are laughing about and we don’t tell him.

CHAPTER THREE

"THE HILL"

Artillery Hill is a small hill about twelve miles northwest of Pleiku in the central highlands of Vietnam. It's not very high, maybe a couple of hundred feet. A statue of the Virgin Mary sits on the top of the hill with the date March 1961 carved into the base. The statue, defiled by the attachment of several radio antennas, is referred to as "The Lady on the Hill" by all the units in the Pleiku area. Parked next to the statue is the million-candle-power searchlight used to sweep the vast expanse of defoliated land that stretches between the hill and Pleiku Air base several miles away. The main road leads up from the gate, circles the base of the hill and branches off to several small roads that lead down to the perimeter or wind their way up to the top of the hill.

It was only thirty days ago that Jim Fishe, Jim Farmly and I first arrived in Pleiku. We had spent two days and a night at Camp Alpha down around Saigon waiting to be transported to our unit.

It was April 6th, 1966 When a C-141 Starlifter deposited us at Ton Son Nhut airbase after an excruciating sixteen hour flight. A dusty ten-minute ride in a bus, windows open, barbed wire covering them, transported us to the Camp Alpha processing center, then, after a brief processing we were billeted and directed to the mess hall.

My eyes look at the food plopped down so delicately by the servers in the chow line. Roast beef, mashed potatoes, corn, baked beans, Jell-O and a glass of milk. The beef looks edible but I find it to be as tough and tasteless as the tongue of my GI boots. The potatoes are instant and taste like soupy cardboard. The Jell-O melts before I can get to it and the milk is a reconstituted powdered concoction that is never likely to spoil regardless of how long it is left out. This particular batch must have been out for quite some time…it's room temperature. It's chalky tasting and gags me when I try to drink it. None of us actually get past the first mouthful.

"It must be an acquired taste." Jim says as he spits a mouthful onto the dirt floor.

Instead, we drink several glasses of water in a desperate attempt to wash down the meal. At the stopover in Guam, a Staff Sergeant, our chaperone on the flight, warned us that the mess hall there would be our last opportunity to eat real food for the next twelve months. Now I understand what he was talking about.

Our hooch is situated just at the end of a Huey landing strip. We park our butts on a sand bag wall to watch all the activity on the airstrip. Six Hueys drop out of the sky just before dusk, hover for a second or two, gracefully pirouette and gently settle on the tarmac. They are not troop transports, they're Gunships. Each one heavily armed with Gatling guns or rocket launchers. The only troops they carry are their crews. The crews dismount and begin tending to their ships. The flight crews and ground crews work together busying themselves refueling, re-arming, inspecting engines and performing maintenance. They're like a swarm of ants all focused on the same objective…getting the ships ready to fly. I'm impressed by the fact that the flight crews had not walked away when the choppers landed but were still there working alongside the ground crews.

As darkness approaches I have my first intimate contact with one of the local residents…a damned mosquito. They're buzzing around our cots like a squadron of B-17's on a bomb run to Berlin. They're fucking huge! I've never seen such big mosquitoes. I flip down my cot's mosquito netting and stare at them. I swear they're circling the cot like vultures over a dead carcass. I fear they're just waiting for me to fall asleep so they can bring in the engineers and breech the netting that is keeping them from their feast. Even though it is hotter than hell, I opt to put my shirt back on. I want to cover as much exposed skin as possible.

I wake suddenly. I'm groggy and I shake my head trying to focus. I feel the ground shaking and sense a lot of activity. There is a deafening explosion just outside the hooch. The explosion snaps my mind into complete alertness. A siren screeches in the background and someone is screaming... *"Incoming!"* I'm flushed all over; the hair on my arms tingles, and my nostrils flare as the sudden need for increased levels of oxygen makes my respiration skyrocket. *What the hell am I supposed to do?* I'm scared shitless. Then *Wham* ...another loud explosion. I feel the shock wave and realize I'm face down on the floor of the hooch. A Sergeant is tugging at me shouting instructions, I can barely hear what he is saying but don't need any translation. The last explosion must have been close because my ears are ringing and I can barely hear. I jump to my feet and start running after the Sergeant. People are scrambling all over the place. Most of us are shitting in our pants. *Jesus,* I think, *I'm gonna die my first day here.* Outside another Sergeant is yelling, "Get to the bunkers!" Again, an explosion sends me diving for the ground.

"C'mon, let's go, let's go." Someone is tugging at my shirt.

I spring to my feet and follow him to a bunker about fifty yards from the hooch. We pile in, seven of us. There are already six guys in the bunker but it doesn't matter we squeeze in. The sandbags help muffle the sound of the explosions going off three or four at a time, but the presumed safety of the bunker doesn't make any of us relax.

I'm overwhelmed with the sudden realization that I have no weapon. As a matter of fact, no one in the bunker has a weapon. We're as naked as a soldier can get. No rifle, no pistol, no knife, no fucking ammo, nothing! *Holy shit,* I think, *what if the camp is assaulted?*

Anxiety overwhelms me and I yell out, "Where the hell do you get a weapon around here?"

It's dark in the bunker and I can't tell who says it, but someone says, matter-of-factly, we won't get weapons till we reach our units.

This elicits a response from another bunker inhabitant, a black guy, who doesn't seem to appreciate the candor. His response, "The hell you say mother fucker!" The explanation offered up is there have been too many instances of replacements panicking and shooting each other, so a decision was made not to issue weapons.

"What? Man, that's bullshit!" The black guy responds. "You sayin' it's okay to get shot by some Cong mother fucker rather than give us guns?"

"Say, my brother, I don't make the rules, I'm just lettin' you know what's up."

"Man, I ain't your mother fuckin' brother and don't be tryin' to talk like no brother, 'cause you ain't nothin' but a jive turkey."

"Hey, sinh loi my friend."

It's the second time I've heard the phrase; it bothers me not knowing what the hell it means. I blurt, "Man, just what the fuck is that supposed to mean?" I'm agitated, scared, and can't believe someone can be so laid back in our current situation.

"It means too fuckin' bad, my friend, just too fuckin' bad." He repeats it as if to put an explanation point on it.

Fifteen or twenty minutes elapse. I can hear Hueys flying over the camp and in the distance an enormous amount of automatic weapons fire and rocket explosions.

"Sounds like the Gunships have found the mortar positions." Sergeant Gerard comments as he stands with his head outside the bunker looking around. He goes on to say the VC try to mortar the helicopters sitting on the strip a couple of times a month. Unfortunately, for us, their marksmanship is poor and they tend to drop more rounds on the replacement camp than they do on the landing strip. *Christ,* I think, *I won't be doing much sleeping the rest of this night.*

Nearly an hour passes before I decide to leave the bunker. The Sergeant and several others are already gone. I don't see any pressing need to make it back to the hooch and actually consider sleeping in the bunker but change my mind when I start getting bitten by those damned mosquitoes.

Walking back to the hooch I pass an ambulance and a couple of guys loading a body on the back. There's blood all over the place. It looks black and glistens in the moonlight. The two guys doing the loading are pissing and moaning. One of them yells out, "Hey, this fucking jerk ain't wearin' his tags! Anybody know who this guy is?"

A few guys walk over, look, and back away shaking their heads. When I'm close enough to see, my stomach twists into a ball and I have to do everything humanly possible to keep from retching. The guy has no face! His nose is gone, there is a huge chunk of his head missing; he is totally unrecognizable. I turn and quickly move away almost running back to the hooch. It's the first time I've ever seen a dead person. I'd never been to a wake, and have never seen a body. Suddenly, I'm overwhelmed with the realization that the odds of my making it another three hundred and sixty-four days are a lot lower than I would have liked. It's a frightening moment.

Lying in my cot I can't stop thinking about it. After a few minutes I realize there are tears running down my face. I wipe them and resist the temptation to sniffle. I don't want anybody to know I'm crying. I'm more frightened than I have ever been before. Death, for the first time in my life is not just something I read about in the newspaper.

The next day is uneventful. We're out of the sack at 06:30. They don't have anything for most of us to do, so we sit around all day picking our noses. A few guys get grabbed for KP and a few get picked for a clean-up detail.

I wake to find the mosquito engineers have done their jobs. My body is riddled with mosquito bites. They aren't like the little red pimples I'd get back in the States, they're huge welts, large reddish mounds all over my body that itch beyond belief. Desperately seeking relief, I manage to find the medical tent where the medics are gracious enough to give me a small bottle of diluted ammonia; they tell me to dab it on the bites. Amazingly, it relieves the itching almost immediately and it doesn't even burn all that much. They throw in a bottle of mosquito repellant and send me on my way.

The repellent comes in a small plastic bottle and holds about one or two ounces. This stuff looks, smells and tastes like kerosene. It's oily and feels slick when I rub it between my fingers. When applied, it gives me a very acrid taste in my mouth and makes my skin feel creepy. Now that I have the stuff, I notice most of the GIs walking around the camp keep a bottle of it stuck under the elastic band used to hold the camouflage cover to their helmets.

There is a PX not far from the hooch and I am in desperate need of some smokes. When I walk in, I immediately notice an ample supply of civilian clothes hanging from several racks and folded neatly on shelves. There are Hawaiian shirts, an assortment of trousers, shoes, socks, etc. I'm surprised because the Army dumped our duffel bags and confiscated all our civvies and dress greens before we left the States. I can't help thinking, *why the hell did they take our stuff back in Oakland?* I shake my head and grab a couple of cartons of Pall Malls and try to pay for them.

A sweaty Spec 4, immersed in an issue of Playboy, doesn't even look up when he asks, "You got a ration card chief?" I begin to believe that

Specialist 4th class is a rank the Army gives to everybody that's a big pain in the ass.

"What ration card?"

"Can't buy cigarettes or liquor without a ration card."

"Where do I get one?"

"They'll issue one when you get to your unit."

"What the hell am I supposed to do till then? Man, I'm outta smokes and ain't shippin' outta here till tomorrow!"

"Okay, Okay, take a carton, but don't let me see you back here trying to buy more." The fuckin' guy acts like he just gave up six pints of blood and a kidney by allowing me to buy the cigarettes.

The cigarettes are ninety cents a carton. I paid forty cents a pack back in the States. I pay for them with a one-dollar MPC certificate. MPC is *Military Pay Currency*, funny money reminiscent of Monopoly script. They took our greenbacks away from us when they took our clothes and replaced it with the MPC funny money. This is the military's attempt to discourage black-marketeering. Presumably, the MPC is not negotiable with civilians, so the only place it can be used is in military establishments.

As a Private First-Class, a PFC, the Army feels my services are worth about a hundred thirty-seven bucks a month. Wandering back to the hooch, I light a Pall Mall take a deep drag and exhale.

"My God, a hundred thirty-seven bucks a month," I mumble under my breath. Then I remember I'll be getting sixty-five bucks Hazardous Duty pay and few extra bucks for overseas pay. *Sheesh, a couple of hundred bucks a month*...after last night, it doesn't seem like very much compensation. *My life ought to be worth more than that.*

The *Caribou,* a twin engine back loading airplane, is not a large aircraft, it has the wings attached above the fuselage and about a dozen porthole sized windows along each side. There are no actual seats. Instead, there is harness seating that hangs from the walls. The harness is made from two-inch wide canvass or nylon strapping making it simple to push out of the way and accommodate cargo loading.

The plane is shaking and vibrating. It creaks and strains, and at times, I wonder if it is going to make it. One of the two engines is spewing a constant stream of faint bluish smoke from the exhaust and we're flying low. The cargo door at the back is partially open which increases the noise level in the plane. The plane reeks from the smell of gasoline; I surmise this might be why they leave the cargo door slightly open.

There are twelve of us on the plane destined for different parts of the country. Our first stop is An Khe home to the 1st Cav. Three of us, Fishe, Farmly and myself, are destined for Pleiku. The other six are marines headed to Da Nang.

The view of the landscape is quite spectacular. Saigon is far behind us, so the only thing visible is the jungle and large expanses of rice fields. It seems surprisingly uncluttered and sedate, rarely seeing a building of any kind. The jungle itself has a bright-green neon hue to it and the rice paddies reflect the glint of the recently risen sun like mirrors set into the bright green landscape. Occasionally, a water buffalo accompanied by several Vietnamese farmers is visible.

Paa...zzzziiiing!

"What the hell was that?" Fishe asks with a trace of panic in his voice.

"Someone taking pot shots at us," The crew chief yells out, "Happens all the time. Every gook with a pop gun feels it's his obligation to bring down an American aircraft." His demeanor is matter of fact. He doesn't seem the least bit concerned about it. *Maybe the pilot should gain some altitude.*

"Hey, aren't you going to tell the pilot?" I yell.

"He knows! Hell, man, don't sweat it. We're long gone."

I guess this means the plane is already out of range. Jeez, I think, if you have to be an asshole to be a Spec 4, this guy, a Spec 5, must really be a piece of work.

"Most guys sit on their steel pot just in case," he informs us with a little smirk on his face. Since none of us actually have a helmet yet, I interpret his statement as, *Gee, too bad you bozos don't have steel pots yet, or you could sit on them to keep from getting your nuts shot off.*

We're airborne for forty-five minutes, maybe more, when I sense the plane slowing and starting to descend. When the landing gear is lowered, it makes a huge racket and instantly puts a noticeable drag on the plane. As we near the ground, the crew chief starts opening the already partially open ramp at the back of the plane. When it is almost completely open, he alerts the three guys destined for An Khe to get ready; a few seconds later the plane touches down. It hits hard, actually bouncing up off the ground a couple of times before it starts rolling down the airstrip. The plane is still rolling and the chief opens the rear door so the lower ramp is almost touching the ground. When it is about six inches from touching the ground, he motions for the three to get up and move closer. They stand at the threshold of the ramp holding straps hanging from the bulkhead. Up ahead there is a building, I assume it's the terminal, there are three GIs crouched next to the runway waiting for the plane. They're wearing steel pots, flak jackets and carrying M-16 rifles. The plane taxis down the runway at a pretty good clip, as we near the terminal, the chief points out the back and yells, "Jump off."

"The plane hasn't stopped yet!"

"It ain't gonna stop! Just get the hell off!"

"No fuckin' way, man!"

"The pilot'll shove your ass out the door before he'll stop this plane. You better get your asses out!" With that, he tosses their duffel bags out the back. Two of the guys take a couple of steps and hop off the ramp, they're unable to move their legs fast enough to keep from tumbling and before they are twenty feet from the still moving plane, the chief pushes the other guy off the ramp.

The men waiting next to the runway spring to a crouched run and grab the three poor bastards. They start pulling them towards the building, encouraging them to run, the engines immediately start revving and the plane accelerates down the runway. No stopping; no turning around, just full throttle and get the hell out. We're in the air in less than a minute. After the crew chief returns the cargo door to the almost closed position, he leans over and yells, "An Khe is always hot, man, we don't like flying in there. Pleiku is much safer." A bit of information that at least makes me feel like I won't get shot the minute I get off the plane.

When we land at Pleiku we come to a complete stop before unloading. There are several other planes bunkered around the runway. Several C-130's, a C-47, which amazes even me, and about a dozen A1E attack planes. The A1Es are single engine prop driven fighter planes that resemble a Jap zero, or some other WWII fighter. They are much larger than I would ever have imagined. As we mill around waiting for someone to tell us what to do, I grab an airman and ask him about the A1Es. They're called *Sandies* and discover they're actually quite fast. The airman says they're far more effective supporting ground troops than some of the big boys, like the F-4 phantoms we saw sitting on the airstrip in Guam.

Inside the Quonset-hut terminal we try to find out what the hell we're supposed to do.

"Ahem, excuse me?" We stand at the counter for about a minute but the Airman behind it doesn't acknowledge our presence.

Finally, he asks, "What'ya guys want?"

"We just got off a plane from Saigon. We're going to a mechanized self-propelled artillery unit." I point at the Caribou sitting on the strip.

"Oh, fresh meat...hold on." We look at one another with disgust, none of us particularly enamored by the term, *Fresh Meat.*

The Airman picks up the phone and cranks it a couple of times.

"Yeah, get me Smasher," he says. A few seconds elapse. "Yeah, this is Halberg over at the PAB (Pleiku Air Base) terminal. I got some fresh meat for you guys." He pauses a moment, reaches up and asks for our orders. I hand him mine. He gives them a cursory look, then continues. "Yeah, I got three guys for the Hill." He listens for a few seconds then returns the phone to its cradle.

I'm still thinking about the term, *fresh meat;* it's making me think about the guy who had his face blown off back at Camp Alpha.

Halberg looks at us and informs us we'll be picked up in about twenty minutes. We walk outside and plop down on the ground, sitting with our backs against the wall of the terminal. No one has much to say. The airfield is not unlike the one at Ton Son Nhut, but there are more planes here. Off in the distance, almost as if painted against the horizon, is a mountain range of considerable size. I love the sight of it. California had been the first time I'd ever seen them. Though, the skyline and the lakefront in Chicago hold their own picturesque mystique, mountains seem to be of divine making. They seem unspoiled and majestic, monuments to the creativity of God. These are not nearly as big, but the blanket of bright green vegetation that covers them radiates a beauty that would etch itself onto the canvas of anyone's memory.

A constant stream of helicopters comes and goes from a pad at the other end of the airstrip. They're noisy as hell. Every time one flies by a large cloud of red dust is stirred up, the same is true of vehicles that drive by. I take off my cap and try brushing it away, but it doesn't seem to matter. We go back inside the terminal.

Twenty minutes pass quickly. A Jeep pulls up out front; I'm the only one who gets up to see who it is. The Jeep is driven by a stern looking Staff Sergeant who dismounts and heads for the terminal door, I know he's there for us.

The Staff Sergeant, his name is Dick, his last name not his first, walks through the door, sees us, and says, "Let's go." Fishe and Farmly beat me out the door, so Fishe takes shotgun. Farmly and I are left to the back seat. There are four cases of C rations lying on the floor in the back of the Jeep.

"I have to make a stop before we take off." Sergeant Dick turns his head slightly to share this tidbit of information. We drive down a couple of dirt roads, make a few turns and stop in front of a house trailer. Sergeant Dick takes off his steel pot and tosses it on the seat.

"You," he looks at me, "Gimme a hand with these boxes."

I hand two of the boxes to Sergeant Dick and take the others myself, then follow Sgt. Dick to the door of the trailer where he neglects knocking and just barges in. I am amazed to find the inside of the trailer air-conditioned. Hell, we didn't even have air-conditioning back home so it is a welcome contrast to the steam bath outside.

Inside, sitting on one of the bunks are two Air Force Sergeants.

"Okay, where's the beer, dickhead?" Sergeant Dick barks at the one whose nametag identifies him as Anderson. I smirk at the irony of someone named Dick calling somebody else a dickhead. I think no one else would probably see the irony.

"Right here, buddy." Anderson bends over and pulls up the overhanging blanket from his bed and reveals about ten cases of Budweiser beer neatly stashed under the bed.

He pulls out four cases; Dick motions and we pick them up and head out the door.

"Nice doin' business with ya," one of them says as we walk out.

Somehow, I would have expected the transaction to have gone differently. Four cases of beer for four cases of C rations, it didn't make a lot of sense. *Why would anyone make an even trade of beer for C rations?*

Once outside the gate of the compound Sergeant Dick stops for a moment, pulls a bandana out of his pocket and ties it around his face. He unlatches the M-16 rifle from the holder, hands it to Fishe, and we drive away. The first couple of miles are pretty dusty, but soon we move on to a blacktop road. My sense of direction and the position of the sun make me think we're going north. The road actually has quite a bit of traffic moving in each direction, not like in the States, but enough so the road doesn't seem deserted. The civilian vehicles are either old French cars, banged up trucks or three wheeled Lambretta scooters designed to carry about four passengers in the back. The Vietnamese however, manage to squeeze about ten people into them. There is so much crap tied to the top of them, the scooters are dangerously top-heavy. It's easy to see it wouldn't take very much to make one of them flip over on its side. We're forced to ride behind one of these for ten minutes as a convoy of Jeeps and APC's passes us on the left side of the road. The vehicles in the convoy are covered with dust, as are all the GIs riding on them. The convoy prevents us from passing the Lambretta which keeps moving slower and slower. We're on a grade, not very steep, but enough to stall the severely overloaded vehicle. Four of the people riding on the back jump off and start pushing.

"God damn gooks!" Sergeant Dick vehemently voices his frustration.

"*Come on ya little bastards, get that piece of shit moving!*" Sergeant Dick, half-standing behind the steering wheel, yells at the melee in front of us while violently motioning with his arm to move the vehicle off the road. Farmly, who's from Boston and has a certain snobbish air about him, makes a huge mistake and suggests Sergeant Dick calm down.

"What'd you say to me, boy?" Farmly's attempt to calm down Sergeant Dick has the opposite effect.

"Hey, Sarge, yelling at them ain't gonna make them move any faster. I just don't see any use in abusing them because their scooter won't make it up the hill." A poor attempt at rationalization.

"Look, dip wad, when shit like this happens, you become a target. You get it? They could be slowin' down on purpose because there's a sniper out in the field waiting to pop us. It happens all the fuckin' time, asshole, so keep your mouth shut until you know what's goin' on."

Farmly looks away and shakes his head. I'm sure if I could read his mind he'd be thinking, *Sgt. Dick is a dick!* I, on the other hand, begin anxiously looking around and Fishe starts holding the M-16 at a more ready posture. I think to myself, *sniper, Jesus, what next?*

The convoy finishes passing and Sergeant Dick gooses the accelerator. He swings the Jeep out around the Lambretta to pass, as we do, he yells, "Assholes!" Some of them yell back, "Number ten! GI number ten." I decide this isn't a good time to ask Sergeant Dick what *Number Ten* means. Besides, I have a pretty good idea.

Sergeant Dick pulls down his bandana and points to a small hill. "That's 'Artillery Hill,' your new home."

Several hooches and a few large tents are scattered around the hill. Two gun emplacements are visible on the side of the hill facing us. There is a perimeter made up of concertina wire. There are three fences of concertina, each about six feet high. The fences are about five or six feet apart. In other words, as someone walks towards or away from the hill, they encounter a six-foot high fence of concertina, then a six-foot expanse of ground, a second fence, and then six or eight more feet to the third fence. There are signs warning the area between the concertina is mined.

We pause at the gate and wait for the guard to swing it open so we can pass. The gate is framed from large steel struts and embroidered with yards of barbed wire. Bunkers flank each end of the gate. The bunkers look like they're only about four feet tall, but as the guard emerges from the back of one I realize it is partially dug into the ground. Just outside the gate to the right is a large corrugated building with a roof slanted from front to back and an old-fashioned barber pole sitting next to the door. A wooden sign hanging over the door reads, "*LAUNDRY and MASSAGE*." Sgt. Dick follows a dusty dirt road up from the gate and makes his way around the hill parking next to a half-assed structure about the size of a garage...The Orderly room.

Inside a First Sergeant emerges from one of the two offices. A first Sergeant is nearly a god-like entity to enlisted men; a Sergeant Major is actually considered to be God. Stenciled to the tag over his shirt pocket is the name Neuman. He picks up our orders and gives them a cursory look glancing up at us momentarily. He doesn't introduce himself or ask us our names.

Looking up he says, "Simon, you report to the commo bunker and see Sergeant Bennett. Fishe, you go with Simon. Farmly, says here you're a crypto man, you must be educated. Tell me you're not gonna let all that learnin' get in the way of stayin' alive."

A crypto man is a code guy. All the important messages that come and go are encrypted. These messages generally fall into four categories: Confidential, Secret, Top Secret, and super duper Top Secret known as Top Secret Flash.

"You'll be working for Sergeant Dick." Farmly rolls his eyes and grimaces, knowing he's already made such a good impression with Sergeant Dick.

"Farmly, you'll bunk with Varant and Sergeant Dick in that bunker right there." He points to a sand bagged hooch kitty corner to the orderly room about forty yards up the hill. The term *Orderly Room* always sounds like a place for guys who change bedpans at a hospital, but that's what the army calls the office that houses the Company Commander, First Sergeant and Company Clerk.

We report to Sergeant Bennett and he points us at the S-4 supply tent so we can pickup our issue of equipment. The S-4 tent is probably the largest structure on the hill. There are literally mountains of supplies stacked next to it. Everything from pallets of C rations to stacks and stacks of every type of ammunition imaginable. Everything from M-16 rounds to the huge rounds used by the Howitzers. The supply Sergeant, a guy named Bast, gives us a choice of weapons. I take an M-14 because it is the weapon I'm most familiar with. I can break down an M-14 and reassemble it in about thirty seconds. It is - at least from my limited experience - an extremely accurate weapon with tremendous stopping power. The round is a 7.62 millimeter projectile with a full metal jacket and is fired with enough velocity to knock down a full grown man five-hundred yards away. Fishe and Farmly take M-16's. We're issued eight empty magazines and a crate of ammunition, a steel pot with helmet liner and camouflage cover. We're given six pair of jungle fatigues and two pair of jungle boots, a flak jacket, along with a field pack and harness, two bottles of mosquito repellant and two sets of earplugs. Bast tosses us a pistol belt, canteen, first aid kit and two ammo pouches, a new bayonet with scabbard, a poncho, and a snakebite kit. The last item is a lightweight sleeping bag and a pillow.

The S-4 tent is located about a hundred yards behind the orderly room so we have to drag all this equipment back to the commo hooch, a good two hundred yard stretch.

The ground is dry and hard. Each step kicks up a little puff of red dust that leads me to conclude that it hasn't rained in quite awhile. On the Caribou ride from Camp Alpha, I had seen vast expanses of rice paddies. I saw them again during the Jeep ride from Pleiku Air Base. Pleiku is not as hot as Saigon had been, but it's warm enough to make me wonder how the farmers keep the water in those paddies from drying out.

Our hooch is just above the road that encircles the camp, maybe two hundred yards up from the perimeter. The hooch is just a large tent erected on top of a wooden floor. Outside, a wall of sandbags protects the sides of the tent. A screen door serves as entrance to the tent and all the cots have mosquito-netting hanging above them. There are several empty cots in the hooch, none of them seeming any more desirable than the other. I just drop my gear on the first one I come to. There is a foot locker at the end of each cot and we start stowing our gear as best as we can. The hooch is set up for eight or ten people, but there are only five of us. Fishe, a big Swede from Minnesota named Leighton "Lee" Lindlay, a chatterbox named Tom "Red" Smitt, James Pinetti and myself. Pinetti flew into Camp Alpha with us but hasn't been shipped up to Pleiku yet. Evidently the NCOs, with the exception of Sergeant Dick, are all housed together in another hooch about fifty more yards down the road.

"Where the hell do they get this stuff?" I ask, removing a grizzled piece of meat from my mouth. It's my first trip to the mess hall on the hill.

"I don't think it's real beef. I think its water buffalo," Lindlay offers. Fishe is gnawing determinedly on a mouthful of the meat.

"Generally, I only come here for breakfast. I chow down on C rations the rest of the time." Lindlay goes on to say he's been in country for about a month and has quit trying to digest the food from the mess tent. We learn that fried chicken or baked ham are the only decent things they serve. The beer trade starts making sense.

After chow Lee gives us a tour of the hill. The PX is located just up the hill from the gate. The chapel is right next to it. On the other side of the hill Bravo Battery has three big guns, two 175mm's and one 8 inch self-propelled howitzer, all three firmly emplaced and primed for fire missions. The large spade at the back of each gun is firmly dug in and all three guns are encircled with a four-foot high wall of sandbags. Canisters of shells and powder are neatly stacked at the rear of each gun. The Howitzers are big, really big. The muzzles of the 175s have to be fifteen or twenty feet long, at least that's what they appear to be.

"We call that Bunker up there the *Crow's Nest.* Lindlay points to a bunker just below the top of the hill. There's two of 'em. They have a fifty caliber in each one, but all the perimeter bunkers have M-60s."

"What's the story on the statue?" I had seen the statue from the road coming from Pleiku a couple of miles away. It is a statue of the Madonna and the Christ Child.

"The local gooks say there was a Catholic mission here when this was occupied by the French. I'm not sure why the statue was left after they moved away. You'd think they would have taken it with them." Lindlay offers, looking up at the statue shaking his head.

"We get to see movies every Tuesday and Friday. Tuesday is always an episode of *Combat* and *Gunsmoke* and Friday we get to see a real movie. Dey hang a sheet on da side of the chapel to use as a screen."

"What about stuff like laundry?" Fishe asks.

"We take our fatigues and stuff to the shack at the entrance; we get dem back in two or three days. They'll also develop film for ya and we all get our haircuts there, haircuts about a buck. Laundry is ten cents an item." Lindlay cracks a huge smile and informs us we can also get a massage for two bucks and a tip. The length and detail of the massage usually depend on the size of the tip. This, strangely enough, is the first thing I've heard since being in country that hasn't sent me spinning down the road to gloom and doom.

CHAPTER FOUR

"DUTY"

As part of the commo platoon my main duties include laying field wire and setting up landline communications between our unit and other units in the area. Sgt. Bennett also pointed out that occasionally we'd be shuttled back and forth to our fire-support bases to help set up the commo when they relocate. Bennett is also kind enough to point out when we're out laying wire we're pretty much on our own.

"So far," he says, "the wire teams 'ave only been ambushed a couple of times." I feel so reassured hearing that.

Outside of our commo duties, we pull guard, go on patrols, and labor around the hill. So pretty much we do any of the crap Bennett is kind enough to volunteer us to do. According to Bennett, our unit is also the main source of cover and support for a local engineering battalion camped adjacent to our perimeter at the bottom of the hill. About the only thing he doesn't have us doing is pulling KP. Local Vietnamese are used for KP and a lot of other menial duties around the hill. They're paid about five bucks a day, for most Vietnamese that's about a months pay.

Positioned around the perimeter are twelve defensive bunkers. Each partially dug in and set back about ten yards from the inside of the perimeter wire. During normal guard they only man every other bunker with a team of three people. The other bunkers are only manned during periods of high alert. There is also a series of trenches that ties some of the bunkers together. Tonight I get my first indoctrination with guard duty.

I report for guard at seventeen-thirty in the front of the orderly room. The Sergeant of the Guard makes a quick inspection, gives us the skinny on some intelligence information and then doles out the assignments. I'm assigned to bunker number six with "Red" Smitt and Harold Varant. Smitty is from Oklahoma. He's a good old boy with a serious Oklahoma drawl. The nickname "Red" is a product of his bright orange colored hair, though there isn't very much of it left. Male pattern-baldness has taken a serious hold on our Oklahoma friend. He was shipped here from Fort Sill, where the army thought his best use was to be an ammo-humper. One of the poor bastards who have to feed two hundred pound shells to the gun crews during a fire mission. Somehow or another he's managed to get himself assigned to the commo platoon, a welcome change I'm sure. He's been in country for a couple of months.

Varant is from the Los Angeles area. I haven't been able to get a good read on him. He doesn't say much and tends to think everything is a joke. His wit seems as dry as most of the ground around here. I haven't decided whether or not I like him. Either way, I'm going to be living with him for the next twelve months and in order to survive I'm going to have to be as tolerant as possible, especially considering everyone here is walking around with a loaded weapon. Hell, you never know what will send someone over the edge. Back in Chicago, I knew guys who'd cut ya just because you were walking down the wrong side of the street. Being flexible was a good idea then, it's a better idea now; I won't be alienating anybody I really don't have too. Who knows, maybe he'll turn out to be okay…you just never know about these things.

We break the guard duty into three shifts: six-till-ten, ten-till-two, and two-till-six. We flip coins to determine who will pull the ten-to-two shift and I lose.

Smitty and I lie on cots inside the bunker and shoot the bull for a while, well, he does, I just listen. Smitty is one of those guys who will never shut up. Finally, at eight, I beg him to be quiet so I can get a couple of hours sleep.

"*Simon! Simon! C'mon get your ass up!*" It's ten o'clock. I've just fallen into a deep sleep, just deep enough to start dreaming.

"What? Huh? Yeah, yeah, I'm up." I roll up to a sitting position on the side of the cot and try to open my eyes.

"C'mon, let's go." Varant is indignant. I stand up, put my flak jacket on and follow Varant out the door. On top of the bunker he flips open the breech of the M-60 to check the belt.

"Okay, the sixty is ready. These are the detonators for the Claymore mines." He hands me the four detonators. They're small, gray-plastic, hand-pumps just a little bigger than my hand.

"You've got to pump each one three times before it'll blow. Don't blow 'em unless we got gooks in the wire." I acknowledge and he continues, "You've got to call in every half hour, say this is post six and let 'em know what's going on. You remember the password?"

"Mouseketeer," I mumble.

"All the posts are on a common line, so you can hear everybody. If you think you see something you can fire the flare pistol or call for illumination. The flares don't show you shit unless something is moving. If a gook freezes out there till the flare burns out, you probably won't see him."

This confuses me. "Then what the hell are the flares good for?"

"We use the flares to try and spook the gooks."

"Anything happens, get on the horn and start yellin'. One last bit of advice, keep sharp. You'll hear 'em before you see 'em. If a gook gets through our area and caps somebody, your name will be dogshit around here, buddy." Varant disappears down into the bunker.

Sitting on top of the bunker I look out over the wire at the empty expanse of field. There is only a sliver of moon so the blackness seems thick. Millions of bright specs are sprayed across the sky and produce what little light there is. In Chicago, where the air is thick with smog, it's a rare occasion to see more than a handful of stars.

I stare into the darkness for about fifteen minutes and realize that after a time I can actually discern the details of the landscape. In basic training we were introduced to *Night Vision* during our night firing exercise. We were taught to guard our eyes from light and our eyes would acclimate themselves to the darkness. One burst of light, the pupils recede, and night vision is gone for several minutes.

I light up a smoke and gaze at the stars. The field phone startles me when it rings. I grab it and respond, "Post six...all clear...nothing to report."

The Sergeant of the guard prompts each of the other posts.

"Post two?"

"Post two, all clear."

"Post four?"

"Post four, all clear." He continues till all the posts report.

"Post six, don't respond till I ask, you got it?"

"I got it, I got it."

Two hours pass. The darkness, the quiet, and the lack of sleep sneak up on me. One moment I'm staring out into the blackness, then…"*Son-of-a-bitch!*" I jump up shaking my hand and instinctively bring the burned fingers to my mouth wetting them with saliva. "Damn it," I mumble. I must have dozed off. My cigarette burned all the way down to my fingers. *How long had I nodded off?* I did a mental estimate thinking it could have only been three or four minutes.

God, damn it, I think to myself. Sleeping on guard is bad, real bad. Article fifteen for sure; maybe court marshal if something happens.

"Okay, Okay. I've only got another hour to go," I mumble trying to convince myself I'll make it. I stand up, shake my head and sit back down. I force my eyes open as far as I can get them. I want to start whistling, but know I shouldn't. I catch myself just as my eyelids are about to shut.

"*Fuck!*" Again, I stand up and try to shake it off. I sit down and slap myself hard on the side of my face. A few seconds later, the phone rings again.

"This is post four, I heard somethin' out in the wire, gimme the spot."

The huge searchlight at the top of the hill illuminates the wire just to my left.

"Okay, scan right, man." The searchlight responds. "Okay, hold it there. No, that's nothin' go back to the left. Okay, sweep the field in front of five and six." I see the searchlight swing back and forth across the field outside the wire, but nothing is discernible.

"Must have been a rat, go ahead and kill the light."

At least the incident brings me back from my stupor. I sit for several minutes, more alert; stimulated by the possibility that post four did see something, when it dawns on me. "Shit!" I mumble, suddenly overcome with the thought that I might have been the "sound" that they heard. I reach up and slap myself hard in the face and wait. Sure enough, five or six seconds elapse and post four calls in.

"Gimme the light again, there's something out there, man."

The searchlight again lights up the field in front of post four. For an instant I actually think of telling them it was just me doing the - *I can't stay awake face slap* - but don't.

"Swing the light over here to post eight I think I've got movement."

The light sweeps past my post and over to the right. It weaves a pattern back and forth across the field, but there is nothing to see. The light is once again put to rest. I'm sure the guys over at post four are going to be sleeping with their eyes open the rest of the night. I smile and light another cigarette.

My watch says it is 01:55. Five more minutes and I can finally get some sleep. I stand up and climb off the back of the bunker. Just as I do, a trip flare shoots off near the main gate and the phone rings.

"Post two...post two... we got gooks in the wire! We got gooks in the wire!"

Immediately the M-60 machine gun from post two starts firing short bursts into the wire right of the front gate. A few seconds later, post four's M-60 chimes in. The searchlight is on and people are firing flares and shooting their weapons. The loud methodical firing of the fifty-caliber from the crow's nest sends tracers flying over my head. *Jesus Christ, everyone is shooting!* Men are piling out of the bunkers and others are running down from the hooches in their underwear and flak jackets, guns blazing.

Holy Shit! Smitty and Varant start firing from the gun slit inside the bunker.

"Simon, why the hell ain't you using that sixty?" Varant yells from inside the bunker. "Are they close enough for the Claymores?"

"Close enough for the Claymores? Man, I don't see shit," I yell back in frustration. A couple of the Bouncing Betty mines go off inside the wire. I aim the M-60 at that location and start firing. I pull the trigger and pour out a continuous stream of rounds.

"Short bursts! Short bursts!" Smitty is pulling at my shoulder.

"God damn it, short bursts, Simon." I stop firing and look back at him. "Man, you want to burn up that barrel," Smitty asks? "Let it cool down. Then only fire short bursts. Did you fire the Claymores?"

"Hell, no, man. I'm still not sure what the fuck everybody is shootin' at. I haven't seen shit. I only started shooting 'cause a couple of the mines went off."

The searchlight is panning all along the perimeter; everywhere else it's as black as a bottle of ink. The blackness interrupted only for split seconds by the muzzle flashes of our weapons. Smitty grabs a flare and fires it out in front of our bunker and immediately gunfire erupts from all around us. The trenches are full of guys all with itchy trigger fingers. The gunfire lasts three or four minutes then ends as abruptly as it started.

"*Hold your fire. Hold your fire.*" The duty officer is running behind the bunkers yelling, it is the only sound that disturbs the dead silence. The searchlight keeps panning all around the outside of the perimeter. The ring of the field phone startles me and I snap up the handset.

"This is Lt. Duke, where was the initial contact?"

"Post two, sir. We had mucho movement in the wire down around the gate."

"Anyone else see anything?"

"We heard the tin cans rattling in the wire at post four, sir. It looks like there's a dead body in the outer perimeter, but it's hard to tell."

"Anyone hit?" No one answers.

"Anyone get any incoming fire?" Again, no one answers.

"Okay, listen up. I want everyone to stay put. No one fires their weapon unless you can actually see a gook, got it? He emphasizes the word see and we all acknowledge. Sergeant Keelerhall is going to take some men out by the gate to check it out."

I can see Sgt. Keelerhall coming towards our position with several men following. He looks into the trench and points, "You, you're with me." Then he looks up at me and repeats his order.

I fall in behind the squad as it moves towards the front gate, stopping only to draft two more volunteers. We pause near bunker two; Keelerhall motions us all down. Crouching behind the bunker Keelerhall huddles us up for instructions. He uses his finger to draw a little diagram in the dirt illuminating it with a flashlight that has a red lens.

"Okay, I'm gonna send you four out the gate." He passes a hand radio to a little guy known as Frenchy. "I want you guys to take position in front of the skin palace. You two," he points at Frenchy and me, "sweep around the building and you two cover. Once you're around the corner of the building, if it's clear, signal and move back out to the front."

"What if it's not?" Frenchy asks.

"Then you can walk up and ask those mean Vietcong to go away, oh, and make sure you say please." The raspy sarcasm in Keelerhall's voice makes us feel like idiots. He reaches across and whacks Frenchy on the side of the helmet.

"What'ya think, you idiot! Hit the dirt; use the radio! If it's clear, move back out in front of the skin palace. Then we'll join up and sweep the outside of the perimeter."

"Okay, I'll have 'em hit the lights and you go on my signal." He uses his radio to request the lights. Almost immediately both searchlights hit the area around the gate.

Keelerhall barks into the radio, "Move 'em out away from the gate asshole. We don't want them shining on us." He has the lights train in on the road and move along the ditches just out and away from the gate.

The four of us move over just to the right of the gate. We use the gate bunker for protection. My heart is pounding; I can hardly breathe. I pull back the operating lever of my M-14 to make sure I have a round chambered. I look at Frenchy and realize he must have dressed in a hurry. Pants, no belt, tee shirt and flack jacket. I see his boot laces are untied and motion at him to get his attention; I point to his boots. He looks down and says, "Fuck." He drops the radio and bends over to make a quick attempt at tying the laces. They're still half-undone, but at least he won't trip over 'em. Our attention is focused on Frenchy and we don't realize Keelerhall is motioning for us to move out. Keelerhall throws a rock that hits Frenchy on the side of the helmet. We turn around and see him thrusting his arm repeatedly in the direction of the laundry. I don't know the other two guys and neither have shirts on, so there are no nametags to read. One of them says, "Okay, me and Bobby will open the gate…you guys cover till it's open." We nod.

"What's your name?" I grab his arm and ask as he turns to move away.

"Thompson."

They move to the middle of the gate where the two halves meet. Bobby stays crouched with his M-16 ready to fire. Thompson starts removing the chain that's holding the gate halves together. He crouches and pushes the gate away from him. He and Bobby scoot over to the door of the laundry building and motion for us to come. Frenchy leads the way. We crouch down and run through the gate. When we reach the door of the barbershop, Frenchy stands up with Thompson and Bobby, but I stay crouched.

"Okay, you two sweep around the building. We'll come up behind to cover."

Fuck, is all I can think. Frenchy moves in behind me as we inch our way along the wall till we reach the corner of the building. With my back glued to the wall I slide down till I am crouched as low as I can get. I roll my head around the corner with my helmet glued to the wall. *Shit! I can't see a damned thing.* I snap my head back.

"I can't see shit," I whisper. The spotlight falls across the roof of the building as it focuses on the road, creating a pitch-black shadow on the roadside wall of the building.

"Shit, man, let me take a look." I move back and Frenchy snaps his head out around the corner, and snaps it back quickly. He moves down and does it again. "You're right dammit, you can't see a damned thing."

We slide back towards the front door to let the other two guys know. Frenchy puts the radio against his ear and keys it. "Sarge, it's dark as hell out there. We can't see shit."

"Okay, okay. Move back to the corner and get down. I'll fire a flare out over the road that should light up the back of the building."

As we move back to the corner of the building, I can actually hear my heart beating. We get to the edge and crawl halfway around the corner. I know the flare is also going to make us visible.

Several seconds pass and I hear the thwack of the flare being fired. It goes off out over the main road. It hangs in the air from the little parachute that deploys when it ignites and begins its slow fiery descent back to the ground. We sweep our eyes back and forth across everything in our field of vision…nothing. We get up and plaster our backs against the wall again, then slide down to the back corner of the building. We take a turn at peering around the corner then we move around the back of the building and sweep down the wire for about forty our fifty yards hoping someone on the inside of the wire doesn't get an itchy trigger finger and mistake us for VC. We pause so Frenchy can call back to Keelerhall.

"Ain't nothin' out here Sarge, no bodies or nothin'."

We cautiously return to the back of the laundry where Bobby and Thompson have taken positions to cover us. The radio buzzes with Keelerhall's voice telling us to return.

"You guys move out two by two...keep your spacing about fifteen feet. We'll move out as you pass us." Keelerhall's deploys half of us just outside the gate and we begin inching our way down the wire. Thompson is in front this time, I'm right behind him; Frenchy and Bobby are just behind me. We move slowly, staying crouched low to the ground following the searchlight that's slowly moving down the perimeter just ahead of us. As we reach the area in front of bunker three, one of the unmanned bunkers, Thompson abruptly stands up, lowers his weapon and says, "Son-of-a-bitch!" He motions for the rest of us. Keelerhall instructs his men stay put and trots down the wire till he's standing next to Thompson.

"Jesus H. Christ!" Keelerhall looks into the perimeter at the carcass of a dead water buffalo. It's blown to hell. It's just a big lump of flesh. The only way you can actually tell it is a water buffalo is from the horns.

It must have been shot a thousand times and mines have blown two of its legs off.

"Man, who's gonna go in there and drag that carcass out." Thompson voices what we're all thinking. The mines aren't going to make getting it out very easy.

Keelerhall is on the phone, presumably with the duty officer or someone up in the operations bunker. Shortly thereafter, I hear whistles blowing and people yelling, "All clear!" An exodus from the trenches and bunkers returns people to their hooches. The rest of us return to our bunkers to finish out the guard shift. Lying on the cot waiting for the adrenaline rush to subside, I look over at Varant, he says, "You know they'll report contact with the VC tomorrow."

"Huh, what the heck are you talking about?"

"They'll have to report some contact to explain all the gunfire here tonight. They'll also want to requisition replacement ammo. So in the morning they'll report that we were hit by some sappers, or some other bullshit."

"A sapper? What's a sapper?"

"Sappers are like Vietnamese Kamikaze. They come running in with a satchel full of C4, pull the detonator, and 'Adios Muchachos'."

Shit! Another fucking way to get killed. The more I find out, the more I worry about completing my tour.

Varant continues, "I get to send all that shit out every day. I see it before it gets encrypted and I see the incoming stuff after it gets decrypted." He pauses for a second, as if something has just occurred to him. "I shouldn't be saying anything, so don't go shootin' your mouth off."

"Hey, no problem." Before I fall asleep, I think long and hard about everything that's occurred. I smile a little knowing my attempts to keep myself awake had spooked the guys on the neighboring bunker. It is a short-lived smile because I start wondering what I would have done if there really had been VC out there when we were sweeping the perimeter. Would I even be here thinking this at all? It's a chilling thought.

Chapter Five

"Squeaky Clean"

We sleep till noon. Pinetti was sent in by Bennett to wake us. Turns out, Pinetti is becoming a real pain in the ass. He's a real wise-ass who spends more time tryin' to get out of doing things than it would take him to actually do them. I know somewhere, in some dictionary, the term Kiss-Ass and the name Pinetti are intimately connected. We figure Sergeant Bennett will never have to worry about running out of ass-wipe as long as he's got Pinetti around. What is especially irritating is his phony baloney southern accent. The little bastard is from Champaign, Illinois, for Christ sake, but to hear him talk you'd swear he was from Alabama or Tennessee. The fact that almost our entire cadre is of southern persuasion leads me to believe it's just more ass kissing.

Red Smitt and I have to report to Bennett over at the commo bunker.

"So you boys had a little excitement last night, hope none of you pissed your pants," he says laughingly. Of all the people I've seen around here he appears to be the oldest. If I had to guess, it'd be near fifty.

"What'd they do about the water buffalo?" I ask motioning in the direction of the wire.

"Drug it out with a tank retriever this morning, hell they didn't even set off any of the mines. Red, you and Sis here got the short end of the straw and pulled latrine duty." Bennett started calling me Sis because he thinks I sound like a girl on the phone. I hate it.

"God damn it, Sarge, we pulled guard last night and your gonna stick us with burnin' shit?" Smitty's disdain is reflected in the distasteful tone he uses to voice his objection.

"You two are the only ones left not doin' anything." *Yeah, everyone but kiss ass Pinetti.* I think rolling my eyes.

Smitty, mumbling and bitching, is already heading out of the hooch.

"What's latrine duty?" I ask.

"It pretty damn disgusting," is all he says.

Latrine duty stateside means scrubbing the latrines from top to bottom, here we don't have latrines, only outhouses.

I follow Smitty to the motor pool, wondering what this has to do with latrine duty. We pick up two five-gallon cans of JP4 jet fuel, grab two shovels, some work gloves and head to the outhouse just south of the orderly room - it's a four-holer.

"Well, first thing we do, is pull these out," Smitty puts on the work gloves and flips up the little door behind hole number one. He reaches in and pulls out the can. It's half of a fifty-five gallon drum filled nearly brim high with twenty-five gallons of crap, urine, and toilet paper. The smell is ghastly! I almost vomit.

"Jesus…Man…This is fucking gross," I gag, all the while trying to hold my breath. As we pull the can away from the outhouse the contents slosh back and forth and slops over the edges.

"God damn it!" Smitty jumps back to keep from getting splashed again. My stomach is retching.

"Why don't they pay the damned gooks to do this?" We drag the can about ten yards away, towards the perimeter wire.

"We're supposed to pour the piss out before you burn it," so we each grab a side and tilt the can so the liquid pours over the side onto the ground. Fuck! Smitty pours three gallons of JP4 into the can, lights a match and throws it in. The fuel ignites immediately, but not like gasoline, it's much less volatile. Plumes of thick black smoke roll into the air accompanied by a stench so foul, if we could bottle it, we could drive every VC back to North Vietnam without firing a shot.

"Now I know why those monks set themselves on fire, they were scheduled for latrine duty."

We pull out the second can and repeat the exercise. My eyes are watering and I can no longer control the retching. I bend over and vomit next to the can.

It is near four when the fires burn out. While they burned, we busted our nuts digging a five-foot pit. We empty the contents of the cans into the pit, spread it around and cover it with the dirt.

Walking away, I turn towards Smitty and state the obvious, "my God, we stink beyond comprehension."

"The barnyards back home don't smell this fuckin' bad." Smitty says removing his shirt.

At the entrance to the hooch, we strip down to our skivvies and leave the clothes outside. We grab soap and towels and head for the shower. The shower is actually a thousand-pound bomb canister. The ends are welded shut, the top is cut open to accommodate filling and four shower heads are connected underneath with pull chains for controlling the water flow.

Standing under one of the shower heads I grimace in anticipation, then pull the chain. "Jesus! Shit!" The water is always ice cold. I shower as fast as I can. There's no getting used to it...it just stays cold.

Today is fried chicken day so this will be a meal I will actually enjoy eating. Uncharacteristically, everything served with the meal is actually edible. The chicken is the best thing I've eaten since coming here. It is served with corn bread, corn and chocolate pudding. The pudding comes from a can and has a chemical taste to it, but it is still a welcome change.

Outside, after the meal, we pause to light up. While mindlessly smoking the cigarette, I watch the Vietnamese scrape the trays into the garbage. They hand them down to another worker who is washing them in a thirty-gallon garbage drum. The water in the drum is hot; small wisps of steam rising from the can. Stuck in the can, firmly clamped to the side, an immersion heater is burning kerosene or bunker fuel and heating the water to what appears to be a very warm temperature. The stack from the heater rises three feet above the can and sends a steady plume of dark smoke rising into the air. I guess the fuel is probably JP4, the same stuff we burned the shit with earlier. Then, without any conscious reasoning, a light bulb switches on in my head.

"Smitty, look." I point towards the gook washing the trays.

"Yeah, so what?"

"No, look at the heater. Don't you get it?"

Red stares at it for several seconds then the skin on his brow stretches back and his mouth falls open. "No more cold showers!" Smitty starts chuckling. Fishe has just finished handing his tray to one of the gooks and instantly wonders why Smitty is so excited.

"What's going on?" Smitty is hopping up and down like a four-year-old.

"The heater, man, the heater." I point at the tower that holds the promise of a creature comfort not enjoyed since we left the States.

"If we can get one of those we can have hot showers."

"And just where do you propose we get one of those?" There is a tone of cynicism in Jimbo's voice.

"Man, I don't know, but somewhere in this country, there's an immersion heater with our name on it."

Back in the hooch, Fishe breaks out a six-pack of *33* beer. *33*, *OB* and *Carling's Black label* are the only beers available in our PX. All three taste like shit. *OB* beer is especially rancid. It still has crap floating around the bottom of the bottle.

The beer is warm. There are no coolers or refrigerators. The temperature of the beer, though undesirable, does not prohibit or minimize our consumption. We drink it anyway. One bonus, *33* and *OB* have much higher alcohol content than the *Black label.* After you drink a couple, the bad taste doesn't seem to matter that much anymore. Jim opens up his footlocker and produces a CO_2 fire extinguisher. He puts the six-pack on the floor and empties the extinguisher on the beer cans. He passes around the beer; they are surprisingly cool.

"Let's steal one from the mess hall." Pinetti has opened his mouth, and as usual, neglected to think about the words coming out of it.

My God, what an idiot! I roll my eyes, laugh and say, "Yeah, that's a great idea. Don't you think they might notice that our shower mysteriously gets a heater right after theirs disappears?" I look around waiting for someone to offer a suggestion.

"The engineers have their own mess tent. If we took one of theirs, how would they know? We've got several runs of wire going through their camp…"

Before Smitty can finish I add, "Yeah, we could cut the line going to their switchboard just after dark. Then a couple of us will have to drive down and troubleshoot the wire."

"That's a good idea." Fishe, who we consider the most sensible one of our group has blessed the plan by acknowledging that he believes not only is it feasible, but is actually a good plan. "Most everybody will be in their hooches by dark. We should be able to grab it pretty easily."

"Anybody got any other ideas?" I ask.

Varant, who just walked in, grabs a beer, listens to our attempts to devise a plot then offers his own opinion, "You can always bribe Sergeant Bast. You can get anything out of him if the price is right."

"Or you can trade. See what he needs and make a deal." Lindlay offers.

"I'm leaning towards the engineer heist myself," I again voice my preference, but ask, "What about those Air Force guys?" I explain the deal Sergeant Dick had transacted my first day here.

"Yeah, I hear those bastards will trade anything for the right price," Smitty adds.

A new topic pops into my head and blurt out a question totally unrelated to the topic. "So what's the story on Pleiku?"

Smitty plops down on a cot, leans back on his elbows, "Well, there's a rumor floating around that claims some guy got his pecker cut off by one of the whores so right now it's off limits."

"Man, you got to be shittin' me. Some whore cuts my dick she ain't never seeing the light of day again." Fishe points his finger and cocks his thumb to mimic a pistol. He snaps the thumb down, pulls the hand back and adds, "Pow!"

"Doesn't look like anybody here's gonna get a pass for awhile. The brass can't make up their minds...off-limits...not off-limits." Varant grumbles.

"Hey, there's always the little massage girls at the laundry." Smitty says, licking his lips and rubbing his crotch.

"Yeah, but those little bitches always want ten bucks for a lay and fifteen for a blow job," Varant grumbles.

Pinetti's head snaps up, his eyes widen and he asks, "You can get a blow job from the girls at the laundry?"

"Yeah, I'm guessing that's the reason they call it the skin palace," I add as I remove my boots and tee shirt. Ever since I've seen guys scrambling down to the bunkers in their underwear, and then spending several uncomfortable hours rooting around in the trenches, I've taken to sleeping with my pants on. I lay my M-14 on the floor just under my bunk; my flak jacket is hanging next to the bunk. Hell, Lindlay actually sleeps with his boots on, but I would never be able to stand doing that.

By Saturday we've pursued all of our alternatives except the heist. The benevolent Sergeant Bast said he'd get us an immersion heater for the low bargain price of *two hundred bucks!* The son-of-a-bitch said that would only be about ten bucks a piece from everybody that uses our shower.

Yesterday, Fishe and I accompanied Sergeant Bennett over to Pleiku Air Base to pick up wiring supplies at the airstrip. While Bennett lunched in the Air force mess hall, Fishe and I went knocking on the trailer door of the guys who'd made the deal with Sergeant Dick.

"So whata'ya you guys want?" It was the airman Sergeant Dick had called a dickhead.

"Don't you remember me? I was here with Sgt. Dick. Ya know beer for C rations."

"Sure, I remember, come on in and close the door you're lettin' in the hot air."

"We were told you could deal just about anything. We're looking for an immersion heater."

"An immersion heater? What the hell you want one of those for?"

Fishe says, "We're tired of taking cold showers."

"Ah yes, that would be a real pain in the ass, wouldn't it? I don't know, it's not something I've had much call for. I'll have to check around to see if I can get one." He brings his hand up to his mouth and runs his thumbnail up and down the edge of his front teeth. It makes his statement seem sincere.

"Hey, you guys interested in a nice Air Force, thirty-eight *Smith and Wesson* with a six inch barrel? He turns away, picks up a wax-papered package, unwraps it, then lays it down in front of us. It is brand-spanking new. Hell, it still has the Cosmoline on it.

"I'll let you guys have 'em for seventy-five each?"

"What about ammo?" Fishe is already reaching in his pocket.

"I'll throw in a hundred rounds, but you'll have to buy it in the future. If you make it eighty-five, I'll throw in a shoulder holster."

Fishe divvies up the money and takes the pistol and holster.

I have to ask, "Ya know, I was curious, why would you guys trade beer for C rations?"

"It's too damned hot."

"Huh?"

"We can't draw C rations here, so if we want to eat, we have to go to the mess. Hell, it's a ten minute walk from here. With the C-rats we can stay in the trailer, drink beer and stay cool. So we trade with you guys."

I add, "...and sell them to the gooks on the black market."

"Yeah, that too."

Thus, our most logical course of action…hit the engineers.

Fishe, Smitty and I hang around the front of the mess hall trying not to allow our larcenous plans show on our faces. Sergeant Dick is dressing down the guard formation for the night. I look at Fishe, he looks at Smitty and Smitty looks at me. We nod and Smitty heads off in the direction of the operations bunker. A large container at the back, dug into the side of the hill, houses the switchboard. When Smitty is sure no one is paying any attention to him he disappears behind the switchboard container where a bundle of wires emerges from the back, travels down the hill, and either enters the ground or goes up a pole and splits off in different directions.

Smitty re-emerges from the back of the operations bunker and nonchalantly walks back down to join us. Together we meander around till we end up back in front of the commo bunker. We try not to look too conspicuous.

About forty minutes pass when we see Sergeant Bennett's hunching frame meandering up the rode from the NCO hooch.

"There's something wrong with the wire down to the engineering camp. Why don't you take Sis here and go check it out." Bennett has his hand on my shoulder as he talks to Smitty. *Damn it, I hate when he calls me Sis.*

"You mind if I go with 'em?" Fishe asks.

"No, go right on ahead." He turns and walks back in the direction of the NCO hooch.

"Man, how sweet was that?" I am elated that our scheme is unfolding just the way we planned it. Smitty is displaying a smug smile of accomplishment.

At the motor pool Smitty checks out a three-quarter ton truck. It's like a pick-up with a canvas-covered bed. Jim jumps in the back, Smitty drives and I ride shotgun. Smitty grabs a tool belt on the way to the motor pool because we have to at least give the impression we're actually troubleshooting the wire. We pass through our gate only after the guard calls operations to confirm we are troubleshooting a phone wire. We take the road down and around the hill and pull up to the engineering gate.

The guard walks up to the driver side window, looks in and says, "Okay, what are you guys tryin' to steal?" I stiffen and avoid looking at him. Smitty, in his inimitable way, informs him the phone line is down and we're here to check it out. The gate swings open and we're allowed to pass. We park the truck near the mess hall, which is only fifteen feet or so from their orderly room. A light is on and I can see the Staff Duty NCO sitting at the desk. He has a clear view through the screened window. He glances up momentarily, then goes back to his issue of "Stars and Stripes".

"Shit, man, the *First Shirt* has a clear view of us. What are we going to do?" Smitty turns his head and whispers guarding against being overheard.

I motion for Smitty to move to the back of the truck. "Don't whisper, man, or he'll think we're up to something." I look at both of my co-conspirators and comment, "We're going to have to figure out a way to distract him."

Under the canopy extending out from the mess hall are two trash cans filled with water. Clamped to the side of each can and rising up like two glistening jewels are the immersion heaters idly waiting for us to grab one.

"Fishe, you wait in the back of the truck. Smitty and I will wander around acting like we're checking the wire." I pause for a second trying to think of what to do next, "We're gonna need some kind of a signal, any ideas?"

"Yeah, yeah, how about when he hears one of us yell out, 'I think the break's over here,' that'll be the signal the coast is clear."

"Sounds good to me." Jim moves back into the darkness of the truck.

"Let's go over this way." I point in the direction of the hill taking us right past the orderly room. As we pass, I stop, turn and walk in the door.

"Excuse me, Top." Top is an endearing term First Sergeants actually seem to like. "We're here from up the hill because the wire to your board is down." The Sergeant looks up at me. I can't tell anything from the expression on his face.

"I'm wondering Top, was there any digging going on around here today? That would be a good place for us to start looking."

"Son, this here's a maintenance and engineering battalion. Hell, there's diggin' goin' on around here all the damn time."

"Well, thanks anyway. We'll just have to dig it up in a couple of places to try and find the break."

"Well, you boys better get to diggin', we don't want that line bein' down too long. Hell, there might be someone tryin' to get through to us right now. No tellin' what emergencies we're missin'."

A sudden rush of guilt washes over me. We hadn't considered cutting the line would delay a response or interfere with something that might cost lives.

Outside, as Smitty and I walk away from the orderly room, I ask, "Shit, man, what if they miss some important call while we're out here fucking around?"

"Don't be a dipshit. If there was a big emergency, they could always call on the radio, the first shirt was just tryin'ta motivate ya, you dumb ass."

"Okay, okay…I didn't think of the radio. How are we gonna get him out of the orderly room?"

"Look, the wire runs right along the side of the road here then it cuts over in that direction to their commo bunker." Smitty points to the side of the rode that goes right past the front of the orderly room. "Let's start digging. It's only about a foot underground."

I dig up the wire with Smitty holding a flashlight. I pull the wire up and clear away the dirt. I look at the wire in my hand, look at Smitty, look at the field phone and look back at the wire. The standard method for tracking down a break is to cut the wire, then test each end of the cut wire by connecting it to a field phone and cranking the phone's generator. If you've connected the good end of the wire, the crank will have normal resistance to the cranking. If the crank turns effortlessly it means there is a break somewhere in that piece of line. If the crank is really hard to turn, it means there's a short. We already know where the break is, so there is no real purpose in going to the trouble of cutting and splicing the wire, but I have an idea!

I cut the wire and hook the phone up to the good end. Smitty looks at me like I'm an idiot. I grab the handset and am about to crank the phone.

"What the hell are you doing?" Smitty is tugging rapidly at my sleeve.

"Hold on, I know what I'm doing." I crank the phone a couple of times and wait for a response.

"Erector, sir." The switch board operator answers. Erector is the call sign for the engineers.

"Yeah, get me the orderly room." Mentally, I can see the board operator pull a plug up from the panel and plug it into a socket on the board with some innocuous label that stands for orderly room. Then he will push a button that sends a small charge through the wire to make the phone in the orderly room ring.

"First Sergeant Franklin, what can I do for you?"

I try to lower the pitch of my voice, that Sis thing is making me paranoid, "Sergeant Franklin, this PFC Pinetti.

"What's on your mind, son?"

"There's a PFC Simon and Smitt down there doing some wire troubleshooting. Any chance you can get a message to them?"

"You're in luck, son, I can see them from here. Would you like me to have 'em come to the phone?"

"No need Sarge, if you can just let them know they need to check the phone at our guard shack on the way back."

"I'll pass it along, son." He hangs up the phone and gets out from behind the desk.

I disconnect the phone and start skinning back the insulation to splice the wire. I can see Sergeant Franklin coming through the door. When he is about ten feet away, I say loudly, "*I think the breaks just over here!*"

"Say, boy, we got people tryin' to sleep around here how about you try to hold it down? Your people want you to check the phone at your guard shack on the way back."

"Hey, thanks a lot, Sarge. They didn't say what was wrong, did they?"

"No, boy, they just asked that you check it out." Sergeant Franklin turns and starts to walk away. He stops and turns to look at us. There's a look of bewilderment on his face, like something's bugging him. He starts to say something, shakes his head, then turns back and goes on his way.

"Good thing it didn't dawn on him he couldn't have gotten a call from Pinetti if the wire is out, you dumb-ass." Smitty whacks me on the side of the helmet.

I feel like an idiot. "Holy shit, I never thought about that."

"Next time you get a brainstorm, let someone else in on it."

We quickly cover up the wire and scurry back to the truck like two kids who've just pulled a fast one. We aren't quite running, but we're walking conspicuously fast. As we near the truck we're almost laughing. We jump in, Smitty starts the truck and we pull away. As we approach the gate, I turn and look through the little plastic window into the back of the truck...panic sets in.

"Stop the truck! Stop the truck!"

"What? What?"

"Jim's not back there!"

"What! Where the hell is he?"

"How the fuck am I supposed to know?" I can see the guard from the gate already walking in our direction.

"Just tell him we left a tool and we have to go back."

Smitty tells the guard the story then turns the truck around and heads back to the mess hall. Smitty walks back to where we'd been working and pretends to be looking around. I skulk around the mess hall.

"Jim? Jim? Where the hell are you?" I'm whispering as loud as I can. I can see that one of the immersion heaters is gone.

"He's not here." I look at Smitty and shrug my shoulders.

"He's got to be around here some fucking place." We move around the area whispering, "Jim?" There is no answer. After about five minutes neither of us knows what to do.

"What the hell are we gonna do?"

"How should I know?" Smitty keeps moving his head around in a desperate attempt to locate Jim.

"Okay, look. Something must have spooked him. He's got to be around here someplace. Let's take the truck down that way and then come back up over there." I'm pointing at another road that feeds back up to the main road leading to the gate.

"What if they grabbed him when he was taking the heater?"

"Do you really think we'd be standin' here if they grabbed him? Look he's got to be around here somewhere. Let's just cruise the road...I can't think of anything else."

"Fuck me!" Smitty gets back into the truck and we roll down the road looking as hard as we can for Jim. The truck's headlights give off little or no light through the little slits that remain uncovered. This is to make the truck more undetectable at night.

We move as slow as humanly possible, get to the end of the road and turn to the left…still no Jim.

"Maybe he slipped out and walked back?" I was desperate; grabbing at straws.

"Would *you* try walking back *at night*?"

"Well, then he's got to be here."

We move back up to the main road that leads to the gate. Every ten or twenty feet Smitty pauses, I stick my head out the window and try to whisper loud enough for Jim to hear, no luck. Finally, as we near the gate, the guard looks at us and waves for us to pass, but Smitty stops the truck.

"What're ya stopping for?" The guard starts moving towards us.

"Look over there."

"Where?"

"Over there, just to the right of the guard shack." Smitty nods his head in the direction of some sandbags that are about five feet from the guard shack. I squint as hard as I can. There is a silhouette of a man waving his arms back and forth over his head. It has to be Fishe.

"What the hell is wrong with you guys?" The guard shines his light into the cab of the truck.

"Something ain't right here. Just hold it, I'm gonna have to check the back."

"Be my guest." Smitty snaps his head towards the back of the truck.

The guard moves to the back of the truck, all the while I'm frantically making motions for Jim to go through the gate. We hear the guard lift the tarpaulin flap and lower the tailgate. Almost simultaneously, we can make out Jim's silhouette moving through the gate.

"Okay, you guys are clean. Get the hell out of here."

"Hey, just doin' our jobs, man," Smitty yells with his head hanging out the window as we pull away. When we turn onto the main road, Smitty slows to a crawl. A couple of loud slaps against the side of the truck and Smitty stops. Fishe drops the heater into the back and climbs in.

"Man, let's get the hell out of here!" Fishe starts laughing like hell.

Back in the compound, Smitty drops us off at the hooch and goes up to the operations bunker to repair the wire he cut earlier. While we're waiting, I ask Jim what happened.

"When you went in to talk to the first shirt, I thought it would be a good chance to grab the heater."

"So what the hell happened?"

"I couldn't get the damn thing loose. Then, just as I get it loose, it bangs against the can. I see the Sergeant get up and I think he's heard me. So I grab the heater and slip to the back of the mess hall."

"Why didn't you get back in the truck?"

"Before I feel it is safe enough to go back, you two bozos jump in the truck and take off. I hear someone coming and I figure I'm screwed. I grab the heater and run like hell trying to catch you guys, but you stop. I see the guard heading your way so I duck behind those sandbags. I figured I'd jump in or use the truck as a screen when you went through the gate, but you guys turned around and went back!"

"Yeah, we found out you weren't in the truck."

It's about ten-thirty, still early by our standards, but all three of us hit the rack. Unconsciously, we are all looking forward to sunrise with great expectation.

At four A.M., before the sun has started to spill light over the edge of the horizon, we're up, and with the aid of a couple of flashlights, install the heater. Jim lights it and we go back to the hooch. At five-thirty, just after sunrise, the three of us, wrapped in towels, laden with expectations, stand under the thousand pound bomb canister watching the plume of smoke rising from the heater. Ironically, the smoke is blowing in the direction of the engineers. We look at each other, hang the towels, and walk under the shower heads. Simultaneously, we reach up and pull the chains that allow hot water to flow through the shower heads. The hot water cascades down onto my face washing over my body. Standing there, I hold the chain so the warm water will continue to flow. The warmth enshrouds my body; I can't help but feel elated. The hot water beats a soothing rhythm on my face and stimulates every nerve in my body. After so many cold showers, this is life reminding me once again that the things we take for granted are the real pleasures. Smitty begins giggling and I turn to look at him. The giggling is accompanied by a smirk of contentment which quickly turns into a bout of infectious laughter. We roar!

"Hey! Hot water!" Turner is standing at the shower entrance, wrapped in a towel and yelling back in the direction of the hooch.

As we lavish ourselves in the warm relaxing flow, a small crowd gathers at the entrance to watch. Everyone has the glint of expectation in their eyes. Watching them, seeing the eagerness on their faces, I know, for some period of time, regardless of how long or short it may be, we will be heroes whether we see action or not. Sometimes life is good.

CHAPTER SIX

"CREATURES"

A commotion in the hooch rouses me from my sleep. A quick glimpse at my watch reveals it's 04:30. "You gotta be shittin' me," I grumble and roll over in my cot.

"Wake up, Sis!" Sergeant Bennett shakes me.

"Huh, what? Leave me alone."

"Come-on, soldier, on your feet!" There is an insistence in Bennett's voice. I roll to a sitting position and swing my legs over the edge of the cot. My eyelids are stuck half-closed with eye scum so I ball up my hands and rub the crap out of my eyes, then slowly focus on the activity in the hooch. Sergeant Bennett and Sergeant Dick are rudely rousing everybody out of their cots. Again, I look at my watch.

What the hell? Man, it's only four-thirty!

Everybody is dumbfounded looking around and wondering what the hell is going on. Sergeant Dick looks around to make sure everybody is still up and he has their attention.

"You boys get your gear together and fall out in front of the orderly room at oh-five-thirty."

Pinetti is the first to ask, "What's goin' on, Sarge?"

Dick's eyes give Pinetti the once over and he says, "Jesus, boy, you look like hell. What the hell's wrong with you son?"

Pinetti is still wearing the vomit stained pants he wore just four hours earlier when he had downed about ten bottles of OB beer, gotten sick and vomited outside the hooch. His hair is all fucked up and he has chunks of vomit still stuck to his face.

"Christ, I don't believe I've ever seen a sorrier excuse for a soldier. You best be getting your shit together." Dick and Bennett start walking out but Dick hesitates at the door, looks at Pinetti, shakes his head, says "Jesus," and walks out.

None of us shower, hell, most of us sleep in our pants anyway. Sitting on the edge of my cot I pull on my boots and lace them up. *What the fuck? Shit, four-thirty in the damned morning, shit, this must be bad, though, Bennett and Dick don't seem all that upset… maybe it's just some army bullshit.*

"Fuck it." I finish lacing my boots and pull on my jungle fatigue blouse.

"Bring lots of ammo," Fishe says as he pulls his flak jacket on over his shoulder holster. The thirty-eight has yet to be fired, though he's taken it apart and cleaned it a couple of dozen times.

"Why? What is it that you know and we don't?"

"Just that Dick said we're going somewhere hot." Jim picks up the first aid pouch and mentally contemplates adding it to the pistol belt, then tosses it on the cot.

"I wouldn't do that if I were you." I comment offhandedly.

"Why's that?" He's already reconsidered and is reaching for the pouch when I respond.

"Hell, you might need that bandage to patch my ass up; shit, if you're worried about ammo, you can carry all you want by throwing a couple of bandoleers over your shoulder."

Yeah, maybe you're right."

I have pre-loaded ten magazines for my M-14. I slip two into the ammo pouch on my pistol belt then loosen my pistol belt and add a second ammo pouch with two additional magazines. I stick another under the elastic band of my steel pot, then decide against it and put one into each of my jungle fatigue thigh pockets. I take four bandoleers from the case of ammo I have stashed and lay them on the cot. Smitty is using electrical tape to fasten two magazines together bottom to bottom. "Man, what the hell are you doing?" I know what he's trying to do, and instinctively recognize the flaw in his thinking.

He explains, "When one magazine is empty, all I gotta do is flip it over. I'll be able to change a lot faster." Smitty gives a quick demonstration to validate his point.

"Hey, ya know what. I'm new to this shit, but it seems to me that the bottom magazine is probably gonna get all fouled with crap being open like that." Smitty doesn't even consider my argument and leaves the magazines taped together. *Hey, what do I know?*

I stick my bayonet into the scabbard on the front strap of my pack harness. I stash the other four magazines into my pack. I finish my preparations by hanging two grenades on the harness and check to make sure everything is tight. I pull a Pall Mall out of the pack with my lips, light it up and lay down on the cot…I'm ready.

Lindlay stops at the end of my cot and asks, "You goin' for chow?"

"No, I'm gonna stay here." Lee nods, then follows everyone else out of the hooch. I finish the cigarette and instinctively light another. The temperature is still cool, but I can see small beads of sweat on the back of my hand as I lift the cigarette to my mouth. I feel a droplet roll down behind my ear as I stare at the netting strung across my cot. My mind is momentarily blank, but slowly it begins filling with questions and hypothetical answers that may explain why we're all up and waiting to ship out.

I lay in the cot for some time, how long, I'm not sure; I don't even notice everyone else returning. I only become aware of the activity in the hooch when Fishe yells, "Yo…Simon…lets go!"

The crowd in front of the orderly room reinforces my thoughts that something big is going on. There are about sixty people loitering around waiting for someone to bring order to the scene. Everyone is in full gear; no one has a clue.

Frenchy, my partner on the perimeter sweep, sees us, walks over, and asks, "Hey, you got any idea what's goin' on?"

I had thought about this long and hard while lying in my cot. Concluding that if it is related to our artillery unit, it must be related to Delta battery; I voice my opinion.

"What makes you say that? You hear something from Varant?" Townsend asks insistently.

"No, I haven't heard shit."

"Then what are you talking about?"

"Look, man, at night the sky directly east of here is being lit up for hours with flashes from big guns. When the Howitzers aren't firing it's filled with streams of tracers."

"Yeah, so what?"

"Look, I don't have a clue. You want me to guess? Then all I know is the only thing due east of us is An Khe and Qui Nhon. Delta Battery has a fire base somewhere east of here, somewhere between Pleiku and Qui Nhon. Varant mentioned something last week about a lot of NVA activity out there, so I'm just making a logical conclusion."

Our hypothesizing is interrupted by Sgt. Dick. "All right, let's get some kind of formation going here. This is still the Army. "Dick is walking through the crowd trying to get us organized.

Looking at the diversity of the assembled group leads me to conclude we have no fixed purpose…it's more like we're just a large group of bodies, numbers. Wherever we're going they just need bodies.

After Sergeant Dick gets us organized, First Sergeant Neuman addresses the formation. "Okay, men, you're going to be airlifted from Camp Holloway by chopper to Delta Battery," several of the guys turn and look at me. I shrug my shoulders and Sergeant Neuman continues. "They've been hit pretty hard and the Colonel has ordered them to abandon the fire base and re-deploy to a position near Dragon Mountain."

We call it Titty Mountain because the shape of the mountain consists of two large humps that closely resemble the silhouette of a woman's bust.

"We want the camp completely razed and moved to the Dragon Mountain fire base before nightfall. If you're still farting around at nightfall you're going to get your asses kicked by an NVA regiment that the 25th and 1st Cav are trying to drive out of the area."

Sgt. Dick takes over as Neuman walks away. "Our intelligence reports indicate the pull out should encounter very little, if any, enemy contact. Hell, they'll probably be glad to see the battery pull out."

I'm not sure I share Sergeant Dick's optimism. All I know is we're leaving the relative safety of our base camp, a camp situated mere miles from the 25th infantry's base camp and mere minutes from all the air support Pleiku Air Base offers.

"When the new fire base is set up at Dragon Mountain, non-essential personnel will return here to HQ Battery."

That's it. That's all the information they give us.

"Sarge?" Frenchy, who is always at the front of the formations because he's so short, tugs on Dick's sleeve like a little kid wanting his mother's attention.

"What is it, Frenchy?"

"Will there be enough ammo for us at Delta Battery?" Actually, it's a pretty damn good question. We have a mixture of weapons, M-14s, M-16s, hell there's even a couple of M1 carbines floating around.

"There are regular supply flights to all our batteries everyday. If you guys do your job right, you should be out of there and back here in a couple of days…mount up."

Dick turns and heads for the Jeep that will lead our little convoy to Camp Holloway.

The ride to Holloway is like being in a coma. I try to take my mind off what may be waiting for us. This isn't my first time off the hill, nor my first field assignment, but we all know that they don't call 'em fire bases for nothin'. In a poor attempt to distract myself, I get a look of annoyance and ask, "Jesus, doesn't it ever rain around here? How the hell can you have jungle with no stinkin' rain?" No one bothers to answer. The somberness on the faces of everyone needs no interpretation. Most of these guys have fallen into the trap of believing that assignment to an artillery unit means they will be removed from the action, behind the lines so to speak. We have all become comfortable in our daily routines, devoid of any real combat. Combat is something that the 25th infantry and the Air Cav are involved in. I want to say, *our lives are about to change,* think better of it, light up a cigarette and just stare out the back of the truck.

The sun is just above the horizon as we pull up to the airstrip. It is alive with activity. Eight Hueys are lined up on the tarmac, rotors spinning, seemingly anxious to load and lift off. We pile out of the trucks and huddle in a large group at the edge of the tarmac. Sergeant Dick brings his hands up to his mouth to yell something, but no one can hear him. Everyone starts yelling, "What?" Finally, he just starts pointing. He starts grabbing sleeves and points in the direction of a chopper, assigning eight guys to each chopper. Once you're under the rotor the noise level actually seems to drop. The door gunner is waving us onto the chopper with quick motions. We pile in and a couple minutes later we're in the air. This is the first chopper ride for most of the guys.

The rush of cool air through the side doors has a chilling effect and makes me shiver. The door gunner loads his M-60 almost as soon as we lift off.

"We'll fly at about a thousand feet till we get within a few miles of our destination, then the pilot will drop to tree top level till we reach the LZ." The door gunner turns back to the door and his M-60. Five minutes into the flight he turns to us and says, "Watch this." He takes a grenade, sticks the grenade into a large paper cup which prevents the operating lever from coming off, pulls the pin, then tosses it out the door. Our eyes follow the cup and its deadly contents all the way to the ground. At first I think nothing is going to happen, then, after several seconds, *Wham!* Under normal circumstances, especially if you're high enough, a grenade will detonate long before it hits the ground. In this case the cup holds the lever arm in place till it hits the ground and the cup bursts, allowing the lever to fly off and detonate the grenade. Ya gotta love it.

We're airborne twenty minutes when the chopper starts to drop down. The terrain has changed significantly. I can see only jungle, and the craggy hills that indicate we're near An Khe. The chopper is at tree top level now and the trees flash past the bottom of the chopper faster than my eyes can focus on them. This, combined with the occasional banking back and forth of the chopper, creates a stomach churning sensation and makes me close my eyes and grimace. It's like being on a roller coaster. Everybody else seems to be experiencing the same sensations so I know my stomach is not alone in its desire to discharge its contents. Fishe has his head tilted back, plastered against the bulkhead and is taking deep breaths trying to overcome the nausea. The door gunner loves it. Hell, he's half-hanging out the door. He turns his head back towards us laughing at the sight of our green faces, then looks back out the door and begins yelling: "*Yeeeeeeee Haaaaah! Yeah, baby, I love this ride!*"

The copilot glances back at us, his smiling face shows he shares the door gunner's sentiments.

"Saddle Up! We'll be touching down in two (he holds up two fingers) minutes." We grab our helmets, check our equipment and prepare ourselves. All of a sudden the chopper banks hard left, it flattens out and moves into a clearing. The chopper bucks its nose up in a breaking action slamming some of us back against the bulkhead. Then it slowly lowers itself to the ground with the nose tilted up. The heel of the skids hit first, then the chopper plops down hard. The door gunner begins shouting, "Okay, let's go! Let's go!"

We pile out of the chopper, squat, and wait while the chopper lifts-off nose down and moves off swiftly over the treetops. All the choppers duplicate this maneuver, so all eight are in, out, and gone in an amazingly short amount of time.

We're fifty yards outside the perimeter of the fire base. There's an officer coming through the makeshift gate and heading in our direction. I decide not to wait and start walking in his direction…everyone instinctively follows.

1st Lieutenant Chianelli steps up and asks, "Who's in charge?"

I salute, "I'm not sure sir, we haven't got an NCO with us." Chianelli laughs, turns towards the fire base waving his arm for us to follow. Inside the camp Chianelli breaks out sixteen men turns them over to a Staff

Sergeant named Grazianni. I didn't even have to ask, I could tell by Grazianni's voice, swagger and attitude, he was from Chicago, probably around Taylor Street.

"Okay, Dennis (Grazianni), use these guys to relieve your perimeter fire teams." Chianelli passes the rest of us off to Sergeant Jones. He posts four of us at each of the six perimeter bunkers.

"Okay, these bunkers need to be dismembered. Every sandbag needs to be cut and emptied. Toss the empty bags in the hole. When you're done fill in the hole. We don't need to be leaving anything that Charlie can use." Just the way we like instructions, short, to the point, and nothing left unclear.

I drop my pack and remove the trenching tool. I flip the spade to the open position and lock it into place with the lock nut at the base of the handle. Fishe and Turner drop their packs, but Fishe leaves his shoulder holster in place. I take the shovel and in a chopping motion, hack into the side of a sandbag, pick it up and let the red dirt drain out.

"I don't know why they call 'em sandbags, they're always filled with dirt." I shake it to remove the remainder of the dirt, then toss it into the middle of the bunker hole. A large cloud of red dust makes me gag and squint to keep the dirt out of my eyes.

"Jesus!" Turner, standing downwind, turns his head away.

Merkley, our fourth team member adds, "Man, this really sucks. I ain't done nothin' but burn shit, fill sandbags and hump ammo ever since I got here." Merkley is an ammo humper back at the hill.

"How many man?" Jim asks as he empties a bag.

"Two-nineteen and a wake up baby."

"No shit." I look away and longingly add, "Damn, I wish I was two-nineteen and a wake up." I stop a moment to study him. "Where you from, Merkley? What do they call you?" He looks old, I know he's not, but his bad teeth, weathered skin and pouchy jowls give him the look of someone who's been working on the farm for about thirty years. His hair is thinning and he has bad posture, like Bennett.

"Ya all can just call me 'Murky,' that's what they call me back home."

"Where's that?" I ask knowing it's got to be from the south somewhere.

"I'm from Camden, Alabama. It's the county seat. Hell, I lived there my whole life till the army drafted me."

"How old *are* you?" A look of astonishment is on Jim's face.

"I turned twenty back in Feb'ary." No one says it, but by the looks we give each other, it's easy to see everyone has misjudged his age.

Keeping at it, we work till the sun gets high in the sky; it beats down on us, torturing us for being so foolish. One by one, it forces each of us to peel off our shirt, but Jim dons the shoulder holster over his bare chest. Man, he loves that gun.

The last two or three rows of sandbags are all that remain when a couple of guys show up in a Jeep full of C rations.

"Man, I sure hope you don't have any of that ham and lima beans crap," Jim says as he starts to pick through the boxes.

"Hey, don't worry, I'll take the ham and lima beans," Merkley says, "Okay, let's see what we got?" We sift through the boxes on the back of the Jeep; I grab a BBQ beef, not that I particularly care for it, but it comes with a tin of cheese and crackers.

"So how bad has it been out here?" It's my first opportunity to really talk to any of these Delta battery guys and I'm anxious to get some first hand information and satisfy my curiosity.

"The fucking bastards have been hitting us every goddamn night. First couple of nights they hit us with mortars and rocket barrages. Then they send a couple of squads at us. We lost everybody in that bunker to a sapper a couple of nights ago." He points at what remains of a perimeter bunker about a hundred yards away.

"Sappers? You kiddin'? I thought that was just bullshit."

"No, man, it ain't no bullshit. They grab a kid from some village and tell him if he don't do it they'll execute his family. They strap the bag to him and head him in our direction...the cocksuckers!"

"How come they don't hit you during the day?" Turner is already chewing on the cookies from his box of C rations.

"The 7th Cav is supposed to have a regiment pinned down about seven or eight miles from here. We've been pouring in the H & I all day long for ten days. We figure they've been sending the local Cong at us to take the heat off, but for some reason the Cong haven't been bothering us during the day."

"Jeez, sounds like you guys have been in the shit," Jim says.

As the Jeep starts to pull away, I yell after them, "Hey, thanks for the chow."

I look at Merkley and ask, "What's H & I?"

"Harassment and Interdiction," Merkley says while he tries to warm his entree can with a Zippo lighter.

"Okay, what's Harassment and Interdiction?"

"Basically, we just keep lobbing shells at suspected VC positions every now and then to bug the living shit out of them. They just keep doing it all day long at no set intervals. Works real good when they're pinned down, it makes the bastards stay in their holes. Hell, half the guys we nail die from the concussion."

I look at the contents of the BBQ beef can. It's shredded, has blotches of red stuff and big lumps of lard. I rummage through the box looking for the Sterno tablet that's supposed to be in each box. "Shit, man, I haven't gotten a damned Sterno tablet yet." I pull out the little pack of four Chesterfield cigarettes.

"How the fuck come all I ever get is Chesterfields and Camels?"

"Sergeant Bast steals all the Sterno. He sells it in Pleiku along with all the other stuff he scams." Merkley is a surprising source of information.

"What other stuff you talking about, Murky?"

"Cigarettes, fatigues, boots, you name it."

"I thought you could only get six cartons a month?"

"Yeah, but he gets non-smokers to sell him their ration for two bucks a carton. Then he sells them to the gooks for five or six bucks a carton."

"Six bucks a carton!"

"Yeah, but only for Salems. They'll pay five bucks for filtered and won't buy non-filtered at all."

"What a sneaky little prick! He sells our fucking fatigues and boots?"

"No, he's made some kind of deal with the grave diggers and gets them from dead bodies. He has the gooks clean 'em up and barters them on the black market."

I toss the can and what's left of my rations into the hole. I pick up the trenching tool and get back to finishing our bunker demolition. Merkley tosses in the last empty bag and begins shoveling the dirt back into the hole. When we finish we grab our gear and walk over to help Lee. The bunker Lee is working on is near done but there are still three or four rows of sandbags to go.

"Man, you guys are slow!" I chide. "What's taking so long?"

"Hey, screw you." It's obvious Frenchy isn't happy with this detail.

"I guess we better give these bozos a hand, huh?"

We take turns helping out and make fast work of the sandbags. Frenchy and Lee are pulling up the last couple of bags when Lee springs up, stumbling and falling on his back.

"Mother Fucker," he says as he falls.

Just as he hits the ground, Frenchy screams, pulls his arm up and starts snapping it back and forth violently.

"Damn it, damn it, somebody help me. Help me."

He reaches up and grabs something hanging from his arm. He pulls it off, throws it into the hole, then falls to the ground screaming.

"Aaaah! My arm's on fire."

Fishe grabs Frenchy and holds him to the ground. Turner grasps his arm and flips it around so we can see. It is already turning colors and has bright red streaks shooting up the forearm.

"Medic! Medic! Someone, get a fucking medic over here."

I'm frozen. I don't know what the hell is going on. I look into the bunker hole and see three small iridescent green snakes squirming around…they're small, maybe twenty inches long. They almost look like garden snakes but are like neon green.

Merkley and Fishe are holding Frenchy who is still thrashing around and screaming in pain. It only takes a few seconds for the medic to arrive. He drops to his knees next to Frenchy, takes one look at the arm, sees the snakes in the pit and says, "Holy shit, Bamboo viper bite!" He jumps up and yells in the direction of Lt. Chianelli.

"Get a Medivac in here!"

Frenchy is carried in the direction of one of the vacated gun emplacements. I'm dumbfounded. I can't believe what's going on. Jim pulls out his thirty-eight and starts firing at the snakes. It takes him all six shots to kill two of them. I'm overcome…furious…helpless…I grab the trenching tool start hacking. Again, and again, and again, I hack at the slithering little creature. "Man, how many… *Whack*…fucking ways… *Whack*… are there to die in this shit-hole country?" I continue hacking furiously, uncontrollably, like a madman, till Jim finally grabs the tool from my shaking hands.

Turner stares at the dead snakes and grumbles, "Bamboo vipers, shit, man, that's the *'One step and you're dead'* snake." Turner's face is pale.

"That's all bullshit." A second medic is picking up the head of one of the dead snakes. "No one's died from a viper bite that I know of, usually the venom just destroys the tissue around the bite area. It's painful as hell. Some guys end up losing an arm or leg because of clotting, but as far as I know it isn't normally fatal." He turns and walks away.

Jesus, fucking, Christ! Is all I can think.

At fourteen hundred hours, everything is ready for us to move out. Lt. Chianelli and Cpt. Blowhole are organizing the order of the convoy. The Captain's name is really Bloesoe, but everybody here refers to him as Blowhole. I'm sure there is a good reason for it.

We hear the chopper well before we see it emerge from over the tree tops. It's a Medivac with a big Red Cross painted against a white background; it flies right into the middle of the fire base. Frenchy is strapped to a stretcher that's loaded on the chopper. A few seconds later, it lifts off and disappears to the east over the trees. I watch intently till it is out of sight and continue staring till I can no longer hear the thwacking sound of its blades. "Fuck," I mumble, then return to the task at hand hoping it will help put the incident out of my mind. It's time to move out.

The self-propelled howitzers are big and cumbersome. They have to use a tank retriever to pull one out of its pit. The tank retriever is a big tow truck for tanks except it's not a truck. It's a bulky tracked vehicle with a large boom. It looks like it weighs about a million pounds.

The convoy lines up on a dirt road that is barely visible, two ruts really, overgrown with vegetation. The road probably wasn't even a road till our guys moved in here. Chianelli's Jeep pauses next to Cpt. Bloesoe's, they exchange some words and the order is given to move out. Chianelli moves up the side of the column and assumes the lead position.

The convoy starts to move with the self-propelled howitzers setting the pace. They aren't built for speed and they're moving pretty damn slow. It feels like the convoy is going about five miles per hour. Most of the men ride in the back of deuce-and-a-halves; some of us are riding on top of the howitzers. Fishe has a map he managed to swipe from the operations bunker back at the hill. Using it, we guesstimate it is about sixty miles to Dragon Mountain. If this is as fast as we move, it will be long after dark when we arrive…not a pleasant prospect.

Twenty minutes into the trip, gunfire erupts from the jungle. Instinctively, we start scrambling off the howitzers to take cover behind them, but before the convoy can come to a halt, Chianelli's voice comes over the radio, "Keep 'em moving! Keep 'em moving! Do not stop, I repeat do not stop!"

Some of the guys who've already dismounted are returning fire from their cover positions behind the vehicles and Sgt. Grazianni is scrambling down the line trying to get everybody back into their vehicles. Chianelli's

Jeep is flying back along the right side of the convoy, he's standing and waving at everybody to keep moving. Most of us keep firing blindly into the jungle as we pull away. Behind us, I can see Chianelli has formed a fire team of about sixteen or twenty men and is moving into the jungle.

"Hey, how does he know he isn't walking into a trap or something?" I yell into the driver's ear.

"Well, if anybody around here knows what they're doing, it's Chianelli." The driver yells back.

We continue on the jungle road for another twenty-five minutes. The jungle is starting to thin out and we can see a blacktop road ahead. The convoy turns onto the blacktop of Highway 19 and heads west increasing speed.

"How fast are we going?" I have to cup my hands around my mouth so the crew chief can hear me over the noise of the engine.

"About twenty or twenty-five."

"How much farther we got to go?"

"It's about fifty miles to Dragon Mountain. It should be clear sailing once we get past the An Khe pass." The chief has his head cocked in my direction, his eyes snapping back and forth between the road and me.

"Man, we don't like flying into An Khe, it's always hot there!" The Caribou's crew chief's words ring in my head like a fire bell. Fishe and I are sitting with our backs against the muzzle of the eight-incher…the muzzle bounces up and down with every little crack in the road.

An hour's passed. Six Hueys zip out of the western sky, two of them are Gunships, the other four are carrying troops. All of them are headed in the direction of the abandoned fire base.

"Chianelli's pinned down twenty or thirty VC."

"What about the VC?" I just catch the last bit as the Chief flips his head in our direction.

"Chianelli! They've gotten some VC pinned down. He called for the choppers!" I move closer to the drivers hatch so I can hear all the squawking on the radio.

"Anybody take a hit?"

"I think I heard there are four wounded and no casualties…the 7th Cav have got two fire teams enroute."

Still perplexed why Chianelli went venturing into the jungle, I yell in the driver's ear, "How come Chianelli went after them? Why didn't they just call in the Cav from the gitgo?"

"Chianelli's an animal, man. He's only a lieutenant because he got himself a battlefield commission. When we were being overrun, he gathered a bunch of guys and re-took the fire base even though he was wounded; held it till reinforcements arrived. They put him in for a Silver Star. Chianelli capped about ten gooks single-handed."

"Fuck!" It sounded like something out of a Hollywood movie.

A couple of miles east of the An Khe pass the convoy pulls to the side of the road and halts. Finally, a chance to stretch our legs.

Before I hop off, I lean over and ask the driver, "Why'd we stop?"

"From the radio chatter I gather we're waiting for Chianelli's team to rejoin us." In an effort to hear better, the driver presses his headset against his ear.

Grazianni begins posting people along the sides of the road near the brush and bushes. He's already had the two little shacks up near the front of the convoy searched.

My ass is killing me and I've been gagging on red dust all day. I've finished all the water in my canteen and every muscle in my body is getting stiff from working on those bunkers and loading trucks. Jim and I are standing next to the Howitzer, cigarettes hanging from our mouths, puffing away. Though, I'm glad for the chance to stretch my legs, I'm uncomfortable about the convoy just stopping in the middle of fucking nowhere. The hills rise above us on both sides of the road and there's plenty of vegetation to provide cover for the VC. You never want to give the enemy the high ground if you can avoid it.

Two cigarettes later, four Hueys roar in from the east, one of them continues heading west, the other three land up near the front of the convoy. Chianelli and his squad of men scramble out of the choppers and a few minutes later the convoy is once again moving.

The rest of the move is uneventful. Going through the An Khe pass we hear the constant drone of gunfire and small artillery to the southwest. At about sixteen-thirty we turn off Highway 19 and proceed down a red dirt road directly towards Titty (Dragon) Mountain. The dust is unbearable. We can barely see the vehicle in front of us. We push our way down the road till we are near the base of the hills. The red dirt gives way to vegetation and elephant grass. A large scorched area marks the real estate designated to be the new fire base. Dragon Mountain is about a quarter mile behind. A perimeter is already in place and some bunkers are already standing. It's easy to see this site has been vacated just recently, maybe even today. Obviously, some other unit has used it as a fire base.

"Okay, let's go, shake your asses!" Grazianni is motioning for everyone to dismount.

"Okay, who are the commo guys?" We raise our hands.

"We need a common wire run to all the bunkers on the perimeter, then tie it in to the operations bunker." He points to a bunker in the middle of the compound. "We'll need it up and working before dark. We'll also need a line going to each of the gun positions and eventually a line run over to the 4th Infantry on the other side of the mountain. You can get everything you need from that deuce-and-a-half," again he points. "When you're done with the wire report back to me for guard duty; get some chow before you start."

We walk over to the deuce-and-a-half where they're dishing out the C rations, grab a box and park our behinds on the roof of a bunker.

"Fuck, man, this place makes me feel naked." I pop the top of my roast beef with my P-38, a little thumb and forefinger can opener that is supposed to be in every pack of C rations, but, like the Sterno tablets, is never there, so most of us keep one hanging on the chain that holds our dog tags.

"Shit!" Once again there's no damn Sterno. "Just once I'd like to open one of these boxes and find the damned Sterno tablet. Chesterfields again? Crap!"

Jim smiles and looks through his box hoping I've made a mistake.

"As long as Bast is around, I wouldn't be putting any money on finding one of those in your C rations.

"Boy, you'd think the officers would bitch about it," I comment.

"They probably do. I'm sure Bast has got some cock and bull story to feed them." Jim laughs and fills his mouth with a peanut butter covered cracker.

I toss my cans and offhandedly mention, "We got about an hour maybe an hour-and-a-half of daylight left so we better start stringin' some wire, we can bullshit later."

We grab a new reel of wire from the truck and begin stringing wire along the trenches and bunkers. Lee and Smitty follow us burying the wire as we go. On the bunkers, the wire is concealed under the sandbags. Pinetti disappears, but none of us want to waste time looking for him.

We've made the complete three-sixty, staked the wire and ran it up to the operations bunker. The sun is near down when we meet up with

Smitty and Lee. We grab ten field phones from one of the trucks and head off in different directions to make quick work of getting them connected. I step down into one of the bunkers and there he is...Pinetti! He's sound asleep using his pack as a pillow.

Son-of-a-bitch, I think. I pull my leg back and am about to kick him when I notice something out of the corner of my eye. Sitting in the middle of the gun port is a huge fucking tarantula. *Holy shit!*

Slowly, I open one of my ammo pouches and remove the magazines. I unfasten my pistol belt so I can remove the ammo pouch. I pull my bayonet out of its scabbard and slowly move towards the window. Pinetti is still snoring. I slowly lift the ammo pouch so it is out in front of my body and ever so slowly inch my way to the gun port. As I near, the spider moves back just a little; it looks like it cocks its legs...I stop and wait. When the spider relaxes, I resume my approach, but even more slowly. *Man, look at the size of that fucking thing,* I think to myself. Sweat is beginning to form on my brow. It takes an eternity, but I manage to lower the ammo pouch onto the sandbag about ten inches away from the spider, my eyes glued to hairy monster. If I see a hair on his legs move, I freeze, remaining as motionless as possible. I have the bayonet raised up level with the spider. I move slowly towards him with the blade trying to get him to back him into the ammo pouch. As the bayonet moves towards him, he rotates a little so he can see both me and the bayonet then he backs up a couple of inches.

"That's it, that's it, come on baby, just move back a little more." I'm breathing the words without moving my lips. The bayonet keeps advancing, and the spider keeps backing away. The spider is at the opening to the ammo pouch...I stop...the spider suddenly squats down and I know it isn't good.

"Shit!" I duck just as the Spider flies past my head. The damn thing lands on Pinetti's chest right between the pockets.

"Jesus!" I mumble.

Pinetti starts to rouse.

"Don't move! Don't move!" I have my hands out in front of me motioning for him to stay down.

"Huh, what?"

"Man, don't fucking move!" I point at the spider sitting on his chest.

Pinetti's head bends forward slightly and I see his eyes move down and widen. I know what is going to happen and am already moving towards the door.

"Oooooaaah Shiiiiiit! Pinetti shaking, his eyes bulging more than normal, starts crawling backwards as if he's going to crawl out from under the spider. His hand has latched onto his helmet liner and he swipes at the spider as he moves back. He misses. The spider moves up Pinetti's chest just below his chin.

"Ah…! Somebody help me!" Pinetti slides up the wall to an erect position. His eyes are glued to the spider; his arms plastered against the wall and tears are running down his face.

"Damn, look at the size of that thing!" Fishe says as he moves through the door of the bunker. Pinetti's cries for help have drawn a small crowd to the entrance.

Pinetti is sliding sideways along the wall.

"Man, I wouldn't fucking move if I were you." I say as calmly as I can. Pinetti's eyes are filled with terror and he's looking in our direction wanting us desperately to help him. Fishe is trying his best not to laugh. Merkley pushes his way past and walks up to Pinetti as calmly as if he was going to take a crap. He pulls a red kerchief out of his pocket, throws it over the spider and brushes it away all in one fluid movement. The kerchief with the spider underneath starts moving across the floor.

"Jesus, it ain't no big thang. It won't strike ya, less ya tries to grab at it." Merkley nonchalantly steps on the kerchief squashing the spider. It sounds gross and makes a large mess.

"Man, you are one big fucking pussy!" Merkley says, laughing at Pinetti who's blubbering like an idiot.

"C'mon, let's get these phones finished, it's almost dark." Jim says walking past everyone standing around the entrance to the bunker. Pinetti isn't going to live this down for a long time; he pushes his way past us and disappears.

"Man, did you see the size of that thing?" I laugh and follow Jim out the entrance.

"Yeah, baby, and I'll never forget the look on Pinetti's face."

"Okay, you four take the bunker where that pussy pissed in his pants over that spider. The existing bunkers are a little too far apart and they all have a pretty wide field of fire, so I want two men awake all the time. No single man shifts! You guys work it out. Get the claymores setup like I have illustrated here on this diagram and remember: *point them in the right direction!"* Grazianni passes out the hand written sketches showing how he wants us to set up the claymores and dismisses us.

We decide to work in two-hour shifts. Turner and Merkley take the first shift and we'll just keep switching off every two hours.

"Damn, it's darker than hell." Fishe says.

Staring out into the blackness of the night I have my poncho over my head so that I can smoke without anybody being able to see the ember from the cigarette.

"Yeah, it is *really* fucking dark out here," I joke. I finish the smoke and come out from under my little teepee. We continue staring out past the perimeter trying to detect anything that resembles movement.

Knowing Jim is from Detroit I comment, "You know, I actually worked in Detroit in the summer of '64."

"No shit."

"Yeah, I dated some girl named Judy Opinowski. She lived out around Schoolcraft."

"Opinowski! You sure she wasn't from Hamtramck?" Hamtramck is a suburb of Detroit with a predominately Polish population. The WASPs around Detroit have ten million Polish jokes they tell about Hamtramck.

"No she wasn't from Hamtramck, but she has a lot of relatives out there. Man, she was built like a brick shithouse."

"So what happened?" Jim asked.

"Man, I was seventeen, I didn't know shit."

"Yeah, we still don't."

"I think I just got scared off." I formed a vivid visual image of Judy in my mind.

"Scared off? What are you talkin' about?"

"She was too classy for me. She looked like she was headed for college and I was headed nowhere. My mother pissed away all the money I saved for school."

"That's a shame, man, but I know what ya mean. It looked like the Dearborn car plants for me so I wasn't all that upset about being drafted, except for ending up here. When I get out, I'm gettin' back in school. Maybe I can get me some of that free love I keep hearin' about."

The ring of the field phone startles us. I pick up the handset and a flare shoots off from our right, ignites, and starts floating to the ground. My muscles tense and my body stiffens. My eyes peer through the shadows searching for anything that looks like it shouldn't be there. Jim has the detonators for the claymores in his hands and is ready to start squeezing.

"I saw a Tiger! I saw a Tiger!" The panicked voice belongs to Red Smitt.

Grazianni says, "Identify yourself," his Chicago accent is unmistakable.

"This is Smitt at post seven. *Man, oh, man, I just saw a tiger!"* Immediately I relax.

"Jim, you've got to hear this!" I pass him the phone.

"You're full of shit," someone chimes in, someone else says, "You been smokin' bad weed man," another says, "What've you been drinkin' over there boy?" The comments come simultaneously from all the bunker positions, making it difficult for Smitty to actually respond to any of them. It wouldn't make any difference if he could, his reputation for embellishment is renowned at the hill.

"I ain't bullshittin', a big ass tiger just walked right past the front of my bunker." Smitty is jabbering like an idiot. He's trying to convince everyone he's serious.

"You better watch that shit or they're gonna bust ya for sleepin' on guard." Everybody on the line is laughing like hyenas.

"Pipe down, pipe down! I don't want you guys giving away your positions...put a lid on it." Grazianni tries to be serious, but is having a tough time of it.

"Son, if that tiger comes back, see if you can put out a saucer of that shitty milk they've been tryin' to poison us with." You can almost hear the laugh in Grazianni's voice.

"Screw all you guys! I'm tellin' ya I seen a tiger!" Smitty slams the phone down and breaks the connection.

"Jeez, that Smitty comes up with the weirdest damn things." I still have my eyes glued out across our field of fire.

"Hell, he probably started dozing and needed something to wake himself up." Jim says as he climbs down from the bunker.

Having spent nearly thirty percent of my time in country doing perimeter guard, I know if you stare at something in the dark long enough, you start seeing almost anything you can imagine. Poor Smitty, he's going to get ribbed about this forever.

I feel like crap. The two hour shifts were great for staying awake, but somewhere during the second shift, my body decided it was going to make me pay for it. So any detail we get today is going to be a real pain in the ass.

There is mucho activity around the camp. Guys are busy setting up the gun emplacements, trucks are still being unloaded, sandbags are being filled and there's a Chinook full of ammo and supplies that's being unloaded. There's a big tent being set up as a mess, but there will be no hot food today. A flying crane hovers over the camp gently lowering a gigantic blivet full of water. It looks like a huge, big, fat, tire.

Chianelli is rounding up a squad of volunteers to patrol the base of the mountain. He doesn't feel comfortable having higher ground above the fire base, even though the 4th division occupies the other side of the mountain. He wants to forage for tunnels and signs of VC activity. None of us are in the hero mood, so we go back to setting up the phones around the camp.

Sergeant Grazianni shows up with a scribbled plan for re-arranging some of the bunkers. Chianelli feels there are blind spots the way they are currently set up.

"Okay we want to put a bunker over there and get rid of that one."

"How about we dig a hole and just move the sandbags?"

"I don't have a problem with that. We can use the old hole to bury the shit we burn from the latrines."

Murky starts to recite his signature phrase, "Man, I ain't done nothin' but…."

"…burn shit and hump ammo ever since you been here." We chime in and finish Merkley's sentence for him. He looks up and smiles.

Merkley and Turner set about digging the hole. Fishe and I start toting the sandbags from the old bunker.

"*Over here, over here!*" Someone working on one of the three unmanned semi-collapsed bunkers is jumping up and down waving his arms frantically. People start walking in his direction slowly, then faster and faster, till a mob of people are running towards him.

"There's a tiger in the bunker!"

"You got to be shittin'." The crowd approaches the bunker reluctantly. A guy with an M-16 inches around each side of the bunker till they have the doorway flanked on both sides. Sergeant Grazianni moves towards the bunker ever so slowly. His forty-five in front of him he rolls his head around to look into the bunker. Instantly, a blood-curdling roar emerges from the inside that sends Grazianni reeling backwards.

"Jesus, it's nursing a couple of cubs in there. Damn, it must be hurt or somethin' or we'd never be able to get this close without it chargin'."

One of the guys huddling next to the entrance asks, "How we gonna get it out and what are we gonna do when it does come out?" He never takes his eyes off the entrance.

"How the hell do I know?" Grazianni doesn't have a clue how he's gonna deal with this.

"See, I told ya, I told ya. You pricks didn't believe me, but I told ya." Smitty is hopping around like a Mexican jumping bean. "I told ya, I told ya."

"Yeah, yeah, yeah," Fishe is trying to get Smitty to shut up so we can hear what's going on. Smitty on the other hand keeps hopping around like he has a jock full of fire ants.

Captain Blowhole pushes his way through the crowd.

"Sergeant Grazianni what's going on here?"

"Sir, looks like we've got a wounded tiger nursing some cubs in the bunker; we're trying to figure out how we can get it out."

"Sergeant, what the hell would we do if we did get it out? Use your fucking head." Grazianni turns his head and rolls his eyes. Blowhole bends over and peeks in, again a roar sends the potential intruder reeling backwards.

"You," Blowhole points at Coleman who's crouched next to the entrance.

"Me, sir?"

"Yeah, you, soldier. Toss one of your grenades in there and kill it."

"Huh? Toss a grenade in, Sir?" There is an instant response from the crowd, most of it under the breath mumbling, all of it anti-Blowhole.

Someone yells out, "Don't be an asshole."

Blowhole snaps his head around trying to identify his detractor. "Soldier, I gave you an order." Blowhole glares down at Coleman.

Coleman stands up, his eyes locked in a glaring war with Blowhole's. "Just a mother tryin' to protect her cubs, *Sir!*" Coleman is now face to face with Blowhole.

"I gave you an order...*private!*" Coleman pulls a grenade off his harness without removing his eyes from Blowhole's.

"Sir, maybe we can..."

"Stow it, Sergeant." Blowhole cuts off Grazianni's attempt to intervene.

Coleman pulls the pin on the grenade, holds the lever arm in place, and just stands defiantly holding it. Blowhole wants to move away, but Coleman reaches out and grabs him by the web belt. The rest of us are tripping over ourselves trying to get out of the way. He takes the grenade, lets the lever arm fly off and sticks it into Blowholes hand, all the while staring Blowhole in the eye. Blowhole instantly tosses the grenade into the hole and dives for the ground.

"Wha…blam!" The grenade detonates and Blowhole springs to feet.

"You're dead, you're done. Arrest him! I want this prick up on charges. I want him burned. He's going to the stockade. You hear me, Sergeant? You hear me?" Grazianni is pushing Blowhole away from the crowd.

"Dickhead!" "Asshole!" Derogatory comments follow him all the way back to his bunker.

Coleman walks away to the cheers of the crowd. The rest of us are anxious to see what happened to the tigers.

Inside the bunker the adult is blown to hell, one of the cubs lays lifeless in the corner.

"Hey, this one's alive!" Coleman's partner in arms comes out of the bunker with the baby tiger - it's about the size of a stuffed teddy bear. You can't even make out its stripes yet. It hasn't got a mark on it…it's untouched…it's a damned miracle! We can't believe it. The animal is scared and gnawing on the GIs harness.

"What are we gonna do with it?" someone asks.

"Fuck, we should keep it and make it a mascot," someone says. "They've got a huge Monitor lizard for a mascot over at the 25th."

"I don't give a shit what you do with it just get it out of sight." Grazianni has returned from ushering Blowhole back to his bunker.

"Where's Coleman?" There is note of panic in Grazianni's voice.

Coleman is over by the bunker we started dismantling. His shirt is off and he's sitting in the *Lotus Position* with his eyes closed.

"Coleman! Coleman, you did it this time. Blowhole's gonna have you skinned. Chianelli ain't gonna be able to save ya, ya stupid bastard."

Coleman gets up, stands with his legs spread and starts doing moves with his arms. He balls up both fists up next to his body, steps and thrusts one out, then the other. Sweeps one arm up and around in a precise movement and again follows with the other. He keeps moving, making a variety of sharp purposeful movements, continuing the routine as if Grazianni isn't there.

"That Karate shit ain't gonna keep your ass out of the stockade Coleman."

Coleman stops bends forward as if bowing to some unseen person, and turns to face Grazianni.

"Fuck 'em."

"Coleman you are one big stupid asshole. Blowhole's in there on the radio telling Chianelli to call the MP's ya dumb prick." Grazianni turns and walks away.

"Holy shit man, are you fucking nuts?" I have a completely bewildered look on my face.

"Man, your balls must be the size of cannon shells," Fishe says as he shakes Coleman's hand. "Why the hell did you do it?"

"Blowhole's an asshole. Last time I was out here all he was doin' was tryin' to get us killed. He hasn't got a brain in his fucking head."

"When were you with Delta?" Jim asks.

"Two months ago."

"Do ya think they'll bring you up on charges?"

"Nah, they'll probably bust me to E-2 again and transfer me to another unit.

"Again?"

"Yeah, I had a run in with that prick before. He wanted us to cap some kid he thought was VC. We just wanted to send him back to G-2. I told him to go fuck himself."

"So how come they didn't move you out then?"

"You kidding? I *wanted* him to bring me up on charges so someone would find out what a jackass he is. He just gave me an article fifteen. That way it never gets out of the battery."

It takes three more days to get the fire base secure and operational. We are trucked back to the hill; Coleman is with us. Blowhole wanted a court martial but Chianelli threatened to transfer out of the unit, which of course meant Blowhole would have to get off his dead ass and do something for a change so he backed off and just insisted that Coleman leave his fire base. Coleman would be one of us permanently.

Chapter Seven

"Up close and Personal"

The setting sun casts a golden yellow hue over the countryside in front of the hill. The charred expanse of recently burned elephant grass takes on a mystic, eerie quality. There's a rumor this may be the last time we have to burn the grass, the Army is going to be spraying it with a defoliant in the future, something called *Agent Orange*, the army's version of weed killer.

Early on it became evident everything in the army is given a cryptic name or designator that often belies its true function. A good example is a P-38. If I were in the Air force, a P-38 would be a vintage World War II twin-engine fighter plane. To a cop a P-38 is a handgun, but in the army, it's the little thumb and forefinger operated can opener we use to open C rations.

Earlier today, up at the top of the hill I got a picture of *The Lady on the Hill.* Carved into the base of the statue is the date 1961. I kinda thought that the French pulled out in the fifties, and if that's true, it shoots holes in the French Catholic Mission theory. In an unavoidable, guilt ridden, Catholic, knee-jerk reaction on my part, I have a momentary rush of remorse for my obvious lack of control and eagerness to partake in what Sister Mary Consumata would deem *Sinful Practices* and decided it might not be a bad idea to see how mass is on Sunday.

Tonight, everybody is in the hooch. No one has guard, no one has duty and no one is in the field. They're all self-absorbed and oddly enough, hardly any of the normal hooch banter is going on. Fishe is busy disassembling the new reel-to-reel stereo he recently picked up at the PX. When he tried to play some of his tapes, the music sounded like the Chipmunks recorded it. He has recorder parts strewn all over his cot. My curiosity gets the best of me and I'm compelled to ask, "Jimbo, what the hell are you taking that apart for? Didn't you just buy it?"

"Yeah, I did but Varant says the reason it doesn't work right is because the electricity over here operates at 50 hertz, but our electricity is 60 hertz." Jim keeps removing screws as he talks.

"So what? We aren't using gook electricity. We've got our own generators, they must run at 60 hertz or nothing would work, right?" I thought this was a pretty good rationalization, for me at least.

"No, no. It isn't that our electricity is wrong. The stereo is set up for 50 hertz, so when you plug it into 60 hertz, it runs too fast. Look, according to Varant, all I've got to do is switch out this capstan – he points to a little rubber wheel that drives one of the tape reels – with the one he gave me and it'll work fine." Jim shows me the drive wheel Varant supplied.

"Where'd he get it?" I ask.

"Fuck, I don't know." Jim is trying to determine which screw to remove next, so I amble back to my cot and sit with my back against the wall and my hands folded behind my head. The hardships we endure from day to day and the fact that Jim can walk up to the PX and buy a stereo is a dichotomy to say the least. It's as if this war exists in two different dimensions. The face-down-in-the-mud, hope-you-make-it-through the night dimension and the one filled with things to distract you from its reality. *I wonder if Rod Serling knows about this?*

Looking around the hooch, everybody is busy tinkering, reading or sleeping. Lindlay is sitting on the edge of his cot wearing a cowboy hat, practicing the four guitar chords Townsend taught him. Lee, short for Leighton, is a really good hearted guy. He's a farmer and we often think of him as naïve and there are a lot of things he doesn't have a clue about. He's a mom, pop and apple pie kind of guy. Though, we're often amazed by his naïveté, he has a very good grasp on life as a whole and loves to simplify the things the rest of us allow to clutter up our lives. He accepts many things as second nature, things us *City Boys* would regard as gross or unspeakable. Lee frequently turns our faces green with detailed explanations of delivering calves, beheading chickens, or digging through cow manure looking for grub worms to use as bait. His dreams and aspirations are not of big cars, fast women or lots of money. He knows when he goes home, he'll work on his dad's dairy farm, and someday, if the banks don't fuck him out of it, he'll inherit the farm.

His is a small tight knit community where everyone knows everyone. He's known his fiancée her whole life. They played together as infants and attended school together, though she's gone on to college, Lee has been the only boy she has ever dated and both know they will marry someday. Though, Lee just turned twenty, Lee's father is near seventy. Of anyone in the hooch, or maybe even the battery, Lee is the one that has shown the most disdain and remorse about killing. It bothers him (not that it doesn't bother the rest of us) and it is easy to tell he will never really get used to it.

Lee is not an opinionated man. His life on the farm has sheltered him from the propaganda bombardment that fills the television airways or pours out of the radio all morning on Sunday. The depth of his family's political alliances is to vote for the guy who claims to be in favor of farmer friendly legislation. Using farmer-related rationalizations is the only way he can justify the killing to himself. This natural allegiance to farming, the life that most of the South Vietnamese lead, is probably the only thing that gives Lee the edge he needs to pull the trigger. These poor farmers are presumably being murdered and pillaged by the VC. If the Americans and the South Vietnamese are not allowed to win the war most of them will lose control of their land. This concept hits close to home with Lee. According to Lee, the *Right to Bear Arms* was put into the Constitution just so farmers would be able to defend their land. That sums it up. He doesn't want to be a movie star or a famous athlete. He has no dreams of fame and fortune...he just wants to be a farmer.

I look back over at Fishe still working on his stereo. Jim is from Detroit City...Motown. He is proud of it and loves to talk about it all the time. He is, for lack of a better word, mellow. I don't believe I have ever seen him pissed-off about anything. Things that send me right over the top propel Jim into fits of deep bellowing laughter. His demeanor is generally so positive that it gets harder and harder to get pissed at some of the annoyances life manages to put into our lives each day. It isn't that he is incapable of anger, it is his nature to let absurdities roll off him. As a friend, he is always ready to counsel when one of us loses control over something asinine. Jim is the first one to offer advice, laughing and saying things like: "Man, if you blinked your eyes, you wouldn't have even seen that, how important can it be? Damn, man, there's songs that need singin', beer that needs drinkin' and women that need lovin', forget about that shit!"

Jim is from a family of autoworkers, blue collar through and through. He had a job with GM as an assembly line worker just after high school, worked about a year then decided he needed to re-evaluate the whole blue collar career path. Not that he thought it was dishonorable, or too much work, but because he thought being involved in the design of cars was far more attractive than being the one who assembled them. He plans to return to school and get a degree in engineering as soon as he gets out of the service. His mind is made up; I know he'll finish if he starts.

Jim has three girl friends. His devotion to any one of them is closely related to which one has sent him the most recent letter, or in some cases, how much beer he's consumed. My instinct tells me his deepest feelings are for a girl named Judy. She's the one who always receives the highest editorials after about two six packs. One of the girls, Carol, is the one we, as a group, have all become interested in. She sends him letters that are so hot, they shouldn't be handled with bare hands. The entire content of each letter is dedicated to describing in every detail some sexual encounter they've had, or some sexual experience she wishes they were going to have. After listening to Jim read a couple of these letters out loud, some of the guys have had to make emergency trips to the laundry/massage parlor.

Pinetti is also sitting in his cot with his back against the wall reading a letter he believes has come from a Playboy Centerfold. He wrote a letter to Playboy with a sob story about how much he missed reading those wonderful articles and admiring the beautiful women. He was hoping they would fork over some freebies. Playboy responded with a letter supposedly written by one of last year's centerfolds. The letter is full of appreciative remarks for the service that Pinetti and the rest of us boys are doing for our country and baloney like that. The sad thing is, no matter how hard any of us try to convince him it is a form letter, he's going to go on believing the letter was actually typed and signed by a real live Playboy Bunny. Hell, who knows, maybe it was.

Pinetti also claims to have come from a farming family. He is from central Illinois, but his thick twangy drawl is always mistaken for Deep South. Pinetti is by far the biggest bullshit artist I have ever met in my life, even worse than Red Smitt. Smitty's embellishments are always good natured and meant to make whatever he talks about more colorful or interesting and are rarely used as a measure to discredit or defame anybody. Pinetti's on the other hand border on libel. He likes talking about people, putting them down, talking behind their backs, and criticizing them in general, as if defiling others somehow raises his own self-esteem. I classify him as a mindless hypocrite. We think of him as a big ass-kissing weasel. If he could ever forget the Peyton Place rhetoric and just try to be one of the guys, he might not be too bad. There are moments – very short ones – when he is actually personable. But just when I start thinking maybe he's not so bad after all, he'll start shoveling out a big load of bullshit or demean someone from the battery and I realize I'm wasting my time with him.

Farmer or not, Pinetti is one dumb hick. For someone who supposedly knows everything, it's amazing how little he actually knows. People in the platoon bait him regularly and are usually astonished by his responses. Once, when we were talking politics, Pinetti actually argued that State assembly representatives and senators and congressional representatives and senators, were one and the same! He loves to bet that he is right, as if this will somehow validate his position and back down his detractors. Anytime someone disagrees with him, the first thing out of his mouth is, "You wanna bet?" Then of course, he never believes anyone who corroborates an opinion contrary to his own. Consequently, he never pays off on any of his bets.

Unlike Lindlay, Pinetti has no aspirations of becoming a farmer. He's gonna get himself a Corvette and lots of money, the two ingredients Pinetti believes will make him totally irresistible to women. He has never mentioned how he will make this sky rocketing climb up the social ladder and none of us really want to know. The one thing I know for certain is I don't trust him. For the most part I've been glad he's managed to weasel out of most of the shitty assignments, I'd be worried if I had to depend on him to cover my ass. Jim feels the same way. Even though Coleman will never say it, we know he hates Pinetti. Pinetti's racial slurs and obvious disdain at having to sleep in the same hooch with a black man are surely the sources of those feelings. I often think Pinetti will end up in jail.

Coleman is at the other end of the hooch doing his karate exercises. For the most part he is quiet and rarely says anything just for the sake of talking. His first name is Ronald. He doesn't want to be called Ron, Ronald, or anything else, just Coleman. When he told me his first name, I opened my mouth to say it, but before I could even utter a syllable, he said, "Now don't be telling me about the famous actor Ronald Coleman, I done heard it a thousand times." So I didn't.

He hails from Philadelphia where he worked at a refinery for two years before being drafted. At the refinery he was a general laborer, it doesn't sound very glamorous, but it paid well and he enjoyed it. Laborers are the guys who climb up and down those huge towers and refining vessels to open valves, perform maintenance, take samples, and do insulating. He liked it. He felt it was a dignified job, better than most black men could get, and he plans to return to the job when he gets back home.

Coleman is from a family of eight. He has five brothers and a sister and a widowed mother. Before he was drafted he was pretty much the sole supporter of the family. His father died four years earlier and he took on the responsibility of providing for his family. Even now he sends home nearly his entire monthly pay. The edge of bitterness he wields against authority is tied to his attempts to avoid the draft. He applied for deferments, knowing that his family would surely suffer financial hardship if he were drafted. The draft board turned down his requests. He tried to get his local committeeman to intervene, but was once again denied. All in all, every authoritative person or agency he approached turned him down, so his attitude toward the army and authority are weighted heavily on the hostile side. Coleman's character doesn't let this resentment interfere with his responsibilities as a soldier or to his comrades. He might tell the battery commander to kiss his ass, but he will be the person of choice if the Captain needs someone he can count on.

Red Smitt, Smitty, is an Oklahoma boy and a character to say the least. At the ripe old age of twenty, he has pretty much lost most of the hair on top of his head, but the hair on the sides is a fiery bright orange. The hair color is accentuated by a complexion that has an orange hue to it, his body being covered with a layer of heavily freckled skin.

Red is a yarn spinner. He loves to have the floor and if he thinks someone is listening, he'll follow 'em into the shithouse just so he won't lose his audience. He also has a good sense of humor, but yucks like an animal when he laughs. He has a nervousness about him and any increase or change in his emotional demeanor sends him into a chattering, jittery state of alarm. He'll make weird sounds, flailing his arms, with his feet moving back and forth even though he doesn't move an inch, sometimes even spinning around in circles. He looks like a Howdy Doody marionette that is out of control.

Smitty went through training at Fort Sill Oklahoma. Fort Sill is one of the Army's artillery training sites. He claims the only reason he requested artillery was so he would be stationed at Fort Sill and be close to home. Smitty worked in his father's Phillips 66 gas station doing tune-ups and lube jobs. He has no idea what he wants to do with his life. I'm coming to the conclusion if he makes it through the war he's going to be a lifer. He's already talked about becoming an MP, so if he does leave the service, it would help him land a job as a state trooper.

He has a fiancée back in his hometown, Bartlesville, which also just happens to be the home of Phillips 66. According to Smitty, Phillips pretty much owns the town. He's made it clear that whatever happens from here on out, he has no intention of working in a gas station the rest of his life. Probably why I'm convinced he'll re-up.

Turner has joined my short list of good friends. He's a college dropout from Altoona Pennsylvania. He's pretty intelligent and is a good source of political banter. I suppose it is unusual for someone from Chicago, but I have never thought about politics in any way shape or form. Before talking to Turner, the scope of my political interaction revolved solely around two things: I cried when J.F.K. was assassinated and I knew Richard Daly would be mayor of Chicago forever. Turner's the type of guy that always reads the editorials and national news in the paper. I'm the type that reads the funnies. His rationalizations have started me thinking about things, that before now, were not important to me in any way, shape, or form.

Me, well I'm just a schmo from a middle class blue-collar family in Chicago. My father, an honest, hard working man, spends sixty or seventy hours a week trying to support his wife and six kids.

My mother, at times, is a certified nut case. Though, she occasionally abused us physically, beatings with anything she could get her hands on, she is also a master of mental abuse, utilizing guilt and character assassination to keep us feeling inadequate. Her antics provide the motive for my older sister moving out at the age of seventeen and the reason I was anxious to enlist in the service. We had to get away from her.

I was an *A* student at O'Toole grammar school but faltered in high school. I still managed A's in math and science, but only C's in the other subjects. The subject material wasn't that difficult, I just didn't spend enough time in class. My out of control hormonal urges were a constant distraction. A girl in a cashmere sweater could completely disable my ability to think about anything other than what she looked like without it. For some reason, math and science always seemed easy and I rarely had to study or think about it.

I had aspirations of attending college, but the plan didn't develop the way I envisioned. From the time I was fourteen, I worked an assortment of jobs with the intention of socking money away for school. My mother, a true matriarch in the sense she ruled our house with an iron fist, diligently collected my paychecks assuring me the money was being saved. When the time came, it turned out she pissed it all away.

In all fairness, I must admit I was no angel, especially when I was a teenager. I hung out with guys who were constantly in trouble. We weren't criminals, just rotten kids. We were often involved in fistfights with guys from other neighborhoods. We'd pull stunts like blowing up mailboxes with cherry bombs, or putting Volkswagens on porches. Behind our house, across the alley, was the garage where Dressel's bakery parked their delivery trucks. Their main products were frozen bakery goods. The drivers would fill their trucks at the bakery in the evening and park them in the garage so they could get a four A.M. start on their delivery routes. We'd climb up on the roof of the garage, remove a pane from the skylight and drop down onto the top of a truck. We'd steal a couple of cases of eclairs or cream puffs, eat till the filling was coming out of our ears and then use the rest to have cream puff fights.

Jim's stereo breaks my train of thought. The hooch is filled with the blaring sounds of *Mitch Ryder and the Detroit Wheels*; Jim's doing the Cool Jerk dance and mouthing the words to *C.C. Ryder*. He plays the same songs over and over and by the end of the evening the words to *C.C. Ryder, Devil with the Blue Dress On* and *Good Golly Miss Molly* are permanently scribed into our long-term memory.

Thursday morning... Two eighty-eight and a wake up. Walking through the door of the mess hall we sense that something's not right. Missing is the smell of frying bacon and burnt toast.

"Sorry, no chow, just grab a box of C rations." We look down at Sergeant Pace, the mess Sergeant, sitting at a table reading a two-week-old copy of "Stars and Stripes".

"How come 'dere's no chow?" Lee asks with an obvious tone of disappointment, he is one of the few people who actually like the crap they serve.

"No water."

"Whata'ya mean, no water?" Smitty asks with a look of astonishment.

"Well, most of our water is pumped and processed from a small lake over on the other side of Pleiku. When I sent the water trucks over for a refill, the filtration station was shut down. Gooks poisoned the lake; all the fish are belly up. Supposedly several people have died drinking the water."

I shake my head in disbelief.

Coleman's brow furrows, the muscles in his neck tighten and he says, "So what the hell are we supposed to do?"

"They'll have blivets flown in once or twice a week to supply us with water. It ain't just us ya know, a lot of the units around here are gonna be strapped. It'll be a far cry from our normal supply of water. Standing order'll be two canteens a day, one for drinkin' one for shavin'."

"What about showers?" I ask.

"Weren't you listening? Two canteens a day is all you're gonna get. The showers are filled from the water trucks, no water trucks, no showers." Sergeant Pace is surprisingly calm and doesn't seem the least bit disturbed by the situation. Then again, this means he's not going to have to be preparing meals for some unknown period of time. Hell, he's probably glad.

"You have got to be shittin' me! No goddamn shower water. Man, this is bullshit." I've never seen Coleman so pissed off. He stops and whips around, saying, "Wait a damn minute, I know there's another lake over on the other side of Pleiku somewhere, why aren't they pumping out of there?"

"I only know what I'm told." Pace just goes back to reading his paper.

"Shit! I don't give a damn about the hot chow, but no showers, man, that's bullshit."

Mentally, I'm glad I managed to get a shower this morning; I'm worried it might be a while before I can get another.

At about eight thirty a formation is held and everyone on the Hill gets the bad news. The brass seems to think the situation will be resolved in a week or so. *A week...that's not so bad. We go without showers for a week in the field all the time. The hot chow ain't all that good anyway.*

Saturday July 2nd, it's been over two weeks since most of us have been able to shower...*So much for the cock-and-bull story about the water situation lasting only a week.* As a stop gap the battery is trucked in bunches of fifty to a small lake near Kontum to bathe in the lake. The forty-mile ride back is so dusty it makes the whole trip a waste of time. Even so, I will admit, it was nice to wash my balls for a change. We believe the only reason the trip was organized was because there's been an outbreak of crotch rot and jungle rot throughout the camp. Crotch rot and jungle rot are pretty much the same, both are caused by fungus. One you get on your feet, the other you get in the crease of your legs next to your balls. It itches like crazy and smells horrendous. While we were at the lake I asked why we didn't bring our water trucks along and did not receive any credible answer. Even if it couldn't be filtered for drinking, we could still use it for bathing. "Too long of a haul," was the only response I got. Sometimes you gotta wonder what kind thinking goes into some of the decision making.

Fishe is putting the final wrap of electrical tape on the wire he's just spliced. The line from one of the bunkers was cut when some digging was done. "That's it...let's put it back in the ground." Fishe drops the wire, then bends over to nestle it back into its trench. I push the dirt in over the wire and start tamping it with my foot. I pause a second to look at my hands and again start thinking about the shower situation.

"Man, this shower thing is getting out of hand. How the hell are the locals getting water to bathe with?"

Jim looks up with a smile and says, "Hell, man, the way some of them smell, I don't think they bathe that often anyway."

"There's got to be someplace to get water. I can't believe all the officers over at MACV and PAB are going without showers."

Jim helps tamp the dirt while he seemingly ponders my observations. After several seconds of contemplation he says, "Ya know, most of the people in town are probably getting their water from wells."

"Then how come we don't just buy it from them? Hell, why aren't we digging our own wells?"

"Hell, man, what do you think the Cong would do to a villager that sells us water?" Jim stops when he sees Sergeant Bennett sauntering in our direction. Bennett has terrible posture. He kind of lumbers over when he walks and when he's standing erect it looks like he's leaning over. We know he's volunteered us for something.

"Hey, Sis, you boys all done here?" Bennett has a sheepish grin on his face that signals he is about to confirm our suspicions and it doesn't take him long to do it.

"Yeah, we're done here. Ya know, Sarge, I do have a name. How about not calling me Sis? It's fucking embarrassing."

"Sure thing, Sis."

I know he isn't going to stop, so I just let it go.

"What's up?" We ask, waiting for the bomb to drop.

"Well, boys, I just need ya to ride shotgun on the garbage trucks. They'll be moving out in about twenty minutes up by the mess hall." Bennett starts laughing and walks away.

"What the hell's so funny?" I look to Jim for an explanation. Jim just shrugs his shoulders and we head back to the hooch.

I put my harness on, but no pack. This limits me to about six magazines. I think, *how bad can it be? Hell, it's only a trip to the garbage dump.* Grabbing my helmet and flak jacket, I head for the mess hall.

In front of the mess hall a deuce-and-a-half is being loaded with a half dozen thirty gallon garbage cans. Frenchy, just back from the hospital in Japan, is on the back of the truck. The cans are hoisted up to the bed and fastened to the side railings with rope.

"Hey, Frenchy! Man, when'd you get back? How's the arm?" Frenchy reaches out with his good arm to help lift me up. He's only been back two days. The MASH unit here put him on a plane to Japan the day after the snakebite. When the guys at the Hill found out, there was a lot of the, "What a lucky bastard," comments floating around. Personally, I didn't think he was all that lucky.

"Muh arms still pretty weak and them doctors say the damaged muscle will never grow back, but I'm getting' along. I was hopin' the bastards would send me home, but they didn't."

That fact is obvious, but I refrain from making the smart-ass reply. He rolls up his sleeve and shows me the large indentation on his forearm where the muscle has deteriorated. *Christ,* I think*, it must have hurt like hell.*

The smell from the garbage cans is overwhelming. Some of these cans have been sitting around for a week in ninety-degree weather. Sergeant Pace emerges from the mess hall with an M-16, a pistol belt, and a helmet. I don't know why this strikes me as peculiar, but it does. Maybe, it seems weird because he's a cook.

Pace takes the passenger seat in the Jeep parked in front of us, his helper, Carl Lea, a Spec 4, is driving the Jeep. Lea has always been a pretty good guy, never unwilling to give extra helpings if you wanted them - not that anybody ever does.

Once the truck is moving, the aroma isn't quite as bad; the breeze feels good and cools our faces. The canvas canopy that normally covers the back of the truck is missing.

We drive about twenty minutes, pass MACV and turn onto a dirt road heading east. As usual, both vehicles create a cloud of dust that chokes us and makes it impossible to see. By this time we're smart enough to prepare ourselves by carrying goggles and a kerchief. At least the goggles allow us to keep our eyes open. The kerchief helps, but doesn't keep us from choking.

Shortly after turning onto the road I realize it isn't the dust that's gagging me, it's the smell. The closer we get to the dump, the more horrendous it gets. As the truck nears the dump, I'm awed by the expanse of rotting garbage.

I can't make out Jim's expression, but I know what it must be, especially, when he says, "God almighty, man, *the smell*, I can't fucking breathe!"

A massive hoard of people agglomerates and moves towards the gate of the dump, there are hundreds. I pull down the kerchief and raise my goggles letting them rest on the front of my helmet.

"What the…?"

As we move through the gate, the people are all over the truck. They are jumping up and grabbing the tailgate, climbing up the sides. They're like a swarm of roaches.

"Get down! What the fuck's wrong with you people? You're gonna get killed. Get down!" Jim yells as he pushes them off the back of the still moving truck.

As we pull away from the crowd, they mass and follow us like a swarm of insects. We drive around one of the mountains of garbage and come to a stop.

I look at Jim. "What the fuck was that?" I'm about to hop down and lower the tailgate, but Pace pulls up next to us and tells us to stay on the back of the truck.

"Stay up there, stay up there, if we have to go in a hurry, we can get the hell out of here." Pace turns around to look at the advancing horde.

"Drivers gonna move slowly, you guys just empty the cans off the back. Anybody starts pullin' at you, remember, you've got to protect yourselves. You don't want to die deliverin' garbage." A chilling thought. Pace pulls up next to the cab and motions to the driver. He drops the truck into low gear and the truck starts crawling forward. We untie a can, slide it to the back and knock it on its side, then up-end it to get all the garbage out.

The advancing crowd catches up and some of them stop and begin picking through the garbage we've just dumped, grabbing pieces of uneaten food or half empty cans of C rations. Some of them are actually eating the crap.

Jim gets a look of contempt on his face and says, "Are you fucking kiddin' me?"

They start to swarm the truck again and while trying to up-end another one of the cans, it's grabbed right out of our hands.

"Mother fucker!" I'm really beginning to get freaked out. I knock two people off the truck.

"Stay down, assholes, stay down!" I'm repelling so many of them we can't get to another can. They're pulling on my pant legs trying to climb up. Jim fires three bursts into the air, which freezes them momentarily, but then, they start climbing up again. Jim has to use his rifle butt to knock a couple of guys off the truck. It doesn't seem to matter at all, they just keep dogging at the back of the truck. "Fuck this." I pick up my M-14, jump off the truck, and empty a magazine into the ground. As I fire, the mob scatters like a bunch of cockroaches when you turn on the lights. I change magazines and once again fire into the dirt.

"Dee dee mou! Dee dee mou!" I yell. Loosely interpreted, it means get the fuck outta here. I remain off the truck while Jim starts dumping the cans. Two kids ignore my threats and start picking through the garbage. They latch onto a couple of unopened cans of C rations and as they wipe the slop and maggots off the cans, they are accosted by an old man and an old woman who try to take the cans away from them. The old man keeps whacking one of the kids in the side of the head. I push the old man away holding my rifle across my chest, then do the same thing to the old woman. As they move away, she defiles me with a string of boing-boing profanities emerging from her mouth with the same screeching tone finger nails make on a chalk board. It makes me want to club her just to shut her up, but I know it'll be something I'll regret so I resist the

temptation. Instead, guilt sets in. I reach into my pocket, pull out the four hundred piasters I have, jam them in the old woman's hand and tell her to dee-dee.

Lea appears at my side and comments, "Man, this is totally fucked."

"No shit. I can't fucking believe this shit. You do this often?"

"Every goddamn week. The first time I did this I felt sorry for them, so the next time I brought about ten cases of C rations and started tossing them off the truck. It made it worse. They pulled me off the truck to get at the rations, ripped my fucking clothes off and tried to steal my rifle. I thought they were going to kill me. The goddamn women are the worst."

"Fuck! That's scary." I turn my head in his direction but never take my eyes off the crowd of people.

"Even after they got the C rations, they still picked through the garbage, so I figured screw it."

Jim dumps the last can, leaving a very large pile of garbage behind the truck. Lea backs away and I quickly climb back up on the truck.

As we pull away we watch the revolting display of people pulling garbage soaked clothes out of the trash, picking up portions of uneaten food, some infested with maggots, wiping off the maggots, and depositing the find into a sack or a pocket. It makes me sick to my stomach. I yell at the driver, "Man, let's get the fuck outta here!" *I won't be eating any supper tonight.*

We have to get back on the blacktop before we can breathe again, Jim laughs and yells in my ear, "Ya know, I think I saw the woman who ran that restaurant where you guys ate in Pleiku. I could swear she was stuffing her bag with rotten meat."

"Real funny."

It's sixteen hundred when we get back to the hill. Bennett meets us at the hooch with a big shit eatin' grin on his face.

"Glad to see you boys made it, it's really somethin', ain't it?" Bennett acts as if he's somehow done us a favor.

The image of the revolting display is still fresh in my mind. "Damn, Sarge, that was fucking disgusting. Why the hell doesn't the brass do something to feed those people? Isn't it sort of counter productive to let people be starving over here? Don't we want them to think we're their friends? What the hell's the story?"

"Well, Sis, there's always a lot of sufferin' in a war, and it ain't always from getting' shot or wounded. I'd guess most of the kids are orphans and the old people, probably homeless. Who the fuck knows." It's the first time I've seen Bennett serious about anything since I've been here.

As an afterthought, I wonder how much food could be bought with just a portion of the money spent on the guns we give to the South Vietnamese. Would the North Vietnamese or the Vietcong be trying to kick out Nguyem Key if the country was more prosperous? Why the fuck don't we just toss out Key? He sure as hell ain't doing any more for these people than Diem did. These are questions I have no answers for, nor do I have the information or facts to derive any sensible conclusion. I know it and push the thoughts out of my head. I look at Jim; we shake our heads, then turn and walk away.

"Hold up a minute boys, there's a formation at 17:00 that I want both of you to attend. Ya'll need to go change, you guys smell like shit."

I look at Jim, "Why the hell are they having a formation?" I try to remember if I even have any clean fatigues. Laundry is starting to become a problem since the water problem started.

We saunter over to the orderly room at about five minutes to five. A few minutes later, the door of the orderly room opens; Neuman and Solomon walk out. Bennett is actually standing in front of the platoon, a first. I don't think I've ever actually seen him show up for a formation prior to this.

Neuman has us fall in and Solomon addresses the group.

"We received word from MACV today that the water situation is likely to last for another couple of weeks." Everybody groans. "We'll try to arrange more trips to the Kontum for bathing and laundry. Once the Monsoon starts, water won't be a problem."

I turn slightly and ask, "Monsoon?"

Coleman leans over, "I'll tell ya later,"

Solomon continues, "Pleiku is once again off limits and will remain off limits until intelligence feels that it is again safe to open up the town."

"Okay, next order of business, we have four promotions." He looks at Neuman who calls out, "Sergeant Bennett." Bennett takes the sets of orders from Neuman and they both turn towards the company. Bennett begins to rattle off all the standard jargon.

"Special order number…something and so forth, the following people have been promoted to the rank of Specialist Fourth class, grade

E-4. Fishe, James E. and Simon, William J." Then Sergeant Dick advances and reads off promotions for Varant and Farmly. Bennett hands us the orders and shakes our hands.

Solomon calls us to attention and dismisses the formation.

"Nice goin', Sis, you boys deserve it." Bennett shakes our hands and walks away.

"You boys must have been doin' some pretty heavy ass kissin' if you ask me." This, coming out of Pinetti, seems pretty ridiculous.

Jim's response is, "Ya know, we wanted to do some ass kissin', but every time we did, we had to get in line behind you...dickhead." Jim bursts into laughter.

"Assholes." Pinetti noticeably disturbed over our promotions, stomps away.

We make a beeline for the PX to get chevrons for our fatigues. We're not anxious to flaunt it, though, I'm not above rubbing it in Pinetti's face, we're just a little proud of the accomplishment.

Varant suggests checking out the NCO club.

"Huh?"

"Yeah," Varant says, "Spec 4's can get into the NCO club. Let's see how the other half lives." He has a little glint in his eye.

"Hell, yeah, I'm up for that," Fishe says as he stands and pulls on his shirt in one fluid movement.

"Hey, I have a thought."

They look at me, waiting for me to elaborate.

"Now that we're Spec 4's, does this mean we're all assholes?"

I smile and Farmly laughs. He knows my theory about every Spec 4 in the army being an asshole.

Varant looks bewildered and asks, "What's so funny?"

Fishe stands up, laughs, and adds, "Hell, we're all assholes. Let's go see what the inside of that NCO club looks like."

It's not quite dark as we walk over to the club. Ironically, it is situated just down the hill from the chapel.

The NCO club is about twice the size of our hooch, maybe a little bigger. Pushing our way through the screen door and looking around, I can see six tables, like picnic tables, occupied by the twenty or so guys drinking beer and listening to country music. The music blares out of speakers attached to a reel-to-reel tape recorder. There's a bar with six stools on one side of the room; Sergeant Pace is tending bar.

"Well, Sis, you boys didn't waste any time, come on I'll buy the first round." Sgt. Bennett stands us to a can of Carling's Black Label and joins us at one of the tables.

"So what did you boys think of the dump?" Bennett asks.

Jim answers. "Sarge that was the most disgusting damn thing I have ever seen in my life. Man, I hope we don't ever have to pull that duty again."

Bennett assures us it will be months before we will have to pull the duty again. He chats for a while, and then excuses himself so he can join Bast and Neuman.

Varant is working on his third can of beer. I realize that we know nothing about him. He is the tight-lipped one of the group.

I probe a little. "So Hal, where you from?"

"The sunny state of California. I'm from Anaheim, baby, you know,

Disneyland." According to Varant, he actually had a scholarship to UCLA where he was studying Electrical Engineering. He lost his scholarship because of personal problems that interfered with his studies, he doesn't elaborate and we don't ask. Later, after a couple of more beers have loosened his inhibitions, we find out his step father beat the crap out of his mother, so Hal left school to go home with the intent of kicking his step father's ass. Unfortunately, it didn't work out the way he intended. So he did the next best thing, he took a sledgehammer to his step dad's car and was arrested. The judge gave him thirty days and a year's probation. When he lost his scholarship, he had to drop out and lost his draft deferment. Next thing he knows he gets the old "Greetings" letter from Uncle Sam. The army found he had an IQ of about 135, and wanted him to go to Officers Candidate School, but he turned them down. It would have meant adding a couple of years to his stay in the army. Varant thought that being in radio and crypto might land him at some missile site in the states, but why expect his luck to change at that point.

Varant has a sarcastic edge and a *fuck everything* attitude. He's not easy to warm up to, but once you do, you feel like he's your brother. Hal is blatantly honest; he never withholds anything. I think it is his honesty that makes him seem so sarcastic. He doesn't beat around the bush and is always ready and willing to call a spade a spade.

At first I felt Varant and Farmly were both snobbish, but turns out I was wrong about both of them. Farmly is not as snobbish as he had first come across, though he still has an air about him. He likes to ask questions and delve into the thought processes one uses to arrive at a decision, especially if he believes it is a wrong decision. Abstractly, it is his way of telling someone he thinks they're full of crap.

Farmly comes from upper middle class, way upper middle class; his family has some money, or at least what I'd call money. He dropped out of Boston College because he wasn't doing very well, which enraged his father. Farmly is obviously quite intelligent, but he just didn't want to follow in his father's footsteps and become a banker. As a matter of fact, he wanted to study theatre and do drama on Broadway, which really pissed off his old man. Before he could convince his father to finance his acting career he was offered the opportunity of a lifetime by the Selective Service system. Maybe he isn't all that different from the rest of us after all.

Friday morning while I'm preparing to take my whore's bath with my little ration of water, I notice Lindlay sitting on the edge of his cot with his pants down around his ankles. Lee has his schlong in his hand and he's twisting it all around inspecting it.

I smile and yell, "Lee, quit playing with yourself, you want to go blind?"

Lee's head snaps around, surprised that I've caught him. He bolts to his feet pulling his pants and shorts up as he rises. I half expect him to have that shit eatin' grin he carries around with him, but he doesn't…a signal that something is wrong.

"Lee, what's up?"

He looks around to see who's within earshot, then tells me he thinks he has the clap.

"What the hell are you talking about? It's been weeks since we went to Pleiku?"

"My dick's dripping and it burns when I take a piss. I got to get over to the medics."

"Shit, man, how the hell did you get the clap?" Lee, embarrassed, tells me they stopped at a roadside shack on the way to MACV to pick up supplies. The shack of course had a couple of girls ready to service anyone who stopped in.

"Well, get your ass over to the hospital at Pleiku bonehead. They'll give you a couple of shots of penicillin and fix you right up." I didn't have to twist his arm.

Lee grabs his gear and hurries out the door. *Damn,* I think, *rubbers, I got to wear rubbers.*

Friday is spent stringing wire back and forth to Delta Battery. They've just returned from Plei Me and are setting up on the far side of the hill. When we're done we try to grab a couple of hours of sleep in anticipation of guard duty.

At 17:30 the guard assembles in front of the orderly room. Frenchy, Jim, Turner and I are assigned to bunker four, right in front of a newly placed Delta Battery 175 Howitzer. Guard manning has been stepped up from three men per bunker to four. For a change, the brass have actually thought about our well being, rationalizing that a three-hour shift is easier on the men and the probability of someone falling asleep is reduced. I think they're right.

Jim takes the first shift, six to nine, Frenchy takes second, nine to midnight, I get stuck with midnight to three and Turner gets cleanup.

The sun has just gone down; it's about 20:30. Frenchy, Turner and I are still up. Frenchy is giving us the lowdown on the nurses at the hospitals in Japan and Cam Rahn Bay. He's feeding us a load of bullshit about nailing an American nurse while he was in Japan.

"Damn, all them nurses were fine as hell. They'd rub your back, give you them sponge baths, every now and then they'd tickle your balls for ya, then, when I'd get a boner, they'd walk away laughin'. Teases, most of 'em was nothin' but teases. Always leanin' over with them titties almost fallin' out, hell, I think I suffered more from blue balls than I did from the snake bite."

Turner says, "Hey, I thought you said you got laid."

Frenchy continues, "Well, after all that teasin', I was getting' the blue balls, just like I said, so I started complaining to the night nurse about it. Then one night she comes in and starts playin' with me while I'm sleepin'.

"Yeah, yeah, yeah…while you were asleep. She just couldn't resist that huge slab of man meat you carry around, could she?" I know the likelihood of this happening was so remote it was exceedingly hard to believe. Frenchy isn't exactly Paul Newman; he's more like Walter Matthau's midget twin brother.

"No, no, really, I swear on my momma's grave. I wake up and there she is with a big smile on her face. She says, for fifty bucks she'll take care of me."

"Bull-fucking-shit!"

"Honest, I ain't a shittin'. I fork over the fifty, she pulls the curtain, takes off them panties, which I kept as a souvenir, and screws the livin' hell out of me. Man, she got money outa me three more times before I shipped out. Damn, that was some good pussy."

Frenchy isn't looking at us anymore. A mesmerized look has washed over his face, his eyes staring off somewhere that prevents them from focusing on anything in the bunker. He has mentally transported himself back in time to that very moment when the nurse was ministering to his needs. Just seeing that look instinctively convinces me he's telling the truth.

Turner sees it too. "Man, I'd give a months pay for some round eye pussy."

Frenchy replies, "I did."

Turner lies on the cot with his hands folded behind his head, a big smile on his face and a glint in his eye. I know exactly what is going though his mind.

Turner continues, "Yeah, if I was back home, me and Alice would be havin' a picnic. We'd be sittin' by the lake waitin' for the fireworks to start, roll ourselves up in the blanket, so nobody could see what our hands were doing…ahhhhh yes."

"Holy shit, tomorrow's the Fourth of July!" It hadn't even crossed my mind till Turner made his comment.

Frenchy is on his feet preparing to relieve Jim. "Damn, Fourth of July, I plum forgot about it. How come we ain't celebrating?"

"Well one reason is because we're on guard duty ten thousand miles from home. Need another one?"

Frenchy walks out the door; a minute later Jim is inside removing his gear. He says, "Frenchy said I should tell you guys it isn't a good enough reason not to celebrate." Not much is thought of it and we just go to sleep.

"Simon! Simon! Come on, wake up, it's your shift, man." I reluctantly open my eyes and am shocked into consciousness by the contorted muzzle Frenchy calls a face.

"Yeah, yeah, I'm up." Man, do I hate guard duty.

"I'm coming, I'm coming, man, don't piss in your pants." I put on my flak jacket, grab my gear, and follow Frenchy out the door.

On top of the bunker, Frenchy checks the M-60. He flips open the top, checks the belt, closes it, and picks up the weapon.

He stands holding the M-60 with a devilish look on his smiling face.

"What the hell are you doing?"

"We got about a minute-and-a-half to go," Frenchy informs me.

"A minute-and-a-half till what?" The smile on his face spreads into a toothy grin.

"About a minute-and-a-half till it's midnight...then it'll be the fourth."

"Yeah, so what?"

"Man, it's all worked out. Everybody agreed to it." Frenchy still hasn't answered my question.

"Agreed to what?"

"At midnight we're gonna have our own little Fourth of July fireworks celebration." Before I can press him for more information weapons begin firing all around the perimeter. Frenchy is off the bunker pointing the M-60 up in the air out over the wire. He laughs, pulls the trigger and the M-60 starts chattering away. A snake like trail of tracers pours into the sky all around the hill. Several small *Pows* signal flares are being fired. Every swinging dick on guard is participating and I can't avoid getting caught up in the frenzy. I start firing bursts from my M-14. Fishe and Turner charge out of the bunker, realize what's going on, and begin firing their weapons. Guys are laughing and shooting, almost dancing around to the bizarre rhythm created by the recoil of their weapons. From out over the dark expanse in front of our position, out towards Titty Mountain, there is a wave of tracers pouring into the sky. They're doing the same damn thing.

The field phone begins ringing. I barely hear it over the sound of weapons firing. The guys over at bunker eight start yelling. *"O.D.! O.D.! The O.D.'s coming down."* Everyone scrambles to get back in their bunkers. I look back up the hill and see the O.D. (Officer on Duty), Lt. Duke, running down the hill in his shorts, flak jacket and steel pot. His boots are untied and he isn't wearing a shirt.

I poke Jim in the side. He stops laughing and looks at me with a big smile. I point towards Duke. He grabs Turner and they scramble down into the bunker. Frenchy is still firing the M-60. He has expended the contents of an entire can of ammunition. The barrel of the M-60 is so hot I swear I can detect a slight glow of red.

I yell, "Frenchy!" He looks at me and I point at Duke who is about twenty yards away.

Frenchy turns, looks, and says, "Shit!"

Duke, out of breath, sweating and looking ridiculous, runs directly up to him. "*Did you fire that weapon private?*" Duke towers over Frenchy, Frenchy is about five-six if he wears lifts.

"Fuck no, I ain't fired no weapon, Sir." Frenchy says in a defiant "Kiss-my-ass" tone of voice.

The obvious lie enrages Duke. He looks first at the still glowing barrel of the M-60, then at the pile of brass shell casings at Frenchy's feet. "Well, where did all that come from?"

Frenchy responds, "How the hell am I supposed to know, I just walked up and picked up the weapon. I fired off a couple of short bursts to test fire the weapon sir."

Duke looks up at me. "I suppose you didn't fire your weapon either, did you?"

"Hell, sir, I just started my shift. Though, I did notice a lot of fire coming from over near Titty Mountain." I have to fight to keep from laughing. Duke looks at me, then Frenchy, then at me again. He starts to say something, stops and stomps off in the direction of bunker twelve.

Frenchy and I look at each other unable to control the urge to laugh and just start roaring. Frenchy is laughing so hard he falls to his knees with tears streaking down his cheeks. Jim's head pops out of the bunker, he looks around and comes out when he feels it is safe.

I look out towards Pleiku and see several streams of tracers rising into the darkness of the night sky. These are accompanied by dozens of flares visible in almost any direction I look. The four of us sit with our legs dangling over the side of the bunker, chuckling and watching the fireworks. For each of us it's a little touch of home.

Two days later, the entire guard, everyone on duty that infamous night, is assembled by Capt. Solomon and informed that Article Fifteens were considered, but dismissed because it is not clear who or what parties were responsible for initiating the fireworks display. An Article Fifteen is unit punishment dispensed by the company commander. I'd compare it to a misdemeanor drunk and disorderly violation or a speeding ticket.

Instead, we're all fined equally to "pay" for the cost of the ammunition that was expended. An estimate of twenty thousand rounds at seven cents a round meant all forty-eight guys on guard are getting fined twenty-nine bucks apiece. That's pretty substantial when you made less than two hundred a month.

Chapter Eight

"Good Guys and Bad"

July 25th – Two forty and a wake up. I lay a carton of Marlboros on my poncho and roll the poncho up as tightly as possible. I stuff the poncho into my duffel on top of my gear. A towel, four pair of socks, two changes of underwear, twelve loaded magazines, my shaving gear and a two sets of fatigues. At the very bottom, I have three extra bottles of mosquito repellant. There is methodology to the way things get packed. If the repellant leaks, having it on the bottom insures it won't contaminate the clean clothes. The magazines, the next layer, are kept clean and dry by the layer of clothing and poncho packed in above them. The poncho also protects the cigarettes, the second most valuable item in the duffel.

Everybody in the hooch, with the exception of Farmly, is busy packing their gear. I watch Pinetti fill half his duffel with Playboy magazines and some junk food he got from home.

"Hey, Pinetti."

"Huh?"

"That's not quite what we meant when we said pack lots of magazines. Aren't you gonna bring underwear or socks or any necessities?"

"Hell, yeah, I got room here for some skivvies. Why, what else should I bring?"

I'd forgotten up to this point, the only time Pinetti has been off this hill was to go to the whorehouse and the little stint relocating Delta battery.

"You need to bring dry socks, underwear, one or two changes of fatigues, a bed roll, a poncho, mosquito repellant, and all the fucking ammo you can carry."

"Ya'all are kiddin' me, right? Hell, we're only gonna be gone three or four days."

"Bennett says up to a month."

What a dickhead, I think. Bennett says up to a month and he thinks we're only gonna be gone a couple of days. How can he even presume that? Hell, why am I even trying to help the prick? I have no reasonable answer to either question so I resume my own preparations.

Jim puts on his helmet, grabs his gear and says, "Let's go outside and wait."

Sitting on the sandbag wall that surrounds our hooch, I sense that Jim is not happy about this assignment, which is completely out of character for him. I'm pretty sure his disdain is tied to the water situation. Recently, the 4th Infantry Division with a base camp near Titty Mountain set up a filtration station at a small lake near there. Water trucks are once again supplying the local units with water for drinking and bathing. Everybody is anxious to have their supply reestablished, but the filtration unit is only capable of producing so many gallons per day, so a schedule has been set up for re-supplying the water. We're scheduled to get a tanker full tomorrow. It'll be the first real water supply we've gotten in a month. So as fate would have it, we won't be here.

"Man, no shower water for over a month," Jim's legs are repeatedly kicking back and forth against the sandbags like a nervous little kid, "and the day before the damn water starts flowing again, we've gotta ship out with Delta Battery. Damn it, I've already got things startin' to grow between my toes, and if you ask me, we're all startin' to smell like Mary-Jane rotten crotch." Jim shakes his head, looks at Lindlay and adds, "Ya know, I'm startin' to have trouble distinguishing you guys from Coleman."

Coleman laughs. He holds his arm up next to mine, "Ya know he's right. 'Tween the dust and the sun tan, I wouldn't be attending any Klan meetings if I were you." Coleman shoots a look over at Pinetti with a little smile on his face, waiting for a reaction.

Pinetti can't resist. The bait has been thrown out and he bites down hard.

"Ya'all know my cousin is a Klan member and you guys got it all wrong. Klan ain't against nig…, ah, black men, no sir. Matter a fact, I believe Charlie's got himself a couple of black friends. "Pinetti's eyes always seem to have a slight bulge and the eyelids never reveal more than half of the man's cornea. When he smiles, it seems to stretch the eye openings to mere slits. He has that look on his face now.

Coleman asks, "Is that a fact?" Then he looks at me and says, "Damn, I didn't realize the Klan was so active in Illinois." Coleman is toying with him but Pinetti doesn't realize it.

"Oh, hell, yes, Klan's got a big following in Illinois." Pinetti is on the line and doesn't know he's about to be reeled in.

Jim has a look of disbelief on his face, but feels compelled to ask, "No shit? You been to meetings?"

"Damn straight, and we never once even mentioned black men, not even once." Pinetti's eyes shoot a look over at Coleman to see if he seemed disturbed in any way.

Coleman knows he's hooked himself a whopper, so he lets out some line. "Well, me being a black man…" He pauses for a moment, then says, "You knew I was a black man didn't you?"

Jim doesn't let Pinetti answer, he jumps in with, "Hell no, I thought we were all enlisted men."

Coleman continues, "Well, just to keep the record straight, I am a black man and since I have always been under the obvious misconception that, 'The Klan' is a racist organization, maybe you'll enlighten me as to the real function of the Klan?"

Pinetti just can't resist, "Well, at the meetins' I been to, we never talk about hatin' black people, they just believe that white people should keep the white race pure and there shouldn't be any of that interracial stuff." Pinetti is dancing around like Fred Astaire.

"Well, I can't see anything wrong with that," Coleman says. We wonder where he's going. "Hell, no, I sure as hell wouldn't want my sisters hitchin' up with no red neck hillbilly."

Pinetti doesn't get the dig, and continues, "That's right. See, you understand." He's tap dancing all over the place now. "Yeah, we just think that everybody should stick to their own kind is all. You know, spics should only marry spics, Jews should only marry Jews, and like that."

"What about all that back of the bus bullshit and signs that say *No Niggers*. How about all that school segregation and what about not letting black people vote? What's the Klan think about all that?"

There's almost fervor in Pinetti's voice. This is probably the first time since he's been here that any of us have ever acted like we were interested in anything he had to say. He doesn't realize the band's been fired up and he's being led all around the dance floor like a cheap date.

"I ain't never seen a 'No Niggers' sign, I don't believe that'd be right."

"I have," Coleman says.

"Hell, I had two black boys in my high school class, I never had no problem with that."

"Yeah, I remember I had a white boy in my high school. No, no, I'm wrong, he was a teacher." Coleman's is enjoying this immensely.

"So what would 'The Klan' think if you brought yourself home one of these little Vietnamese girls?"

Pinetti looks unsettled. "Hell, man, I would never want to marry one of these slanty eyed little whores. They're okay for fuckin' but who'd want a house full of little slopes runnin' around."

"Oh, I see. So you're sayin' it'd be okay to fuck black girls, but you'd never want to marry one. Damn, they were doin' that before the civil war."

"No, no, that's not what I'm sayin'."

"Oh, so are you sayin' black girls are too repulsive to screw?" Coleman has a little gleam in his eye.

"No, you're not getting' what I'm tryin' to say." Frustration is starting to show on Pinetti's face.

"Are you sayin you would like to be screwin' black girls, but you wouldn't want to marry one? Coleman is almost in Pinetti's face.

"God damn it! That ain't what I'm sayin'! You're just twistin' my words all around. I'm just sayin' that the Klan believes in that Tower of Babel stuff is all."

"Tower of Babel? Man, what the fuck *are you* babblin' about?" I can't resist the small play on words.

"You know, the 'Tower of Babel.' Where God got mad and made all the different races and languages, so's people wouldn't intermix."

I will never need any further evidence that Pinetti is an idiot. "I think you missed the point of that story." I shake my head and let Coleman move in for the kill.

"Okay, let me get this here Klan stuff straight. It'd be okay if you had yourself a couple of black boy friends, as long as you weren't plannin' to marry 'em, is that right?" Realizing that he's being played like a fiddle at a barn dance, Pinetti tries to save face.

"Yeah, that's right, but you wouldn't have to worry 'cause you ain't my type." He tries to make a joke, but Coleman won't let him off the hook.

"Oh, so if I was a white boy, you'd want to marry me? Damn, we didn't realize you liked boys. Man, I'm gonna half-ta start sleepin' with one eye open." Our laughing causes Pinetti to glare at each of us with a look of disgust...the fish is in the net.

"Aw, fuck you guys!" Pinetti starts to stomp off, stops, turns around, grabs his gear, then continues in the direction of the mess hall. We're still laughing.

I shake my head. "Man, is that guy dumb."

Sergeant Grazianni's Jeep turns off the main road, rolls down the hill and comes to rest in front of us. He doesn't bother getting out, just asks, "You guys ready?"

We grab our gear and hop into a three-quarter loaded with all the wiring equipment. We remember Grazianni from the Qui Nhon relocation. He and Coleman seem to be pretty good pals. Coleman says he's a real straight guy and we should be glad Chianelli and him are in charge. Cpt. Blowhole rotated back to the States and hasn't been replaced yet, so Chianelli's been temporarily put in charge.

The trip to Plei Djerang is tedious and uneventful. According to the map, we're knocking on the door of Cambodia. When we arrive we are surprised to find a nearly completed fire base setup and waiting to be occupied. A company of men from the 25th infantry and a detachment from the 488th engineers were in ahead of us and cleared out the area. The engineers are using heavy equipment for deforestation and have already leveled the ground. A dozen waist high bunkers have been constructed and trenches were dug to connect them. A concertina wire perimeter is in place complete with Claymore mines. A pleasant change from the last time we helped Delta Battery relocate.

The guns are activated at about twenty-three hundred on the second night. They fire H & I missions all night long. The interval between firings is just long enough to keep me from falling into a deep sleep. Every time I'm on the verge of real sleep... *Wham*...they fire off a couple of more rounds. A brilliant flash of light fills the bunker a split second before the thunderous roar jars it. The ground shakes and loose dirt rains down on me from the roof of the bunker.

During the day the infantry sends out "Search and Destroy" patrols and they've had skirmishes with VC every time they've gone out. Twice, Gunships are called in for support.

After a week, Sky cranes, big ass helicopters, are brought in to airlift the two dozers back to a main road where they will be trucked back to Pleiku. Once the heavy equipment is gone, the engineers pack up the rest of their gear and leave.

"Yo, Simon! Twenty-three and a wake up and I'm outta here! Any women you want me to take care of when I get back?" It's Merkley. We haven't seen much of him because he's up all night humpin' ammo and spends all day sleeping.

I smile at the sight of our scrawny friend and ask, "Man, what the hell you doin' up? You sleep so much during the day we were startin' to think you were a vampire or somethin'." Coleman walks out of the bunker when he hears us talking.

"Say, my man, nice to see you still walkin'." Coleman walks up to Merkley, grabs his shoulders and shakes him. Merkley is as thin as a rail and his stature is diminished by Coleman's physique.

Merkley smiles at Coleman, then asks him, "So now that Blowhole is gone, is Grazianni tryin' to get you back?"

"No fuckin' way, man. I like being back at base camp. Shit, I actually have days when I'm not worrying about getting' my ass shot off. Can you believe that?"

"I know what you're sayin', man. I'll probably be going back with you guys, I rotate out of this fucking hole in twenty-three days."

"So where's your short-timer's stick?"

This is something new to me, but I'm not going to ask. It seems pretty obvious what it represents.

Merkley lifts up a bamboo shaft he's carrying. The shaft is adorned with names of people and places that have been carefully etched into the bamboo. On one side is a series of numbers that starts at one hundred and ends at one. The numbers one hundred through twenty-four have all been struck out with a line burned across each number.

"Looky here, I got all your names burned in." He holds up the stick and shows us.

"Damn, Merkley, what did ya do that for? Shit, you had a perfectly good short timers stick till you ruined it by puttin' all our names on it."

Sergeant Grazianni materializes and puts an arm on Coleman's shoulder. "Tell me Coleman, who the hell is stickin' their neck out to protect your black ass back at the hill? I know you must be missin' me by now. Want me to arrange to get ya back?"

"Hell, no, man! Who'd want to be transferred to a unit run by a couple of Wops?" Coleman smiles.

"Yeah, maybe you're right. The only thing you were good for was guard duty and patrol and that's because no one can see you at night unless you're smiling." Pleasantries aside, Grazianni gets down to business.

"Okay, guys, the infantry is gonna start puttin' out a couple of ambush patrols at night. This means you guys are gonna have to start pullin' watches. I put Coleman, Merkley and Pinetti down for bunker six. Simon, Lindlay and Fishe take bunker seven…any questions?"

Guard duty isn't anything new to us, so nothing is said. I've actually been surprised we haven't been asked to pull it before this. Pulling duty out here is different than at the hill - no shifts. Everyone stays awake till two in the morning when another crew takes over. No one sleeps.

We man the bunkers at five, by eight-thirty a concealing blanket of darkness falls over the countryside. Occasionally, there is a momentary flash of light when someone pushes open the doorway flap of a bunker or tent. Other than that, there is barely enough light to make out silhouettes. It'll be hard to see things moving even with good night vision.

I tilt my head in Jim's direction and ask, "What time is it?"

Jim uses the dim red light from his flashlight to illuminate the face of his watch, "Quarter to twelve"

"Whata'ya think?" I ask.

"I don't know…it's been over an hour?" An hour earlier, the symphonic overtures of the night creatures were interrupted by several volleys of gunfire. We couldn't tell how far away they were, but they were close enough for us to see flashes. Guard duty in the bush has an eerie perspective about it, especially if there is no moonlight. Generally, I attribute this to an absence of background light. It's just plain spooky. Back at the hill, there are always lights off in the distance from other camps and Pleiku.

"I'm goin' down for a smoke." I hop off the bunker just as Lindlay comes back from the head. "I'm goin' for a smoke," I say as he walks past.

Inside the bunker, I extract a Pall Mall and light it up being careful to hide the light from my Zippo. "Well at least they haven't been firing those damn guns tonight," I mumble, even though I am the only person in the bunker.

What the fuck! Springing to my feet and looking out the gun port I see a trip flare has gone off about a hundred yards outside our position. I toss the cigarette and run out of the bunker moving through the trench around to the side of the bunker. Jim is already on the field phone.

From our right, an RPG rocket screams out of the night across the perimeter and detonates just short of one of the gun emplacements.

Someone yells, "*In…com…ing!*" Multiple rockets rip out of the darkness from several different positions. Gunfire erupts. It's coming from everywhere. Jim and Lindlay are firing short bursts from the M-60. I can't see anything; I peer and peer, looking for something to shoot at. Every flash of weapons fire illuminates an area for a fraction of a second so I peer through the darkness trying to draw a bead on one of the flashes as they appear. I'm straining my eyes trying to find targets in the darkness, suddenly, several VC materialize just outside the wire in front of our bunker. A long wooden plank is thrown over the wire to crush it down and make a path through the perimeter. They start charging across the plank, and claymores detonate blowing the VC out of existence. Almost instantly, more materialize and once again begin crossing the perimeter.

"Christ almighty!" I pump rounds in their direction as fast as I can pull the trigger. "*Gooks in the wire...gooks in the wire!*" Jim yells into the field phone. Lindlay works the tracers from the M-60 across our field of fire towards the breach in the perimeter. I have the Claymore detonators in my hand and am cranking them like crazy. "*Wham! Wham! Wham!*" One moment a gook is running across the board then his body is wrenched and thrown out of the perimeter almost as if there was an invisible rope yanking him back.

The trenches began filling with people a few seconds after the first round hit. Out of the corner of my eye, I see two VC at one of the gun emplacements hurling a satchel charge over the short wall of sandbags. The charge detonates just as they are cut down by men running to reinforce the trenches.

"*Your left...on your left!*" Jim points as he swings the M-60 around. Ten or twelve VC are advancing on Coleman's bunker. Two of them fall to a wave of automatic weapons fire from Coleman's M-60. Two of them manage to slip into the trench. I push my way past the guys next to me, yelling, "*They're in the Trench*! *They're in the Trench!*" I run with no thought of what I'm doing...all of a sudden, there he is, one of the VC. His AK-47 is at his hip, firing; his legs spread apart bracing himself. He's screaming at the top of his lungs and firing right at me. I hear his rounds zipping past me, some of the rounds so close to my face that I can feel the heat as they pass. I fire repeatedly. I see rounds hit him in the chest, two, three, four hits. He collapses to the floor of the trench, a twisted lifeless heap. I have to run over the body to get to Coleman's bunker. Ten more lengthy strides and I'm there. Pinetti is struggling with another VC who uses his rifle to knock Pinetti's weapon out of his hand. Then he smashes the butt of his rifle into Pinetti's forehead.

Just as I am about to shoot, Coleman blows his head off with a burst of several rounds fired point blank from his M-60. Coleman reaches down and tries to pull Pinetti up, but Pinetti resists and Coleman turns his attention back to the VC.

"What the fuck you doin' here?" He neglects looking at me, concentrating on the VC; continuing his rate of fire. I duck my head below the top of the trench, drop an empty magazine insert another.

"Ruinin' my chances for getting' in the clan by riskin' my fucking neck for a big dumb ass nigger." I look out over the trench wall, *Jesus, the VC are all over the fucking place.* Pinetti is still cowering down in the bottom of the trench so I lean over and scream in his face, "Man, you better get your fuckin' ass up and start using that weapon, or we're gonna fuckin' die!"

Pinetti stands up, lays his M-16 on top of the sandbags, turns his head away and starts pulling the trigger. I want to slap him, but dare not take my eyes away long enough to do it.

Merkley slides down into the trench as two guys from the 25th take up positions on top of the bunker. One of them is popping out M-79 grenades; the other is bringing a second M-60 into service.

"Mother Fuckers! Come on you little bastards. Look what I got for ya, ya little cocksuckers! Profanities spill out of his mouth almost as fast as rounds spew from the machine gun.

Merkley's weapon jams. He opens it up and tries to clear it twice but it won't fire. *Thwap! Thwap! Thwap! Joink!* I see the first three rounds hit the dirt as if they marking a trail directly towards Merkley. The fourth round hits Merkley's helmet. It flies off and blood immediately covers his face. He falls at Pinetti's feet.

Coleman screams at the top of his voice. *"Me…dic!"* Pinetti freaks. He drops his weapon, climbs out of the trench and starts running. I fall to my knees and grab Merkley.

"Come on, come on, it's only a fuckin' scratch. They just creased ya. Come on, you only got two weeks, you'll be home fuckin' round eye pussy in no time. Merkley is face up; a big chunk is missing from the side of his head. I don't know if he can hear me or not.

"Merkley! Come on, you fucking hillbilly, open them eyes! I shout at the top of my voice. The sound of the gunfire and screaming seem muffled. Merkley's eyes are open but lifeless. I pull off my pot and bury my ear against his chest. I hear his heart pounding. *Please, God, don't let him die, please, not after lasting this long.*

"Simon! We need you." Coleman yells then turns and again yells for a medic. "He repeats his urging, *"Come on Simon."* He's looking down at me and shooting at the same time. A medic, running in a low crouch, dives into the trench head first. He starts working on Merkley immediately, attempting to dress the head wound.

I see tracers and gunfire coming out of the darkness from all over the damn place. I don't see any more gooks running around, but there has to be a couple hundred of them out there.

The unmistakable sound of choppers comes out of the eastern darkness and moments later three Gunships roar right over the camp. After they make their pass, flares are fired out past the perimeter and the Gunships return from the south, strafing the VC positions. Three passes are made with rockets and mini-guns chewing up the field and shredding the jungle behind it. It's hard to believe that anything could live through the strafing, but the incoming fire proves otherwise. The fire is relentless. Our position is reinforced with a squad of infantry. They bring word that our two ambush teams have joined up with a Special Forces MIKE force and are maneuvering to flank the VC from the east.

"Coleman." I grab his shoulder and we drop our heads below the top edge of the trench.

"Speak to me." Coleman looks me in the eye.

"Man, I'm down to my last magazine. I gotta get back to Jim's bunker to get some ammo for my M-14." I bend down and pick up my five empty magazines.

"I'm with ya," Coleman says.

We slide past everybody and make our way back. Fishe and Lindlay are both in the trench. The top of the bunker collapsed after being hit with an RPG round. Miraculously, neither Jim nor Lee has been hit.

"Man, I was startin' to worry about you," Jim yells as he crouches down next to me.

"Merkley took it bad, and, well, we just don't know…his heart was still beating but a big chunk of his head was gone...Damn it! I gotta get some ammo." On the other side of the bunker I find three men lying on top of the fallen sandbags. They've been patched up by the medics and by the oblivious looks on their faces, two of them have received ample doses of morphine. The third guy is more coherent, but immobile, both of his feet bandaged. I don't have time to ask what happened.

I start tossing sandbags around trying to get down to the bandoleers of 7.62 mm ammo I carried to the bunker earlier that night. I find them and start removing the little clips from a bandoleer and start shoving the rounds into my magazines as fast as I can. It's still dark and I'm fumbling a lot. The guy with the bandaged feet sits up, grabs a couple of my empty magazines and starts helping me load them. I look into his eyes and can see desperation and helplessness. He'd rather be killing VC.

"Thanks man." He just nods his head, grabs a bandoleer, and keeps loading. I grab six magazines and leave three empties with the wounded guy knowing he'll load them for me. As I turn to walk away, I toss him my sidearm, a 45 automatic, and make my way back out front. *Damn it, why the fuck didn't you ask his name?*

The incoming fire is still quite heavy but the effort to overrun the camp has stopped. The incoming fire is coming from all directions. Peeking over the top of the trench I try to pinpoint gun flashes, then wait for the flash to repeat and fire three or four rounds at the position.

We've been at it for over an hour. Then we hear it...the unmistakable *Whump* of mortars launching their rockets. The sound comes first from one position, then from several. We hear, *Whump, Whump, Whump, Whump,* and scrunch down into the trench, put our heads between our knees and cover up. A couple of agonizing seconds later, the ground shakes and the explosions rain debris and shrapnel across the base. The detonations compress the air and send out shock waves that make your eardrums feel like they are about to burst. The mortar rounds are landing all over the place. They're trying to knock out the big guns, but as usual the little bastards are hitting everything but their targets.

From off to the right we suddenly see and hear gunfire. The VC gunfire shifts in that direction. It's got to be the MIKE force.

A Staff Sergeant from the 25th works his way through the trench, gathering us together in small bunches, "Okay, look, we need to lay down a heavy blanket of fire to the west," He points and moves his arm to indicate the field of fire. "That'll cut off the VC trying to retreat in that direction. With the MIKE force driving from the east, the only direction they can go is north. We're trying to herd them towards an area that's been targeted for an air strike."

The roar of the F-4 Phantom afterburners can be heard screaming out of the east, flames shooting out of their twin engines. They make their pass coming in just above the treetops, then snap into a steep vertical climb just as they unload their napalm. They circle around and disappear back to the southeast. The detonating napalm lights up the night and creates an intense blast of heat that singes my eyebrows. A wall of fire, maybe two or three hundred feet across, torches the countryside in front of us. The sight is mesmerizing, I just stare, hypnotized, at the incredible sea of fire. It's the first time I've ever seen napalm used; I can't help but think, w*hat a horrible fucking way to die.* The flames burn for several minutes sending plumes of acrid, eye watering, clouds of smoke drifting over our position, it has the unmistakable smell of burning foliage and for a brief moment, it reminds me of burning leaves back home during the fall.

There is still gunfire, but the incoming rounds have diminished to short scattered bursts, the exchanges between the MIKE force and the VC is still heavy.

Most of us are sitting now, our backs against the front wall of the bunker. I pull out my canteen and guzzle several mouthfuls of warm water. My eyes hurt, and my throat is dry. I splash some water into my eyes to try and relieve the burning. Lindlay watches me, then pulls out his canteen and does the same thing.

I light a cigarette and pull the smoke into my lungs with a long slow drag on the cigarette.

"Do you think it's over?" I look questioningly at Coleman and Fishe.

Coleman looks in the direction of a corporal from the 25th, "Hey, you, Corporal," Coleman waits. The corporal looks in our direction, then works his way over, being careful not to stick his head up over the top of the trench.

"Yeah, what?"

"You hear anything man? What's the scoop? What did they tell ya on the phone a few minutes ago?" Coleman fires off the questions never pausing long enough for the guy to answer.

Finally, the corporal says, "Word is the VC are falling back but we'll probably be out here all fucking night if that's what you're interested in."

"No, man, we weren't planning on going anywhere, we're just wondering whether anybody thinks the VC are gonna launch another attack."

"I don't think so. They were probably trying to knock out the guns, I know the sappers got one, but I don't think the mortars hit any of the others. A lot of them got barbecued and the rest are probably hauling ass."

"Doesn't sound like they've left to me," Jim gives the corporal his opinion as he points over his shoulder in the direction of the still present gunfire.

"That's just VC they leave behind to cover their withdrawal. They'll harass us for the rest of the night then disappear down some tunnel when the sun comes up. By the way, be careful to watch your asses in the morning, they'll leave snipers out there waiting for us to come out of our holes."

At three in the morning, a sudden flurry of gunfire erupts between the MIKE force and the VC. It lasts about thirty seconds. At four-fifteen, three small explosions go off in the distance, followed by several minutes of automatic weapons firing.

Light starts spilling over the eastern horizon at about ten minutes after five. It sweeps its way across the landscape like water spreading across a freshly polished car. The sun's light illuminates the charred terrain and the dead bodies tangled in the perimeter wire. There are bodies lying all around the camp. The Howitzer just behind us has had one of its hydraulic positioning pistons severely damaged. The track of the vehicle is also damaged, but overall the gun doesn't look like it is damaged beyond repair.

There are instructions to hold fire while the MIKE force sweeps the area. I'm still sitting with my back against the wall and am having difficulty staying awake so I pull out my canteen, take two pulls and splash the remains of the water on my face.

"I wonder what happened to that chicken-shit Pinetti?"

Jim and Lindlay have no idea what I'm talking about so Lee asks, "Why, what's going on?"

"Well, Coleman pretty much saves his life by cappin' a VC who was about to drill the little bastard, then when Merkley gets hit, he climbs out of the trench and takes off running. The fucking weasel!"

Down the line someone says, "I'm goin' to take a shit." I turn to look just as he stands up. Two of his buddies try to grab him, but they are too late. As he stands and turns, a single shot cracks through the air and hits him in the side of his face. It blows his jaw off and he falls into the outstretched arms of the men trying to pull him down.

One of them screams, *"Medic,"* as he lowers his friend to the ground.

I mumble, "Mother Fucker," then turn my head away and grimace.

Lindlay plants his rifle and starts firing out past the perimeter. I know he really doesn't have a clue where the shot came from, but there is a need to do something. Then, as if prompted by some unseen signal, everyone is up and firing. Thousands of rounds are being fired randomly, strafing the jungle and trees or anyplace that could conceal a sniper. The firing continues for several minutes and then just as quickly as it started, it stops. Everyone poised, weapons ready, eyes moving back and forth, attempting to detect movement in the jungle a couple of hundred meters away. Little by little, we slide back down into the trenches.

Twenty minutes pass, I'm losing the ability to stay awake. I feel the dampness of the ground seeping through the seat of my pants. My feet are flat on the ground, my knees up and my arms resting between them. My hands hang loosely out over the knees. An eerie silence surrounds me. I hear voices and movement, but it is muffled and undistinguishable. I vaguely realize everything around me, all the sounds, voices, and movement is fading away, as if an early morning fog is slowly masking them from my consciousness. My head ever so slowly begins tilting more and more forward until some unidentified sound manages to crack through the foggy mist clouding my consciousness. My head snaps up and back and my eyes open wide. I try to shake off the drowsiness by removing my helmet and violently shaking my head back and forth.

"Shit!"

Several seconds later, the fogginess returns. My mind decides it will no longer respond to the nerve impulses that register sensory inputs; my head droops forward, my eyes close, and just like that, I'm asleep.

My mind begins wandering through a series of surreal images which make no sense, but somehow seem tied together. Images with meanings I wrestle to understand.

My father is sitting outside the oxygen tent I spent several days in when I was seven. I'd been stricken with a severe case of pneumonia and my father is trying to reassure me; encouraging me to be strong. His words are muffled through the tent, but I am drawn to his strength. He removes me from the enclosure and we walk out of the hospital hand in hand, me still in my PJs. The image fogs up and I am suddenly aware that I am snuggled safely between my Grandmother and Grandfather on the bed they keep on the enclosed back porch of their house. The weight of the thick feather comforter warms me against a cool fall night. It is peaceful, no words are spoken, my Grandfather's dog Knobby is lying at my feet. Then, I'm playing in front of my Grandmother's house and eating a Good Humor bar. Some kid runs by and snatches it out of my hand, so I pursue him and tackle him to the ground. The kid on the ground is Carl Schramm; all of a sudden I'm a teenager. Carl Schramm is a high school adversary. I'm pounding him, hitting him repeatedly, smashing my fist into his bloody face, cursing him. I look up and see my reflection in a mirror or pane of glass. I can see his blood on my hands and as I hold them up in front of me, my teenage facial features mutate into a hideous, dark, sullen image with sunken eyes, disheveled hair, and sinewy arms. My clothing is torn and dirty and my body is scarred. I turn and run from the image finding myself running up the front stairs of my home and through the front door. I'm afraid...afraid of what I saw in the reflection. I cry out for my mother while I dart through the rooms of the house, but am unable to find her. I see myself run out of the house and try to run through the narrow passage that separates our house from our neighbor's. Halfway through the passage I become stuck. I'm wedged between the two houses and struggle to free myself, but cannot. I begin calling out for help, "Mom! Dad! Someone help me!" No one comes. I continue struggling. Behind me I hear something and turn to see a hideous creature trying to squeeze between the two houses to get at me. It has slanted, red, glowing eyes, hideous dirty yellow skin, grotesquely enlarged crooked teeth; there is a trickle of blood running down the side of its mouth. It is slowly working its way towards me and I'm frightened beyond belief. I look up and find I am opposite the dining room window. Again, I can see my hideous features in the reflection, even more exaggerated than before, more hideous than the slanty-eyed creature trying to get to me. Then…I am free. I can no longer feel the pressure of the two buildings restricting my movements. I turn to face the creature, raising the AK-47 now in the grip of my left hand. As I raise the weapon, the evil red glow in the creature's eyes is gone. Instead, I see them fill with fear; it tries to back away, but cannot. I pull the trigger and…*CRACK!*

My eyes instantly open. My M-14 is cradled against my chest in the fold of my left arm. My right hand is gripped over the stock and my thumb is on the trigger. People are yelling, falling away from me, tripping over themselves.

"Simon! Wake up you asshole!" I turn my head back and forth, then, as things become more focused I see a wisp of smoke curling up from the flash suppressor of my rifle. Jim grabs the M-14 just below the flash suppressor and pulls it away. "Hey numb-nuts, you awake?"

"Yeah…yeah, I'm awake." Christ almighty, I must have fired my rifle while I was asleep.

Jim plops down next to me. "You dumb-ass, you could have capped one of us."

There's drool dripping from the side of my mouth; I reach up and wipe it away. I glance up and down the trench. Everybody is looking at me and either laughing or making some kind of comment to the person next to them.

"Fuck, man, how long have I been sleeping?" It feels like I've been out for hours.

"Hell, man you've only been out about five minutes. Shit, you were just sitting there with your head hangin' and mumbling. Then picked up your rifle and pulled the trigger you asshole. Ya probably wouldn't have be able to shoot yourself, but you could have easily shot one of us."

"...five minutes, sheesh."

There are dozens of wounded, all Medivac'd to the hospital at MACV. A couple of hours are spent collecting bodies. The Americans are bagged and flown back to Pleiku, the VC are loaded on the back of deuce-and-a-halves and trucked off to Old Plei Djereng, why I don't know.

The perimeter is repaired and duty rosters are made. We're finally able to sleep around noon. A rifle company from the 25th is flown in to reinforce the fire base. Hot food is flown in with them. The MIKE force is fed, they sleep for a couple of hours, pack their gear and disappear into the jungle.

Lying on my cot I am physically and emotionally drained. Before I close my eyes, I grab the small shaving mirror from my gear, hold it in front of my face and study my features. My eyes are slightly sunken and puffy dark circles surround them. The stubble from my unshaven face makes me look older. I keep staring into the mirror knowing deep down inside what I'm trying to see. I stow the mirror and go to sleep.

Chapter Nine

"The Rain, the Mud, the Bugs and the Rats"

The Jeep ride to MACV is intolerable. The cloud of dust stirred up by the vehicles ahead is so bad I spend most of the time trying to hold my breath. It is so thick we have trouble seeing through it and drive tentatively. It is a huge relief when we make the transition to blacktop.

I can't remember the last time it rained, as a matter of fact I don't think its rained one goddamned time since I've been here and we still have no shower water. The new pumping station operates only sporadically. Every few days the VC lob in a few mortars and the station shuts down.

We pass through the main gate at Pleiku Airbase and maneuver our way around till we reach the 71st Evac Hospital. We park in front of the Hospital, dismount and try to knock the dust off our clothes. We enter the large tent serving as a hospital ward but are turned back by a female nurse who looks better suited to be a stevedore or tank mechanic.

"Hey, no weapons in here boys!" She moves quickly up the aisle waving her arms as if to shoo us away. "No weapons in here."

We leave our weapons outside with Turner and Farmly. Back inside, we find Merkley in a bed near the end of the tent. It's a real bed, not a cot, complete with clean sheets and a pillow! Merkley is awake and seems alert. His head is bandaged in a way that leaves only the right side of his face exposed; an IV is pumping something into his arm. As we walk towards the bunk I feel my eyes being drawn to each bed we pass, each one occupied by someone not unlike myself, my eyes quick to focus on each man's injury. A missing leg, two head wounds, a chest wound, and a burn victim...all their lives changed forever.

Jim reaches out and grabs Merkley's hand to shake it. The fact that Merkley is able to exert some force is reassuring. "Man, I sure hope that she-man nurse you got ain't the one givin' you sponge baths?" We smile.

Merkley tries to say something, but it comes out all broken and raspy. He clears his throat and tries again. "What…the …heck…you... guys…been doin'…without me?" The words are labored and he pauses between each word.

I lean over close to his ear and whisper, "Hell, man, I ain't been doin' anything since you left but *'burnin' shit and humpin' ammo*!" He smiles. We talk a while longer, but it seems difficult for him and we want to give Farmly and Turner a chance to visit. On the way out we ask the Gestapo nurse about his status. He is doing well and is scheduled to ship back to the States in a couple of weeks. The doctors don't think he will regain sight in his left eye, other than that, it doesn't appear the brain damage has had any other effect on him.

After Farmly and Turner visit, we set out to find Pinetti. Turns out, after Pinetti bailed, he got himself shot trying to help a wounded man get back to one of the bunkers. The Sergeant he helped actually put him in for a commendation. At least he found the nerve to do something right. He still might be an asshole, but he was one of us, and he took one in the ass trying to help someone. I knew instinctively we would go easier on him if it was at all possible.

We find him two wards (tents) over. He's up on crutches and is returning from the head. A male nurse is helping him back to his bed.

I break the ice. "Hey, good thing Coleman isn't here to see you cavorting with the male nurses." We laugh and Pinetti uncharacteristically takes it in stride.

"Hell, man, you guys should see the nurse that comes on at four. Damn, she got titties out to here." He braces himself with the crutches stuck under his armpits and holds his arms and hands out in front of him to indicate the nurse's chest size.

"So how long you gonna be able to use that scratch as an excuse for sleepin' on a real bed?" Jim asks, pointing at the bed.

Pinetti actually seems human for a change.

"Damn, you guys should try to stick around and get into the mess hall.

The food here is damn good. Better than the slop we get at the hill, that's for sure."

With a more serious tone, Jim asks, "So, Pinetti, how you doin'?"

"I guess I'm doin' okay," Pinetti turns his head a little and looks away, "but I'm having difficulty dealing with myself. Man, when I saw Merkley get it, I snapped. Fuck, man, I'm sorry I ran, hell, I'm not sure I even knew what I was doing."

"Well, you ended up doin' good."

"Yeah, I guess so. Ya know I never really believed you guys when you talked about the killin', I thought it was all bullshit. I was so scared; I just knew we were all goin' to die. Then, when I was runnin' and saw our guys gettin' hit, I knew I had to do somethin'. I was actually gonna go back to the trench, but got nailed." So how about not tossin' me out of the hooch, okay?"

We look at each other and nod our heads. "Yeah, I guess you're pretty much one of the squad now." Jim says with a tone of sincerity.

"Hey, one more thing before you guys take off." Pinetti is lying on his left side (he took it in his right).

"What's that?" I ask.

"Hey, tell Coleman thanks for savin' my life. Tell him I'm turnin' in my hood." We smile and walk away.

"You know he's still gonna be an asshole, don't ya?" I say as we climb into the Jeep.

"Yeah, I know, but at least we can give him the benefit of the doubt."

"Yeah, we can do that."

We drive over to the air base to pick up some ammo for Jim's thirty-eight. Since the opportunity presents itself, I plop down a hundred twenty bucks and buy one myself. Spencer claims the price increase is because his supplier raised the price. It's probably a load of bullshit, but I pay it anyway.

We're anxious to get back because we're on the duty roster for guard and want to try and log a couple of hours of sleep. Driving back we're behind an ARVN (are vin) Jeep that is following a severely overloaded Lambretta. It is barely making it up the grade. The ARVN Jeep swings out to pass the Lambretta, then, as they pass, the guy in the passenger seat sticks out his leg and gives the Lambretta a push on the side. It is just enough to make it rock back and forth, then start to topple sideways. The Lambretta driver is using one hand to make obscene gestures at the ARVN Jeep and the other to try and turn in the direction that his cart is falling. He doesn't save it. It flops over on its side, baskets flying all over the damn place; people scrambling to free themselves from the mass of bodies stuck in the back. The driver and many of the occupants are jumping up and down and shaking their fists at the ARVN Jeep speeding down the road. We stop momentarily to see if anybody is hurt.

As we drive away, I shake my head and comment, "Jesus, can you believe that shit, it's their own damn people."

"Nothing surprises me about this country anymore. The stories I've heard about the ARVNs make them seem almost as bad as the VC." Farmly expresses his disgust.

For a change, I actually get to pull the first shift, six to ten, so I'm looking forward to getting a decent night of sleep. There are no guns on the hill at the moment, so the hill isn't a very strategic target and we know it.

I hit the rack at ten, talk with Lindlay for a while and drift off to sleep. At about four-fifty in the morning Lindlay wakes us.

"Hey, Simon, come on…somethin's happening, it's weird man, come on."

I sit, grab my weapon, and bolt for the door thinking Lee got us up because of some threat.

"No, no, it's not VC, it's something else." He grabs me by the arm and tugs me out the door.

Jim looks at him quizzically and asks, "Then what the hell are you waking us for?"

"Come on, come on, I've never seen anything like it." Outside, the ground is covered with something that crunches under our feet.

"What the...?" I look around trying to discern what we're walking on, then become aware of a droning which seems to emanate from all around us. It isn't loud, so to speak, but seems to be coming from everywhere.

"Look!" Lee points at the sky. There is a faint hint of light from the soon to be rising sun. It reveals an immense moving mass…bugs! The sky is filled with them. Staring up at the phenomenon, we are being hit by a constant deluge of dead insects. They are the source of the mysterious material that crunches under our feet. We stand, looking up at the sky, sheltering our faces from the hail of falling insects. They cover the camp like a blanket. They're everywhere.

"What the fuck *is* this? Where the hell are they coming from?" Jim voices his bewilderment.

I spend several more moments watching and decide the sleep I'm missing is far more interesting to me at the moment. "To hell with this, I'm going back inside."

A couple of hours later I step out of the bunker and am amazed to see the ground carpeted with a thick layer of dead bugs. The sky is clear to the northeast, but from the southwest a wall of dark clouds is moving in. It's a storm.

The insects are the talk of the camp. In the mess hall it is the topic of conversation at every table.

Sergeant Bennett lumbers up to our table and plops down on the bench to join us for breakfast. Turns out, he knows exactly what's behind the bizarre phenomenon. The onslaught of insects signals the coming monsoons.

"Monsoons? What the hell are monsoons?" I haven't a clue what monsoons are; as a matter of fact, I've only heard the word mentioned once before and Coleman never did tell me what it meant.

"Hell, Sis, monsoon is the rainy season." Bennett has his sheepish country boy grin on his face; he's waiting for me to object and I don't disappoint him.

"Damn it, Sarge, will ya quit calling me Sis! I pause, sort of waiting for an acknowledgment, but none follows. I continue, "Rainy season? Is that kinda like spring back in the States?"

"Not hardly. When it rains here, it rains and rains and doesn't stop for days, maybe even weeks. It don't look like we'll have to wait long to find out either." Bennett points at the darkening skies.

The rain starts before we're finished with breakfast. I'm anxious to get back to the hooch and get the four hours of sleep we have coming before we have to go to work. It starts pouring just as I remove my shirt and climb into the rack. The rain chatters against the corrugated roof of the hooch. It taps out a rhythm that makes me remember how much I always loved to listen to the rain as a kid, remembering how I'd beg to sleep on the porch during a summer rain just so I could be put to sleep by the memorizing rhythm.

When I wake, Farmly is standing in the door of the hooch watching the rain. It's coming down in torrents. It's coming straight down, there's no wind, no lightning, no thunder, just rain. I know we aren't going to be working today.

I stand up and begin stripping off my clothes. Jim sees me, knows what I'm up to and begins doing the same. He looks at me, first smiling, then laughing. I grab a bar of soap and head for the door. Farmly turns, starts to say something but just backs away and gawks. I step out into the downpour, naked, and turn my face skyward.

"Goddammmmmmn, it's cold!" I stand there dancing in a circle, the longer I stand there, the less chilling it feels. Looking up I can see the statue at the top of the hill and as I stand there, naked in the downpour, I almost feel as if she is staring back at me. I feel as if I should be ashamed for being naked, but I'm not. Instead, I feel cleansed. I feel her gaze bathing me, not my body, but my soul. That somehow the stench and guilt of war are being stripped from me and I feel a small twinge of innocence. I continue to stare and begin lathering up.

"My grandmother used to collect rainwater to bathe with at her farm." Jim says, washing his hair. "I wonder if she ever did this?"

Turner and Coleman join Farmly at the door of the hooch. "How's the water?" Turner yells through the screen.

"It's wet, man, real wet!" The rain rinses the lather off me almost as fast as I can make it. I wash my hair twice. I sit down on the sand bag wall lift my feet up and wash them, over and over.

Coleman, Farmly and Turner run out of the hooch fully dressed. They start removing their clothes as they dance around in the rain.

"You're right baby, this stuff is pretty wet, let me have your soap." I toss my soap to Turner. What a sight, the five of us standing here, completely naked in the heavy downpour, taking our first real shower in weeks. It's not long before people start emerging from hooches all over the hill, all of them naked, all of them bathing.

As I towel myself off, I know the shower water problem is going away. A bunch of us built a cement cistern up the hill, six feet deep, six feet wide, and eight feet long. It was formed with cement, all mixed by hand, poured into the form one wheel barrel at a time. It should hold a couple of thousand gallons. We piped the tank to the bomb canister we use as a shower hoping the cistern will collect rainwater or even better, get filled from the water trucks when they start running again.

I put on clean shorts and socks and flop back on the cot. "Man, there aren't too many things that feel as good as a clean pair of socks." I don't say it to anybody in particular, but just blurt it out.

"You got that right, nothin' 'cept maybe some pussy." Jim says.

Lindlay sits on his footlocker wrapped in a towel. "Yeah, I haven't had pussy longer than I haven't had a shower."

I couldn't resist giving him a shot. "Hey, you're one guy I'd guess wouldn't be thinking about pussy…still got the clap?" Lindlay winces.

"Ya know, dem medics can just give ya a few shots and some pills and just like that (Lee snaps his fingers), it's gone, great stuff, that penicillin."

Lee's comments send my thoughts back to our Pleiku visit and the women. I admit to myself, Lee and Jim are right.

Varant comes through the door of the hooch in a dripping poncho jibing us about our escapades.

"So are all you little pixies done dancin' around in the rain? You sure you guys don't belong in the Garden of Eden?" He smirks waiting for our reply.

Jim chimes in, "Well, this place is just like the Garden of Eden."

"What? Are you crazy?"

"No, really, Frenchy got bit by a snake but the only fruit anybody's seen around here lately, is you." Jim says laughingly. Varant knows he's been outgunned and further rebuttals will only instigate even more demeaning comments…he capitulates.

"Yeah, yeah, very funny. Hey, Bast's got himself a two-dollar card game goin' over at the NCO hooch. Anybody interested?"

"Hell, yeah, I'm interested!" I dress, pull on my poncho and follow Hal out the door.

The NCO hooch isn't to unlike our own, except they've partitioned the hooch into five rooms. At the east end of the hooch there is a screened in room furnished with a table and some chairs. This is where they're playing. A standard army-green wool blanket covers the table where Bast, Neuman, Pace, Keelerhall, Bennett and Thompson are all deeply involved in the current hand of poker.

Bast glances up, "We've got room for one right now."

I motion to Varant, "Go ahead."

Varant takes a seat as the current hand ends. I sense it isn't exactly a *friendly* game, sometimes it seems downright vicious. Bennett is the first to go; I'd have to guess he dropped about eighty or ninety bucks. Bast asks me if I want to play, but I decline. I'm a little short after laying out the money for the thirty-eight, so I want to watch for a while before I decide to risk my money.

After several trips around the table it's clear that Bast is the one raking in the dough. The game is predominantly seven-card stud, with an occasional hand of Jacks or better. Keelerhall is doing okay, but it never seems like he can beat Bast. If Keelerhall has a good hand, Bast never sticks around till the end, even if Keelerhall's hand isn't obvious he never seems to be able to draw Bast into it. Twice, I see Bast fold fairly strong hands, once with jacks over sevens, and once with three of a kind, both times there is nothing showing that would make somebody fold those hands. Yet, in both cases, Bast would have lost. It finally dawns on me…he's got to be cheating somehow. The cards have to be marked!

The cards are diamond backs. I've seen a marked deck of Bicycle cards once; those cards were marked using the spokes of the wheels, but diamond backs are an entirely different thing. There is no elaborate design that can be used to conceal a mark. The design is just rows and rows of tiny diamonds that alternate between blue and white. I look at the other four decks stacked on the side of the table. They're all blue, no red. Whatever it is Bast did to the cards, it must have been harder to do with red cards. I decide it's time to sit in.

"Deal me in." I toss in the one-dollar ante and wait. As Pace deals the cards, I can see Bast intently watching the cards as they are passed out. Pace starts by dealing two cards down and then goes around the table dealing the first up card. As I receive the down cards I cup my hands over them, peel up the corner and see a queen and a six. I lay them on the table and immediately cover them with my left hand. I look for a reaction from Bast, but he doesn't seem concerned. Pace deals out the second up card, and blesses me with a pair of fives showing. Bast has a pair of jacks showing and that makes him the bettor. He bets the two-buck limit and everybody calls. I still have my down cards covered, so if Bast can read 'em, he has to be Superman. By the time the fourth up card is dealt, I have three pair, Queens, sixes and fives. Bast still has Jacks but Pace pairs up aces. If Pace has two pair, I know that Bast will know it, so I watch him. The odds that he has the third Jack are slim. Neuman had one showing before he folded. If Bast bets into Pace, it'll tell me two things. One, it'll mean Pace has a naked pair of aces, and two, that Bast has at least two pair. I quickly scan all the up cards trying to eliminate any other possibilities or a hidden powerhouse, but the best I can see is two pair for Bast.

Pace bets the two bucks, I call and Thompson folds. Bast picks up his hole cards, looks at them, acts beleaguered, as if he isn't sure, then he stretches his head out over the table as if he is studying the up cards. I know what he is really looking for and still have my cards covered.

"Aw, what the hell, I think I'm gonna raise ya two bucks."

Pace calls, then I raise. "Make it two more." It's an attention-getter.

"What the hell you got over there?" Bast again acts like he is studying my up cards, but I can see him trying to see my hole cards.

"Well, ya can't have that third five, I done seen both of them already. Haven't seen any sixes though, so what, you've got yourself two small pair over there, huh, boy?" It is the first time since I walked in the door that Bast appears unsure. He hesitates a second or two then throws in the two bucks.

The last card is dealt...it's the moment of truth. Pace still is the bettor and he is the only one playing that doesn't have an edge. Bast obviously has an edge. He knows exactly what Pace has and I know that Bast knows. All I have to do is watch him. If Pace connects, Bast won't even wait, he'll act like he didn't hit and throw his cards in.

"Well, my aces didn't get any weaker, two bucks." Pace throws the money in and starts shuffling his three hole cards as if trying to change them somehow.

I call. This must convince Bast I don't have shit, so he raises. Pace thinks about it a few seconds then turns his hand over.

I smile and say, "Well, hell, if the aces fold, I must have the best hand. I raise two bucks." This disturbs Bast.

"Damn, boy, you're awful proud of them two shitty pair ain'tch ya?"

"Damn, straight. Two pair looks like a pretty good hand to me, I ain't gonna let ya buy it with a pair of Jacks." I know he doesn't have three of them the other two have been dealt and folded.

"I believe you're right, two pair is gonna win, but I don't think you got 'em so I raise two bucks. Bast takes the last raise and flips over his cards. He shows Jacks and tens and is anxious to drag the pot.

"Damn, Sarge, I didn't think you had another pair." His grin gets a little bigger. I flip over my hole cards and say, "Good thing I got me a pair of ladies to go with them fives."

I reach across the table and grab the cash knowing I've just thrown a huge monkey wrench into Sergeant Bast's plans. He's got to be distraught about never getting the opportunity to see my hole cards. We play another hour and half; I'm the only one that can ever beat him. After a while he must be wondering if I've somehow figured out how he had marked the cards...I haven't, not yet anyway. Each time it's my turn to deal I scrutinize the cards as closely as possible without being too obvious.

Pace asks, "Hey, how about a new deck?" I'm dealing so I take the deck of cards Bast tosses in my direction. I remove them from the box and start counting them.

"Hey, how come there are no red cards?" I continue counting waiting for his reply.

"PX only had blue. Besides, red ones is bad luck."

Neuman quips, "Bad luck? What the hell are you talkin' about?"

Pace adds, "Well, hell, next time we play I'm bringing nothing but red cards, 'cause you is the luckiest bastard I've ever seen."

I finish counting, shuffle the cards and start dealing out a hand of seven-card stud. I've figured out a way to conceal my hole cards while dealing. I manipulate the deck using two hands till I deal my own card. I set down the deck, slide my card off the top trying to block Bast's vision as well as possible, cup my hands around the card, look at it, then set my cigarette pack on top of it.

Bast folds right off the start; Varant has a king showing and immediately takes off betting the limit. I don't think a pair of kings is strong enough to scare Bast out after three cards, so I surmise he must have three of them. My two hole cards are aces, so I'm compelled to stick around. Bast uses the opportunity to get up and go to the head. By the time we get to the fourth up card, Varant still only has the one king and no other pair showing, if he's going to get a full house, it's got to be on the last card. I've added a second pair so I'm still alive and can still fill the house. Pace has a potential straight or a flush. I think, *Yeah, me and Varant are betting like idiots, neither of us will hit and Pace will walk away with the pot.* Since Bast is gone, I don't have to spend so much energy trying to conceal my hole cards. I pick them up and slowly riffle them in my hands then lay them back on the table. I haven't looked at my third card yet. After once again reviewing everybody's up cards I look down at the backs of the cards on the table. As I stare at them; something sticks out at me. I have to look away and look back a few times till I realize what it is. In the upper left-hand corner of each card, the first blue diamond on the top row is larger. It is larger on all three of my down cards. It is only evident, because the white ones surrounding it are ever so slightly smaller. The betting has started and I still haven't looked at my hole card. My eyes move around the table gazing at all the hole cards. I act as if I'm studying the up cards just like Bast did. In every case, there is a blue diamond that stands out along the edges of the cards. I look at Varant's cards. I can see the second blue diamond across the top row on two of them is enlarged. After looking several times and staring at the deck, it becomes evident that the enlarged diamond is key to identifying the card. I surmise that the face cards are marked across the top row and the number cards are marked using the left most column of diamonds. Then, all I have to do is count across or down to determine what value the card has. The number cards marked vertically going down the left edge with ten at the top and two at the bottom. I can't believe it! Once you see what to look for, the diamond stands out like the searchlight at top of the hill. They scream at you, "Hey look I'm an ace."

"Hey, you gonna bet or what?" Pace breaks my trance.

"Huh, oh yeah, sorry, what's the bet?"

"It's four bucks to you." Varant is anxious. He has no pairs showing, and after checking his hole cards, I can see he has two kings and a nine turned down, pair these with the king and nine showing, he has the boat. Pace, I see, has a straight to the jack. I don't even look at my last hole card, I can easily see it is an ace, I raise. Pace immediately begins bitching and moaning.

"First goddamn decent hand all night and I know I'm gonna lose... damn it!" He throws in his four bucks, turns over his cards and declares his straight.

"Kings full!" Hal is eager to drag his first pot.

"Whoa, whoa, sorry bud, Aces full." I flip over my cards and sure enough, I have 'em. Bast comes back just as I am dragging in the dough.

"Shit, looks like I missed a good one." He flops back down in his chair.

I think about divulging my discovery, but decide against it. I realize I might be able to use this information to our advantage.

We play another hour or so; Bast and I turn out to be the only winners. If Bast is out of the hand I'd try to avoid reading the cards, but the temptation was too great. The only weakness to Bast's system was trying to determine suits. If there was a way to tell, I had not figured out how it was done.

Outside, it's still raining, not hard, but steady. It has been raining non-stop for about ten hours now. We step down into the doorway of Varant's hooch, it's more a bunker than hooch, essentially a sand bagged bunker sunk into the side of the hill.

"Man, you and Bast are two lucky-motha-fuckers."

"How much you lose?" I ask.

"About a hundred ten bucks, how about floating me twenty till payday?"

"I pull the wad of MPC out of my pocket and count off a hundred twenty bucks and hand it to Varant. "Here, take this."

"No, you won fair and square, just lend me the twenty."

"That's the problem, it wasn't fair and square, Bast was using marked cards."

"Marked cards! Are you fucking shittin' me? The little bastard! That fucking cocksucker! Man, wait till everybody finds out."

"Calm down, calm down, we've got to be cool about this. We can use this to our advantage." I hope I haven't blown my opportunity by telling Varant. "Look, there are two things we need to do: One, make sure the prick doesn't cheat anymore and two, get whatever we can get out of him to keep us quiet. Besides, if we tell everyone, they'll kick his ass and transfer him out of the unit. He'll just end up screwing over someone else." Varant knows I'm right and agrees.

At one in the morning I lay awake contemplating my course of action, running several different scenarios through my mind. I'm not disciplined enough to lay out anything specific, but after all, this isn't going to be some major covert operation.

The next morning I bring Jim in on our plot. I figure I have to let him in on it and I know I can trust him not to spread it around. We check with Varant and I tell him about my ideas. We agree they're worth pursuing. Next, I have to think of a good excuse for Jim and I to get over to Pleiku to talk to my favorite Air Force person, Sergeant Spencer.

"Man, you guys got it made! Shit, I'd pay just to sit in this air conditioning all day." I see Spencer's eyes light up when I say it and know he is actually trying to decide whether or not there is a possibility he might be able to cash in on the idea.

"So, what's up? You guys haven't used up all that ammo I sold you already, have you?" Spencer knows we're here for something and wants us to get to the point.

"Well, I, we, want to know what the deal with the beer for C rations is?"

"You mean, like how many cases of C's for each case of beer?"

"Yeah, that's it and what's the limit?"

"Limit? What do you mean limit?"

"Well, we want to make one big score. Say like fifty or sixty cases of beer."

"*Fifty Cases!* All at once?"

"Yeah, fifty cases and we want to get a couple hundred pounds of steak too."

Spencer stands up and starts pacing. His eyes are oblivious to everything in the room. We can almost hear the wheels turning. Finally, he stops, sits back down and looks at us.

"Okay, this isn't going to be easy, but it shouldn't be all that hard either and we're way beyond C rations for beer."

Jim shrugs his shoulders. "Okay, what do we have to cough up?"

"Okay, I can arrange to get you a pallet of beer. I don't know how many cases are on a pallet, but that's the best I can do."

"Sounds good, but we want American beer, not that *'O.B.'* or *'33'* crap."

"No Problem. I'm gonna want fifty cases of C rations..." Spencer stops, runs over to a table to get paper and a pen, he does some figuring, then continues, "Yeah, fifty cases and I want forty pair of Jungle fatigues, new ones not used. I want twenty pair of jungle boots, sizes ten or eleven nothing bigger, twenty cartons of *Salems* and five forty-fives."

"You mean pistols?"

"Yeah, forty-five automatics, I believe that's normal army issue."

"No more than five cartons of smokes. We have to use our own ration cards for those."

"Okay five cartons."

"Okay, it's a deal. We need to make some arrangements. How much notice do you need to hold up your end?"

"Two days." He writes some instructions on piece of paper. "Here, you can call me through the terminal at PAB (Pleiku Air Base). I know all the board operators so you just have to tell them you want to leave me a message. Just say something like, Simon called and the repair parts are in stock."

The deal is struck. Now we just have to back Bast into a corner and get him to cough up the supplies.

We're up early. We wait till we see Bast leave the NCO hooch and head to his office in the S-4 tent. We nonchalantly mosey across the road and enter the NCO hooch through the back door realizing we could easily get nailed for being where we don't belong. We try to act like we actually have a reason for being there.

"Sergeant Bennett? Sergeant Bennett you in here?" We wait...no response. We look around the screened-in porch but the playing cards are no longer perched on one of the two-by-four cross members.

"Shit! Bast must keep them in his room."

Varant isn't surprised, "Whad'ja think, he was gonna leave them out so everybody can see them in the daylight?"

"Yeah, yeah, I'm an idiot. You watch and I'll look in his room." I walk down the corridor and find, fortunately for us, all the doors are marked with the occupant's name. I slip into Bast's room. The little rat has a bed! There are boxes of merchandise stacked neatly all over the room, several cases of Budweiser, at least twenty cartons of cigarettes, cases of canned fruit and boxes that I have no inclination to investigate. I just want to get the cards and get out.

My eyes fix themselves on the mirror just above a makeshift dresser. There is a shaving mirror surrounded by a collage of pictures of Bast and a bevy of different Vietnamese girls. There's also a couple of pictures that must be his family. The wife looks beat up. She has a long drawn face that leers from behind a pair of black horned rim glasses. Her hair is piled and ratted on top of her head in a beehive that has to be a foot high. It may be the lighting, but it sure looks like she has a mustache to me.

A footlocker is on the floor next to the dresser; the inside is surprisingly neat. In one corner of the footlocker is a pile of postal money-orders four or five inches thick secured with a rubber band. I pick them up and thumb through them. "Damn, there must be ten or fifteen thousand bucks here!" All of them are made out to Bast. I replace them, and grab a deck of cards from a stack neatly placed next to the money orders. I open the deck just to make sure it isn't a clean deck. I'm not disappointed.

With cards in hand we head for the S-4 tent. Weber, a PFC, is working the counter. He's always been a dickhead, a real weenie. Everybody dislikes him, partly because he's Bast's little weenie boy and mostly because he's just a big asshole. He was probably one of those guys everybody beat the crap out of in high school and now that he actually has some limited control over the issuing of supplies, he wants to flex his muscles and be the one pushing people around.

"What do you guys want?" He asks with his usual sarcastic tone. Today, though, we aren't putting up with his bullshit, we can see Bast sitting in his make-shift office in the back, so we walk around the end of the counter.

"Hey! Where do you think you're going?" We don't even pause. "You can't go back there." Weber grabs Varant's arm and realizes instantly this is a mistake and releases Hal's arm.

"You *ever* put your hands on me again and I'll kick your fucking ass!" Weber backs away.

Bast sees what's going on and is on his feet heading in our direction. "What's goin' on here?" Bast asks sternly, probably more for Weber's sake than ours.

I manage a half-smile, look Bast directly in the eye and say, "We need to talk to you about a very important matter."

Bast guesses it probably isn't something he'd want Weber to hear. "Okay, come on back to my desk." We follow him to the desk where he flops into his chair and leans back. He neglects to offer us a seat.

"Well, what is it?"

I look at Varant and take a quick glimpse to make sure Weber is out of earshot. I pull the deck of cards out of my pocket, and fan them out on the table. I reach in and put my finger on a card, "Six," I say. I flip the card to reveal the six. "King," again, I flip the card to reveal the king. I repeat this four more times but Bast doesn't flinch. He's got to be wondering what we're after. He makes a half-assed attempt to act like he doesn't know what's going on.

"Nice trick. You gonna show me how you do that?"

"These are *your* cards Sergeant Bast. We took them from your foot locker."

Bast springs to his feet and starts to protest, "Why you little pricks. Who the hell do..." but Varant cuts him off.

"You're a cheatin' little bastard, so don't even attempt any of that self-righteous bullshit or we march right over to Neuman's office."

"Okay, just what is it that you guys want your money back or what?"

I take over. "No, I'm afraid it's a little more complicated than that. We figure if Neuman and some of your buddies find out, your ass is grass. Hell, Keelerhall would probably cut your throat." I pause a second so his imagination can bring that image into focus. "Who knows, Neuman or Dick might turn your ass in to CID for some of your other activities."

"Look, we know you've got a sweet deal here and we're willing to let bygones be bygones, we just need a few things we feel you're in a position to supply."

Bast senses it isn't going to be a nickel and dime payoff and also has to realize if we got the cards from the footlocker, we've seen the stack of money orders. "Okay, you made your point let's hear your pitch."

"Okay, first, no more fucking cheating. Right now only three people know about this, Varant, me and a third person who will remain unnamed. You try to have us transferred or anything like that the third person is going to blow the whistle. If we find out you've cheated again, we're going straight to Neuman."

"That's it?" Bast relaxes a bit thinking our demands are going to be a piece of cake.

"Not hardly," I reply. We know you've got a 'Preferred customer list' because certain people can get things out of you we can't. Everybody on this list just moved up to preferred status." I hand him a piece of paper that contains the names of everybody in our hooch.

Varant jumps in before I can continue. "And from now on, we want those damned Sterno tablets that are supposed to come with the C rations."

I look at Varant like he's an idiot...the tablets were something we hadn't discussed. I turn back to Bast. "By the looks of it you've made a nice chunk of change off us and we want a little pay back." Bast stiffens, anticipating our asking for money, but I surprise him. "Ok this is what we want..." I go over the list of things Spencer gave us. Bast looks at us like we are out of our minds.

"What the hell you gonna do with all this crap?"

"Before I forget, add six bottles of whiskey."

"Hey, I have to account for all this stuff, there are reports and inventories. What the fuck am I supposed to do about that?" Bast is trying to side step, but we're not about to let him wiggle his way out of this.

"I still want to know what you're gonna do with all this?"

"We're plannin' on havin' a barbecue. You know, grilled steaks, beer, shit like that."

"Are you guys fucking goofy? Where the hell you gonna get steaks, and what are you gonna barbecue them on?" Bast's demeanor is no longer defensive he's suddenly taken an interest.

"We made a deal with someone over at Pleiku Airbase. That's a list of the things he requested in trade. We've already figured we can cut a bomb canister in half to use as a barbecue...charcoal, well, that's another issue."

"So who are you guys dealin' with over at Pleiku?" Bast seems to have forgotten the fact we're blackmailing him.

"We'd rather not say."

"Look, you guys got me over a barrel and you know it. I was going to try to negotiate the terms a little, but I think you guys have actually come up with a good idea." Bast begins smiling, the warning light in my brain starts flashing.

"I'd hate to think you've somehow figured out a scam in all of this, we have no intention of allowing you to fuck over everybody."

"Hey...*hey!* The one damn time I actually buy into something with good intentions and you guys are gonna bust my balls? You should have come to me before you made your deal with Spencer. I could have probably gotten a much better deal."

How the hell did he know it was Spencer? Then again, he probably deals with him all the time. At least I knew I could trust Spencer, he hadn't warned Bast that someone in his group was cutting in on his action.

"So when are you guys planning to have this weenie roast?"

"In a few weeks, when the rainy season ends."

"You mean *if* the rainy season ends. Hell, last time I was over here it rained till the middle of October. Look, we have to plan this for a day when the old man is away from the hill if we can. There's a lot of logistics involved, and, nothing personal, but you guys are sure to fuck it up. Here's my terms: I'm in, but I want everyone to think I arranged for the barbecue. That's for your sake, not mine. If everyone thinks you did it, you'll be heroes till the old man finds out and starts askin' questions. If they think it was me I can always provide a paper trail to account for everything. I want you guys to make all the arrangements through me. Spencer's okay, but he'll screw ya if he gets the chance. When the bash is over, we're even, clean slate and all that shit...deal?"

Varant and I look at each other for a second and in unison we say, "Deal."

Chapter Ten

"Expendables"

"Son-of-a-bitch! Damn it!" I strain as I try to pull my right leg out of the mud but there's nothing I can grab to brace myself. Instinctively, I reach down with my hands in a vain attempt to create enough leverage to pull out one of my legs. "God damn it!" My arms immediately sink in the mud up to my elbows. I pull them out and try to shake the mud off. I stand there twisting and pulling like an idiot.

"Hey, you gonna help me or what?" I irritatedly yell at Smitty while struggling in the mud.

"Yeah, yeah, hold on." Smitty is fishing out the winch cable mounted to the front of the three-quarter. We came out here to repair a couple of broken lines, but were welcomed with a toppled pole and a mess of broken wires. Twenty some wires snapped and were in need of splicing. I gathered all the broken ends and brought them together so I could stand in one place to splice them. Getting the pole back up was entirely out of the question. We should have brought some hay or something to spread over the muddy ground, but we didn't. I lost both of my rubber boot shells in the mud when I collected the wires. They came off when I pulled my feet out of the mud, first one, then a couple of steps later, the other. I couldn't retrieve them. It turns out standing in one spot for forty minutes was an incredibly stupid thing to do. After about ten minutes, my legs sunk all the way to my knees. Now, no matter how hard I try, I can't pull either leg out. All my struggling has managed to do is get me more deeply imbedded.

"Here, grab a hold of this." Smitty tosses me the end of the winch cable and walks back to the truck. "Okay, here we go." The winch begins taking up the slack, as it does, I wind the cable around my forearm and grab it with both hands. The cable tightens and starts pulling me forward. It's pulling faster than my legs are yielding and I can't unwrap the cable from my arm fast enough and I start to pitch forward, yelling, "Turn it off! Turn it off!" Smitty is too slow and I end up face down in the mud.

"Damn it!" I try to stand several times before I can get to an erect position. Once up, I pull myself slowly forward using the winch cable till I finally extricate myself from the mud.

"Christ, you are lookin' mighty bad." Smitty says, laughing at me with that stupid-ass grin he always gets on his face.

I grab a rag and start wiping the mud from my face, "Yeah, kinda reminds ya of sloppin' the hogs back home don't it?" It's intended as an insult, but Smitty just looks at me and says, "Ya know, it does kinda remind me of getting' all greased up workin' in the garage."

I strip off my fatigue blouse and tee shirt and throw them into the back of the truck. When we drove out here we were very cautious, thinking this could easily have been an ambush. Now that we're leaving, I think, *what a stupid way to die this would have been. Wallowing around, stuck in the mud like an idiot.* Naked from the waist up, I climb into the cab of the truck. Screwing around out here in the rain and mud makes me really start to feel for the poor bastards in the infantry. They have to slug their way through this shit every single day.

It's August 31st and it's been raining for fourteen days straight. I don't believe it has ever stopped. It slows to a drizzle for hours on end, but it hasn't ever actually stopped.

"Ya know, that Noah story from the Bible's got to be a load of bull."

"Huh? What? The Bible? What the hell you talking about?"

"The Bible, you know, raining for forty days and forty nights and all that crap. Hell, man, it's rained for two weeks straight already and It'll have to rain a lot longer than forty days to flood the world." I don't know why I feel compelled to bring up this obviously moronic point of view.

"Yeah, but you don't know how hard it rained for those forty days, right?" Smitty makes a very reasonable observation. "Plus, it was raining everywhere in the Bible story."

"Yeah, yeah, I know you're right. I guess I'm just trying to say I'm sick of the rain already." I continue trying to clean the mud off my face.

Smitty looks at me and smiles, "Jeez, you're the same guy who was pissin' and moanin' about it never raining over here a few of weeks ago, right?"

"Hey, blow me! I'm just aggravated because this has gotta be the most fucked up country in the world. Everything here is fucked. Nothing ever seems to be proportioned correctly."

Smitty doesn't take his eyes off the road, but echoes my sentiment. "Yeah, you're right about that, this is one fucked up country."

"It's always too damn hot, the damn mosquitoes are too big, people are always tryin' to kill me, it doesn't rain every now and then, you've gotta get the whole years rain fall all at one time. Ya know what the worst thing is?"

"What's that?"

"It's the people." I mean, not only are they living in the dark ages, but they don't seem to have any character."

Smitty furrows his brow a little, "I'm not sure I know what you mean?"

"Character, ya know, like what makes someone a stand-up person."

"They're just different is all." Smitty rarely says anything intentionally bad about anybody.

"No, it's more than that. Think about it. How many men do you know back in the States would sell their fourteen-year-old daughters to the local whorehouse? Hell, most men I know would kill ya for even suggesting it." I pause a moment then add, "Every native I've come in contact with over here was either trying to kill me, or screw me out of my money."

"Almost as bad as Bast, right?"

"Well, Bast ain't trying to kill me."

"Maybe not, but back in the States there are guys who'd kill ya for five bucks and you know it."

"Yeah, there are guys back there, but over here it seems like everybody is trying to kill me."

Smitty thinks about this for a few minutes and then says, "I'm not sure if you're right or not. You gotta remember the only people we come in contact with are the schemers, the wheeler-dealers. We haven't exactly spent much time with the locals learning their customs. That'd be like me sayin' everybody from Chicago is a hood or gangster. Hell, the only thing I know about Chicago, is Al Capone, the Cubs and some creep that killed a bunch of nurses a few months back."

"Richard Speck."

"Yeah, that's right Speck ."

I mull this over for a few seconds, I know he's probably right, but I look at him and say, "Look, I'm only nineteen, I really don't know much about anything. I only know what seems right to me and I haven't seen too many things over here that fall into that category. Maybe your right, the only people we deal with are the connivers taking advantage of the war to make themselves rich. What I know about local officials, the military and the government over here, makes me think that most of them fall into that schemer category. So, if you're right, you have to wonder if the South Vietnamese are really intent about ending this war. Face it, there's a shit load of people over here making tons of money. Come to think of it, I bet there are a lot of people back in the States who are making a bazillion bucks off this war."

"Wow, Simon, that's some pretty heavy rationalization, but what are we gonna do about it? We're just grunts, man, we just gotta make it from one day to the next."

"Maybe, but think about it. Does anybody really want us to win this war?" The 'Locals,' as you call them, are the poor bastards caught in the middle. The VC and the RVNs tear through villages raping the women, grabbing the men, and stealing the food. They fuck over the kids so bad they grow up just as fucked up as everybody else. When we're shelling a village tagged as a VC stronghold, how many of those 'Locals' get killed. So they end up hating us just as much as they hate VC and the RVNs. Man, this is a fucked up place." I decide I don't want to think about it any longer and just stare out the window for the remainder of the ride.

Monday September 13th, two hundred one and the freedom flight. In two days I will no longer be considered a *Long Timer*. Anyone who can say "One hundred and ..." is almost a short timer.

Thursday…it hasn't rained for about three days. This three-day respite follows twenty-seven straight days of rain. The effects of the rain is seen everywhere. It's nearly impossible to travel anywhere unless you use the main roads. Most of the vehicles in camp are parked down near the motor pool on the back of the hill. Four APCs from the 25th infantry were borrowed just so stuff could be hauled around the hill. Several times a day we have to struggle to pull a vehicle out of the mud.

At oh-nine-hundred the entire hill is assembled on the main road encircling the hill. The new commander, Lt. Colonel Monferes, is going to address the battalion. It's unusual only from the standpoint that most of our formations are generally held by platoon leaders or battery commanders.

Sergeant Major "Jimmy" Jackson emerges from the operations bunker followed by the new commander. The formation is very formal with Battery commanders standing in front of each battery and each platoon leader standing in front of his platoon. All in all, there are almost two hundred and fifty of us assembled on the road.

Lt. Colonel Monferes leans a little forward and says, "Sergeant Major…" Then Sergeant Major Jackson barks out the preparatory order to bring us to attention. "*Battalion!*" This is acknowledged first by the battery commanders, *"Battery!"* then by the platoon leaders, *"Platoon!"* a pause follows till the Sergeant Major barks the command to complete the instruction, *"Aaaaattennnn…shun!"*

The battalion comes to reasonably organized state of military attention, actually, quite impressive for a bunch of guys who have become distanced from normal military decorum.

Lt. Colonel Monferes steps forward and barks the command: "Lt. William Chianelli, front and center!" He rattles off the normal pursuant to this and by declaration of that, Lt. William Chianelli is awarded the Silver Star for his actions during an engagement with the enemy on March 22nd when a superior force of North Vietnamese regulars overran the fire base near Buon Me Thout; with the battery commander disabled and infantry support in retreat, Lt. Chianelli assembled a group of men and re-took the position. Lt. Chianelli personally received two wounds but continued to lead the counter-attack. He was directly responsible for re-taking the position and holding it till air support and reinforcements could arrive to aid in driving off the enemy.

Holy, Jeez, I knew Chianelli was supposed to be a bad ass, but holy shit.

Chianelli advances and Monferes pins the medal on his chest and hands him the order. They shake hands and he steps back. Monferes follows the commendation with orders promoting Chianelli to the rank of Captain making his current position as temporary battery commander permanent. Chianelli salutes and moves back to his position in front of his Battery.

A second citation is presented. PFC Ronald Pinetti (still in the hospital rehab) is awarded the Bronze Star for his actions during the battle for fire base Zebra at Plei Djereng. PFC Pinetti, while engaging the enemy at close quarters, was directly responsible for saving the lives of several wounded men who were defenseless and unable to move. PFC Pinetti intentionally came between one of the wounded and the weapons fire of a charging VC, saving the wounded man's life and sustaining a serious injury to himself.

I turn to look at Coleman and Fishe, my mouth wide open in disbelief. Coleman is shaking his head and Jim rolls his eyes back while muttering, "You gotta be shittin' me."

Sergeant Major Jackson steps forward and puts the unit at ease.

"In two weeks the engineers will be expanding their camp to accommodate another detachment. We'll need to make room by clearing out a section of the perimeter. This is a call for volunteers to help remove the mines from that section of the perimeter. Your platoon Sergeants have the details. Everyone who volunteers will receive the Bronze Star and get an additional five days of R & R in Bangkok. *Commanders…* dismiss your troops."

Back at the commo hooch, Sergeant Bennett elaborates on Jackson's request.

Jim jumps right in with his questions. "Aren't the EOD teams supposed to take care of shit like this?"

"What's EOD?" I interject.

"Explosive Ordinance Disposal...EODs the army's bomb squad, Sis, and yes, they'd normally be the ones taking care of something like this. The Colonel says the EOD refuses to do it." Bennett seems uncomfortable.

Instinct warns me that something is not kosher and compels me to ask, "What do you mean they *refused*? How can you refuse to do a job your unit is specifically designed to do?"

"Well, Sis, seems they're worried all the rain's washed a lot of mud down the hill and covered up the mines. They say our map doesn't properly identify the location of the mines."

"Are you shittin' me? What the hell does that mean? The experts refuse to do it, so let's get a bunch of idiots who know nothing about mines to do it? Someone is fucking crazy."

"You might have a point there, Sis. Don't be spreading it around, but my advice is *not* to volunteer for this, if you get my drift."

Damn, something dangerous that Bennett isn't volunteering us for. I actually smile a little thinking about it.

Fishe looks distressed, "Man, this is bullshit, there's gotta be some other way to clear that mine field."

"Well, believe it or not, Lt. Duke actually came up with a good idea. He wants to make a big roller out of fifty-five gallon drums filled with cement, hook 'em up to the boom on the tank retriever and use the tank retriever to roll the drums over the field and detonate the mines."

"Sounds like a damn good idea to me," Coleman responds. "Why the fuck ain't they gonna do it?"

Bennett tries to take the company line with his words, but you can tell from his tone he thinks its bullshit too. "Colonel Monferes is afraid the tank retriever will get out there and have a mine blow the track off and then we'll have the problem of figuring out how to get the retriever out of the mine field. My guess is Monferes, being new, doesn't want the brass to think he can't handle the situation himself."

I think about this for a minute, "Hey, wait a minute." I pause till I am sure I have everybody's attention. "Aren't those mines Bounding Bettys?"

"That's right, Sis."

"Those are anti-personnel mines. They don't blow up when you step on them - they blow when you step off them. Seems unlikely they'd blow the tread on the tank retriever. They detonate two or three feet out of the ground and probably aren't strong enough to blow the track anyway."

Everybody's eyes immediately go back to Bennett.

"That's not necessarily true, Sis. When the mine is tripped there's a short delay before the ejecting charge shoots it out of the ground, but I believe it will still blow even if it isn't ejected. Still, the roller idea would have worked; the fact that there is a delay actually makes the likelihood of blowing a track even smaller, but it could miss a few."

"Yeah, so what? I'd rather be out there with a mine detector looking for one or two mines, than looking for a couple of hundred...and quit calling me Sis, damn it."

Coleman brings the conversation to a close. "None of this bullshit matters, ain't nobody gonna be dumb enough to volunteer anyway, so screw Monferes."

Coleman is wrong. They find six guys stupid enough to do it. The real surprise is Sergeant Dick. Turns out he actually has some EOD experience. When Monferes found out, Dick was *volunteered* to train and lead the team.

Friday morning Sergeant Dick and his six volunteers assemble down near the wire. The section that needs clearing is staked out and comprises a good hundred yards for sure.

Dick's team is comprised of guys who, to say the least, have very little experience. Most of them have never even been off the hill. PFC Weber - Sergeant Bast's flunky, Dale Pollack - a mechanic, Roger Cook - also a mechanic, Kevin Lesser - a plotter from the operations bunker, Pete Pinasso - one of guys from the searchlight team and the final guy is an ammo-humper from Charlie Battery named Loosy (Lucy). *These guys can't possibly realize what they've gotten themselves into.*

We're near the operations bunker welding shell canisters together to make poles, from this position we have a ringside seat to all of the perimeter activity. The wire has been removed and Sgt. Dick has his group working in two man teams. Lesser and Pollack move into the field sweeping the mine detector back and forth in front of them. They're out for only a few moments when they detect a mine. Pollack operates the detector and Lesser marks the locations. They use two-foot lengths of thin metal rod, each with a little white flag attached to the end and stick one of these into the ground to mark the location of each mine. The mines were planted in groups of four using a diamond shaped pattern, so once all four mines are marked, Cook and Loosy do the unearthing.

We can't see in detail, but it looks like they have a couple of bayonets, a trenching tool and a big serving spoon from the mess hall. They crawl in on their bellies, kneel up and start removing dirt. Dick is barking instructions at them, but we can't hear what he's saying. The main problem is that many of the mines are completely covered with mud and nothing is visible. They're using a bayonet to probe the soil and find the mine. The difficult task of removing the dirt looks to be an excruciatingly slow process. At least the mud has made it easier for them to dig out the mine without exerting too much pressure. Once a mine is cleared the safety pin is re-installed to prevent the fuze and propelling charge from firing, ejecting the mine or setting off the detonators. When the mine is deactivated they carry them back to one of the guard bunkers where they're being stored.

Our attention shifts back and forth between Dick's crew and our welding till we finish what we're doing. It's near lunchtime so we clean-up and head down to the mess tent. Five minutes later Dick and his group of foolishly brave men follow us into the mess. I can tell by the look on their faces they've finally realized what they've gotten themselves into. When they sit, Sgt. Dick stares at the food on his tray the way I would expect a condemned man to stare at his last meal. It sends a shiver up my spine and I spontaneously shake my head.

"Sergeant Dick, how many mines have you guys pulled out so far?" Smitty makes sure he asks with a tone of genuine sincerity, not wanting any of these guys, especially Dick, to think he was making light of their predicament.

Dick doesn't seem sensitive to the question, "Twenty-four. If my estimates are right we've got another hundred-twenty or so to go."

That's it. That was the extent of the conversation. It was obvious that neither Dick nor any of his men wanted to elaborate or discuss the issue any further. Dick's men finish before we do and head back to the minefield. We meander back up the hill and return to the task of making poles.

The novelty of watching the amateur EOD team eventually wears off and little more than an occasional glance is made towards the minefield. The Hill is still a quivering mass of mud and the ninety degree plus temperature is driving the humidity levels up near a hundred percent. I stop to remove my shirt and glance down at Dick's team. They've cleared a sizable path all the way to the outer wire and have begun working their way to the right. I watch for a moment while Cook and Loosy work at unearthing another mine.

Pow! Both of them flatten out and in the same motion grab the back of their helmets. I see the object pop out of the ground and detonate about two feet in the air. At the same instant, Dick and the rest of the group dive for cover. Weber has his back to the field and when he sees everyone diving for the ground he compulsively turns to look.

I'm already running down the hill. *"Medic...Get the Medics!"* By the time I get to the wire Dick is already dragging Cook's unconscious body out of the minefield. Dick seems uninjured. He yells, *"Get Loosy, get Loosy, and don't go outside the fuckin' path!"*

Loosy is face down in the mud and unconscious. His forearms and hands are a mangled bloody mess. The entire back of his lower body is torn up and bloody. His fatigue pants are nearly shredded. I roll him over and use my index and middle finger to check his pulse just below the side of his jaw. *At least he's still breathing,* I think, as I grab his feet and start dragging him out of the minefield. Coleman grabs him under the arms and when he does, I lift him by the legs and we carry him out of the minefield and lay him near the bunker.

Sergeant Dick is kneeling over Weber. Weber's helmet is gone, as is most of his face. A large portion of flesh is gone from the side of his face completely exposing the jaw. The exposed bone and teeth give Weber the appearance of having a sadistic bloody grin.

"God dammit, he's dead! Get something to cover his face." Dick looks like he's on the verge of tears. "Monferes, you cocksucker," he mumbles as he gets up.

The ambulance arrives seconds later. The medics begin treating Loosy and Cook and the Medivac chopper from Camp Holloway can already be heard. Pinasso and Pollack have a couple of superficial wounds and Lesser is unscathed.

The rhetoric flying around the camp for the next couple of days is all focused on the incident. Everyone seems to feel that Monferes will have to force the EOD to come in and finish the job. Unfortunately, this is not the case. It's hard to believe but Monferes solicits for more volunteers and finds six more Bozos stupid enough to do it.

Wednesday morning Dick takes his team out to the minefield again. They work through the day without incident and manage to remove sixty or seventy mines. This group is even more diverse than the last one. It's comprised of Lesser, who we thought would have learned his lesson the first time, Dick, Jones, Mike Shredl, Gerald Washington, Roger Polonsky and "Mick the Spic" McDormand. Jones is an ammo humper from Charlie Battery; Mike Shredl is a cook from Bravo Battery. *Jesus, a fucking cook! They've got a fucking cook disarming mines.* Washington is one of the guys who works in the PX and Polonsky is a tank mechanic who works on the Howitzers. McDormand is the Colonels driver. We call him "Mick the Spic," because his father is Irish and his mother is Mexican.

Per Sgt. Dick's estimate there are about forty or fifty more mines that still need unearthing. His estimate is based on the square footage of the area that still needs to be cleared.

Thursday morning at about nine thirty, the unthinkable happens again. Polonsky and McDormand are killed instantly. Polonsky, kneeling next to McDormand, was digging out a mine, the mine tripped, popped out of the ground and blew up in his face. This set off a chain reaction that detonated three more mines. Shredl received several small wounds and Jones lost an eye. Watching the Huey fly off towards Pleiku Airbase, I can't help thinking, *at least three dead, but that damned tank retriever is still in one fucking piece.*

The NCO club on Friday night could easily be mistaken for a funeral home. At eight in the evening the screen door opens and Sgt. Dick walks in. An eerie silence falls over the club as most everyone stops talking mid-sentence. Every pair of eyes in the club follows Dick as he makes his way to the bar. He sits by himself; no one makes an attempt to talk to him. After several uncomfortable minutes the conversations resume in hushed whispers, the jocularity that is normally the din at the club is missing. If anything, it probably makes Dick more uncomfortable than he already is.

Dick sits for an hour; he consumes four beers and several shots of whiskey. Once, Bast walked up behind him, put his hand on his shoulder and started to say something, but before he could, Dick looked him in the eye and Bast just turned and walked away. Dick leaves the club at nine-thirty. At ten we leave and are halfway back to the hooch when... *Wham!* A second explosion follows almost immediately. Instinctively we hit the dirt after the first explosion. By the time the smoke starts to clear we're on our feet running. There is a cry from somewhere behind us. "*Incoming!*" Flares are popping off out over the perimeter and the searchlight is already sweeping the defoliated fields that surround the camp. People are scrambling all around the camp. With weapons and gear in hand we make a beeline for bunker six. Bunker six flanks the section of perimeter that's being cleared of mines. If there's going to be an attempt to breach the wire, it will be here.

We peer out past the perimeter, but see nothing. Fifteen or twenty minutes elapse; no more explosions, no sign of VC, no nothing. No one has even fired a shot.

"All Clear! All Clear! Alright, everyone back to their hooch." Lt. Duke and Sgt. Pace are working their way around the perimeter sending people back to their hooches. Pace looks at us and says, "You four go with Lt. Duke," then disappears into the bunker.

We follow Duke up the hill to the Colonel's hooch. A gaping hole in the side of the hooch leaves little doubt where the detonations occurred. As we approach, Colonel Monferes charges out of the hooch wearing only trousers.

"*Duke,* I want a complete investigation, you hear me?"

"Yes, Sir, I hear you." Duke's words are thick with complacency.

"I mean it Duke, somebody's going to pay for this. I want this hooch guarded all night. No one sleeps, got it, no one sleeps!"

"Yes, sir, we understand. You should get some sleep," Duke is obviously trying to placate him so that he'll get out of his face.

"*Sleep! Are you fucking kidding?* Someone tosses two grenades in my hooch and you want me to sleep? Monferes disappears back into his hooch.

"Someone threw a couple of grenades in his hooch?" Jim asks.

Lt. Duke seems irritated. "Yeah, lucky for him, he was out taking a shit when they did it." We're surprised to hear this, but he continues, "Okay, I want someone up here all night, one man is all, you guys can work out the shifts."

"Damn, Lieutenant, we were on guard last night."

"Look, I don't want any shit about this, I'll get a couple of more names from Jackson and you guys can break it into two-hour shifts."

We flip and Thompson gets first shift, I get two to four, what a surprise.

In the morning, back in the hooch, "God...damn! Can you fucking believe it?" Smitty seems surprised.

"You kidding? Half the guys on this hill would like a crack at Monferes. He hasn't made any friends around here with this minefield bullshit." I find myself thinking, *too bad he was taking a shit.*

Jim agrees. "You got it there, my man, the brass always thinks we're expendable. Guys like Monferes don't give a shit about anything 'cept how they can advance their careers."

"Who do you think did it?" I look back and forth at Jim and Smitty.

Jim slows up and looks down at the ground, his eyes aren't focused on anything, I can tell he is formulating some theory in his mind. "I'd have to guess it was Sergeant Dick. Yep, Dick would be my guess."

I ask, "Why would you think that?"

"Dick took it pretty hard. He was forced to lead the detail, everyone knew there were alternatives and Monferes didn't even allow him a chance to give those guys a few days of training. Yeah, my money's on Dick."

"Don't you think it could have been a buddy of one of the guys that got killed?"

"Yeah, I thought about that, but I think it was Dick." Jim says with a finality that indicates his mind is made up.

The next day a team of officers from MACV show up and hush-hush meetings are held for most of the morning. At about thirteen-hundred they depart. Two hours later Monferes loads all his gear into a Jeep and leaves. An hour after that word comes down that Monferes is being transferred to the Fourth Infantry Division. Our new Battalion commander will be Colonel Ralph Schoebert who's in route from the Philippines.

In the evening, sittin' around the hooch, Sergeant Dick's normally somber frame appears in our hooch looking for Varant. Uncharacteristically, he's in an exceptionally good mood.

"How you boys doin' tonight?" Dick is smiling and very congenial.

"We're doin' pretty good Sergeant Dick, how about you?"

"I'm feeling pretty damn good tonight, pretty damn good. I need Varant, anybody see him?" Dick hasn't talked this much to us in all the time I've been here.

"Yeah, he's out at the shitter, he'll be back in a few minutes, how about a beer?" I hold out a bottle of *33* and Sergeant Dick takes it.

"Thanks." He takes the bottle and sits down on the cot across from me.

Jim, in an effort to make conversation, brings up Monferes. I cringe when he does, thinking it will pour ice on Dick's good mood.

"So do you think they're gonna kick Monferes out of the Army for getting' those guys killed?"

Dick was surprisingly laid back. "Nope, they didn't transfer him 'cause he got those boys killed, they transferred him because someone tried to kill him. That usually undermines a commander's ability to lead."

"Too bad who ever did it missed," I say as I lift the beer bottle to my lips.

Dick says, "Maybe they didn't."

"Huh? I'm not sure what you mean."

Dick leans forward and he looks directly into my eyes. "Look, whoever tossed the grenades may have known Monferes wasn't in there."

Jim looks at him and makes the comment, "You mean they might just have been trying to scare him?"

"No, someone who's been in the Military for a while knows the Army's response to an attempt like this will be to diffuse the situation by removing the intended victim. So maybe the guy did it just to get rid of Monferes." Sergeant Dick smiles and takes another swig of beer. "Well, when you boys see Varant tell him we need him up at operations to do some deciphering."

I watch Dick disappear through the door of the hooch. I continue staring for several seconds, then turn and look at Jim, "You're right, he's the one who did it."

Lt. Colonel Ralph Schoebert arrives three days later. Instead of having a large formation, Schoebert makes the rounds to each platoon and personally introduces himself to everyone. He follows this up with visits to all the fire bases. Once he has the feel for everything he conducts several staff meetings to lay down his rules and does a little reorganizing. His first official act is to hold a memorial service for the minefield victims. He follows this with Bronze Star presentations. Then he gives the go-ahead to Lt. Duke to implement his plan for using the tank retriever to detonate the mines.

The day of the clearing an audience of seventy or eighty people sits along the road circling the camp and watches the tank retriever do its job. The tank retriever rolls up to the edge of the minefield, extends the boom with the drum roller, drops the drums and then moves backwards perpendicular to the minefield. As the drums roll across the minefield, a steady string of subsequent mine detonations follow. The tank retriever then completes the section by moving in over the cleared section and extending the boom the rest of the way across the field. It repeats the procedure twice over each cleared area as a precaution to insure all or at least most of the mines are cleared. The entire area is cleared in less than two hours. The tank retriever then works the roller back and forth lengthwise several times as a measure of safety.

Next, Schoebert brings in the EOD to sweep the area for any remaining mines. After going over the area several times, they find only one mine that hadn't been detonated. Schoebert personally oversees the entire operation. The end result is everybody in the camp walks away with a very high opinion of the new battalion commander. It is comforting to think the man that leads our unit feels the equipment is far more expendable than the men.

Chapter Eleven

"Tears and Beers"

Friday September 13th, one hundred eighty-three days till I warp back to the twentieth century. The rains have stopped, water supplies are flowing at regular intervals and no one has gotten killed since the minefield incident.

Jim is bouncing rhythmically behind the wheel of the deuce-and-a-half speeding down an empty highway at six in the morning. Like idiots, we're traveling unescorted through territory we know has a high level of VC activity and convoys are ambushed on a daily basis. Not wanting to look away from my surroundings for even a second, I comment, "Man, I sure don't like being out here on the road at this time in the morning."

The tarpaulin that typically covers the bed of the deuce-and-a-half is missing giving Varant and Turner an open field of fire, it also exposes them and makes them prime targets for any ambitious sniper that might be in the area. Being the only truck on the road at six in the morning heading for the hairpin turn at the An Khe pass is unsettling to say the least. We might as well paint a big bull's eye on the top of the truck's cab.

We have an appointment with a pallet of beer at the Qui Nhon ship yards. Sgt. Bast convinced Sgt. Bennett (who knows we're up to something) that he should let us to make a special pickup for him at the Qui Nhon supply depot. So the excuse was made and all that was needed was four morons to make the trip.

"Hell, man, don't sweat it. We've been on this road before and baby, we ain't stopping for nothin'." Fishe seems much more comfortable with the situation than I am.

Somehow, Turner managed to get his hands on an M-79 grenade launcher. None of us have much if any experience with it, but never the less, it does give us a little added firepower. We're just four guys; if the truck gets disabled, we're gonna be up shits-creek. I know it, Jim knows it, Turner knows it and Varant knows it. When they find our mangled dead bodies, riddled with AK-47 rounds, stripped and lying naked in a ditch, someone will ask: "What were these four idiots doing out here at six in the morning?"

My biggest concern is we have no radio. If something happens, we can't even call for help. Unnerving thoughts dart through my adolescent brain. *Fuck! If we get captured, would anybody even look for us?* I know the answer.

It's just one of those things that can't be explained, the hair on the back of my neck charges up with static electricity and adrenaline starts pumping through my veins. There are no outward signs, at least nothing I'm aware of, but I snap up in my seat and grab my rifle. When I do, Jim realizes I sense something so his foot instinctively pushes down on the accelerator pedal, which in turn alerts Turner and Varant that something is up. Jim has the truck doing about forty-five, probably as fast as it will go on this grade. We're fast approaching the An Khe pass; when we get there we'll have to slow to less than ten miles per hour.

Sssssshhhhhhhoooooo... WHAM! A rocket flies past the front of the truck and detonates on the left side of the road.

Varant yells, *"RPG!"*

No, shit, Sherlock. I hate when people state the obvious. Varant has the front of the M-60 resting on one of the side rails and begins firing short bursts.

Sssssshhhhhhhoooooo... WHAM! A second rocket flies past the back of the truck and detonates behind us.

"Fuck, man, where the hell are they!" Varant yells firing several more short bursts. Turner is blindly popping out rounds from the M-79 that detonate seventy-five or eighty yards into the side of the hill on the right side of the road. He is surprisingly quick reloading, taking aim and firing with the weapon.

Thirty seconds pass; there are no subsequent rocket launches. *We must be out of range,* I think.

Turner yells at me over the noise of the truck, "Hey, I think that's it!"

"Yeah," I yell back, "we're probably out of range."

Jim turns and says, "More likely they only had two rockets."

"Lucky us." I respond. I begin questioning the wisdom of the trip. Spencer's come through; we dropped off all the barter goods he requested at five this morning. In exchange we have two names and a list of instructions for getting our beer at Qui Nhon. One contact, an MP, will get us in and out the gate. Another is a Seabee who will get us the beer. Spencer stressed the importance of getting the transaction completed by noon before the gate guard changes. When you think up stupid shit like this, you never really comprehend how stupid it is until you are actually doing it and realize you're risking the lives of four people for some stinkin' beer.

Jim slows the truck down as we approach the hairpin. He glances in my direction and asks, "Well?"

"Well what?"

"Hey, man, you're the one with the built in early warning system, you picked up on those rockets back there, what do you think?"

"Shit, I don't know that was just a freak. I haven't a clue what made me feel that way."

"So what are you *feelin'* now?" Jim says looking at me a little weirdly. The speed of the truck is down to about five miles per hour.

"Nothing…I'm not feeling anything, but I wish we had a radio." Jim relaxes a little as he negotiates his way around the hairpin. As the truck makes its way around the turn, the rest of us sweep our eyes back and forth across the hills, weapons ready and our nerves on edge. Once we're through the pass Jim floors the accelerator and starts charging down the hill. We complete the last leg of the trip to Qui Nhon without any further incident.

There is an underlying fear the transaction won't go as simply as Spencer has led us to believe. We've had reservations and worry about getting busted. Varant is the only one who doesn't seem to care. He says, "Hey, screw 'em…let 'em lock me up, at least no one will be shootin' at me." His rationale doesn't do anything to reduce the anxiety the rest of us are experiencing.

Heynis, the MP, is at the gate checking requisitions and paper work. We hand him the papers Spencer provided and after giving them a cursory glance he directs us to a warehouse where we'll find a guy named Vaughn.

Vaughn is sitting at his desk in the office of the warehouse; he's all business. He knows who we are and doesn't waste any time. He tells Jim where to park and disappears out the back of the building. The dock itself is a hotbed of activity, trucks coming and going, forklifts moving materials and workmen loading and unloading trucks. It's easy to see how things could occasionally get misplaced amidst all this activity. We wait.

Vaughn is gone only a few short minutes. He returns at the wheel of a forklift toting a pallet of Budweiser beer. He maneuvers the forklift around and deposits the pallet on the back of the truck where Varant and Turner immediately cover it with a canvas tarpaulin. The whole transaction has taken less than ten minutes. At the gate, Heynis, after making a cursory inspection of our cargo, takes two cases of beer as an extra-added bonus to whatever deal he'd worked out with Spencer. "Two case toll," he says. There is no objection.

The trip back to Pleiku seems faster than the trip to Qui Nhon had been. The road is busy with both military and civilian traffic so we don't feel quite as naked. Just east of Pleiku, Jim spots a hooch with a "Car Wash" sign mounted just above the doorway and two hookers conspicuously standing by the door. He pulls over. No one asks why we're stopping and before anyone can, Jim says, "Hey, no telling when the next time we'll have an opportunity like this."

We take turns with the girls using the two beds in the hooch. One of the girls is significantly more attractive than the girls we normally encounter. She's bigger than the normal Vietnamese and her features seem more European than oriental. We surmise that she is most likely a French half-breed. Turner is quite taken by the girl and is compelled to share his fascination with the rest of us.

"Man, she was beautiful, I can't believe how good lookin' she was."

I turn my head and yell back at him, "You got that right. Man, if she wasn't a hooker I could go for a girl like that."

"Yeah," Turner says, "She was French Kissin' me the whole time we were screwin'."

"What? Kissin'? Jeez, I sure hope you got some good mouth wash, cause she gave me one heck of a blowjob." Turner had been number two in the saddle.

"You're full of shit!"

"No, honest, she sucked me better than a Hoover. Hell, she swallowed and everything."

"Fuck you."

"Hey, ask Jim, I think he got one too."

Jim plays right along, cocks his head a little and says, "You better believe it. Man, she could suck the chrome off a trailer hitch."

With Turner's face now the color of crimson, Varant leans over and asks him how we tasted. Turner tries real hard to convince himself we're lying, then just says, "Hey, fuck you guys."

We're back at the hill an hour later.

We're still short two items: the steaks and some charcoal. The steaks we'll pick up first thing in the morning at Pleiku Air Base. The charcoal is another matter. Calls are made, people have searched, and as unbelievable as it may sound, there evidently isn't a briquette to be found anywhere in Southeast Asia.

We decide to take Sergeant Pace, our cook, into our confidence figuring the Army must have some contingency for cooking when normal fuel is unavailable.

We explain the barbecue concept to Pace who immediately volunteers to do the cooking. "I don't want you boys fucking up all that good meat," he says, "It would just be a crime. Hell, you don't need any charcoal. You need about twenty good-sized pieces of hard wood, like Hickory, but any hard wood will do. It burns slow and hot, much better than any of that charcoal briquette crap."

"That's great, Sarge, any idea where can we get some?" Jim asks.

"Hell, boy, don't you ever notice the jungles here are full of hardwood trees. Teak, hickory, walnut and god knows what else. You'll have your wood. I'll take care of it."

Pace gets on the horn to the First Sergeant over at the engineering battalion. The engineers are always taking down trees and evidently they've been giving the stuff to a Vietnamese lumber mill. It isn't very difficult for Pace to talk them into sending a load up to us.

Saturday morning we're up early. Bast tries to arrange for us to be put on his detail but Varant has some ciphering to do and Turner has to pull switchboard duty. We gear up even though it is just a short trip to PAB. It's become second nature. We grab a three-quarter from the motor pool and head for the airbase.

At PAB Spencer loads some merchandise on the truck, climbs in the cab and directs us to the rear of the hanger-sized mess hall that serves most of the base. Once there, Spencer takes the goods from the truck and delivers it to one of the cooks. The cook leads us to a big walk in freezer where we each grab three twenty-pound boxes of T-bone steaks…a hundred eighty pounds of meat. No words are exchanged. As soon as the meat is on the truck, everyone is on their way.

Our last stop is to "The Junkyard." It is a large area at the back of the airstrip where pallets, drums and things of that nature are stored.

"What are you guys lookin' for?" The attendant asks, his shirt open and his undershirt soaked with sweat. He looks like he would be more at home at the hill. Over here at PAB most of these Air Force guys walk around with clean fatigues and polished boots which is why this guy looks so out of place.

"What's the biggest canister you guys got?" I ask.

He looks around, then asks, "What are you gonna use it for?"

"A barbecue grill...we're gonna cook up some steaks."

"Why not just use a fifty-five gallon drum?"

"I was thinking of something bigger, but now that you mention it, we could just split the drum lengthwise and make two grills." With that, we grab a couple of empty drums and load them on the truck, thank the airman, and head back to the hill.

At the hill we unload the steaks at the mess hall and take the drums to the maintenance area to be cut. One of the drums is split and legs are welded to each half. We finish by using the torch to cut some iron floor grating to use as the grilling surface. Everything is carried over to the commo hooch where we prepare to get our little party rolling.

In front of the hooch there's a pile of wood the engineers dropped off while we were gone. It's cut neatly into nice eighteen-inch logs, but Pace says we need to split it into nice little chunks about the size of a wallet, so we spend the next hour and a half making little hickory blocks.

The aroma stirs memories of summer picnics and family outings. Plumes of smoke swirl up from the split drums now hot with chunks of glowing red hickory. As the smoke wafts its way around the hill it has a mesmerizing effect on everybody it comes in contact with. Like zombies in an old B movie, the hypnotic smell draws them to the grills of cooking meat. A crowd grows around the grills, most just stand there, hands in their pockets, eyes seemingly glazed over, staring at the slabs of meat sizzling on the gratings.

"Man, look at that," someone says while gazing at the grills. Thirty steaks sizzle away on the grill while Pace is attentively watching over them. All of them have been expertly seasoned by Pace, using his hands to rub a blend of spices into each piece of meat.

Someone asks, "Hey, Sarge, who them steaks for?"

"You bring a mess kit, I'll put a steak in it," Pace replies. Further encouragement is unnecessary; everyone scrambles back to their hooches to grab their mess kit.

Twenty cases of beer are stacked near the barbecue where Pace has Bast dishing out the corn, peas and carrots he prepared in the mess hall.

"Christ, this is unbelievable!" Thompson douses his steak with steak sauce and is eating it with the same enthusiasm as a six-year-old eating a chocolate sundae.

The Coup-de-Gras is the thirty gallons of ice we managed to get from PAB which is now cooling the beer Fishe and I are dispensing.

Watching the smiling faces of everyone sitting around eating steak and drinking beer, it's easy to see we've given them an opportunity to forget about the war, even if it is only for a few short moments. It fills me with a sense of pride.

"Aaaatennnnnnnn...SHUN!" Everyone springs to their feet. The heaving crowd of drooling carnivores separate and allow Colonel Schoebert and Captain Solomon through. Solomon walks up to the grills, looks at the steaks, looks at Pace, then looks around at everybody.

"Who's responsible for this Sergeant?" he asks.

Sergeant Pace replies, "Is that important, sir?"

Schoebert cuts in before Solomon can press the issue. "Weren't you going to invite us to this cookout, Sergeant Pace?"

"Yes, sir, we planned on inviting everybody on the hill, sir." Pace is in the process of flipping a steak. He's the only one not standing at attention. He just keeps tending to his meat and only briefly looks up at Schoebert when he replies.

"I'll have mine medium-well Sergeant, with grilled onions."

"...comin' right up, sir."

Schoebert grabs a can of beer and begins walking around. He whittles his way through the crowd introducing himself and shaking hands. Surprisingly, he actually knows a lot of our names. Eventually, he makes his way to us.

Col. Schoebert introduces himself and asks what kind of assignments we've had, and we give him an earful. When he gets his steak, he sits down next to us to eat. Turns out he's a pretty regular guy. He doesn't have the typical gung-ho army, I'm an officer and you're dogshit attitude prevalent among Army brass. He's from Streeter, Illinois, attended U of I and earned a degree in history. He seems young for a Lt. Colonel, maybe thirty-five.

Someone has a radio playing music from the AFVN (Armed Forces Vietnam Radio). *"I Can't Help Myself"* by The Four Tops is playing and Coleman gets up, starts dancing and begins singing along with the music. Almost immediately he's joined by others. More and more join in till there is a choir of GIs harmonizing the song and enjoying the moment.

The music and the beer keep flowing. At one point, *"My Kind of Town"* by Frank Sinatra plays and as the drunken group sings along off-key, I feel tears welling up in my eyes because I sorely miss being there, Chicago was my whole universe till I came here. I feel like I'm on another planet, like I've been transported to some bizarre alternate universe.

It's dusk. Only a splash of pale orange hue left behind by the setting sun keeps the night from painting the sky black. Before the crowd thins out a couple of people lead cheers of gratitude to Sergeant Pace and Colonel Schoebert. Most of them under the impression the cadre had arranged the bash. We don't care.

Colonel Schoebert says, "Well, I'm not sure who's really responsible for this, and probably don't want to know, but they sure are making me look good." He nods, lifts his bottle of beer and makes a motion as if making some invisible toast and then downs the rest of the beer. We're sitting on the sandbag wall surrounding the hooch. Schoebert just bummed a cigarette and is working on his seventh or eighth beer. Though darkness is setting in, I can see his eyes are glazed and it won't be long before he'll be totally drunk.

As the last few guys wander back to their hooches, I comment. "Well, guys, we did good, didn't we?"

"We sure did." Jim laughs.

Turner, sloshed to the point that everything he says is a jumbled slur of mispronounced words, says, "Yesh, youse guys are oh-fucking-kay!" Farmly, who is only moderately bombed, puts his arm around Turner and helps him back to the hooch.

The rest of us sit around for another hour drinking warm Budweiser (the ice is long gone). Hardly anything is said; we smoke and stare off into the darkness, everyone deep in thought.

“Damn! Where the hell am I gonna sleep?” Colonel Schoebert has passed out on my cot.

“Looks like you’re sleeping on the floor.” Jim laughs.

“Should I wake him? Dammit, I want my cot.”

Jim says, “Hell, no, let ’em sleep. You can’t wake up a drunken man, he’ll spew for sure. Why don’t you go up and sleep in his hooch?” Jim knows I can’t do it, but says it just to needle me.

“Damn it, I ain’t sleeping on the stinking floor.” I mumble. There are reasons we put cans of water under all the legs of our cots. The cans keep all those creepy-crawly things from crawling up the legs and snuggling up to us in our sleep.

I grab my sleeping bag and gear - we all use the sleeping bags more as a mattress than anything else - and head for one of the empty perimeter bunkers. It’s better than sleeping on the damn floor.

On Wednesday, Fishe, Smitty, and I are sent TDY - temporary duty - with a company from the 25th infantry division who are on their way to Dak To. The inside of the APC is hotter than hell; we’re packed in like sardines. We and all of our wiring equipment are jammed in with a squad of infantry. The guys sitting across from me look very serious. If I were guessing their ages, I’d say vastly experienced. One of them has his pack off and is double-checking his gear. He has about thirty magazines for his M-16, a paperback, several packs of smokes, some clean socks, and some writing materials wrapped in saran wrap. He has four grenades hanging from his harness. His flak jacket has several shrapnel tears and his face and forearms display scars most certainly acquired in country. He uses his thumb to test the strength of the spring in each magazine. When he depresses it, it’s easy to tell each one of the magazines is one or two rounds short.

“Hey, man, how come you short load ’em?” I ask.

“The springs in these M-16 magazines aren’t as strong as they should be. You jam ’em full and there’s a chance it won’t feed. What’s your name?”

“Simon, what’s yours?”

“What’s your first name or do you go by Simon?”

“Simon.”

"Mine's Willy." He moves his arm down the row of men seated on each side of the APC reciting their names. "This here's Mad Dog, that's Nestor, Weiner, Franklin, Andy, and the guy with the shotgun is Scatter."

"This is Jim Fishe, and that's Smitty or Red, he answers to both." Everybody nods.

Willy looks at Smitty's M-16, shakes his head and says, "Taping those magazines together like that isn't too good an idea. The bottom magazine gets fouled with dirt and dust and it'll fuck up when you need it most. Yeah, and the weight of the two magazines may be a little too much for the retainer so the top magazine won't line up properly and the weapon'll jam."

Smitty has been doing this all along, and I'm sure he wants to say so, but instead he pulls out the magazine and cuts the tape off with his bayonet.

"You guys been to a fire base or you just been over at the hill all the time?" Willy is trying to decide whether we're going to be a burden if anything happens.

Jim responds. "Yeah, we were at Plei Djereng a few weeks ago, it wasn't pretty."

"Yeah, I heard from a couple of our guys that Plei Djereng was pretty fucking hairy."

I'm not ashamed to admit, "Yeah, it scared the hell out of me."

Jim starts laughing. "Yeah, dick breath over here makes it through the night then almost blows his own head off when he falls asleep in the trench in the morning." He then proceeds to give them all the gory details.

"So, what'd you guys fuck up to draw this assignment?" Weiner wants to know.

I roll my eyes a little and explain, "Yeah that thought crossed our minds too, but the truth is...nothin'. A couple of ours guys are temporarily out of action so we're it. We didn't draw straws or anything like that, Bennett, our platoon Sergeant, felt we had the most experience."

"Next time tell him the other guys need to get some experience too."

Referring to this as a shitty assignment piques my interest and makes me ask, "Is there something about Dak To we need to know?"

"Look, Dak To and Plei Djereng are two areas where the NVA channel into the south from the Ho Chi Minh trail. Neither place has ever been very hospitable." I neglect to mention our little escapade to the sniper's nest or our small encounter with the VC. Probably the real reason we were elected for this.

The inside of the APC is getting unbearable. We're baking. I feel like a piece of pottery inside a kiln. The sweat is pouring off everybody.

Willy yells up at the crew chief. "Hey, Espo, it's getting mighty fuckin' hot in here."

The crew chief ducks down from his position on the fifty.

"Yeah, so what the hell you want me to do about it amigo?"

"C'mon, let's go up top." Willy says as he stands up.

Espo climbs down into the APC and Willy goes up through the hatch onto the top of the moving vehicle; a few of us follow. Esposito sticks his head back out and takes his position on the fifty.

I lean over and yell, "So where are we?"

"We passed through Kontum an hour ago."

The terrain looks brutal. We're traveling on dirt roads now. It still rains a couple of times a week so the dust isn't so bad. The mountains, which seem to rise up all around us, are higher than the ones near Pleiku. A dense layer of jungle covers them from bottom to top. Normally, traveling down these dirt roads leads you from one small village to another, but we haven't encountered any since we climbed out onto the top of the APC.

The assignment, or at least what we've been told, is to help the 25th set up a fire base that will be used to support a MIKE force nearby. The MIKE force, twelve Green Berets and a couple of hundred Montagnard sneak into Cambodia and set up ambushes along the Ho Chi Minh trail where they grab prisoners for intelligence to interrogate. We're supposed to help set up the commo at the fire base and string wire between the fire bases, the Montagnard camp, a couple of outposts, some bunkers and a small airfield. We wondered why the 25th doesn't use their own commo section to do this and were told the division is in the process of relocating to Cu Chi and most of their commo people are tied up with that major relocation. Truth is, when our batteries aren't moving and nothing is going on at the hill, they usually don't have much for us to do, so they volunteer our services to other units.

The convoy turns onto an even narrower dirt road and heads north. Ten minutes later we're at the airstrip where we rendezvous with three tanks and proceed west for about twenty minutes till we come to an area that's been partially cleared. *This must be the place.*

The next two days are spent setting up a perimeter, building bunkers, and filling sandbags. All the same crap we've been through a dozen times before. A day later, all the commo around the camp is up and working.

Lt. Sanderson finishes going over his directions using a map to mark where outposts and bunkers outside the perimeter will be. We mark the route we want to use for our wire to the MIKE base and back to the airstrip. Sanderson is adamant about keeping the wire as concealed as possible.

"Jeez, this ain't gonna be easy," Jim says. "There has to be ten or fifteen miles of wire to be laid and you know most of it is going to have to be buried."

I add, "Yeah, and Sanderson wants duplicate lines so we're going to actually be laying the wires twice in different locations."

"Yeah, that's why I said it could take us a while, at least a good couple of weeks."

Jim has a thought. "Sanderson is worried about the VC cutting the lines, that's why he wants it in duplicate, right?" Smitty and I wait for Jim to provide details. "Why don't we set up a dummy line that's easy to find?"

"I'm not sure I know what you mean?"

He explains. "Look we lay in the first two lines and conceal them really well. Then lay a third that's a little more conspicuous. It might help keep the VC from cutting the real lines. Let's run it by Sanderson."

"Okay, show me what you've got." Sanderson looks at the map we spread out on the table.

"Look, sir, we should lay a third wire. Only we lay this one so that it's easier to find. It should make an easy target and maybe keep the VC from looking for the real lines."

"You know the VC aren't stupid. They'll tap the line first to make sure it's live, you might end up wasting your time."

"That's the beauty of it sir, it won't be a dead wire. We make it a real wire with phones at both ends. If we're smart, it can be used to send dummy messages back and forth several times a day. If the VC are listening, then you can use it to feed them bad information."

Sanderson's expression changes from one of placation to one of interest. "Yeah," he extols, "This *is* a pretty good idea." He's sold. Smitty and I aren't quite as jubilant because it means even more work for us, but we know it is the right thing to do.

"Okay, it's my turn to go up." I look up the tree and try to pick out the best route for ascent. I kneel down and strap on the gaffs. These are different than the ones we used in pole climbing school, they're specifically designed for tree climbing. The gaff is longer than the ones used to climb poles, the extra length allows the gaff to penetrate the bark deep enough to bite into the wood.

We laid our wire, buried it six inches deep and covered it with brush till we reached the jungle, then we began running the wire up the trees and entwining it with the foliage. We surprised ourselves when we realized how difficult it was to see the wire. We patted ourselves on the back and then continued stringing the wire through the jungle along the treetops.

We've been taking turns gaffing up the trees. We string the length of wire out on the ground and braid it with leaves and twigs so it doesn't stand out like a sore thumb. Jim and I do all the tree climbing. Smitty never went to Commo School so he doesn't know how to climb poles; he has no desire to learn.

Sergeant Willy is helping Smitty braid the camouflage into the wire. His squad is providing cover for us, several of them probing the jungle ahead, scouts flanking us on both sides and a couple of guys watching our behind.

Contrary to the army's teaching, I use the safety belt to climb. I gaff three or four small steps up the tree, maybe five or six inches each, lean forward far enough to take the tension off the belt, then slide it up and repeat the process. Ten feet up I reach the first major limb. I have to release the belt so I can climb high enough to step out onto the limb. I lift the 20 x 50 binoculars up to my eyes and scan the area.

Willy and Jim wait for my signal. I give them the thumbs-up and continue climbing another ten feet or so till the trunk of the tree is too small to comfortably continue using the gaffs. I make another sweep of the area with the binoculars then drop one end of a rope down to the ground. Smitty ties it to the wire and I pull it up then fasten it to the tree using some 'U' nails and a hammer.

All in all, it takes almost four days to finish running the first wire into the MIKE camp, then we begin running the second wire back to fire base. It's a duplicate wire we run about seventy yards north of the original.

It's been three days. We're hiking back to the point we stopped the day before, about a mile west of the fire base. Mad Dog's on point and as we near the location we find the camouflage job we did on our equipment was not good enough to keep the VC from finding it. Mad Dog's hand goes up and he drops to the ground. He signals Willy first holding up two fingers spread apart forming a V. Then he uses his thumb and forefinger to form a C. He flashes five fingers, five fingers again, then one finger...a squad of eleven VC.

Willy spreads us out left and right and we advance slowly through the elephant grass. The VC are just inside the tree line of the jungle where our equipment was concealed with brush and leaves. One of them has uncovered the reel of field wire. He is pulling on the end of the wire and following it up the tree. Two others are looking up and visually trying to follow the wire. There's a lot of yelling and pointing. They seem completely absorbed with trying to see the wire running through the trees, and oblivious to everything else, quite unusual for the VC.

Once in position I get anxious about the impending firefight. Willy is directing everybody solely with the use of hand signals most of which I don't understand. I shrug my shoulders a few times trying to indicate I don't have a clue and Willy holds up a finger and moves his lips telling me to hold on.

The VC are moving back towards us as they follow the wire. One of them pulls out a bayonet and is about to cut the wire, but is stopped by one of the others. A lot of conversation is going on and one of them begins meting out instructions. He yells heatedly at the man holding the wire and after a heated discussion the man drops the wire, drops his gear and starts shimmying his way up the tree. He stops to rest on one of the large limbs and yells back down, obviously voicing his dissatisfaction at being chosen to climb the tree.

Sergeant Willy crawls over and whispers, "They know someone is coming back to finish running the wire so they're gonna set up an ambush, they're not going to go away, we're gonna have to take 'em out. Pick out a target and wait for my lead. Dammit, we should've booby trapped the damn equipment." He looks at me then says, "I want you to go for the guy in the tree. You keep firing till you see him fall...got it?" Willy waits for me to acknowledge. I nod my head.

I reach up and pull back the slide on my M-14 slowly and quietly chambering a round then work my way over next to a small bush.

The VC in the tree parks himself on a large limb two thirds of the way up the tree. He lowers a piece of rope and starts pulling up his rifle and a bandoleer of ammo. I know instantly that if we're gonna go, now is going to be the time. Sergeant Willy is thinking the same thing; he gets to his knee and starts firing. I've already lined up the top edge of my sight on the middle of the guy in the tree and centered it in the reticule of the back sight. I squeeze off a round - it misses. I see leaves right of his head fall and instinctively move my aim left. The VC is pulling up his weapon frantically. I squeeze off two more rounds.

"Fuck," I mutter, both shots look high. Wood chips fly off the tree just above his head. Again, I adjust my aim and squeeze off another two rounds. The first one hits his right side and almost knocks him out of the tree. His left arm whips around the trunk in a desperate effort to keep from falling. I empty my magazine; he's hit two more times. He lurches forward and starts to fall but his leg becomes lodged in some branches and he ends up hanging upside down by his left leg.

Whack! A round hits the tree just above my head and a splinter hits me in the face. I've been concentrating so hard on the man in the tree I've been oblivious to everything else going on.

Willy, Weiner and Mad Dog are trying to sweep around the right to flank the VC. They want to pin them down and keep them from breaking off and retreating into the jungle. At least three of the eleven are dead or wounded. The VC are falling back; they'll be running any minute now. Scatter shoulders his ten-gauge and loads the M-79. He pops off two rounds that detonate amidst the VC. Cries are heard as hot pieces of shrapnel rip through flesh. The M-79 is shouldered and the 10 gauge is once again ready to go.

Nestor yells out, *"Cover,"* and everyone starts firing. We lay down a heavy blanket of fire as Nestor and Scatter spring to their feet and cover twenty yards very quickly. We fire till they drop behind some cover.

Four of the VC lay down cover fire while the others start retreating into the jungle. Then like a well-orchestrated football play, all of them are up and running, running very fast, and in the opposite direction.

Willy, Mad Dog and Weiner have positioned themselves to the right of the VC less than twenty yards away; the retreating VC cross right in front of them. A volley of fire brings two of them down. The four trying to cover the retreat have a good angle on Willy and concentrate their fire in his direction. Weiner takes one in the leg and pitches to the ground.

Scatter and Nestor are on their feet yelling, "Let's go! Let's go!"

We're up and running, running and firing, trying to draw the fire away from Willy. The air is alive with bullets flying in different directions and it's becoming difficult to tell where everyone is. Scatter catches up to one of the VC and cuts him in half with the ten-gauge. Another VC stops, turns to draw a bead on Scatter but is distracted by three rounds I fire in his direction...all three miss. He whips around to face me and I see the AK-47 flash, then, seemingly out of nowhere, a sledgehammer hits me in the face. It knocks me back and off my feet. The sounds of the battle are suddenly muted and I can't focus on anything. I try getting up, but can't. I feel something warm flowing down my face. I reach up with my hand and wipe some of the liquid away from my eyes. I look at it. It's red. It's the last thing I see.

"Man, look at that fucking eye, holy shit!" Fishe says jabbing Smitty in the side. I'm in my cot back at the fire base. A whole day's gone by since the firefight. An AK-47 round grazed my right eyebrow and split it like a melon. The wound was closed with six stitches and the whole side of my face is swollen so badly my eye is completely closed. I'll be on the next chopper back to Pleiku.

"You know you pricks are gonna have to lay a whole new line don't ya?" I try to crack a smile, but the swelling is so bad I can't.

"Yeah, we've already started. I guess this means Pinetti isn't going to be our only freeloader, doesn't it?" Jim laughs.

"Yeah, me and him are gonna be taking it easy while your sorry asses are climbing those trees out here in the jungle."

A couple hours later, the medics get me up and help me carry my gear out to a waiting chopper. Pinetti is walking away from the chopper as I hobble up.

"Damn, Simon, you're lucky you didn't lose your eye!"

"Yeah, nice to see you too..." I climb in next to Weiner. He took a round in the thigh and is on his way to the hospital unit in Pleiku. As the chopper lifts us into the sky I lean back, close my good eye and think, *One sixty-eight and a wake up.*

CHAPTER TWELVE

"MESSAGES"

Today is the first day I can actually open my eye. It's been ten days since receiving the wound, the swelling is still severe but most of the soreness is gone. The medics have me on light duty, so all I do is lie around reading all day.

A letter from home arrived today. It's only the third one I've received since getting here. My mother sent two, but this one is from my dad. I've never been all that close to him because I was a rotten kid and was always getting into trouble, most of my memories usually involve me getting an ass whooping from him. It would be unfair to say he was cruel or abusive because I deserved every beating I ever got.

My father is a meat jobber and is on the road fifteen or sixteen hours a day delivering meat. He works his ass off. It's hard work, I know, because he had me work with him a couple of summers. He comes home at seven or eight in the evening, tired as hell, and my mother would start in on him. She'd bitch and moan and brow beat him with all the little annoyances we provided her with till he had no recourse but to beat us. It was the only thing that would make her happy. I know now, she actually was the abusive parent.

Often he'd apologetically offer advice while administering the punishment, "Damn it, why the hell do you get your mother so pissed off, for Christ sake, use your fucking head once in a while." This would be followed by the obligatory, "You know this hurts me as much as it hurts you."

In fairness, there were also cherished memories. The Saturday morning five A.M. trips to the Holsum bakery on South Chicago Avenue. We'd get warm bread and coffeecake, and then back at the house we'd toast up the bread and eat it before the rest of the family was even awake.

I enjoyed our Sunday afternoon drives to Midway Airport where dad would park the car next to the fence on Sixty-Third Street; we'd spend the afternoon watching the planes take off and land. Usually, this followed a stop at the KarmelKorn store to pick up a big box of caramel corn and a couple of pralines. We'd lie on the hood of the car and watch the big four engine prop planes roar over us. There were the trips to see my Grandmother and Grandfather, my dad's parents. I'd walk with my grandfather and his dog Knobby for hours. The memories make me long to be home and make me realize how much I love my father. I start reading the letter:

Dear Bill,

I am very sorry for not having written before this. You know I am not very good at talking about emotional things, and have been really bad at taking the time to write. I've been seeing more and more on TV about Vietnam and it has made me worry. I remember how fragile life was when we hit the beaches at Normandy, and I suddenly came to the realization that you are in a real war over there. I want you to know how proud I am of you. I know that your life here has had its ups and downs. For some reason, your being over there has made me reluctant to discipline your brothers and sisters. It is really pissing your mother off.

Micky, Mike, Skippy, Joe and Kathy all say hi. I'm trying to get them to write you a letter and send you a package. Skippy and Mike are really putting your mother to the test. Sometimes, I almost think they do stuff intentionally just to push your mother over the edge. Bill, we have never enjoyed what most people would call a close relationship. There have been times I know I should have reached out to you and been a more compassionate father and know that I failed miserably. I only hope you will forgive me for those lost moments.

Your Grandparents are fine, and Uncle Freddy is going to have your cousin write to you. I know I should write more often and promise I will try. I don't recall ever telling you, but I want you to know that I love you very much and want you to come home safely. Believe it or not, you have always been my favorite. I made a deal with God. If he protects you, I'll go to church.

Love,
Dad

There are tears welling up in my eyes. I slowly fold the letter and put it back into the envelope.

"How's that eye doin', Sis?" Sergeant Bennett parks himself at our table.

"Not bad, Sarge, hell it almost stays open all by itself now." I lift the bottle of O.B. and take a big swallow.

Bennett continues, "Since you'll be on light duty for a couple of more weeks, I'm gonna have you work on the switchboard rotation. You can work the three to eleven shift."

I almost protest, but don't. It's better than sitting around the hooch all day thinking. When you start thinking, you inevitably begin thinking about dying and it just isn't healthy.

We stay at the NCO club till about twenty-two thirty then head back to the hooch, as we walk, Varant comments, "Man, I can't wait to get the fuck out of here. It seems like more and more guys are getting hit and that's one list I don't want to get on. Shit, man, I'm down to 'Seventy-eight and a wake up' and I haven't even taken R & R yet."

"R & R...where you plan on goin'?"

"Bangkok, for sure. I thought about Japan and Hawaii and I don't think they're letting anybody but officers go to Australia.

"Why not Hawaii?"

"Man, when I go on R & R I'm gonna want to be getting' pussy everyday. I don't want to have to go searching for it, I don't want to be wasting time playing games with some broad who may or may not climb in the sack with me. I ain't gonna find any broads like that in Hawaii." Varant looks up and stares off into the sky. I'm sure he is mentally visualizing himself with a bevy of Thai girls performing all sorts of deviate sexual practices.

October twenty-eighth, it's late, sixteen-thirty; the sun will be setting soon. I've just picked up Sergeant Dick from the strip at Camp Holloway where he returned by chopper from Cu Chi. His trip must have had something to do with his crypto stuff because he's reluctant to talk about it. Holloway is a couple of kilometers east of Pleiku city just off highway nineteen. That's about twelve or thirteen klicks from the hill. Sgt. Dick always prefers driving himself.

"Well, Simon, you guys over in the commo hooch turned out better'n I'd expected. When I picked you guys up at Pleiku Airbase way back when, I had my doubts." Sergeant Dick smiles a little.

"Thanks, Sarge, you turned out to be okay too."

He takes his eyes off the road for a moment and looks at me then returns his focus to the road. We turn off highway 19 onto 14 and pass through a small stretch of Pleiku. Once we're past the edge of the city there is a three or four kilometer stretch of road till we get to Pleiku airbase and MACV. Dick slows as we pull up behind an overloaded Lambretta.

"Christ, here we go again." He swings the Jeep out around the Lambretta and yells as he passes, "Come on, get that piece of shit off the road!"

Crack! Sergeant Dick's helmet flies off and he slumps forward; the Jeep swerves sharply and slams into the drainage ditch on the right side of the road. Instinctively, I dive for the ditch. Once I collect my thoughts, I bring my rifle to bear on the Lambretta. The passengers are sprawled on the ground trying to hide behind the vehicle. *Are they a threat or aren't they?* I decide they're not and crawl to the front of the Jeep. Peeking around the front tire I'm unable to see the shooter. I look up and down the road hoping there is some other military traffic but the road is empty in both directions.

"Damn it! Shit!"

I slide back to the side of the Jeep and reach up to see if Sergeant Dick has a pulse. I check his neck just below the jaw but there is no pulse...he's dead. I grab the mike from the radio on the back of the Jeep.

"Smasher, Smasher, I need help, over." I wait for a response.

"This is Smasher, go ahead, over.

"Smasher, we've been ambushed and Sergeant Dick is dead. I'm pinned down and need help. I'm two miles north of PAB on the highway 14...do you copy, over?"

"Roger we copy. Sit tight help is on the way, over."

I peek around the front of the Jeep again; I still can't see anything. There is motion to my left and snap my head around to look at the Lambretta. Four of the men have jumped up and are running away at full speed. The remaining man is trying to pull a weapon out of one of the baskets but it's snagged on something and he is frantically trying to free it.

"You fucker!" I yell pulling the trigger. My first shot hits the Lambretta; the second strikes him in the side and spins him around knocking him to the ground. Leaping to my feet, I bolt to the Lambretta diving to the ground next to him. His eyes are glazed and he's shaking. For a brief moment I think about giving him first aid, but this thought lasts only a fleeting instant. Blood is pouring out of his side; it's black. This usually means his liver is punctured; it also means he's going to die. *Fuck 'em.*

I slide up the side of the Lambretta till I am almost standing and peer through the cage on the back. I can see three VC moving towards me from the field west of the road. *They want to finish the job before someone else comes along...the cocksuckers.*

I whip around the end of the Lambretta and fire four rounds. I don't have to aim, I just fire randomly; it sends them diving for cover. Again, I look up and down the road. This time I can just barely see a couple of APCs heading my way but they've gotta be a couple of miles away. They'll be traveling slow, maybe ten miles per hour, a typical speed for an APC convoy. It'll be at least four or five minutes before they get here. *Maybe I should fire a couple of shots in their direction? No, that'll probably just make 'em stop and circle the wagons. Damn it!* Instead, I lean on the front corner of the Lambretta and start firing towards the field. I hope the convoy hears it and they'll come faster. I know it's a gamble.

The automatic weapons fire from the VC pelt the Lambretta and are popping all around me. I look down the road and see the convoy pulling off the road and men scrambling out of the trucks.

Damn it! Son-of-a-bitch! The cavalry isn't coming... I gotta do something... shit! I look around; there isn't much cover in any direction. The drainage ditch along the road is the only thing I've got.

Thwap, thwap...thwap, thwap...thwap. Rounds are hitting all over. I peek through the side rails again and see the VC are up and moving again. They're maybe a hundred yards away now. I swing around the front of the Lambretta and fire through the driver's cab. Again, the VC take cover. *What the hell happened to the help I'm supposed to get?* In the distance there are four choppers heading for Camp Holloway. I pull out my bayonet, get down on the ground and puncture the gas tank of the Lambretta. The gas spills out of the tank all over the ground. The wounded VC is unaware of what I am about to do. I look at him a second or two... *Fuck! I can't let the prick burn to death and, I can't pull him to safety without endangering myself. There's only one thing to do...this bastard is gonna die anyway.* I pull out my thirty-eight and shoot him twice in the middle of the chest. I tear off his shirt, now soaked both in gasoline and blood and bolt back to the Jeep. From the safe side of the Jeep, I pop up and fire the rest of the rounds in my magazine. I drop the empty magazine and slide in a full one...it's my last. Again, I jump up and fire. This time on the way down I grab Dick by the shirt and yank him down across the seat. Then, from a crouched position, I pull him out of the Jeep. I reach into the Jeep and move the shifter out of gear. I give it a quick wiggle then slide back down. The VC are as close as a fifty or sixty yards and AK-47 rounds are smacking all around me. I take the gasoline soaked shirt, tie it into a big knot, and ignite it with my Zippo. I toss the burning shirt over to the pool of gasoline by the Lambretta and the gas bursts in flames sending plumes of smoke pouring up into the sky. I reach into the Jeep and flip the ignition switch on, then use my rifle to push the starter switch; the Jeep comes alive. I flatten myself to the ground just before something in the Lambretta blows.

Kaaaa…whaamm! The explosion blows the front of the Lambretta off and pieces of burning metal fly all over the damn place. A large cloud of black smoke rolls into the sky. I hope it will distract the VC and raise the curiosity of the APC convoy. I crawl into the Jeep, jam it into gear and pop the clutch. The Jeep is severely tilted because both right wheels are in the ditch. I yank on the steering wheel trying to pull it onto the road and almost roll it. Hunched over in the seat as low as I can get, I manage to straighten it out, straddle the ditch and have the Jeep running down the ditch kicking up mud and dirt up behind it.

The VC are running now; their guns blazing. Two or three rounds blow out the windshield and another glances the side of my helmet knocking it off. I jam the shifter into third gear…I'm flying. It takes an enormous amount of concentration to keep the Jeep straddling the ditch bouncing all over the damn place lifting me off the seat every time I hit a bump. As the distance between the Jeep and the VC widens the accuracy of their fire diminishes. I still hear rounds whistling past; I know I'm not out of danger. *Come on, I'm almost there, come on…* The bonehead on the APC starts firing at me!

I start pounding on the horn waving my arm and yelling; *"I'm an American, I'm an American!"*

I try getting the Jeep out of the ditch this time engaging the four wheel drive. The Jeep bucks out of the ditch and as soon as I hit the blacktop I'm pedal to the metal. I reach the column a few seconds later. I dismount and take cover behind the APC.

A Lieutenant grabs me by the arm, "What the fuck's going on down there?"

"Ambush, sir, ambush! They slowed us up with a Lambretta and three VC ambushed us from the field, my Sergeant's dead. There was another VC in the Lambretta, but I got him before he got his weapon out."

The Lieutenant and a squad of his men climb into the APC and head for the burning Lambretta, the APC crew chief firing bursts from the fifty caliber.

The VC are gone, they've already escaped, probably disappearing into whatever holes they materialized from. The Lieutenant and his men start sweeping out across the field trying to find them. It'll be a surprise if they do.

An attack Huey is bearing in low from the direction of Camp Holloway, this must be the response to my radio call. It makes a long tilting arc around us then flies almost sideways down the road in the direction of the Lieutenant's patrol.

The rest of the convoy advances down the road and by the time we reach the burning Lambretta, they're dragging a VC body out of the field. When I see the VC's face the hair on the back of my neck stands up.

"Holy Shit! Are you fucking kidding?" A look of disbelief washes over my face.

The Lieutenant grabs my shoulder. "What is it? You know this guy?"

"Yeah, I know him. He's one of the barbers at the shack just outside our camp."

"You sure?"

"No doubt about it."

The Lieutenant is on the radio to his headquarters relaying his situation. When he's done I nod my head towards Sergeant Dick's body and ask, "What about Sergeant Dick, sir? Should I take his body back to the hill?"

"No, we'll take him over to the hospital at PAB they'll take care of the body." He reaches down and snaps the chain and dog tags off Dick's neck, he hands one to me, takes the second and forces it between two of Sergeant Dick's teeth. The body is loaded on the back of a truck.

He hands me Dick's wallet. "Take this back to your company commander, he'll know what to do."

"Jesus, is that it? We just toss his body on the back of a truck, zip him up in a plastic bag and ship him back to the States?"

"Well, what would you have us do?" The Lieutenant looks a little bewildered.

"It just doesn't seem right. It's like this place has not only taken his life, but his identity too. It'll just be another body bag tossed around till he gets shipped back to the States. Christ, it just don't seem right."

Lieutenant James looks like he has a momentary flash of melancholy, but lets it pass.

"Simon, is it?

"Yes sir."

"Simon, all we can do is quietly morn their passing and pray to intervene for their souls. I don't think they'll mind how their bodies are tossed around. If you're still bothered you best get up to see your chaplain. I'll have someone escort you back to the hill.

"I should be able to make it on my own."

"Well, we're gonna escort ya anyway. We have some business there."

Driving back to the hill the memory of our first day in Pleiku and Sergeant Dick's warning to Farmly replays itself in my mind. As we pull up to the gate, our MP's already have the entire staff of the barbershop sitting on the ground with their hands folded on top of their heads. Lt. James and his men are tying their hands. I know without asking they'll all be taken back to MACV for questioning.

The wide-open expanse of defoliated ground stretches out across the front of our bunker and disappears into the blackness. In the distance, lights from MACV and PAB can be seen to our left. To our right exploding mortar rounds, rockets and tracer rounds pierce the darkness around Titty Mountain, the 4th Division's base camp.

"Damn, they really got a shit storm goin' on over there." I pass the binoculars to Smitty so he can have a closer look.

"I sure as hell hope they stay over there." He says peering through the binoculars.

The camp is on high alert, all bunkers are manned and no one can sleep. We knew something was up when they rolled out half the people on the hill to stand in the biggest guard formation I've seen since being in country. During the formation the first shirt gave us the bad news. Word from G-2 was an NVA regiment is planning to hit Camp Holloway, Pleiku Air Base and Artillery hill. The air support out of Holloway supporting the 4th and 25th Division gives us complete control of the central highlands.

We know it, they know it, and till now, they've never been able to do anything about it. Neuman figures Holloway is the most likely target, as it is the main staging area for most of the helicopter activity in the area. The Hill is also a prime target because tonight there are three gun batteries here. Usually, there is only one. There isn't even enough space to deploy all three batteries, so all the vehicles from Alpha battery are just lined up on the road that surrounds the hill. A towed 105mm battery was added to the battalion several weeks back as a defensive unit for the hill and the immediate area.

It is 23:45 hours; the million-candlepower searchlight explodes onto the field surrounding the hill. They do a sweep about every fifteen minutes.

Farmly wanders out of the bunker and stares off in the direction of Titty Mountain.

"Let me have the glasses," he holds out his hand.

"It looks like the incoming at the 4th is starting to tail off," Farmly continues peering through the glasses as he speaks. He's right. The flashes from mortar and rocket detonations have all but stopped.

Why the hell would the VC attack the 4th Division base camp? They've got a whole fucking division over there...it just doesn't make sense. Maybe they're just shelling 'em to keep them from being able to mobilize support for the other units around here.

Out of the corner of my eye, four flashes momentarily light up the sky in the direction of Camp Holloway. Then, a couple of seconds later, *Boom! Boom! Boom! Boom!* Then, more flashes once again followed by the delayed sound of explosions.

With nervous excitement in his voice, Smitty blurts out, "Shit, man, they've started in on Holloway!"

The field phone rings.

All the other bunkers chime in with their acknowledgments.

"This is the OD, I'm just warning you guys, we've got a fire mission, it's gonna get noisy. Keep alert out there." Lieutenant Duke hangs up.

A 175mm-gun emplacement is fifty yards behind our bunker. The gun crew emerges out of the darkness with red flashlights and they set about the task of getting the gun ready to fire.

The barrel is being elevated to a very steep angle. I know this means the targets are close. "Holy shit, they're gonna be shootin' right over our heads. Hell, only one of us needs to stay up here," without hesitating, Farmly and Smitty scramble down into the bunker.

"Pussies!" I yell as loud as I can.

In the background I hear the crew chief barking out orders, repeating azimuths and coordinates.

Baroooooom! A tongue of fire shoots out the muzzle of the 175, the gun rocks back against its spade; the entire vehicle momentarily comes off the ground. The flash from the gun lights up the entire side of the hill for a split second. The blast is loud and starts my ears ringing. The ground rumbles and our bunker trembles. The cans hanging from the rows of barbed wire chime and clank either from the rumbling ground or the concussion of the gun.

"God dammit!" I yell.

Farmly comes out of the bunker covered with dirt. "Damn it, there must be ten tons of dirt fallin' on us in here." He's shaking his head and brushing the dirt off his shoulders.

In the distance, at a point somewhere between Holloway and Titty Mountain, the shells are detonating. It's difficult to tell in the dark but a good guess at the distance would be eight or ten miles out.

Baroooooom! Again, the twenty-foot muzzle spits a two hundred pound shell. *Baroooooom! Baroooooom!* The other two Howitzers in the battery begin firing. I have to press the palms of my hands hard against my ears to muffle the sound. Every time a gun fires it feels like my eyes are going to pop out of my head. Farmly has taken the toilet paper from a box of C rations and jammed it into his ears.

Back out towards Holloway there is still moocho activity. The searchlight kicks on again, sticking to its fifteen-minute cycle. It sweeps back and forth a half-mile out from the perimeter and works its way around the hill.

Baroooom! Cranck! Kachunk! Wham! Something is wrong…I snap my head around. Farmly and Smitty are already off the bunker running towards the gun. I want to go, but one of us has to stay at the bunker.

People are yelling and scrambling all over the place. *"The breach blew, get the medics!"*

The amber red lenses of the flashlights lay motionless around the gun, morbidly marking where each of the dead men lay. The medics are there in seconds; I wonder if Holloway will be able to launch a Medivac chopper in the middle of a mortar bombardment.

Farmly and Smitty are stunned. "Jesus, Sonny Johnson's arm is blown off, Jesus." Farmly keeps repeating it, "Jesus," muttering it over and over.

The grim look on Smitty's face leaves me feeling there is little hope for the crew.

We're surprised that a Medivac chopper does manage to make it ten minutes later. The bodies are loaded on the chopper; it lifts off and disappears eerily into the night. There is nothing left behind but a mangled howitzer and the ghosts of the men who fell, ghosts who will exist as long as there are memories strong enough to sustain them.

I light a cigarette, stand up and stretch. I pull out my canteen and take a big swallow then tilt my head back and let the water run over my face. The sun will be up in an hour. The fire missions stopped a little past midnight. Later there was a flurry of air activity that culminated with a couple of passes by "Puff the Magic Dragon," an AC-47 armed with several Gatling mini-guns. The rumor among GIs is that "Puff" can put a bullet into every square inch of the ground it circles. True or not, the shit storm of tracers that rained out of the sky near Holloway made a believer out of me.

Farmly picks up the phone to make the hourly check-in.

Smitty bums a cigarette, lights up and comments, "Well, looks like we've lucked out."

"Sure looks like it. Damn, I can't even imagine how many rounds were fired during the night." I take one last drag on my cigarette and toss it.

The field phone rings and Farmly moans, "Now what?" He seems irritated so I pick up the phone.

"Post twelve, post twelve...we've got movement, dammit, we've got movement!"

Lieutenant Duke probes him for a better explanation. "Meier! Meier!

Where? Where have you got movement?" Before Meier can answer someone from post eleven fires off a flare.

We yank around trying to see what's going on. Post twelve isn't visible from our bunker, bunker eleven is on the edge of our field of vision, and everything else disappears around the side of the hill.

Lieutenant Duke is still on the phone with Meier, when I detect a sound that makes me lower the phone, whip my head around and stare into the darkness. I stare out past the flare now burning on the ground. It is muffled, barely audible, but Smitty hears it too. He jumps off the bunker, Farmly is on his heels and I bring the phone back up to my mouth and yell, *Incoming!* I grab the phone and jump down into the bunker entrance. We barely make it, before the shells start exploding. *Wham! Wham! Wham!* Mortar shells are dropping all over the goddamn place.

I pick up the phone and press it to my ear.

"Gooks! We got gooks! They're fifty yards outside the wire. Mother of God, there's hundreds of 'em." I don't know who's talking, but someone else jumps in, "Post two, post two, gooks outside the wire, gooks outside the wire."

The searchlight sweeps the northeast side of the hill and weapons fire erupts. The distinctively different sounds made by AK-47s and M-16s make it clear the perimeter on the other side of the hill is under assault. The fifty-caliber machine gun in the crow's nest is alive and a stream of tracers pours down towards the perimeter.

"Man, oh, man, we ain't got shit over here!" Smitty is peering into the darkness trying to detect anything in our field of fire.

Farmly nervously asks, "What the hell should we do? Should we go over and reinforce the guys on the other side of the hill?" Smitty has the M-60 sitting in the gun port, he slaps in the end of an ammo belt from a new can of ammo, cocks the weapon, and once again peers out past the perimeter.

Outside, people are pouring out of their hooches and into the trenches. Mortar rounds are dropping all over the damn place. A couple of mortar rounds detonate near the top of the hill, an obvious attempt to knock out the searchlight. The automatic weapons fire continues filling the void between mortar detonations. An APC with it's mounted fifty caliber heads down towards bunker twelve to reinforce the position and another takes a position behind bunker eleven with its fifty-caliber already chattering away. Someone, I'm not sure who, is moving guys through the trenches towards the front gate where the VC are concentrating their attack.

We hear Gunships coming towards us out of the darkness. We don't see them until they pass overhead. They bank hard left, sweep out in front of us and disappear into the blackness. The searchlight focuses on a large body of VC outside the perimeter making them a target for the unseen choppers. Fire trails follow the rockets all the way to the ground, where they detonate in multiple explosions. There are several quick salvos then the choppers become momentarily visible as they again circle over the hill.

"Holy fuck!" Smitty yells as he cranks up the sixty. "RPG, RPG!" I look out the gun port just in time to see the rocket exhaust shoot out the back of the tube as it's launched. Instinctively, I dive for the ground. I lay on the floor next to Farmly till the rocket detonates on the sandbags of the gun emplacement behind us. They're targeting the 175 unaware that it has been disabled from the blown breach.

Farmly yells, "Christ, they're trying to knock out the gun." He yells out the gun port, "Hey assholes, this gun is already broken!"

The VC are mere silhouettes just thirty yards outside the wire. I cover one of them with my sights and squeeze off a round. I let the weapon drop back into the cradle and fire again. I can't tell how close my rounds are hitting, but I keep firing. Finally, I squeeze, the weapon recoils and as I bring it to bear once again, I see the target has gone down. Another VC picks up the RPG, but Smitty walks his tracer rounds across the field till he smothers him with fire from the M-60. I whip around to Farmly, "Flare! Flare," I yell. Farmly grabs a flare and hustles out the back of the bunker and he fires it out over the perimeter. The flare casts an eerie illumination over the field in front of our position. It reveals several VC just outside the perimeter.

The unmistakable sound of tanks can be heard coming from the west. Two tanks and two APCs take up positions to reinforce our main gate. They're just off the road and are providing a really good crossfire. The first round out the tank is the white phosphorous. WP rounds are used by the tankers to mark and range targets. They don't like having them in the tank and usually get rid of them as soon as they can. A WP round detonates a few yards outside the perimeter. The intense white flash of light from the shell blinds us momentarily. I squeeze my eyelids several times and rub them as hard as I can. I vigorously shake my head trying to refocus. I can hear hideous shrieks of horror and see a VC running wildly, twisting and jerking, a patch of *White Fire* from the phosphorous shell is burning a hole in his back. Another VC mercifully puts him out of his misery with a burst from his AK-47. A convoy of tanks and APCs is coming up highway fourteen, probably from the fourth division. There is activity all over the fucking place and it's getting hard to tell all the players without a scorecard. The arrival of the tanks sends the VC withdrawing to the northeast.

The attack has lasted forty or fifty minutes. A red twinge of light is just barely visible on the horizon. The small sliver of sun washes light over the horizon and begins to illuminate the countryside. The mechanized infantry from the 4th are in full pursuit.

The field phone rings and Smitty answers, "Roger that, sir," is all he says before he cradles the handset. "Colonel Schoebert," Smitty says, as he cocks his head towards the phone, "has ordered a stand down. The 4th infantry is taking over the operation and he doesn't want us accidentally shooting at the wrong guys."

Fifteen minutes later it's daylight. Several miles away there is still gunfire being exchanged as the 4th infantry continues its pursuit of the retreating VC. For us, the night is over.

CHAPTER THIRTEEN

"ROY ROGERS AND ARCHIE WHO?"

October 10th – One forty-three and a wake up.

"Okay, pass up a two-by-six." Standing on a two-by-four header and leaning against the rafter I just nailed in place, I wait for someone to pass me the lumber, Fishe is on the other wall doing the same.

The Hill has been designated as a permanent headquarters facility for the Artillery support in the central Highlands and the 1st Field Forces. What that means to us is we won't be moving off this hill anytime soon. For this reason more permanent housing structures are being built to replace the tent and tin hooches we've called home. Varant said he saw some documents from MACV directing base camp commanders to build more permanent structures. We surmise they're sending a message to the VC that we aren't going to go away or something along those lines. So the last couple of weeks have been spent erecting barracks. A building for the senior officers went up first housing Schoebert and all the senior staff on the hill. Then we knocked one out to replace the NCO hooch.

Frenchy passes up a two-by-six cut to size. I set it on the outside wall header, fitting the header into the notch of the two-by-six and nail it in place. Then I toenail it to the two-by-ten beam that spans the length of the roof.

All the rafters are up before lunch. The sweltering heat makes everybody peal off their shirts and work bare-chested. We were the obvious choice for this work, especially for the two-story barracks, since many of us received pole climbing and elevated work training. The barrack is a two-story building not all that different from the barrack we had at Fort Knox and Fort Dix. Bennett, our hero, felt we'd be more comfortable working and climbing around the structure.

After climbing down from the rafters and wiping the sweat from my neck and forehead, I plop down next to everybody sitting on the floor. Turner passes me the pack of Pall Malls.

"Man, it is fucking hot!" I wring the sweat out of the kerchief I'm using for a headband.

"Brother, you ain't a shittin'." Pinetti echoes my sentiments, then looks at Coleman and says, "Say, what the hell's that boy up to?" Coleman has his shirt off and is in the semi-hypnotic trance he goes into when he does his Karate exercises.

"Yo, Coleman, how about breakin' some boards for us?" Pinetti yells. He's kept a surprisingly low profile since Plei Djereng, but we've been waiting for him to slip back into his *irritating little prick* mode. I think the wait is over.

Coleman just ignores him and continues with his routine.

Pinetti presses, "Hell, how hard can it be? Damn, I bet I could do it." He gets up and walks over to the sawhorses. He looks around and picks up a piece of one-by-four about four feet long.

"Hell, I could break this." He sizes up the board, then lays it across the sawhorses. He looks at it; he isn't sure how far apart to put the horses, so he sets them about three-and-a-half feet apart. He presses down on the board to test it and finds that it has a good spring to it. Pinetti decides this will work against him and pushes the horses closer together.

"I wouldn't be fuckin' with that, you're gonna break your hand bozo." Coleman finishes his routine and nonchalantly offers advice to Pinetti.

Pinetti pauses, looks at the board then turns to Coleman. "Can you break this board?" Coleman nods yes.

"Hell, then, let's see ya do it." Pinetti is trying to back out without looking like a big chicken shit.

"I don't have any reason to break that board. I don't do my Karate for anybody's entertainment." Coleman breaks out his canteen, takes a big swallow and then pours the rest on the back of his neck.

We can tell by the look on Pinetti's face he must be thinking if some black guy can do it he should be able to do it. He takes up what he thinks is a karate stance, leans forward and braces himself on the board with his left hand. Then he lays the edge of his right hand on the board measuring his strike. He pulls his right arm up sharply; then makes a sharp downward movement stopping his hand just before it strikes the board. He repeats this action four or five times. It's hard to say whether he's just chickening out or if he's building up his nerve.

"Come on, ya pussy, either hit it or quit fuckin' around." Varant taunts.

Pinetti casts a quick glance in Varant's direction, releases his left arm, raises back from the waist bringing his right arm and hand behind his head and lunges down at the board with a jerking motion of his right arm. His hand strikes the board hard…it does not break. Instead, it bounces off the sawhorses, snaps up and whacks Pinetti on the side of his face.

"Fuck!" Pinetti grabs his right hand with his left and starts shaking it violently. "Damn it! Son-of-a-bitch!" He spins around, moving his left hand back and forth between his face and holding the right hand.

"You dumb ass," I yell at him. He's hopping up and down like a circus clown.

Turner yells, "Yeah, you sure taught that board a lesson." Jim just sits rocking his head from side to side laughing so hard his belly is shaking.

"Yeah, well I think Coleman's full of shit. You can't break that board with no Karate chop. I think all that breakin' boards crap is bullshit." Pinetti's ego is damaged far worse than his hand.

Coleman stands up, walks over to the scrap pile, picks up a piece of two-by-four about five feet long, sets it across the sawhorses about three feet apart. He stands sideways with his left hip a foot or so from the sawhorse. He doesn't even look at the board, he stares away for a few seconds, closes his eyes momentarily, then in an incredibly fast movement, his knees flex, his upper torso twists and his right hand slices through the two-by-four. It is the fastest movement I have ever seen a human being make. Coleman stands for a couple of seconds, balls up his right hand two or three times - it still must have hurt - then returns to his spot.

"Bozo," is all he says as he walks past Pinetti. We look at each other in disbelief, and then resume laughing.

Frenchy walks over to Pinetti and looks at his hand. It is already swollen and the little finger is turning black and blue.

"Man, you better get over to the medics. That looks like you broke something to me and I wouldn't be telling them how you did it either. They court martial ya for self-inflicted wounds ya know."

Pinetti starts walking towards the first aid tent gingerly carrying his right hand in his left.

"You know he's done it to us again, don't ya?" Fishe says laughingly.

"Done what?" I ask.

"Hell, he probably broke his hand or at least bruised it real bad. They'll take him off this job and put him on light duty."

I only let it bother me for about two seconds…I'm too amused by the look Pinetti had on his face.

Saturday evening after chow we make a beeline over to the NCO Club because the USO is coming around with some entertainment. It's the first time this has happened. We don't know who's coming and we don't care, its a welcome break in our routine.

Sgt. Bennett ambles in and sits down next to me. I take advantage of the opportunity and ask, "So who's coming, Sarge?"

Bennett replies, "Archie Moore."

"Archie Moore?" I look at Fishe, shrug my shoulders and hope someone will enlighten me.

"He's a fighter," Bennett says.

"You ever hear of him?" I look at Fishe.

"Fuck, I don't know. The only fighter I know is Cassius Clay." Jim is just as perplexed.

Coleman lowers himself onto the bench and says, "Archie Moore's a black fighter. He was big in the forties and fifties. He was the light heavyweight champ for years. Moore had more knockouts than any other fighter in history. They call him the "Mongoose" because he has a lightning fast jab. I think his last fight was against Clay but Archie was already way past his prime so Clay got a TKO in the fourth round."

At six o'clock Archie Moore is escorted into the club.

Moore is an elderly black man with whitening hair. His face is puffy and upon closer inspection, I can see his right ear is slightly disfigured. He's big, weighing at least two-fifty or two-sixty and I'd guess his age near fifty. Of course, when you're nineteen, everyone over the age of thirty looks fifty.

Archie tells a couple of jokes and gives us the details on a couple of his more famous fights. He fought Marciano once and actually knocked him down, by the way he was bragging about it, I guess it was pretty hard to do. Marciano is a name I recognize. My father and uncles used to talk about him and another fighter named Jake La Motta. Then they'd argue with my German grandfather about a fighter named Max Schmelling or Schmerling or something along those lines. Actually, the only fights I've ever seen were at the field house of Bessemer Park on the south Side of Chicago. The park district gave boxing lessons and held *Golden Gloves* bouts there.

Archie is going to give us a quick boxing lesson. He has us stand up and walks us through the proper way to throw a jab. It didn't seem like that big a deal. Someone starts jibing Archie about Karate. Coleman's name is ultimately mentioned.

"Karate," he says. "Hell, none of that karate crap could ever be bettern' a good left jab and a right cross. Okay, you guys bring your karate boy up here, come on, bring him here." He looks around the room trying to pick out the Karate expert. We pull Coleman out of his seat and start pushing him towards Moore, Coleman resisting all the way. Finally, Moore puts his hand on Coleman's shoulder and urges him up front.

"Okay, son, show me what ya's got." Moore stands back and watches Coleman do a couple of kicks and fire off a flurry of successive karate punches.

"Damn, boy, you're pretty fast, must be 'cause you're black." Archie laughs; Coleman looks embarrassed. Archie picks a couple of assistants, Neuman and Pace, giving each one an empty beer can. He instructs them to hold the can out next to their body at shoulder length. He turns to Coleman, "Okay, looky here, let's see who can knock the can out of the hand first. Hell, I won't even have anybody say one…two…three. I'll wait for you to go first - loser buys the beer."

No way is Coleman going to lose; we've seen how fast he really is. The audience watches intently. Moore takes his normal boxing stance and Coleman gets into his karate stance. The stances aren't all that different. Moore glances at Pace and the can but his eyes are watching Coleman. I see the muscles in Coleman's neck flinch slightly and then his arm rockets out, but before Coleman's hand actually makes contact with the can in Neuman's hand, the can in Pace's hand flies across the room. A micro second is all that separates the delivery of the two punches, but there is no mistake, Moore was the clear winner.

"I believe you owes me a beer, son. See there, boys, that karate stuff don't do you no good if I knock you out first." Moore laughs and receives a hearty round of applause.

Jesus, no wonder they call him "The Mongoose."

Moore stays long enough to drink the beer he gets from Coleman, shakes a few hands, signs a few autographs and is off to the hospital at PAB. This has been a landmark day for me Moore is the first celebrity I've ever met. We wait around for the second guest to arrive. It takes twenty minutes, and then the door to the NCO club flies open and…"Ye hah!" Bang! Bang! Bang! In one hand is a silver revolver shooting blanks the other hand is waving his cowboy hat in the air. The second he walks through the door everybody knows who he is. He's dressed in the same outfit I'd seen him wear every Saturday morning for years. Same cowboy hat, same pistols, hell, he almost looks the same. Time has not been unkind to him. He's the same Roy Rogers I have always known! His wife Dale Evans follows right behind him dressed in her cowboy attire.

Roy does a few rope tricks and tells stories about the years of doing the TV show and making movies. We find out when his horse trigger died, Dale had it stuffed because Roy loved it so much and they keep it in the trophy room of the ranch. Roy does a quick draw demonstration, does some pistol spinning and tells a couple of more jokes. Then Roy and Dale give us the old we love ya because you're serving your country speech. He uses this to segue into a speech about sobriety.

"Dale and I would like you boys to use some horse sense when you're drinkin' beer with your buddies and be careful not to overdo it. You need to keep your mind clear about what you're doing over here." It would be hard to argue with that logic, but we find the real reason he's giving us the pitch.

"Several years ago our son was drafted into the army. When he finished his training we were very proud of him. The army sent our boy over to Germany and from his letters he seemed to be really enjoying himself. On his birthday his buddies took him out to get him drunk and they took him to a Rathskeller where they serve beer in big one liter glasses," he holds his hands a couple of feet apart to indicate the size of the glass. "Well, his buddies dared him to chug-a-lug a whole stein. So he did. When he finished drinking the beer his heart stopped and he fell over dead." Roy pauses a moment and Dale looks away, it's obvious talking about it is painful.

"Our son was gone." We can see Roy's eyes beginning to water. "He died just from drinking that damn glass of beer." Roy pauses a moment then apologizes. "I'm sorry fellas, I know you didn't come here to hear me preachin,' we just don't want it to ever happen to anybody else." Roy and Dale put their arms around each other and start singing, "Happy Trails to you, until we meet again..." When they finish, they walk through the crowd, shake hands and pose for pictures, wave a few more times and leave.

"Jeez, that was uplifting...lifted my spirits right up." The look on Farmly's face is more morose than usual.

I look at everybody else and say, "Kinda makes you not want to finish these beers, don't it?"

In harmony everybody answers, "Hell no!" Then we lift our beers and empty the remainder of the bottles. The Roy Rogers sermon does not instill enough guilt in us to prevent any of us from getting shit faced. After the evenings festivities, in some strange, bizarre way, I find myself feeling uplifted.

Later, lying in my cot, I feel something I haven't felt in a long, long time; I realize I'm smiling. For some reason, I feel the same sense of excitement I felt the day I went to my first Cubs game. I remember feeling the same way on the last day of school as I'd run across the playground elated with the prospect of being off for the summer. It is the same feeling I get when I think about the hot summer nights sleeping on the front porch to keep cool or running around the park on the fourth of July with sparklers and firecrackers. It is the feeling of hapless freedom every kid feels till it is slowly stripped away by the ever-increasing load of responsibilities that weigh you down as you mature. For reasons I can't understand, the visits by Archie Moore and Roy Rogers have made me feel like a kid again. I haven't thought about the war all night. For a brief moment I forget where I am and only have thoughts of those Saturday mornings watching Roy Rogers, Commander Cody and the Bowery Boys.

I remember my dad once telling me not to be in any hurry to grow up. He told me that once I walk that path, the magic of my youth would disappear. I didn't understand then, but I do now.

Chapter Fourteen

"Mr. Clean"

October 31st...Twenty-two days till I break a hundred. Sitting on the stoop of our newly constructed barrack we watch Sergeant First Class Bennett load his duffel bag into the back of a Jeep. Bennett is down to *the* wake up. Tomorrow, bright and early, he'll wake up in Cam Ranh Bay, board a 707 and be back in the States in thirteen or fourteen hours.

We walk over to the Jeep to say our farewells. Recently, I found out Bennett is forty-two. The way he hunches over and ambles around I always thought the guy might be in his fifties. I guess the uncertainty of how long this war is going to last and the distinct possibility that he could end up back here in the future, have made him decide to take his retirement. So he'll rotate back to the States and put in for discharge.

"Well, Sarge, where ya goin' from here?" I ask sincerely, with a genuine interest in what someone who has spent his entire life in the military does when they quit.

Bennett smiles his big, dumb, hillbilly smile and says, "Well, Sis, I got me about sixty days of leave, then an assignment at Fort Bragg for my last couple of months." He extends his hand to each of us and we shake it in turn. "I'll have my wife pray for you boys. Keep your noses clean and stay sharp, it ain't a'gonna be getting' any easier over here." Bennett seems to be prophesizing, letting us know he senses things are destined to become worse before getting better.

The Jeep rolls down the hill and makes its way out the gate, then down the road in the direction of Pleiku Airbase.

"Lucky bastard!" Lindlay mumbles as we watch the Jeep disappear.

The new barracks is much nicer than sleeping in the old hooch but not nearly as personal and surely not as safe. The walls of the old hooch were sandbagged nearly all the way up which provided excellent protection against shrapnel and weapons fire. The new place is a big wooden barrack. Two stories, just like we had at Fort Knox. We built two of them side by side and nearly all of Headquarters Battery is housed in them. A couple of well-placed rounds and Headquarters Battery is out of business. The first floor is occupied by the commo platoon, the operations boys and of course the crypto geeks. Upstairs are the guys from the motor pool, supply, maintenance and the 105 crews.

Red Smitt is leaning against the wall next to my rack where I am comfortably reposed with my hands folded behind my head, just like Jim in the cot across from me.

Red wants to know, "So what do you think? Think they'll promote one of us to E-5?"

I mull it over for a few minutes before answering. I hadn't actually even considered it being a possibility till Smitty mentioned it.

"No, I don't think they'll do that."

"Why not? We've pulled some pretty nasty duty, all of us have gotten our nicks, hell, Pinetti even got himself a medal!"

I instinctively look Jim in the eye the thought that Pinetti could or would actually ever be our squad leader is chilling. We relax and shake our heads as the realization that there isn't a man alive that would ever put Pinetti in charge of anything.

Sitting up, I say, "Look, I won't even be twenty till January, Jim is barely twenty, hell, you're the oldest guy here!" Smitty is taken back.

"I'm only twenty one, I ain't that fucking old!" We can sense the defensiveness in his voice. He takes exception to the insinuation.

Varant leans up on one elbow. "The only way any of you guys will make E-5 is to volunteer for a second tour."

Somewhat bewildered, we look at Hal and Jim asks, "Why's that?"

"One of the prerequisites for makin' E-5 is three years of service. They'll give you a waiver if you re-up or sign up for another tour."

Smitty is quick to respond. "I don't think that's true. A couple of those guys over at the 25th are E-5s and they're on their first tour." It's pretty apparent that Smitty is secretly hoping to grab the promotion.

"Yeah, you could transfer over to the infantry and probably make E-5 if you live long enough." Varant always has the ability and intelligence to analyze a situation and have the answers waiting on the tip of his tongue. As soon as the situation calls for the information he's ready to deliver.

Usually, his candor has the same effect as throwing a glass of ice water on someone taking a hot shower but rarely is his sage wisdom off the mark.

Rolling on my side I point out a fact that seems obvious to me. "Seems to me you've probably got a pretty good shot at it. You're a pretty smart guy, you think things through, when you're sober, and you're a wise ass like most of the other NCOs around here."

"Yeah, that's exactly why they *won't* promote me. They don't want anybody smart enough to question some of the decisions made around here. Besides they've already got a replacement." Varant smiles, he knows he just tossed a big fat juicy worm into the middle of a bunch of hungry fish.

Immediately everyone closes in on Varant's cot, all our faces masked with an unmistakable look of anticipation, just like a bunch of six-year-olds waiting for the ice cream man.

"Well," Varant hesitates, "When I was delivering some deciphered stuff to Schoebert, I saw some transfer orders and a 201 jacket lying on his desk. Looks like we'll be getting some guy named Fitzpatrick, John Fitzpatrick."

Farmly, who would normally grab the opportunity to chastise Varant for prying or spying, blurts out, "So what did his jacket say?"

"He's twenty-six; he's from Minnesota, he's a college dropout and has been in the service for only three years. He's coming from Fort Sill and this is his first trip to the Nam."

"Wow," I comment, "I guess that was a little more than a glance at his file."

"That's because I know how much you guys depend on me for info," Varant says with an overly smug look, it's a look that's suggests he's not telling us everything.

"What else?" I ask.

"Why, whatever do you mean?" Varant replies coyly, like a girl.

"Come on, dick-breath, I can tell you got something juicy you haven't told us. Quit fucking around and give us the scoop."

Varant looks at everyone, rolls his eyes up at the ceiling then looks back at us with a sadistic smile. "Well," he says, "It might be of some interest to know the school he dropped out of was West Point."

"West Point," several of us mutter at the same time.

"Yeah, West Point," Varant reiterates. "You know what that means, don't ya?" Before he can answer, Farmly answers for him.

"It means he's a frustrated officer wanna-be who's gonna be a real prick and probably has a hero complex," Farmly looks at the floor as he makes the comment, obviously disturbed by the prospect.

"You got it," Varant says. "He's gonna be a real ball buster."

"Great, just what we fucking need: Sergeant Pomp and fucking Circumstance. Well, the Nam will take the edge off him pretty quickly." I mumble.

"Hey, we really don't know jack shit about the guy, don't you think we may be forming some prejudicial opinions before we really know anything about him?" Jim's trying to be fair, probably because he's hoping all our analyses is wrong. "Hell," he says, "Maybe he dropped out of West Point because he didn't like all that chicken shit crap."

It's a possibility, but we won't really know anything till he shows up.

November 1st, 0500 hours, the screen door to the barracks flies open banging loudly against the wall. A man stands in the doorway, barely a silhouette against the little bit of light coming from the mess hall across the road. He starts banging a coffee can with a stick and yells at the top of his lungs, "Drop your cocks and grab your socks! Let's go, let's go! Don't make me have to roll your asses out of those bunks."

Disagreeable comments air from every corner of the hooch.

"What the fuck?"

"What's going on?"

"It's too fuckin' early..."

"Who the fuck is that?"

The man in the doorway strides through the barracks grabbing each cot and shaking it, "Get your asses out of those racks. I want everybody dressed and in formation in ten minutes."

"Yeah, and who the fuck are you?" Varant snaps. Varant is pissed because he was in the crypto trailer till one in the morning.

"I'm Sergeant Fitzpatrick, your new platoon Sergeant, so get your ass out of the rack."

"Fuck you, you ain't my Sergeant, I'm part of operations, asshole." Varant gets back in his cot and pulls his sleeping bag over his head. Fitzpatrick takes his foot and uses it to push Varant out of his cot. Varant springs to his feet and is about to attack Fitzpatrick, but Jim and I grab him before he can.

Fitzpatrick walks up to him, gets right in his face, till they are nose to nose, "I don't give a damn where you work. You don't talk to me that way, boy, ever, you read me?"

"Fuck you…Sergeant! Yeah, and another thing, you forget to brush this morning?" Varant obviously isn't intimidated by Fitzpatrick. Conversely, Fitzpatrick seems flustered. His efforts to impose his authority over Varant are falling far short of his expectations.

"You're ass is mine, soldier, you stand down or I'll have you up on charges." Fitzpatrick doesn't wait for Varant's answer. He turns and heads out the door. "Ten minutes!" He yells as he leaves. At least he was smart enough to realize he was involved in a confrontation on the verge of getting out of control. A situation that would make him appear to be a total jackass.

Not willing to let it go, Varant yells, "*Go ahead…court martial me, ya little cocksucker*!"

We assemble outside the barrack in our usual manner, none of that "Espirit de Corps" formation crap like back in the States, just a relaxed, semi-organized, collection of men waiting for someone to address them.

Fitzpatrick emerges from the mess tent and steps up on a little two step platform he must have taken from up near operations. It's the one the Sergeant Major uses for his formations. In the barracks I hadn't taken in much of his appearance but now I notice: His fatigues are spotless, starched and creased, state-side fatigues, not the jungle fatigues we wear. His boots, all-leather jump boots, are spit shined to a super high gloss. We all wear web sided jungle boots, none of which have ever come into contact with a can of shoe polish. His trousers are bloused, and his back pockets are starched shut; no bulges from a wallet. His belt buckle is shined to mirror finish, we generally spray ours with black primer so it's harder to see or less likely to give off a reflection. He wears his airborne wings, pinned above his left pocket, also highly polished. The guys over at the 101st Airborne, the "*Screaming Eagles,*" have a black wing patch insignia sewn to their fatigues, as is most of our insignia. That way there's nothing white that can reflect moonlight or give away a position.

What a dumb ass, I think. He has a brand new pistol belt, a holstered forty-five and a small ammo pouch for the magazines. Fitzpatrick is a little shorter than I am, he's maybe five-sevenish. His face is pock marked from a bad case of teenage acne. He has jet-black hair and thick eyebrows. He walks stiffly, almost like he has something jammed up his ass, just like Jack Webb used to walk on Dragnet.

He looks back and forth across the formation a couple of times and shakes his head, "What a bunch of sorry-ass lookin' soldiers. Hell, I'm not even sure you guys classify as soldiers."

"Suck my Dick!" Smitty mumbles from the back.

"Who said that? Who said that?" Fitzpatrick's face turns bright red. He paces back and forth across the front of the platoon, evidently thinking this will make one of us confess.

"Look at you guys, just look." He walks up to Jim who is dressed in jungle fatigues with no nametags or insignia. "How the hell am I supposed to know who you are soldier and where's the standing order that says you can rip the sleeves off your fatigues?"

Jim looks past Fitzpatrick, seemingly not bothered, and calmly says, "Well, if you'd been here more than one day, you'd know who I am." It was easy to see Fitzpatrick getting more flustered.

Fitzpatrick steps back from the group calls out, *"Platoon... Attennnnnshun!"* Not being complete idiots and realizing you can only push a guy so far, we make a half-assed attempt to come to attention.

"*Dress riiiiight...Dress!"* Fitzpatrick yells out the command used to dress-up the formation. We all raise our left arms to touch the shoulder of the man immediately to our left and then drop the arm to the side.

"Are you fucking shitting me?" Lindlay mumbles under his breath.

While we stand there under Fitzpatrick's scrutiny other people are making their way to the mess tent. They look at us like we're goofy. We see Sergeant Pace standing outside the mess hall watching, shaking his head and laughing.

"I have no intention of being the platoon Sergeant of a bunch of retards. You guys are gonna get your shit together, do you read me?" He pauses waiting for us to respond; none of us do. "Do you read me?" He repeats his question. Again there is no response.

"Okay, I'm giving you guys sixty minutes. Fall out and be back in formation in one hour. Everybody will have clean, shined boots and a regulation set of fatigues." He turns and walks away.

We're bewildered, it's like a bad dream; we keep hoping we're still asleep. Back inside the hooch we flop down on our cots.

Farmly, normally the reticent man of the hooch looks at the ceiling and says, "Mother of God! The one single thing that's made this screwed up place even minutely tolerable is that we don't have to deal with all the normal military nonsense. Now this?"

"Fuck him, you don't work for the prick anyway." Varant offers his counseling. "Fuck, man, you work with us in operations, what the hell did you even bother falling out for?" We all know the answer to that question; Farmly would never have the Cajones to do what Varant had done.

Pinetti is sitting on the edge of his cot removing his boots. At first I think he's going to climb back into his rack and go back to sleep, but when he pulls a can of shoe polish out of his foot locker, I sit up and ask, "What the hell are you doing?"

"Polishing my shoes, whata'ya think?"

Everybody looks at him like he's retarded.

"Are you nuts?" Jim says as he walks up to him. "Nobody in this hooch is gonna be polishing their boots unless the colonel puts out an order that *every* swingin' dick on the hill is gonna do it!" Jim grabs the can of polish from Pinetti and drops it into the butt can. The butt can, half filled with a muddy concoction of cigarette butts and water, is second only to the cans of crap from the shitter in its degree of grossness. There is no way Pinetti will even attempt to retrieve the polish.

"Hey, I've got an idea!" Lindlay, rarely the one to contribute to our scheming, has a glint in his eye that promises his idea is going to be a pip. We gather around and listen intently as Lee lays out his plan.

We sneak out the back door of the barracks and creep along the wall to the front. We peek around the corner to see if Fitzpatrick is anywhere around. Seeing that it's clear we walk briskly to the latrine and pull one of the half-drums of crap out from under one of the holes. Lindlay and Coleman are already digging a small hole in front of the barracks where we assemble. Pinetti takes the two-step stand between the barracks and knocks off the two top boards. He replaces them with two new boards from the pile of scrap lumber leftover from the construction. The new boards are sawed about ninety percent of the way through, then nailed in place, cut side down. With this done we lower the can of shit into the hole and cover this with the stand. The dirt from the hole is disposed of behind the barracks. All in all it's has taken about fifteen minutes to complete our devious little plot. Fortunately, for us, the view from the NCO hooch is blocked by the new barracks, so Fitzpatrick wouldn't be able to see what we've been up to.

Jim says, “Okay, let’s go.” It’s time to fall out. Jim, our unofficial squad leader, gets up and the rest of us follow. The new guys, Davy Johnson, Mark Moeller, and Whitey Pierce are in on the scheme. They arrived only a few days before; I’m surprised they follow our lead without the least amount of hesitation. I’d have thought they’d need to be here a little longer before they would get enough nerve to do something like this. Farmly follows against the protests of Varant, he doesn’t want to miss the show. Coleman, Smitty and I have all put on blouses with no identification or insignia...a little icing on the cake.

“What’s this? What’s this? Where is everybody else?” Fitzpatrick stands in front of our group, pacing back and forth between *the* platform and us. He’s frantic. “You!” He points at me.

“Me, Sergeant?” I look at him with a sheepish look of innocence.

“Yeah, you. What happened to your name tag?”

“Ah, I spilled some coffee on my shirt when we went back into the hooch to change and this is the only clean one I’ve got.” I turn away and stare forward trying not to smirk.

He stands in front of Coleman, who dwarfs him, and asks, “What about you?”

Coleman replies, “I got some of that same coffee on my shirt too.”

“Me too,” Lindlay says before Fitzpatrick can even ask.

“I believe I ordered you men to have your shoes shined when you fell back out. Why the hell aren’t they shined?”

Coleman raises his hand. “I believe I can answer that for you Mr. Sergeant.”

Fitzpatrick returns to face Coleman. “Well?”

You sees, mister boss man, when dem boots gets too shiny, dey reflect light and make yo’ butt be easier to see. Since none of us will be liken to have dem VC be shootin’ at us, nobody here be shinin’ dem boots, no sir, not even da Sergeant Major. Fact be, we all do what we see Sergeant Major do.” Coleman really lays it on thick. He delivers his recitation in a voice Rochester from the Jack Benny show would have been ashamed of.

Fitzpatrick stands for several seconds trying to decide what to do about the line of shit Coleman is feeding him. He turns his head one way then the other and looks at the rest of us. We’re biting our lips to keep from laughing. Smitty is shaking.

“You guys are a fucking disgrace. You even smell bad. Jesus, what is that fucking smell?” I’m gonna have to help you guys remember what it’s like to be soldiers.”

"What was that, Sergeant? I can't see you very well." Lindlay yells from behind.

Fitzpatrick, probably paranoid about being so short, which would explain him using the little stand in the first place, doesn't even hesitate, he turns and steps up onto the stand.

"Can you see me…" The top boards give way before he can finish the sentence and he drops straight down into the can of grossly disgusting waste. He stands there for several seconds unable to believe he is standing knee deep in a can of shit. The smell is overwhelming. Fitzpatrick's face looks like a Washington State apple. He steps out of the bucket; there is crap and pieces of toilet paper sticking to his pant legs. He reaches down to pull some of it off, but pulls his hand away at the last second.

We're silently laughing out of control. All of our faces are scrunched up and we're biting our lips. Tears are running down Pinetti's face. A couple of guys walking by look at Fitzpatrick and say, "Damn, Sarge, you smell like shit!" They start laughing and keep walking.

Fitzpatrick turns and yells at them, "*Yeah, well you guys look like shit!*" He turns his attention back to us.

"You guys might think you're really fucking funny but you cheese dicks work for me whether you like it or not. You're all going to pay for this. No one in this section is going to be responsible for putting a blemish on my record, got it?" Fitzpatrick is screaming. His face has turned so red I expect blood to start shooting out his nostrils at any second.

Farmly surprises all of us by challenging him. "It's my impression that you've a ready taken care of that."

Fitzpatrick spins around to face him, "What's that supposed to mean?"

"Well, Sergeant, I'm under the impression that you washed out of West Point, I'd have to think that would be a pretty big blemish on anybody's record."

Frustration oozes out from pores on Fitzpatrick's face. "Where'd you get that information? Who told you that? That's personal information. What's your name?"

"Farmly...and it's just a rumor Sergeant."

"Let's go, let's go, Orderly room…*Now!* I'm gonna article fifteen your smart ass."

Farmly and Fitzpatrick take the short walk to the orderly room. Farmly turns and waves with a big smile on his face. It's probably the most rebellious thing he has ever done in his life.

"Man, can you believe that cocksucker?" Smitty says.

I pause to look up out of the hole we're digging, "He'll get over it. We just have to wait a couple of weeks till he gets acclimated."

Jim is shaking his head in disagreement. "Naw, man, I don't think he's gonna come around, not unless something bad happens, that guy's got the 'I want to be a hero syndrome'."

"Yeah, maybe you're right." Fitzpatrick evidently thinks he is punishing us by assigning us to this detail. Six more bunkers are being built around the perimeter, so as usual, we're digging holes and filling sandbags. Hell, this is light duty, I'd much rather be doing this than be out laying wire with a big bull's eye painted to my ass. So far, he hasn't put any of us on shit burning detail, probably because he doesn't know about it yet or maybe because he wants to keep us away from those cans so we don't get any more ideas.

At 1600 hours we quit. Back at the barracks Farmly is getting ready to relieve Varant in the Crypto trailer.

"So what the fuck happened, man? What'd they do?" We're anxious to know because whatever happens to Farmly will have a big impact on how we act around Fitzpatrick.

"Neuman, just told me, and I quote, 'Son, you shouldn't talk disrespectful to any NCO in the army.' Tells me if I do it again I'll get an Article Fifteen, then sends me on my way. Fitzpatrick looked like he was gonna explode. I heard Neuman reading him the riot act as I walked away. When Fitzpatrick left 'Top's' office I heard Top yell after him, 'And another thing Fitzpatrick, you smell like shit!'"

It isn't a surprise that Fitzpatrick may not be welcomed into the fold by the other NCOs, they're a pretty tight knit group and being an NCO that hasn't come up through the ranks might nurture a little resentment.

After chow a few of us head over to club. Inside we find Pace, Bast, Neuman, and Sergeant Major Jackson sitting at a table playing dominoes. Sgt. Castle, an E-5, crew chief of one of the 105 Howitzer's is sitting by himself at another table and Fitzpatrick is sitting at the bar drinking some Black Label.

We ask Castle if we can join him.

"Sure, go ahead and sit."

Fitzpatrick glances in our direction then returns to his beer. He's still stewing.

"I'm Simon...this here's Varant and Big Jim Fishe. Should we call you Sergeant Castle?"

"No, name's Wendell, but everyone calls me Dell."

"What's the scoop, Dell, are you guys permanently attached to us or what?"

"Yeah, and we're glad of it. We spent the last six months being airlifted back and forth from one fire base to another. You know that means a lot of sleeping in holes, eating C rations and not being able to shower. Plus, a lot of them got pretty hairy. Outside of the shelling we had a couple of weeks ago it's been pretty quiet around here. That's the way I like it."

"Amen to that," I raise my glass everybody follows suit.

Fitzpatrick leaves several minutes later without acknowledging anybody in the club. Even though he's pissed it's down right rude to leave and not acknowledge the First Sergeant or Sergeant Major.

It's Thursday morning we're geared up and waiting outside the hooch. Fitzpatrick has been volunteering us for everything, so when Schoebert asked for someone to ride shotgun for some ARVN dump trucks, Fitzpatrick was Johnny on the spot. Ordinarily, we wouldn't have minded shotgun duty if it was for our engineers but these are ARVNs from the South Vietnamese army, hell, half of them could be VC.

Sergeant Fitzpatrick is running the show; that doesn't instill us with overwhelming confidence...he has zero experience.

"Fall in!" Fitzpatrick is still a tight ass trying to play Mr. West Point. "Okay, we're escorting a convoy of dump trucks to the quarry at Kontum. There are twelve trucks and I want two men in the back of each truck."

I raise my hand.

"Yes?"

"Uh, Sarge, why are we riding in the back of the trucks? Why don't we just take a couple of Jeeps and a couple of three-quarters for our guys? That's the way we normally do it."

"Because this is the way I want to do it...anything else?" Fitzpatrick has a small pack, who knows what he has in it. He has no flak jacket, is still wearing a lot of shiny brass, and actually has a helmet with E-6 stripes painted on the front and no camouflage cover.

"What a fucking bonehead," I whisper in Coleman's ear.

Coleman, who's been playing the "Stepin' Fetchit" routine with Fitzpatrick ever since he got here, drops the façade and asks, "Hey, Sarge, if you'd like, I could run over and get a flak jacket for you at the S-4 tent?"

"If I had wanted a flak jacket, I would have gotten one."

"Well how about some gog…" Fitzpatrick cuts Coleman off before he can finish saying goggles.

"Yeah, you're welcome," Coleman mumbles.

Outside the front gate the trucks are lined up along the road. Fitzpatrick is discussing details with an ARVN Sergeant. When they're done, we mount up and head northwest.

The gooks drive like assholes. They tail gate like crazy and the thought of me sailing a hundred feet through the air when this moron rear ends the truck in front is hard to keep out of my mind. A smart VC would only have to hit one of the front trucks and sit back and watch the rest of them pile up.

Just east of Kontum we turn off the black top and start down a dirt road. The road is dry and huge clouds of red dust enshroud the trucks. I cover my face with a wet kerchief and put on my goggles. At least the dust makes the trucks slow down.

Coleman jabs me in the side with his elbow and points. I look at the truck in front of us and barely make out Sergeant Fitzpatrick's silhouette, his arms are waving frantically, he's gagging and constantly turning away trying to get out of the dust. I smile underneath my kerchief, cup my hands up to Coleman's ear and say, "I'll bet the next time someone offers him some advice the prick will listen."

The trucks turn into the quarry amidst the large cloud of red dust. Two of the trucks in front can't stop in time and rear-end the trucks in front of them. Fortunately, the damage is minor. We dismount and start to stretch our legs. Being out in the open with little or no cover is very unsettling. A couple of large gravel hills, a large pit and some heavy machinery and a small shed are the only cover for three hundred yards in any direction.

Fitzpatrick is walking towards us coughing and hacking. His white skin has received its first dose of the red brown pigment that has long since toned most of our skins to an indefinable hue. He stops, turns around and goes back to talk to the ARVN Sergeant. A few minutes later a front loader starts filling the front truck.

Four trucks have been filled when we hear the first round come whistling down on us...Mortars! The first shell explodes forty or fifty yards short of the trucks.

Fitzpatrick yells, "Hit the dirt!" I dive headfirst under the bed of the truck; Coleman flies in from the other side.

Four more shells explode, one nearly hitting the front loader. Another round tears the rear wheels off the lead truck. Then, without warning, the trucks start pulling away, driving off in all directions. I scramble out from under our truck just as he starts to pull away.

"You mother fuckers!" I yell. I barely avoid getting crushed by the wheels and desperately grab at the driver's door but he pushes me off and accelerates.

"You fucking prick!" I bring my gun up, but don't fire. We're scrambling all over the place trying to get on the trucks, but the gooks won't stop.

Three more shells go off sending everyone to the ground, dirt and gravel raining down on us. The big gravel hill is about seventy-five yards away.

"*Let's go!*" I grab Coleman's arm and we spring to our feet sprinting for the hill as fast as our legs will carry us. Everyone else scrambles for the nearest cover. I slam into the gravel hill and roll around to the back.

"Man, those little cock-suckers are dead meat if I ever catch up with them!" I'm out of breath and scared shitless, mentally inventorying the faces of our group to see if anyone is missing.

"Anybody missin'?" I ask Jim as he slides around till he can see out around the pile of stone.

"Fuck!" Jim says with disgust, "Boneheads still out there." Sure enough, Sergeant Fitzpatrick is on the ground trying to crawl to our position.

"*Get up and run!*" We yell. Two more rounds detonate near the entrance of the quarry where the trucks are passing through the gate. One of them takes a hit. The mortar crews seem to be concentrating on the trucks, and so far, there isn't any ground fire.

Fitzpatrick glances around, starts to get up but goes back down when a mortar detonates a hundred yards away from him.

"Get up and run, asshole!" Jim yells.

"Fuck!" Coleman says as he sprints out to grab Fitzpatrick. He yanks on him, almost having to drag him because Fitzpatrick is resisting. Finally, he gets to his feet and follows Coleman. Coleman throws Fitzpatrick against the side of the stone hill as two mortar rounds hit the disabled truck at the gate and blow the shit out of it...then it goes quiet.

We've got to get the hell out of here. We're sitting ducks.

"The mortars have to be coming from that hill a half a click to the northwest," Fishe points. "They obviously have a pretty good view of the area, because they honed in on the trucks pretty accurately, maybe even got an observer calling the shots from right around here. Either way, they know we're out here with our dicks hangin' out so we better get the fuck outta here." Jim says to Fitzpatrick trying to encourage him into doing what we think is best.

Fitzpatrick, who was visually shaken a couple of minutes before, is regaining his composure and asks, "Where's the radio?" He realizes it was left in the back of one of the dump trucks, says, "Fuck! We should have come in our own vehicles, dammit!" I resist saying I told you so, but press the issue for getting out of here.

"Yeah, you guys are right…we've got to move out. How far back to Kontum?"

"About four or five miles...not too far to walk, but this area is usually thick with VC Sarge, it ain't gonna be like a forced march back at Fort Sill." Smitty isn't being sarcastic he just wants to make sure Fitzpatrick knows what's in store for us.

"The trucks are probably already in Kontum, once they alert their camp it will only be another five or ten minutes till the choppers come." Fitzpatrick is hesitating, more like thinking out loud. He isn't sure what to do.

"Sarge, if we don't get the fuck outta here the only thing that's gonna be comin' for us is a boatload of VC. We gotta go, and we gotta go now!" Fishe is in Fitzpatrick's face, his eyes glaring into Fitz's hoping Fitz will see there is no alternative.

"He's right, Sarge, if them gooks were worried about us, they wouldn't have left us here in the first place, they ain't comin' back. We gotta go." Fishe starts walking in the direction of the gate.

Fitzpatrick takes a quick glance around, looks at us then finally makes up his mind. "Okay, let's move out. Maybe we can flag down a Jeep or truck and get a radio call in to the hill."

"Yeah, keep dreamin'," I mumble.

We split up into two squads. Fishe and I get all the new meat. Fitzpatrick graciously lets Coleman take point, their squad moving down the left side of the road along the shoulder. We lag about twenty yards behind on the right shoulder. I take cleanup because we have most of the new guys, and I don't want any VC movin' up behind us.

Coleman stretches the distance between him and his squad to about thirty yards. We move at a rapid pace and are forced back on the road several times when we can't get through the heavy brush along the shoulder. No one has a burning desire to go exploring deeper into the bush.

The first two miles go pretty quickly, but I can tell the new guys are startin' to drag because our squad keeps bunching up.

"Jim, if we don't take a break we're gonna be carrying these guys to Kontum, see if you can get Coleman to take a five minute break." I go back to my position at the rear of the squad. I stop and take a long ponderous look at everything behind us, looking for any telltale signs of pursuit. There are no dust clouds or birds being spooked into flight, no animal shrieks warning other animals of a human intrusion. One last look and I turn to catch up to the squad.

The first squad stops. Jim says, "Okay, we're taking five." I take the opportunity to go over some basic hand signals with the new guys.

The five minutes pass quickly and we're on the move again. As Kontum gets nearer the bush thins out considerably. This gives us a little better command of our surroundings and reduces the possibility for an ambush. Our predicament seems a little less precarious.

Once we reach the blacktop the grade changes; it'll be slightly downhill the rest of the way to Kontum, we can actually see the city off in the distance. There are vehicles on the blacktop; none are American, but vehicles none-the-less.

The first contact with civilization is two Vietnamese hooches just off the road. The squads take up a defensive posture and Coleman, Lindlay and Smitty approach the hooches cautiously. Smitty and Lindlay flank the doorway and Coleman slides up next to the door, with his back to the wall. He bangs loudly on the door with the butt of his rifle, then crouches down and backs away. After a minute or so, Coleman very, very, slowly pushes the latch handle on the door and swings it open. Coleman and Smitty disappear into the hooch for several seconds then emerge and head for the second hooch. This time the door is opened by an elderly Vietnamese woman. She is alone and protests vehemently against Coleman's invasion of her hooch, but he goes in and checks it out anyway. Fifteen minutes later we're closing in on Kontum. We continue to flank both sides of the road and pass several more hooches. They're not searched so we're all the more wary of what's behind us.

As we near Kontum several vehicles pass, a couple of Lambrettas, a broken-down-chunk-of-shit car, and a rickety old pick up. We try to flag them down but none of them stop. As we enter the streets of the city we stop to confer.

Jim says, "When we get into the town be very wary Sarge it's not an open city and there are sure to be VC."

Coleman turns and points off in the direction of Little Lava and says, "There are a couple of fire bases about ten miles west of the town if we get lucky we might run into some American traffic."

"Why can't we just phone someone?" Fitzpatrick asks with a look of bewilderment.

"It's not like there's a phone booth on every corner. Civilian lines into our bases are almost non-existent. Even if we can find one, anybody here know the number?" Jim is intentionally being sarcastic.

"Couldn't we get the operator to..."

"Oh, sorry, Sarge, I didn't realize you could speak boing-boing."

"Boing-boing?" Fitzpatrick asks.

Jim says, "Yeah, Vietnamese."

"Oh," Fitzpatrick says with a look of understanding.

Jim goes on, "Our best hope is to get to the QC station, hope they're not VC and get them to let us use their radio.

"QC?" Again Fitzpatrick looks puzzled.

"Police," three of us answer simultaneously.

Fitzpatrick shakes his head, makes a motion with his arm and we move into the city. We move down the street on both sides. Twice Coleman stops someone and asks for QC, both times getting incoherent rambling and a lot of pointing as a response. We hope we're moving in the right direction.

As we move around a corner, fate, for a change, decides to smile on us. Sitting unattended in front of a local bar are five of the dump trucks that left us to die back at the quarry. The ARVN Sergeant, the same guy Fitzpatrick had talked with back at the hill, is standing next to a truck talking to a hooker and drinking a beer.

"Well I'll be a mother fucker!" Coleman says, "It's payback time!"

Fitzpatrick has the same idea...you can see it in his eyes. "Let's go," he says moving briskly towards the ARVN Sergeant. He walks right up behind him, the hooker's eyes lock in on Fitzpatrick and she smiles, the gook turns to see what she's smiling at just in time to receive a nose crushing right that knocks him to the ground. He gets up on one elbow cupping his other hand over his nose, then, looking up at Fitz he starts yelling Vietnamese obscenities with blood pouring from his mouth and nose. Fitz reaches down to pick him up and the gook starts swinging wildly, so Fitz pummels him with a few more shots to the face.

"You mother fucker, I'm gonna beat you till can't fucking walk," Fitzpatrick wails.

The other drivers charge out of the bar with the intention of interceding, but we're waiting for them. We knock a couple of them on their asses before they make it two steps out of the bar. Jim pulls out his thirty-eight, sticks it in one of their faces and makes it clear it'll be better for them to stay on the ground.

"Let's go, we're getting' out of here," Fitzpatrick says.

"What about the QC radio?" Lindlay asks.

"Fuck the radio, we came here in those trucks and we're goin' back in 'em."

"Fuckin' ay, baby, let's go!" Jim yells. We're worked up nearly to a point of frenzy; we want our pound of flesh. Jim grabs one of the drivers by the neck and stands him up. He sticks his gun under his chin and says, "Strip! Get out of those fucking clothes." He starts pulling off the gook's clothes to get his point across. The others are stood up and stripped. Once they're all naked we toss their clothes into the back of a truck. We tie all their ankles together and rip the spark plug wires out of the other trucks. We pile into the rear of the truck with the clothes and Coleman gets behind the wheel. We pull away yelling obscenities and igniting the clothing with our cigarette lighters. As we toss the burning cloths over the side of the truck I yell, "Sin Loi you little bastards," and give 'em the high sign as we pull away. They're left standing naked in the middle of the street.

We're standing at attention in front of the orderly room. We've been back at the hill for less than twenty minutes. Fitzpatrick hasn't even had time to report to Jackson yet. They were waiting for us when we pulled through the gate, Colonel Schoebert, Sergeant Major Jackson, Sergeant Neuman and some ARVN officer. By the looks of the scowl on the ARVN's face it's easy to see he's pissed off.

"Sergeant Fitzpatrick this is Colonel Hue (way)." Schoebert sort of nods his head in Hue's direction. "Colonel Hue claims you and your men hijacked one of his trucks after severely beating one of his men. He also says that all the clothes and weapons from several of his other men were taken by you and set on fire...is this true, Sergeant Fitzpatrick?"

"Yes, Sir!" Fitzpatrick says point blank. He makes no attempt to elaborate.

Colonel Hue starts chattering like a wounded chicken, Schoebert the target of the bantering. "You see, you see, my men have been disgraced by these gangsters. I cannot let this matter pass. I will have to bring the details of this incident up to the authorities at II Corps and recommend criminal prosecution." Hue, feeling he has the upper hand is trying to lord himself over Schoebert. Schoebert is at a loss and doesn't know how to respond.

"Sergeant Fitzpatrick," Sergeant Major Jackson interrupts Hue's tirade.

"Yes, Sergeant Major?" Fitz waits.

"Would you mind telling me the circumstances that led up to the incident that compelled you to steal a truck and beat Colonel Hue's men?"

"Sergeant Major, Colonel Hue's men deserted us when we came under enemy fire and left us for dead in a hostile area with no communication equipment or any recourse for getting assistance, I would add that even when Colonel Hue's men made it to the safety of Kontum they made no effort to notify anybody we had been stranded back at the quarry." Fitz, still at attention, peers directly into Hue's eyes.

Jackson urges him to continue. "Anything else Sergeant Fitzpatrick?"

"Yes, Sergeant Major. An outside observer might even conclude that the way things transpired it might seem as if Colonel Hue's men intentionally led us into a VC ambush and deserted us. I'm sure, given all the facts, G-2 might conclude that whoever arranged this excursion might well be in league with the VC." With a look of smugness Fitz adds, "I welcome an investigation by II Corps."

Jackson turns to Schoebert and just says, "Sir?"

The worm has definitely turned. Schoebert is on Hue like stink on shit. "Colonel Hue, I will be launching an immediate investigation into this matter! Let us hope that I do not find any complicity on your part in this incident." Schoebert is huffing and puffing and is so worked up his face is red as a beet. I think he's only moments away from grabbing Hue by the throat. Hue, who is about five feet two compared to Schoebert's six feet four, is cowering like a five-year-old caught with his hand in the cookie jar.

"My apologies Colonel Schoebert; I apologize to your men for the behavior of my people. I assure you an external investigation will be unnecessary; everybody involved will be severely disciplined. Again, I apologize."

"Colonel Hue, I think you better take your truck and get the hell off my hill." Schoebert turns his back to Hue and walks away. Hue turns, gives us a short quick half-bow and walks back to his waiting driver.

Jackson looks at Fitz and says, "Sergeant, I want a written detailed report from you and your squad leaders within the hour."

After Jackson leaves, Fitzpatrick dismisses everybody but Fishe, Coleman and me. "Okay, look, maybe we didn't get off to such a good start but never let it be said I'm not a quick learner."

Chapter Fifteen

"Thanks for the Dysentery"

One thirty-four and a wake up. We've been bustin' our nuts all week. Twice we've had to chopper north somewhere around Doc To, a very *Hot* area. The Fourth Division and the 101st Airborne are conducting operations in the area. Charlie Battery has a fire base near Ben Het that gives them the ability to support the entire area. So we've been stringing wire from Charlie Battery all over the damn place.

President Johnson, Secretary of Defense Robert McNamara and the military tacticians have revealed their master plan to save South Vietnam from communist insurgence. The plan relies on setting up a picket line of fire bases across the DMZ and down the Cambodian and Laotian borders that will stem the flow of North Vietnamese troops and weapons into the south. I'm only nineteen but I have enough brains to realize this means we're going to need a hell of a lot of troops to man all those fire bases. President Johnson, according to the "Stars and Stripes," is quoted as saying the number of American troops in Vietnam will grow to over four hundred thousand. If this is true, I suspect Americans are going to be in Vietnam for a long time. Even if the communist flow into the south is stopped, the Vietcong, who are principally South Vietnamese, will continue their guerrilla tactics for years, just like they did with the French. So our presence will surely depend on how well the South Vietnamese Army can contend with the Vietcong. So far, their track record hasn't been that good.

It's Saturday morning and we're back at the hill. For a change, we actually have a whole day off.

Smitty runs into the hooch buzzing with nervous excitement.

"Cease-fire! Cease-fire!" He chatters over and over.

"What the hell you talking about?" Jim asks.

"They're calling a cease fire for the holidays."

"What, what did you say?" Smitty's announcement has captured Farmly's interest.

"Word is an order came down from MACV, all offensive action has been put on hold and we can only fire weapons in defense."

"Sounds to me like Varant has been reading Schoebert's mail again." This is an easy conclusion to make since he's the source of almost all the information on the grapevine.

Just as predicted, a couple of hours later Sergeant Neuman and Sergeant Fitzpatrick announce the cease-fire to the hill confirming Smitty's information.

Sgt. Castle shakes his head, and comments, "Don't get too excited." The disconcerted look on his face gets everyone's attention.

"What's eatin' you, man?" What's eatin' him? Hell, how can you be upset about a cease-fire?

"These cease-fires suck. Look, just think of two groups of kids having a snowball fight. The only way to win is to try to make the other side use up all their snowballs. When they run out, you can move in and pelt the living shit out of them, right? If you stop and let them re-supply every time they run out nobody's ever gonna win and the snowball fight will go on forever."

Kind of a bad analogy…who the hell ever wins a snowball fight?

"The last time we had a cease-fire it just gave the gooks a chance to stockpile and bolster their forces. Once they were ready they launched a huge attack at Buon Me Thout. We kicked their ass but it took three days and we had a lot of casualties. These damn cease-fires have never been very good for the Americans."

I stare at Castle with a blank look on my face. Am I reading him right? Is he saying we're probably gonna get a couple of weeks off from the war, but when it starts back up, it's gonna be worse? We don't know the reason for the cease-fire and after listening to Castle we're leery of what lies ahead. Even so, the prospect of even going a couple of weeks without hostilities is a pleasant thought and I, for one, intend to focus on the positive aspect of the situation.

Tuesday night is movie night. A sheet is hung on the side of the chapel and the movies are projected on it. Sitting on the side of the hill looking down, makes a nice little amphitheater for viewing the films. The playbill for the evening will be "Gunsmoke" and "Combat."

Walking by the chapel I momentarily have a flash of guilt. Okay, God, I know, I know…Okay, Bozo, you make it over here for the movies, but not for the services. Okay, Okay, I'll get to the service once in awhile. Being so near Thanksgiving, and hoping the cease-fire will last, the Catholic in me makes me feel like I should be on my knees giving thanks. It's the deep-seeded Catholic guilt complex fed and nurtured expertly by the nuns in parochial school and continually reinforced by several whacks from "The Board of Education," as the nuns called it. I mention my thoughts to Varant.

Varant looks inquisitive, then says, "Jesus, Simon, I never had you pegged as a Holy Roller."

"Holy roller...yeah, right. Shit, I'm a terrible Catholic. I was so bad, when I was in school, I used to wonder what some of the nuns looked like naked. How sick is that? In fifth grade I was an altar boy, not because I was devoted, but so I could swipe quarters out of the collection basket. They kicked me out when I got caught cheating on a test."

"*You* an alter boy? Wow, that *is* hard to believe, although that bit about getting' kicked off for cheatin', I can see that happening." Varant laughs.

Once we settle in for the movies Varant begins milking a fifth of Vietnamese whiskey. I know the stuff tastes hideous, it is the most rancid crap I've ever put in my mouth. There's a half-an-inch of sediment on the bottom of the bottle. Varant is downing the stuff like it's Kool-Aid.

The episode of "Combat" draws the usual heckling from the mass of men sitting on the side of the hill. Vic Morrow is arguing with one of his men over the fate of a captured German soldier. Morrow, the platoon Sergeant, wants to take the prisoner back for questioning, but his men want to kill him in retribution for the death of one of their pals.

"*Come on ya pussy, shoot the Heimie,*" Someone yells from the crowd. "*Yeah, quit fuckin' around and snuff the bastard,*" someone else adds. It almost seems like these guys actually believe the characters on the screen can hear them. In reality, I know they're really yelling to vent their own frustrations.

"What a bunnnch of pushies." Varant slobbers out the words. The man is wasted, totally smashed. "Man, this is bullshit! Da bashturds that make this crap up don't know anything about real war." Varant's downed over half the bottle of whiskey in less than an hour.

Whether he's right or not, I'm pretty confident no one in this group really wants to see a realistic depiction of war on the screen. I'm glad when the episode ends. I prefer "Gunsmoke" anyway. How could a man not like "Gunsmoke?" It has everything men want to see: A manly good guy, who has no apparent vices; who's respected by everyone. The good guys always win, the bad guys always lose and there's always some good looking babe working for Miss Kitty, and even though they don't show it, we all know Matt is pluggin' Miss Kitty on a regular basis. He has a loyal sidekick, a doctor who still makes house calls, and a nice little office I presume he lives in, as I have no memory of ever seeing his ranch or a house. He never seems to have any problems of conscience because he always does what's right. He's not above bending the law as long as justice is served. "Gunsmoke" is definitely more to my liking. I don't need any flashes of reality - I see enough of those every stinkin' day. Quite out of the ordinary, both episodes play flawlessly without any projector failures. Normally, the film breaks or melts at least two or three times.

The fifth of whiskey is gone; right now the entire contents must be sloshing around in Varant's head. He's talking gibberish and the prick is having trouble standing up.

"Shit, man, this guy must weigh two hundred pounds." Fishe and I are trying to lift Varant up and help him back to the hooch.

"Come on dick-breath, at least *try* to stand up, would ya." Varant is not co-operating and he is babbling and talking nonsense. Then he starts sobbing.

Coleman sees him sobbing and rolls his eyes, "Aw Jeez, here we go."

"So hoisht up the Johns bees shails, she how da main shail sets …" Varant is trying to sing "The Sloop John B." by the Beach Boys.

"Hey, letch schtop at the club for shum beers."

"No way, man, you're too fucked up already." I can't believe he wants something else to drink.

We drop Varant on his cot and he immediately passes out.

"Man, what a bonehead." I grab a six-pack from the stash and go out to sit with the guys.

"Got a light, my lighter's dry?" I ask as I pull a Marlboro out of the pack with my lips. I am beginning to like the filters. At first I thought they were "weak." Now, I prefer them over the Pall Malls.

"Hey, looky here!" Townsend comes out the door with a CO_2 fire extinguisher.

"Where'd you get that man?" Fishe asks. We have long since emptied every fire extinguisher on the hill, all being sacrificed in the name of cold beer.

"I was over at PAB today and swiped it out of an Air force Jeep." Townsend pulls the pin and directs the icy stream of CO_2 over the six-pack of beer.

"Hey, not too bad." Though, it isn't cold, it isn't warm. We sit, smokin' and drinking with Townsend plucking away at his guitar. After a minute or two we recognize the tune he's playin' and Townsend starts singing the words: "Last night I went to sleep in Detroit City…" It makes Fishe ecstatic. When they get to the chorus we join in…"I wanna go home…I wanna go home…Oh, how I wan...na go home."

We sit around enjoying the small dose of melancholy for about an hour or so, then decide to call it a night.

Inside, we find Varant sitting on the floor leaning against his cot with another bottle of bad whiskey in his hand.

"Jeez, this guy is totally fucked," Coleman says. Typically, he isn't very tolerant of people with little or no self-control. I think it has something to do with his karate mojo tojo crap.

He bends down and tries to lift Varant up. Unexpectedly, he lets Varant go and pulls back. Then, in a panic, he rips open Hal's shirt and puts his ear against his chest.

"Get the medics! Get the medics! He ain't breathin'!" The panicked look on Coleman's face convinces us that Hal is in big trouble. I kneel down next to Varant and listen for a heart beat. I can't hear one either. I stick two fingers up under the back of his jaw trying to feel a pulse. *Jesus, Coleman is right…his heart has stopped.* Townsend took off running for the medics immediately and is already running back. The ambulance is coming down the road. We're at a loss. The only training we've ever received is how to put on a field dressing and how to jam an atropine syringe into someone's thigh.

A medic kneels down and tries to take Varant's pulse. "Fuck!"…He pulls out a hypodermic, fills it from a small bottle and injects it into Varant's arm. Then he bends over and places the heel of his hand against Varant's breastbone, he puts his other hand over it and with his arms locked at the elbows and he starts making hard jerky compressions against Varant's chest. After about ten compressions, the medic stops and again listens to Varant's heart.

"I got a beat, I got a beat. How much did this jerk have to drink?" The medic looks at us waiting for a reply.

"I'd have to guess over a fifth of Vietnamese whiskey." Fishe replies.

"When're you fuckin' jerks gonna learn?" The medic sticks an IV into Varant's arm; the other medic lays a stretcher next to him.

"Okay, on three. Ready? One... two...three, *Lift!"* Varant is laid on the stretcher and loaded into the back of the ambulance then rushed over to the hospital at Pleiku Airbase.

"Jesus Christ! What the fuck got into Varant, Jesus!" I can't believe the guy almost drank himself to death. Farmly came down from the Crypto trailer while the medics were trying to revive Varant, he says Varant has been upset all day mumbling something about his girlfriend. Hell, none of us even knew he had a girlfriend.

Farmly starts rifling through Varant's footlocker and finds some letters. He carefully checks the dates on the postmark. "Here, this is the one." He pulls the letter out of the envelope and starts reading it. "Damn, no wonder he's upset. It's a 'Dear John letter, his fiancé dumped him for someone else."

"What...a...fucking...bitch! Why the hell didn't she wait till he got back, hell, he's a fucking short-timer," I mumble.

"Man, that's cold. That is really cold." Coleman is shaking his head. "Sometimes I wonder about you white people."

Tuesday afternoon Fitzpatrick sends Fishe and I over to MACV to pick up Hal. He's waiting for us just inside the sick-call tent at the hospital unit; he looks like shit. He's wearing only a tee shirt and vomit soaked trousers. His eyes are sunken with huge black circles around them and his normally cherubic face is as pale as his lily white ass. We have to help him into the Jeep because he's weak and shaking badly.

"Shit, man, you got the shakes?" I ask as I help him into the Jeep.

"No, man, I'm freezing my ass off!" Varant responds.

"Freezing?" It's about eighty degrees.

"Yeah, I think my blood is a little too thin today."

"Well, that's no fucking surprise." I hop into the driver's seat.

Jim, curious to what medical wonders they performed to save him, asks the highly probing question, "So what did they do to you?"

"They pumped my stomach, or at least they tried. As soon as they started shoving that tube down my throat I launched! God, I hurled vomit all over the damn place. It was so bad the doctors and nurses were cursing me." Varant actually smiles. We decided we wouldn't let on that we know anything about his situation, if he tells us, fine. If he doesn't that'll be okay too.

Thursday we get the turkey roll, dressing, yams, mashed potatoes, beans and pumpkin pie. Everything is pretty damn good for a change. In the morning I sneak off to the chapel and attend the Thanksgiving service. I'm surprised to see about forty or fifty guys there, including Lindlay and Farmly. The service is generically Christian, but it isn't the Catholic mass I'm used to. The Chaplain is a Catholic priest and administers general absolution during the mass, then serves communion to those of us who are Catholic. When I leave I feel better about myself.

Saturday morning Fitzpatrick comes by and gives us news that brings smiles to everyone in the barracks. Bob Hope is putting on his Christmas show over at the Fourth Division Base camp and amazingly, our unit has been picked to sit ringside and protect the stage. I can't help but think this is some sort of reward for having gone to church on Thursday. I turn my head to the sky and say, "Thank you, God!"

The 4th division has managed to build a really good stage facing a couple of small hills so that it forms a natural amphitheater. The Bob Hope band, "Les Brown and his Band of Renown," are already setting up. Captain Solomon and Sergeant Fitzpatrick disperse us around the north side of the stage; our instructions are simple, no one gets up on the stage.

Over the next hour the side of the hill is slowly covered by thousands of anxious men. Twelve Gunships continuously circle the area and I'm sure there are a couple of dozen heavy patrols out making sure the VC aren't going to break the cease fire by trying to bag Bob Hope.

"Thanks for the Memories," begins playing and Bob Hope strolls out from behind the curtain. The hill erupts in a thunderous roar, the throbbing mass of men covering the hill goes berserk. Bob doesn't even get to say anything for about ten minutes. Finally, the crowd quiets and Bob starts shooting out the one-liners. He's dressed in golf slacks and is wearing a jungle fatigue blouse. He's carrying what looks like a three wood and it never leaves his hand. He keeps the crowd laughing with shots at our upper echelon and a couple of slightly off color jokes about some of the bar girls in Vietnam. He follows with several jokes about Ho Chi Minh.

Next, to the delight of everyone, Bob brings out Joey Heatherton. The howling from our guys is so loud I wouldn't be surprised if they hear it in Los Angeles. Joey is dressed in a super-mini-sequined dress cut so low her breasts are almost falling out. While she sings and dances there are a couple of times the material pulls away from her body and anyone with a side angle gets a momentary flash. She knows it and does nothing to stop it from happening. She gets some poor schmo from the 4th Division up on stage and drapes herself all over him. She's singing and blowing in his ear, stroking her arms all around his neck and chest and running her free hand through his hair. The guy is creaming in his pants. The poor bastard looks like he's going to pass out. Anyone who's ever been in the service knows military clothing never fits very well and is usually a bit on the baggy side. This is especially true of jungle fatigues. It becomes very obvious that Miss Heatherton is having a very noticeable effect on this guy. The front of his pants looks like he's pitched a tent big enough to house his whole platoon. He has a huge boner and everybody can see it. The sight of it brings roars. Joey looks down, smiles, and gives the troops a devilish look. When she finishes she gives the guy a full contact fifteen-second smack on the lips and sends him off the stage. I'm guessing the guy is gonna head directly to the john for some serious whacking off. The troops roar for another ten minutes.

The next act is three little Japanese dancers who are also dressed in revealing outfits. They dance and sing a couple of numbers and once again draw the roars from the crowd of drooling GIs.

A few more jokes from Bob and he brings out Miss World...Oh my god, is this babe stacked! I think Bob says she's from India, but it's hard to hear with the crowd roaring. She doesn't sing or dance, but assists Bob in a stand-up routine. He asks her questions that are just set-ups for his jokes; she does an excellent job playing straight man for Bob. I'm really surprised, I hadn't expected him to be this funny, but he's great.

Next he brings out a couple of Playboy Bunnies; they are bra-less in tight shorts and cut off tee shirts. Bob grills them about life in the Playboy Mansion and pokes fun at Hugh Hefner. The girls sing and strut around the stage responding to all the hooting and catcalling of the mesmerized GIs. After a couple of minutes of watching those mounds of quivering flesh bounce around, I figure about ten thousand chickens are going to get choked tonight. Every male on this hill will hit the sack with a smile on his face.

For the finale, Bob brings everyone back out on stage one by one to the applause of the grateful crowd. He thanks them, thanks us and all the cast joins in with Bob to sing, "Thanks for the Memories." When they finish, the two Bunnies stand on the edge of the stage tossing out autographed Playboy tee shirts. Before they toss them, they add a big lipstick stain to each one. We're getting mobbed. We're trying to keep guys from climbing on stage, having to physically pull them down. As the mob pushes me back up against the stage and I wrestle to keep from getting crushed...I look up. Directly over my head, Miss June is leaning out past the edge of the stage shaking hands and tossing shirts. I can see right up underneath her tee shirt. There before me, are the two unencumbered quivering mounds of flesh that have the ability to hypnotize any red-blooded American male. It's a magnificent sight... they're in full view, it's like looking at an American institution like Mount Rushmore, only better. *These mounds have probably been looked at by more men in one month, than any national monument in a year.* I just stare. My mouth open and drool running down the side of my chin. My eyes glaze over and I stand there frozen, oblivious to the mass of men trying to get as close as they can. Then, with out warning, she reaches down, looks me right in the eye, smiles, and gently runs her hand up the side of my face and winks. The only sensation my mind is processing is the caress of her soft fingertips. I know it's something I will remember forever.

A chopper behind the stage begins cranking up its engines and three minutes later they are gone.

"Man, this guy's been struck by lightning." Coleman is talking to Fishe and mocking the distant look in my eyes.

Jim replies. "My friend, I think the man's in love."

I can still smell the perfume she had on her hand. On the way back to Pleiku I sit in the back of the truck in a stupor, the vision of her naked breasts still as fresh in my mind as the actual sighting. I imagine what they must feel like, and I can feel seminal fluid oozing out of my manhood.

It's Wednesday. I check into the medical tent for sick call for the first time since coming to this god-awful place. The medic pulls my chart and looks through it asking what the problem is.

"I've had the shits since Thanksgiving. I need something to plug me up."

"Have you been eating?" He's looking in my ear with one of those lights.

"Man, every time I eat I get sick to my stomach and ten minutes later I'm in the shitter."

"Well, I think I'm gonna have to send you over to the hospital at MACV. Here take this they'll need a stool sample." He hands me a little paper cup with a lid.

I do the best I can for the sample considering nothing solid was coming out. At MACV they take the sample, check my vitals and have me lie on a cot till they get lab results. Jeez, it takes about two hours.

"It appears you have dysentery son." The doctor says as he looks at the results. Your weight is down about twelve pounds since you were here with the eye wound. That's not a good sign." He pauses for a moment and gives the nurse some instructions. "I should keep you here for a few days for observation, but we don't have the beds to do that. I'm putting you on bed rest for a couple of weeks. The nurse here has some medication for you and no matter how bad you feel, you drink at least two full canteens of water every day and stay away from alcohol, that's an order. You read me?"

"Yes, sir, I read you."

Four days of bed rest and I don't feel like I'm making any progress. I have the trots, maybe even worse than before, certainly not any better. I'm weak and at times have trouble getting out of the sack to go to the shithouse. I sleep all day and I sleep all night. I don't get up to go to the mess hall and the guys are trying to force feed me C rations.

It's been ten days, I'm still weak, but today is the first time in a week I actually get out of my cot for something other than going to the shithouse. My hands are shaking and my mouth is dry. I drag myself outside to the shower on wobbly legs having to stop a couple of times to hold myself up. I smell pretty rank and I know it. I haven't showered since I came back from MACV. Its been ten days of being in and out of a semi-waking confused state of consciousness. Today, though, my mind is clear. Though, I'm still weak, I feel a lot better than I've felt in quite awhile.

The shower water is still warm. I shave without a mirror standing under the running water. Once I'm dressed I get Pinetti to drive me up to the medics' tent so I can get more medication. According to them, I'm suffering from dysentery and a bad case of gastritis, whatever the hell that is.

Everybody is glad to see me up and about. At dinnertime, I make it to the mess hall to eat my first solid meal since getting sick…I know I am on the road to recovery.

Later, lying in my cot, waiting to see if my dinner stays down, I'm startled by the roar of the Howitzers on the other side of the hill. All three guns are alive and airmailing their special brand of death to an unseen force fifteen or twenty miles from here. I watch the dust fall from the ceiling each time one of the big guns shoots, when it does, the entire building shakes. As the fire mission continues, I sigh and mumble, "Well, so much for the cease-fire."

CHAPTER SIXTEEN

"IT NEVER SNOWS IN THE JUNGLE"

December 8th...One fifteen and a wake up. It's hot...really hot, especially, for this time of year. Sweat is pouring out of every pore on my body, saturating my fatigues, my tee shirt and my skivvies. The sweat collects on my spine and runs down the crack of my ass, a really uncomfortable feeling. My feet wouldn't be any wetter if I'd spent the last twenty minutes standing in the surf at China beach. For three hours we've been hacking our way up this small mountain through some of the heaviest bush I've ever seen. I guess it's a mountain, maybe just a big hill, I don't know how to tell the difference.

The machete is getting heavy, so heavy it feels like I'm wielding a sledge. I stop for a moment and look at the palm of my left hand. Two large blisters have blossomed; they'll serve as a subtle reminder to use gloves the next time I have to hack through this shit. The largest, on the heel of my hand, is torn and burns like hell.

Lindlay and Fishe are laboring with a reel of wire behind me. The wire strung along the ground is camouflaged using leaves and plants. The rest of the squad is providing cover and humping the extra equipment.

We're southwest of Dak To; the 4th Infantry has a mortar battery on the top of this hill that commands a significant area around the hill and can provide cover for our fire base and a camp the 4th is operating somewhere on the other side of the hill. A mortar battery on top of a hill has a significant strategic advantage, the elevated position actually extends the range capabilities and being situated in the middle of three different units allows them to closely support all of them.

Vietcong activity has been heavy in the Dak To and Ben Het area. All the activity has sparked an escalation of U.S. forces and the construction of several camps, LZs, and fire bases.

Landlines are a necessity for conducting everyday business and keeping the airwaves open for tactical communications. They're also a good back up when radio communications breakdown. Radio reliability can be affected by the weather or by terrain. Operating around these hills and mountains can seriously hamper radio communications. Hell, sometimes the transmissions get crappy if the wind is blowing the wrong way.

My arms feel as if they're made of lead. I signal for a five-minute break, flop down and guzzle water from my canteen. I take off my helmet and run my hand through my hair. It's as if I'd just stepped out of the shower. I pull off the headband and wring it out, then wipe my face and neck and wring it out again. Laying the wire is bad enough, throw on a flak jacket, pack, pistol belt, helmet, a rifle and about a dozen magazines, it's like climbing up this mountain carrying a dead mule. I don't know who has it worse, me hacking away at this shit all day, or the poor guys lugging those fifty-pound reels of wire. The job isn't made any easier knowing the hills are crawling with VC. Running into a VC patrol would be catastrophic. *I can just see hacking my way up through this shit and running into a VC patrol hacking their way down. Okay, okay, so maybe it's a million to one shot.* I convince myself the possibility of this happening is remote, however, I can't convince myself it's impossible. In a sense, it's probably good that I don't. The seed of fear will help keep me a little sharper.

We need to keep moving. Fitzpatrick isn't pushing and our only deadline is to get up to that mortar battery before dark because none of us want to be out here slugging our way through this crap at night.

"Yo, Simon, you want me to take point for awhile?" Coleman kneels next to me and takes the machete before I can answer.

"Yeah, thanks man, I'm not sure my hands can take much more of this." I hand the machete and scabbard to Coleman and a few minutes later we're back on our feet forcing ourselves up the hill. I drop back behind Fitzpatrick and take the rear cover position. Fitzpatrick has become a little more comfortable trusting our instincts and experience. Maybe, because he now trusts us, most of us have begun to trust him. He was right when he said, "He was a fast learner."

The sun is getting ready to set and Coleman has been hacking away for about an hour and a half. We're down to our last reel of wire and near the top of the hill. The Jungle thins, there aren't many trees, but the brush is as bad if not worse.

Coleman breaks out of the bush into a defoliated clearing, his arm goes up and we stop. We move up behind him and can see the perimeter of the mortar battery. Coleman signals Fitzpatrick and he grabs the radio mike from Frenchy's back.

"Rocket, Rocket, this is Smasher, over."

"Roger, Smasher, this is Rocket, go ahead, over."

"Rocket, be advised, I'm bringing in a squad of men and some commo to your position, over."

"Roger, Smasher, bring your men in, over."

"Roger, that, Smasher, out."

Fitzpatrick gives the signal and we move out of the bush. The perimeter is heavily fortified with a machine gun bunker about ever twenty feet. Two layers of Claymores are staggered just inside the wire and set about five yards apart. There looks to be a large contingent of support troops defending the fire base. Being on the top of the hill gives them a strategic advantage if there is an assault.

The wire is brought in through the perimeter; we break out the trenching tools and bury the visible sections of wire. We didn't bury the wire coming up the hill, the trail we hacked through the bush will be completely overgrown in a few days leaving little evidence that anybody had ever passed that way. We finish up by running the wire into the fire control bunker. We ring up Bravo Battery for a commo check and let them know we're stuck for the night.

The mortar battery is a relatively mobile unit that moves around a lot. Unfortunately, for us, they don't take the time to erect hooches or anything that smacks of permanency. Most of these guys are sleeping in tents or holes in the ground…just like we'll be doing tonight. We break up into teams of two and set about digging foxholes, by the time we're done it's close to nine...we're spent.

The night brings cool air; the sky is overcast making the darkness even darker. Fishe and I, both dead tired, share a foxhole. Just before we crash for the night, we watch two squads of infantry head out on ambush patrol.

"What the…?" I open my eyes groggily wondering what the hell is interrupting the sleep I want so desperately. *It's raining.*

"Damn it!" I mumble. I dig out the poncho from my pack. Surprisingly, the rain has not stirred Jim. I grab his pack to remove his poncho. I manage to spread them over the hole and anchor them with some sandbags. I lean back against the dirt wall and close my eyes. The chatter of the rain against the ponchos is hypnotic. The tic...tic...tic of the rain drops sing to me, it muffles the other noises that might keep me awake and lulls me back to sleep.

Whump, Whump! Whump! Whump! The sound the mortar tubes make discharging their rockets is louder than I imagined. I push the poncho cover out of the way and stick my head out of the hole. The pool of water that's collected on top runs off and splashes down the front of my fatigues. *"Damn it!"*

The bustle of activity around the camp is barely visible. The only illumination comes from the red flashlights used by the mortar crews. The momentary flashes made as each rocket is launched momentarily lights up the camp with an eerie, psychedelic, strobe light effect.

I look at my watch…Jesus, it's three o'clock.

Muffled voices respond to instructions coming from the operations bunker. The fire mission is surprisingly short lived. A salvo is fired; corrections are called in, then another salvo, another correction and finally five or six continuous salvos for effect. They pack it up and the camp is dark again.

I slide back into the hole and light a cigarette. *Who the hell is out there operating at three in the morning?* Then I remember the two ambush patrols…I wonder if it's them.

An open can of barbecue beef sits on a pile of stones with a Sterno tablet slowly heating the contents. I squat over the can waiting for the chunks of grease to melt away, a good indication the contents of the can are warm enough and actually edible. Jim's just taken a whore's bath out of his helmet and is lathering up for a cold water shave. Coleman on the other hand is using that crap he puts on his face to dissolve his beard before he scrapes it off.

The contents of my delicious breakfast begin sizzling in the can.

"Man, I just love eatin' barbecue beef for breakfast." I shake my head as I contemplate the prospect of enjoying such a tasty entrée for breakfast.

"Hey, it's better than this crap." Lindlay points at his can of ham and lima beans. "At least you can eat that stuff when it's heated up."

"Yeah, Bast has been kind to us for the past couple of months." I smile, knowing that till Bast rotates we'll continue getting the royal treatment.

Fitzpatrick looks up from his box of C rations and says, "Yeah, I've heard complaints from other guys about Bast always stealing the cigarettes and Sterno tablets from the C rations how come he treats us so good?"

"It's a long story that we're not at liberty to divulge, Sarge." He lets it pass realizing he probably doesn't want to know.

At eight we set out. We expect our descent to be easier if only for the reason our load is about two hundred pounds lighter. Fitz decided we should take the access road down the opposite side of the hill into the valley where the 4th Infantry has their fire base. Once there, we can grab a ride back around the mountain to Bravo Battery. It's a logical plan and none of us have any desire to start hacking our way through the bush again.

We space ourselves five or ten yards apart...Fishe on point. An hour later the sun is creeping its way into the sky, the mist that shrouded the top of the mountain at dawn is finally burning off and the temperature is climbing into the eighties; the humidity is about a hundred fifty percent. The road winds back and forth across the face of the mountain and it often seems like we walk a mile just to get another fifty feet down the hill. Going down hill means everything on our left is uphill when the road is going south and uphill on the right when the road bends back to the north. The Jungle and brush off the road is very heavy, just as it was on the other side of the hill. It makes me extremely nervous. I can tell by the way Fishe is moving I'm not the only one who's nervous. Coleman, who's bringing up the rear, is especially leery and spends most of his time walking backwards.

Jungle noises are absent, the thick air and the rising heat seem to amplify the eerie silence. Missing are the customary bird noises and sounds other animals make to warn each other of an intrusion by two legged predators. Last night I hadn't heard the usual concerto the insects normally make. I attributed the silence to the rain, but even now, I don't hear the chatter of the beetles and crickets, it's spooky.

Jim signals and we drop to a crouch taking refuge in the bush off the side of the road. He backs away to his right peering intently into the jungle. *He must have seen some movement...maybe it's an animal.*

The canopy over the jungle is very heavy. Yesterday, there were times the sun was so obscured it seemed like sunset. Today it isn't quite as bad.

Jim drops to one knee, his M-16 at his shoulder; just as his knee touches the ground he pops off five rounds. The rest of us bring our weapons to bear, anxious to fire, but waiting…nothing happens.

Fitzpatrick signals Johnson and Townsend to move in and check it out. They approach cautiously as they move into the jungle. Townsend uses the muzzle of his M-16 to push the brush out of the way.

"On your left!" Jim yells. Johnson whips around to look at Jim, as he does, his face erupts, spewing blood and flesh as the bullet that punctures the back of his head exits.

Jim empties his magazine before Johnson's body hits the ground. We lay down a heavy blanket of fire towards the unseen enemy.

"I see him! I see him!" I yell firing at the silhouette moving through the darkness of the jungle. Leaves and tree bark fly all over as our rounds hack their way through the dense foliage. The VC takes several hits and crashes to the ground.

Fitzpatrick is juiced. "Let's get in there and check it out!"

Lindlay and I tackle Fitz to keep him from charging into the bush. We have to fight to restrain his struggling body. "Listen, Sarge, listen. We need to pull Townsend and Johnson out of there and call for support.

"We gotta make sure that bastard is dead," Fitzpatrick says as he turns his head up to look at me.

"Look," Lindlay presses, "He may have been trying to suck us into an ambush. We need to call for support, now! We need to get our asses out of here before we all end up dead."

Fitzpatrick's eyes look back and forth between our faces. He's weighing what we've told him against his instincts. He decides we're right. He spreads us out to cover and sends Smitty and Lindlay in to pull out Johnson and Townsend. Townsend went down, we don't know how bad he was hit.

"Townsend, you hit?" Fishe yells.

"Flesh wound."

They drag Johnson's body out. We know he's dead before anybody even looks at him. One eye has been completely blown out of its socket and half his forehead is missing. Townsend is helped to his feet and the three of them run toward our position.

Townsend has a crease across the inside of his left thigh. His pant leg is soaked with blood. Just being able to get up and run means it isn't a bad wound.

Fitz puts in a radio call to the 4th Division.

"Look, maybe we better leave Johnson and start moving out of here. I have a bad, bad, feeling about this." Fishe tells Fitzpatrick. Fishe surprises even me with his sudden reluctance to hold our position and wait for help. Jim normally is the cool confident one. He says, "The hair on the back of my neck has been standing on end all morning."

This time Fitz doesn't hesitate. "Yeah, I agree, let's get the fuck outta here."

From behind us a burst from an automatic weapon cracks through the silence of the jungle, quickly joined by another. Jim breaks into a crouched run sprinting across the road and into the jungle. The rest of us lie in the bush firing. Nothing's visible…we can't see shit!

Fitz darts to his feet following Jim's example, waving his arm and yelling, "Come on, let's go." Jim strafes the jungle trying to cover Fitzpatrick's mad dash across the road. Simultaneously, I yell, *"Cover,"* bringing everybody's weapon to life.

AK-47 rounds zip out of the jungle ripping through leaves and thumping into the ground all around us.

"Man, I can't see any of the mother fuckers!" Smitty yells.

"Ten o'clock, Ten o'clock," I yell.

"Two o'clock, two o'clock," Pinetti yells.

We fire at both targets. Things are escalating quickly, there has to be at least a dozen VC out there. It's hard to believe no one else has been hit; I know it's only a matter of time.

"Damn it, we gotta get the hell out of here!" Moe yells out.

We're well spaced making it difficult for the VC to concentrate on a single area. Pierce is the nearest man to me; from the look on his face he's shitting his pants.

Lindlay hollers, *"Simon!"* I look over and he nods his head towards Pierce then says, *"Go!"* He turns and yells, *"Cover!"* I spring to my feet pulling at Pierce; yelling, *"Let's go!"* We bolt for different spots across the road twenty or thirty yards right of Fitzpatrick. By running to different spots I hope to buy us a second or two. If we randomize our paths of retreat it'll keep the VC from being able to anticipate our moves. Once again, the squad opens up as we bolt. I launch myself head first into the jungle and the protection it offers.

"Jim, Jim?"

"Back here!"

I peer through the heavy foliage and see Jim waving at us. I turn towards Pierce, "Stay here…I'll be right back. Try not to shoot unless you have something to shoot at." I don't want him to give away our position. Pierce nods.

Fitz says, "Let's get everybody across the road and get the hell out of here.

"Yeah, and we'd better keep our eyes open, we don't want any VC coming up from behind us."

"The Fourth's sending help, there's no way to tell how long it will take them to get here."

Fitz wants us to work our way down the hill staying within sight of the road. The cavalry should be here in ten or fifteen minutes, but if the VC cut us off and block our retreat we'll have to abandon the road and take the express down the mountain. Fitz is scared, I can see it in his eyes. Fifteen minutes can be an eternity.

I rejoin Pierce; he's blindly popping off rounds across the road. I tell him to take it easy with the ammo.

Lindlay yells, *"Cover!"* then he, Pinetti, Frenchy and Moe spring to their feet. We strafe the jungle to cover their dash. They sprint across the road in different directions splitting the enemy fire.

When Coleman, Smitty and Townsend try to cross, they're cut off by heavy fire from down the road. *The VC have worked their way past us and gotten downhill!*

Damn it, they're getting in position to flank us and cut us off, I spin around and look behind us...nothing but jungle and brush. At least they're still on the other side of the road.

We're weak on ordinance; we have no M-60, no grenade launcher, nothing to compensate for being outnumbered. Not only that, we've been using a lot of ammo covering each other, firing blindly at invisible targets. I reach down and grab Pierce's shoulder, "Come on!" We weave our way through the bushes back to Fitzpatrick.

Fitz is intense...he's trying to figure out what to do.

"Sarge, we gotta stop that crossfire. We've got to take the heat off Coleman long enough to get them over here."

"I know, I know."

"Let me and Lee get down the road and try to circle in behind the VC, all we gotta do is distract them long enough to get our guys over here."

"Go."

It's a dumb plan and we know it, but it's something we can do quickly because we don't have a lot of time.

Lee and I are poised to make a dash back across the road. We're flat on our bellies and well hidden in the brush. We've worked our way about fifty or sixty yards south of the VC flanking Coleman. As long as the VC keep our three guys pinned down they know it prevents the rest of us from withdrawing. The VC will be able to maneuver into positions to surround everybody. They're using their advantage to run us out of ammo.

Lee and I have no intention of taking on a bunch of VC. We just want to distract them, draw their fire long enough for our guys to get back on our side of the road. In the back of my mind I know the idea of drawing their fire isn't exactly something I am particularly looking forward to. *Man, oh man, what the hell am I doing?*

We peer up and down the road then into the jungle, but see nothing. It would be foolish to just dart across the road and we know it; we don't want them to know we're here.

Lee goes first, flat on his belly, the very same way we did it in basic training. I'm right behind him. The brush around the road gives us some cover, but crawling across the road leaves our asses hangin' out big time. The only thing that would make it worse would be a big bull's-eye painted on the back of our pants.

We fly across the road like a couple of cockroaches scurrying around the kitchen floor when someone turns on a light. Amazingly, we make it undetected. Once in the jungle we spread out and advance. We'll try to get up above VC. They can't be very deep in the jungle or they wouldn't be able to keep our guys pinned down.

The sound of the AK-47 fire is close, we have to be within twenty or thirty yards, but we still can't see them. Lee and I are only a few yards apart and we can hear Fitzpatrick yelling at Coleman.

"Fuck!" I mumble under my breath. *Cracka, cracka, cracka.* A burst from an AK gives up the position of a VC. Another burst and we have two spotted. Two more fire from positions we can't see, then another two. We hear more, but can't tell how many or where they are.

Lindlay signals and we slowly withdraw.

"Shit, there's too many for us to take on, we might save Coleman, but we'll be fucked." Lee wipes the sweat from his forehead. "We gotta do something." Lindlay keeps his eyes focused in the direction of the VC.

I grab his shoulder and say, "Look, let's just stick with the original plan; we distract them and get the fuck outta here. We can use the grenades to slow 'em up."

Lee has the, *you gotta be shittin' me* look on his face, but says, "Okay, let's do it."

Cautiously, we creep back to within twenty or so yards of the VC. We have three grenades between us. We pull the pins and jam them into the elbow of two low hanging limbs. We wedge a rock in on top off them to keep the grenades in place and prevent the lever arms from ejecting. Once the grenades are in place we withdraw to a position that'll allow me to shoot the grenades out of their perches.

The amount of gunfire is increasing, we know we have to do whatever it is we're gonna do and do it quickly. I position myself behind a tree and go through a dry-fire test moving from one grenade to another just to get the feel of homing in on the targets.

I take aim at the first grenade and say, "Go!"

Lee starts firing, short bursts, and yelling. The joint of my right thumb is jammed into my cheek and my view through the back reticule of the gun sight shows the tip of the forward sight about six inches below the rock...I wait anxiously. Lindlay keeps firing. The VC will have to break off their crossfire just to cover their backs; it doesn't take long to respond. Rounds start zipping past us as they begin to return fire; there are a lot of rounds. In the distance I hear Fitzpatrick yell, *"Cover!"* It means they're scrambling across the road.

I'm not watching the jungle at all. I have my eye glued to grenade number one. I'm depending on Lindlay to let me know when to fire. Lindlay drops a magazine and reloads. He must be getting low because I'm down to my last four magazines...I started with ten. I have two bandoleers, but don't exactly have time to start reloading. Lee pops off another short burst. The AK-47 rounds are spitting all around us and the reports from the weapons are definitely closer. I can hear the VC barking at each other.

"Now!" Lindlay yells. I squeeze the trigger. The recoil jams the joint of my thumb into my cheek, hard. I bring the weapon back on line and still see the rock sitting on top of the grenade. I know instantly the round had to have been high or I would have seen bark flying. I drop the aim another couple of inches and fire again. The rock and grenade are knocked out of the niche in the tree. Before the first grenade detonates, I already have taken aim on the second rock, fire and the grenade disappears from its resting-place. *Whump!* The first grenade detonates. I sight the third and as soon as I dislodge it, Lindlay and I are up and moving.

Whump, Whump! We're moving as fast as the dense jungle will allow, we don't even stop to fire, we just keep running. When we've covered sixty yards, we stop, catch our breath, and make the dash across the road. This time we aren't unseen and bullets are zipping all around us. We don't know what Fitzpatrick's doing and don't want to start moving back in that direction. If we do, the VC will be crossing the road behind us and everyone will be pinned down. *Where the hell are those guys from the 4th?*

We hold our ground and try to keep the VC from getting to our side of the road. Minimally, it will at least stretch them out and minimize their ability to concentrate fire at one position. We exchange rounds with the VC for a few seconds then hear movement to our left. Smitty and Jim emerge from the heavy bush, followed by the rest of the squad. Lee and I hold our position as they pass firing several volleys across the road. When our guys are ten or fifteen yards past us, we spring up and follow. This time, Jim and Smitty take the cover position as the squad moves past. We keep leap-frogging our way through the jungle in this manner with the VC in close pursuit. Looking back up the road about six VC cross over to our side firing as they cross; they'll be coming up behind us through the bush.

"Where are those dickheads from the fourth division?" I mumble as I drop a magazine and insert one of the two I have left. I pick up the empty and stick it in my pack. I might need to be reloading the empties soon. Pinetti has a horrified look on his face. He's out of ammo. I throw him one of the bandoleers. "Here, use this, spread it around."

"Smasher, Smasher, this is Big Lightning over!" Fitzpatrick grabs the mike from the radio on Frenchy's back.

"Roger, Big Lightning, this is Smasher." Fitzpatrick has his little acetate-covered map out and starts squawking out coordinates. "Bird dog we have mucho VC in close pursuit, do you copy?"

"Roger, Smasher, no where to land for a dust-off, how about some cover fire? Mark your position, over."

"Roger, Bird dog, we'll drop smoke."

Fitzpatrick doesn't have to say anything. Smitty pulls the pin and tosses a canister of green smoke. Thirty seconds pass; we see the choppers thunder across the treetops. They disappear up the road as they bank around the mountain.

We can't see them but we can hear them...two choppers thundering over the treetops on a strafing run. The jungle behind us erupts from multiple rocket strikes. The door gunners blanket the jungle with fire from the chattering M-60's. The choppers make a second pass delivering another salvo of ground shaking rocket detonations. We don't know how many, if any, VC have been hit. All we know is that this is an opportunity to put some distance between VC and us.

As the sound of the choppers fades into the distance it is replaced by the unmistakable sound of heavy AK-47 fire from up the road, down the road and across the road. *Fuck! We're surrounded.*

Fitz yells, "Okay, let's dig in, we ain't gonna outrun them." We pair off in two-man fire teams and try to set up a perimeter. Hopefully, we have enough ammo to hold off the VC till help arrives.

"There!" Lindlay yells and points. We see the bushes rustling and Lindlay starts firing…I pop off three rounds. Frenchy and Pierce are downhill guarding the left flank and our backs.

Some rounds zip by us from the left. Simultaneously our heads whip around to see Frenchy and Pierce firing at an unseen target down the hill.

Fuck! The VC have gotten a couple of guys downhill. "Man, we are in big fucking trouble here." I yell, popping off a couple of more rounds.

"This is fucked, dis is really fucked!" Lindlay blurts out uncharacteristically.

We have to keep firing. It's a catch-22. If we wait for targets and don't fire, it gives the VC a chance to close in on us. If we keep up a steady rate of fire we run out of ammo.

Frenchy yells, "Pierce is hit! Pierce is hit! Someone get down here!"

I glance towards Fitzpatrick but they're under heavy fire from across the road. Coleman is the closest. I cup my hands around my mouth and yell, *"Coleman!"* He doesn't hear me. *"Coleman!"* This time he turns. "Pierce's been hit, I gotta help Frenchy, get your ass over here." Without waiting for a response I rustle my way down to Frenchy.

Pierce is lying on the ground. His eyes are open but glazed over. Frenchy has his hand pushed against Pierce's neck. He pulls it away momentarily, a round has gone completely through and the blood spurts out with every heartbeat. I know instantly he's going to black out at any second, the blood pouring out of his neck is blood that isn't making it to his brain. I know without getting medical help in the next couple of minutes, Pierce is gonna die.

"Shit…here, let me try to put a bandage on it. You keep our asses covered." I tear open the little square package with the first aid bandage inside. I cover the wound and wrap the tails around his neck and tie them off...they can't be tied very tight or they'll choke him. Frenchy keeps firing sporadically while sneaking quick looks down at Pierce.

"I don't think the round punctured his throat or he'd be gagging on the blood...but Jesus!" Pierce blacks out. The blood continues oozing from the saturated bandage.

Cracka, Cracka, Cracka. Fifteen yards downhill is a VC moving up fast.

"Get him! Drop that bastard!" I empty my magazine.

"What's that?" Frenchy says.

"What? What's what?"

"That sound, did you hear it? It sounded like a dog."

"A dog? Are you fucking goofy?'

Then I hear it. It *is* a dog, making that whining sound a dog makes. Out of the corner of my eye I see the bushes rustle; I pull out my thirty-eight and am about to fire, my finger already putting pressure on the trigger. *Come on you little prick, come on.* Then I see it...a yellow Lab crawling out of the brush, it moves past us then freezes into a pointing position. His handler and four other GIs creep out the bush behind him.

"How many?" The dog handler asks. I hold up two fingers.

One of the men pops off an M-79 grenade, reloads, and fires another. Wham! Wham! The rounds detonate spewing smoke dirt into the air. The handler signals the dog and it moves through the bush towards the VC position.

All of a sudden there is an enormous amount of gunfire is being exchanged. Most of it has the unmistakable sound of M-16 rifles. A couple dozen GIs have emerged out of the jungle, there are more, I just can't see them. The cavalry has finally arrived.

After the grenades, the dog disappears into the bush. He's barking now, so the handler and his men move in. I yell back to Coleman, "Medic, we need a medic." Coleman acknowledges with a nod and heads off to find one. The dog and his handler return. "Is he still alive?" He bends over to look at Pierce.

"Yeah, I think so."

He stands up and looks back towards Fitzpatrick and yells, *"Get a medic over here!"*

The jungle is alive with troops now. They're on both sides of the road. There is still a lot of rifle firing going on, but most of it is from M-16's with only a rare volley from an AK-47. The VC are masters of getting out of situations when the tide turns against them.

"I gotta get my dog back in action, the damn VC are probably already crawling back into their holes, so we'll need Elvis here to sniff 'em out."

A medic crashes his way through the brush and starts attending to Pierce.

"Is he gonna make it?"

He doesn't answer. He starts an IV and says, "Come on, let's get him on the stretcher." Part of his equipment was a portable rolled up stretcher. It's unrolled and Pierce is laid on it, then Lee and I carry it back to the road.

Fitzpatrick, Fishe, and the rest of the squad are sitting there. They're spent...used up...emotionally exhausted. All of us have the same look in our eyes. The pensively blank stare that signals each of us is contemplating just how close this came to being the last day of our lives.

I look at my watch and think, *I can't believe it's only been less than thirty minutes.* I flop down on the edge of the road next to Fishe. I pull the magazine out of my weapon and clear the chamber. I take the round and push into the magazine with my thumb. *Jesus, only six rounds left.* Both my ammo pouches are empty and I gave one of my bandoleers to Pinetti. I take the other one and start pushing the rounds off the clips and into my empty magazines.

"Fuck, it was a good thing these guys showed up. I only had about seven rounds left, after that it would have been hand-to-hand." Fishe says with the distinctive tone of exasperation in his voice.

"Yeah, I'm almost out too," Fitzpatrick says as he pulls out his magazine and looks at it.

Pinetti's head is rolled back, his bulging eyes closed with a tear running down the side of his face. "Jesus, how'd we let this happen to us?"

The medic is still attending to Pierce, he turns his head, and bitterly tells Pinetti, "Welcome to the Nam man."

Six APCs are advancing up the road, two pull to the side and the others continue up the road. The rear of the APC opens and a Captain, Captain Bedaas, steps out with a radio mike in hand. An E-6 is at his side holding a map, which Bedaas is staring at intently. There is a lot of radio chatter, and Bedaas is in constant contact with his fire teams and squad leaders. There is still an occasional exchange of gunfire off in the distance.

Thirty or forty minutes pass. The jungle is quiet once again; only muffled conversations and radio chatter break the unnatural silence that has been the trademark of this mountain.

Four Sergeants and three Lieutenants huddle around Bedaas, all are seasoned, it's clear that all of them have spent a lot of time in the bush. One of the E-5s, a black guy, has a grease gun hanging from his neck by a thin leather strap. This is in addition to the M-16 he carries along with a 45-caliber automatic. He has at least six magazines for the grease gun, several for the M-16, and has four bandoleers of ammo hanging from his shoulder. I count six grenades and of course a bayonet. *Jeez, this guy must be carrying a hundred pounds of weapons and ammo.*

I jab Jim with my elbow, when he looks at me I nod my head in the Sergeant's direction. "Where do you think he got the grease gun?" The grease gun is a 45-caliber automatic weapon produced in the Second World War to replace the Thompson sub-machine gun. It uses a standard forty-five caliber round.

Jim looks, then says, "Hell, man, I don't know but I wouldn't mind having one."

"Sir, we've got tunnels here, here and here. It's got to be a complex all tied together." The E-6 points to spots on the Captain's map.

"That's right, sir, and we found a bunker here. My guess is there's a horde of VC holed up all around the area." Jefferson makes a small circle on the map.

"Well, we ain't gonna get 'em out of those holes, let's get the fly boys in here and burn 'em out." Bedaas gets on his radio and instructs Lieutenant Powers to get his men out of the bush.

"Burn 'em out..." That means napalm. It probably won't burn the VC out of their tunnels, but sometimes, or at least someone told me, the intense heat and fire literally sucks all the oxygen out of the tunnels and can asphyxiate any VC unfortunate enough to be in them.

Once all his men are recovered, Bedaas yells, "Okay, let's mount up." His arm is stuck up in the air rotating it in a sharp circle.

Fitzpatrick interrupts, "Sir, I've got a casualty three-quarters of a mile up the road."

Bedaas says, "Sergeant, in about ten minutes everything on the side of this hill is gonna be dead. We can come back for the body later."

Fitzpatrick, Fishe, Lindlay and I are aboard the last APC in the column. It takes about ten minutes to break out into the open, out from the heavy jungle. The crew chief puts his hand up to the side of his helmet to push the earpiece of his radio tighter so he can hear.

"Hey..." he yells to get our attention. Then he points to the north.

Our heads turn in unison, coming in hot and low are four F4 Phantoms. They're screaming down the valley between the hills and for one small instant it looks like they are going to fly right into the side of the mountain. At the last second they pull up and go vertical, as they do, they eject their load of napalm. The large pods tumble into the side of the hill and detonate.

"Holy Mother of God!" I gape in amazement at the spectacle unfolding before my eyes. The side of the hill erupts into a wall of bright orange flame. Plumes of black smoke billow into the sky. It is almost unimaginable. We have to be a half-mile away and I can feel the heat on my face.

"God...damn!" Fitzpatrick is just as mesmerized.

The APCs stop and everyone, seasoned or not, just stares. Whether they admit it or not, anyone who sees and feels napalm has the same morbid train of thought. It makes me shudder.

The jungle is ablaze and the acrid smell of burning organic material burns our nostrils. We stand staring at the inferno scorching the side of the hill. I remember the napalming at Plei Djereng, but that was at night and for some strange reason, it seems much more spectacular in the daylight. Large clouds of smoke are carried away from the burning jungle by the prevailing wind. It blows and swirls around us. As we stand there ashes begin falling out of the smoke wafting over our heads. I turn my head to the sky, the smoke irritating the membranes in my throat and lungs. I have to squint to keep the ash out of my eyes. I hold out my hand and watch as the ashes slowly collect. Staring at my hand it occurs to me that back home winter is setting in and the streets of Chicago are probably covered with snow. Snow, that when it falls, has an air of purity about it. A mental picture of a vast field covered by a virgin white blanket of snow fills my mind. I remember how clean and unadulterated fresh fallen snow always looks. How it always masks the dinginess and filth of the city, knowing full well that in a few short hours, the purity will become tainted and impure, just like everything else in life.

"Hey, bozo, you awake? You hypnotized or what?" Coleman is shaking my shoulder.

"Kind of reminds you of snow, don't it?" I hold the hand full of ashes out towards him.

"Man, it don't never snow in the jungle." He just turns away and I turn my hand over and watch the ashes float to the ground.

The crew chief yells, "Yo, Fitzpatrick?"

"Yeah, what's up?"

"Captain wants you up front." He points towards the front of the column.

Fitzpatrick walks over to confer with Bedaas and two minutes later he's back.

"Bedaas is going to take his crew back up the hill. They'll do a body count and recover Johnson's body, or what's left of it. We'll be transported down in one of the APCs," Fitz pauses, takes a deep breath then says, "Pierce died a couple of minutes ago." He turns and walks toward the rear of the column; we follow.

During our ride we avoid looking at each other and no one speaks. Finally, for some strange reason, Coleman just shakes his head and repeats, "It never snows in the jungle, man, it never snows in the jungle."

Chapter Seventeen

".....I ain't getting' nothin' for Christmas, 'cause I ain't been nothin' but bad!"

December nineteenth...spirits are picking up a little the last couple of days. Things have been pretty morose since Dak To. Pierce and Johnson were part of *our* group. Losing one of your own is always worse than just losing someone from the unit. There is a personal attachment that exists between people who share each and every day together. You sleep together, eat together, laugh together and cry together. Even losing the guy least liked by everyone else in the platoon is worse than losing someone from another platoon, almost like having a finger cut off. We were just getting to know them, and in a moment, they're gone.

For the past two weeks I contemplated their deaths. I realized that whatever energy or thought, whatever deed, accomplishment or contribution their existence might have made is lost forever. Who's to say that Pierce wouldn't have been the man who found a cure for cancer? Who's to say Johnson's son wouldn't have grown up to become the president that erased all hunger and injustice from the face of the earth? No one could say otherwise. How many great men have been taken from us by the unbiased cruelty of war? How much better of a place would the world be today? Perhaps, among the dead, strewn across the battlefields of history, are those who would have eventually eliminated war, a paradox to say the least. I surprise myself thinking such things, I realize questions of this nature will perplex me and remain unanswered for the rest of my life.

The last week or so, people around the camp have begun receiving Christmas packages from home, almost all of them teeming with baked goods, candy, and canned food. There are even occasional articles of clothing. Hell, Farmly got a sweater!

I read the note my father sent along with the package I received today.

Dear Bill,

Sorry, I haven't written much, but as you know we love you and can't wait for you to get home. I sent you some of the things I know you like. I hope you enjoy them. Your Grandma and Grandpa say hi. Merry Christmas!

Love

Dad

I open the package. Two full lengths of hard salami, a large tin of my Grandmother's horseshoe cookies, and six cans of Spam.

"Spam? Someone sent you Spam?" Fishe picks up a can and holds it up. "Hey, look, somebody sent Simon Spam!"

I reach up and grab it. "Man, I love Spam! That's why my father sent it."

"You actually eat Spam! Jesus, man, what's wrong with you?" Fishe is laughing.

"We've been eatin' Spam at my house since I was a kid. My mother used to fry it with a mustard and sugar sauce. It was good, honest. Hell, man, I grew up eatin' Spam sandwiches."

I pull my bayonet out of its scabbard and start slicing the salami. Turner has a big chunk of cheddar that he offers up as a companion. We stuff ourselves washing the food down with warm beer.

"Simon, you know what I miss most about home?" Lindlay asks, stretched out on his cot with his hands behind his head staring at the ceiling.

"Everything," I say with a snicker.

"No, I miss Christmas. Up in Minnesota, when it's Christmas time, there's a foot of snow covering all the fields. It ain't like when it snows in da city, man, the snow lays white on the fields for months, sometimes all winter. Dere's nothin' around to soil it and make it dirty. The fireplace will be goin' all the time," he pauses as he conjures up the mental image, "and the farmhouse will be smellin' of my mom's cookin', she bakes almost every day and getting' up at five to help my dad with the animals. Sometimes I'm up early just so I can take my horse Norstad out for a gallop in the snow. That's what I miss."

"Jesus, does Norman Rockwell know about your family?" Everybody laughs. Then I add, "You named your horse Norstad?"

"Who's Norman Rockwell?" Lindlay asks. Everybody looks at him like he's from another planet. He stares back at us with a questioning look on his face.

"You're kidding, right?" Farmly asks, looking at Lindlay like he's an idiot. I know he's thinking to himself, "How could anybody not know who Norman Rockwell is."

"Hey, look at this," Pinetti says. "Some guy named Oliver got the 'Medal of Honor' for jumping on a grenade to save five of his buddies." Pinetti is reading the latest issue of "Stars and Stripes."

"Wait a minute, this can't be right." Pinetti's brow gets all scrunched up. "Says here, Oliver was a black guy."

"Yeah, what's your point?" Farmly asks.

"Look at the names of the five guys, they all sound like they're white. Ain't no nig…I mean black guy, gonna jump on a grenade to save a bunch of white boys." We can see the leer on his face and we know what he's thinking.

"Why not? Wouldn't you throw yourself on a grenade to save us?" Farmly presses.

"Hell, no! Damn, man, I wouldn't throw myself on a grenade to save myself." Pinetti seems smug about his idiotic answer.

"Huh? What?" We chime in unison. Farmly, however, isn't going to let him off that easily.

"Do you realize what you just said? Look you dumb ass, you *couldn't* save your own ass if *you* jumped on a grenade. Get it?"

It dawns on Pinetti he's made a stupid analogy so he says, "Well, ya'all know what I meant," and goes back to his cot before we can deride him any further.

"Ya know, Pinetti might be right, it does seem kinda fishy that a brother would throw himself on a grenade to save a bunch of white boys." I comment softly, not wanting Pinetti to know I actually am agreeing with him. By the way Farmly looks at me and I can tell he also thinks there might be credence to what Pinetti thought, but we'll never admit it to him.

I silently think about it for another few minutes. I remember Plei Djereng when I instinctively ran from my bunker to Coleman's, thinking they were in danger. I remember how Coleman capped the VC who was about to snuff Pinetti. Then I knew that what Oliver did, he did unselfishly and instinctively. I know that whatever Pinetti was implying is wrong. I realize Oliver did what he did out of instinct…he truly was a hero.

"You know what?" Lindlay blurts out, "We need to get us a Christmas tree. Ya, that's what we need to do." Lindlay must have really been visualizing that Norman Rockwell Minnesota Christmas.

"Hey, maybe I can do something about it." From their looks, I get the distinctive feeling no one thinks I can do it.

"Simon, where the hell you gonna get a Christmas tree?" Fishe asks sarcastically.

"Hell, I don't know, but if there's one in this country to be gotten, I'm gonna get it!"

The next morning before we report for duty, I go over to the NCO hooch looking for Sergeant Bast.

"You want what?"

"A Christmas tree," I say.

"Why don't you guys go out in the jungle and cut yourselves down a small bush or something? It'd be a hell of a lot easier."

"Look, I know there's got to be generals and Colonels that at this very moment have a Christmas tree standing in their office. I just want to know where and how they got 'em is all."

"All right, I'll see what I can do, but I'm outta here on December twenty fourth, so you're gonna have to find yourselves another benefactor."

"You're leaving, Sarge?"

"Fuckin' aay buddy, I'm outa here! Four days and a wake up, you can't be any shorter than I am. I already got my gear packed. Hell, even if I could find somewhere to get a tree, it's only five days till Christmas, we probably couldn't get it here in time."

"Hey, I'm not tryin' to blackmail ya or anything like that. You're too short. What could we possibly do at this point that would have any impact on you, nothin', right? So we're just askin' you to use your long list of contacts to try to help us out. That's all, just a little help. Besides, I know nobody over here is in the least bit interested in the six inch stack of money orders you got." I know the last comment is probably more effective than if I had threatened him with a gun.

"Man, you are one little prick! You're fucking worse than me. You're just too dumb to make any money off that devious little mind of yours. How do you know I didn't already send them home?"

"Somehow or another, Sarge, I just don't see you trusting your wife with all that money. It's your stash, would any red-blooded American man, ever tell his wife? No, man, I don't think so, you've still got 'em. Quite frankly, I don't know whether I'm a big enough prick to blow the whistle, but you have to at least know the possibility exists."

"Yeah, yeah, I'll see what I can do."

I leave the hooch and head for the S-4 tent. I know Fitzpatrick is there taking inventory of our latest shipment of commo gear. I need to get permission from him to go over to MACV and hit the PX. I have a Christmas list and want to do my shopping.

On the road back from MACV, I decide to make a slight detour and turn up the road towards Camp Enari, the 4th Division's base camp. Frenchy and I are waved through the front gate and once inside I stop for a moment to decide how I'll go about finding the item in question. Getting it could easily land me in the shithouse. We drive up and down the roads of the camp till I spot a squad of guys wearing flak jackets, carrying weapons and covered with the infamous red dust. From their appearance I know these guys have just come back from a patrol or just returned from a fire base. Two of the guys are carrying just what I'm looking for so I park and walk up to one of them; we talk for a couple of minutes and I'm enlightened on how to fulfill my quest. This results in another fifteen-minute detour. Before we leave, I stop at an orderly room and pick up something I think Fitzpatrick might appreciate.

On the way back we stop in Pleiku for a couple of reasons. We both decide we need to get laid, but I also want to pick up a couple of things from a shop I'd seen on a previous trip.

I park the Jeep right near the bar next to blowjob alley.

"Go ahead, you go first, I'll stay here and watch all the stuff in the Jeep." I pull out a cigarette and lean back in the seat. "Hey," I yell after Frenchy, "Don't take all fucking day, huh."

I sit back in the Jeep and curiously espy all the seemingly senseless activity taking place around me. It is mid-afternoon and the streets are filled with civilians, a few GIs, street vendors, ARVNs and about ten thousand kids. The kids are like insects, scurrying all around, begging and panhandling. I've long since become immune to the begging and grabbing.

It's warm, but not hot, I have the temptation to take off my flak jacket, but resist. Most of the GIs floating around are weaponless. We aren't supposed to carry weapons into town on a pass, but we aren't on a pass, our weapons are firmly affixed to the rifle holders in the Jeep. I have my thirty-eight on, and know I'll have to stash it in my boot before I go back to get laid. I lean back in the seat.

Frenchy returns after about ten minutes. "Damn, I needed that. Hell, I wanted to go twice, but I spent all my money."

Without hesitating, I say, "Don't even think about it man, I blew all my dough, I barely got enough to pay for the pussy myself."

"I wasn't gonna ask you for money." Frenchy tries to look offended, but doesn't do a very good job.

"Yeah, bullshit." I take off the holster and jam the thirty-eight into my boot, then drop the pant leg over it. "I'll be back in ten minutes."

As I walk back I remember my first trip to this place and have to crack a smile. As I approach the door, I notice in the daylight, most of the women look much older than they do at night in the dim porch light. I pick one out, negotiate the price down to six bucks and in we go. The inside hasn't changed; it still has the beds with the curtains surrounding them. There doesn't seem to be any activity going on at the moment.

As we walk towards one of the beds, another girl is walking out. She is very attractive and both women notice my fixation.

The girl I'm with says, "You like? You want two girl? You pay for two girl?" She has her arm around my waist and sort of tugs me towards the other girl. The attractive girl opens her blouse to reveal two perfectly shaped breasts. "You like?"

"Oh yeah, I like, baby. Okay, I pay for both."

"You pay ten dollar more," she says.

I don't even argue. I just hand over the ten bucks.

The two women take me to one of the cots, and begin undressing me. I just stand and let them do it. The older one isn't very happy when she finds the thirty-eight, but I take it and lay it near the pillow. The other girl is running her fingers ever so lightly all over my body, just barely touching me. It's incredible. The other girl (the older one) is on her knees in front of me doing the same thing to my pecker. She runs her fingers up and down its length, then tickles under my scrotum. Then, suddenly, out of nowhere, she takes me in her mouth and I almost lose it, but she is doing the same thing with her mouth she had done with her fingers, just barely touching. I can feel the warmth of her breath and the ever so light touch of her tongue. They push me back on the cot laughing and return to their manipulations. The young girl lingers above me brushing my naked torso with the hair hanging from her head. She leans over and gently blows in my ear. My eyes are closed and I feel her nipples tracing their way down my face and then moving across my chest. The older girl has returned to touching me. It's fucking incredible! The good-looking girl leans over and gently kisses me on the lips. I can smell the food she's eaten, and strangely it doesn't offend me. While she's doing this, the older girl, climbs on me and starts to lower herself. She only lets the head penetrate, then rotates her hips in a circular motion. I try thrusting my hips to get full penetration, but she skillfully prevents it from happening. The first girl is still kissing me. Then she starts licking her way down my body. She stands up and I open my eyes, she stops to remove her clothes, then returns to the touching. Now both of them are doing it. The young one is stroking my boner and the older woman is running her fingers up and down the inside of my thighs. I'm dying. I am already holding back desperately. The young girl senses this and really begins working the instrument.

"Damn! Hold it! Stop!" Too late, I start ejaculating. Both girls are laughing as the young girl pumps me rapidly. Though the experience was fantastically erotic, it's also anti-climatic. My dick wants to be inside a pussy and these girls know it. The young girl climbs on top of me, I am still hard, and lowers herself on me. Then she leans forward and whispers in my ear, "You boom-boom again...ten dollar?" She blows the words in my ear, my dick is not going to let me refuse and I'm certainly not going to stop to haggle.

"I boom-boom, ten dollar." She starts pumping away and the older woman is still stroking me and touching me all over. I let the young girl grind away for three or four minutes. I'm much more in control now that I've already come once. I watch her moving around, her hair obscuring her face and her breasts bounce up and down in time with her gyrations. Her head from time to time is thrown back almost as if she is enjoying herself, but even if she isn't, I sure am. She raises herself up off her knees, and squats over me with her feet firmly planted on the bed. She raises and lowers herself on me so I am almost completely out, then she lowers herself ever so slowly till I am completely embedded. She keeps doing this till she senses it is time to get the job done. When she does, she slams down on me and rocks her hips back and forth till I once again explode, this time inside her. I jerk and cringe and laugh.

Finally, she climbs off and the older girl starts cleaning me off with a wet rag.

"Hey! Simon! Wake up!" Frenchy is shaking my shoulder violently.

"Huh, what?" I reluctantly start opening my eyes, my mind fighting to stay immersed in my psycho-erotic dreamland, but as my eyes open and reality displaces my imagination, I begrudgingly return to consciousness.

"What's wrong with you dickhead. Shit, some VC could have walked up and cut your throat. Hell, I'm surprised all these little gook bastards didn't steal everything out of the Jeep."

"Goddamn it! Shit!" Disappointment immediately washes over me when I realize the whole episode took place in my head.

Frenchy climbs into the Jeep and looks at me, "Well?"

"What?" I reply.

"Aren't you gonna go get laid?"

"Yeah, I'm going." I already know I'm in for a big let down, but I still have a huge boner from my dreamland encounter. It desperately needs some attention. I'm back in the Jeep eight minutes later.

December 24th, Bast is leaving today and we still have no Christmas tree.

"Hey, I did everything I could, I'm not superman, you know." Bast actually seems disappointed.

"Yeah, well, I'm glad you tried. Here, I'll help you with your gear." I grab his duffel bag and take it out to the Jeep. Neuman, Jackson, Fitzpatrick, Duke and a few other guys are waiting for him outside. Everybody shakes his hand and wishes him well.

While Bast shakes Fitzpatrick's hand he asks, "Hey, you mind if Simon here drives me over to the air base?"

"No, go ahead." Fitzpatrick nods towards me.

"Hey, ain't no way I'm goin' alone, how about Varant going with?"

"Yeah, sure," Neuman says. You boys get this old hillbilly on that plane.

The ride to PAB is quiet, and dusty. Bast is going to catch a C-130 to Cam Ranh Bay, where he'll board a 707 bound for the States in the morning. We clear the gate at the airbase and drive to the very same terminal where I sat and waited for Sergeant Dick to pick us up nine months ago. Bast's ride isn't due for another fifteen minutes, so we sit there and keep him company.

"Sarge, I gotta ask you, I mean, I saw the stack, but I really don't have any idea how much is there. What's that pile of money orders worth?"

Bast looks at me pondering what the consequences of telling me will be. Evidently he doesn't think it matters at this point, or his ego wants to make sure someone knows how successful his schemes have turned out. "'Bout thirty-eight thousand." He says matter-of-factly, like it is no big deal.

"*Holy Jesus! Thirty-eight thousand! That's incredible.*" I can't believe it. Hell, back in the States, two or three hundred bucks a week is a good wage.

"Damn, Sarge, that's like making like fifty thousand before taxes." I'm still having difficulty comprehending that much money. "What the hell you gonna do with all that dough?"

"Son, I spent the last twenty-seven years hoppin' around the world from one army base to another. The army always took care of me, but ya know what? There was never any opportunity. No way to make it big. If I stay in three more years, I can draw full retirement that'd be about five hundred bucks a month. Figure it out, that's six grand a year. Most people are already making ten. Moving around and drawing that huge army salary never allowed me to buy a house anywhere, so even if I did retire I'd still have to get some kinda shit job just to be respectable." He pauses a moment, and looks around. "Yep, when I get back to South Carolina, I'm gonna take my pension, use this money to buy a house with a little land and open up a driving range near Myrtle Beach. I love the ocean and it doesn't get all that cold there in the winter."

The C-130 drops out of the sky as it makes its normal steep descent towards the end of the runway. It hits the tarmac and immediately the engines rev as they use them to help slow the plane. The plane taxis down the runway and comes to rest right near the terminal. They don't shut down the engines, so they aren't going to be here very long. Once the rear cargo door is open several people start unloading crates from the back. Bast shakes our hand one more time and heads for the plane. He makes us promise to sit there and watch his plane take off, "for luck," he says.

We watch Bast stop on the ramp and talk to one of the guys involved with unloading the cargo. There is hand shaking and it looks like Bast hands him some money. Then Bast points in our direction and the Air force guy turns to look at us. He shakes his head, then they shake hands again and Bast disappears into the plane.

As we watch the plane accelerate down the runway the guys who unloaded the plane pull up next to us in a deuce-and-a-half. The driver sticks his head out the window, "You Simon?"

"Yeah," I reply.

The driver gets out and leads me to the back of the truck. He climbs up and pushes out a crate that's five feet long and two feet square. "It's all yours, compliments of Sergeant Bast." He taps the brim of his hat in a courtesy salute, gets in the truck and leaves.

"What the hell is it?" Varant asks.

"How the hell how am I supposed to know."

"Should we open it here?"

"Hell, no! Shit there's no telling what Bast has in there. We'd better wait till we get back."

We strap it to the back of the Jeep and dee-dee back to the hill. The temptation to stop and open it is great, but I'm not going to pull off the side of the road to do it.

We pull up in front of the barracks and drop the crate. Varant agrees to take the Jeep back to the motor pool, but only after we promise not to open the crate till he gets back. By the time he gets back nearly everybody from barracks is outside standing around anxiously waiting for us to open up the box.

"Come on, let's get it open." Smitty is nervous as a tick.

"Alright, alright, someone get a hammer or something."

Smitty runs into the barrack and emerges with a trenching tool, the most versatile instrument the army has ever developed. It is a handy little shovel; you can lock the spade at a ninety-degree angle and use it as a pick or hoe. We've used them to chop down small trees and bamboo; in a pinch it makes an excellent weapon. For this, we'll use it as a crow bar. I pry the top open and lift it off. We huddle around the crate and stare at its contents.

"Well I'll be..." Jim says.

I lean over and take the note attached to the short balsam Christmas tree.

"Merry Christmas to all you little bastards. I had this flown in from the Philippines. If I was still there, I would have bled you guys big time for this."

SSergeant R.J.Bast

"Can you fucking believe it?" Smitty is mesmerized.

"Look." Frenchy reaches in and pulls out a string of Christmas lights. We take the tree into the barracks.

"How we gonna set it up?" I hold the tree by the top and stand it in the corner. Coleman and Pinetti run down to the S-4 tent and return about twenty minutes later with a makeshift tree stand they made from the packing crate. We stand the tree up and string the lights. At chow, Fishe talks Sergeant Pace into making a bowl of popcorn. We use thread from our little sewing kits to string the popcorn then hang it on the tree. An hour later we're through. The tree is as decorated as it is going to get, not too bad, considering.

Turner suggests heading over to the chapel where the film for the night is some Christmas movie. He didn't have to twist our arms.

Someone catcalls from behind us. "Boooo, what is this shit! We thought you had a Christmas movie!" The film's started and low and behold it's "Gunsmoke."

"It is a Christmas movie, it's the Christmas episode of 'Gunsmoke,'" the projectionist yells back.

It doesn't matter, everybody is going to watch it anyway. Midway through the episode of "Combat," I get up and leave. Back in the barracks, I get out all the gifts I picked up and use pages from the "Stars and Stripes" to wrap them. When I finish, I stash them in my footlocker.

Back at the chapel, the episode of "Combat" is coming to a close. As the crowd of about eighty or ninety starts to disperse and shuffle back to their areas, there is air of sullenness that hangs over the hill. Rather than everyone being cheery and excited because it's Christmas, everyone is actually depressed. We all want to be at home with our families, not in some shit-hole country where no one gives a damn about us. Another thought crosses my mind and I know as soon as the thought goes through my mind, the same exact thought has passed through the mind of each and every man on this hill... *Will I ever spend another Christmas back home?* Yeah, I think, looking at the faces of my comrades, we're all thinking the same thing, no matter how optimistic we try to be.

"Hey, get your cup," Farmly holds out a bottle of wine he's just opened. His father, or someone, sent him three bottles in a Christmas package.

I hold out my canteen cup for Farmly, as he pours, I comment, "Ya, know, I don't think I've ever actually had wine before."

"You're kidding! Not even at holidays or weddings?" Farmly looks surprised.

"No, man, I never have. Hell, I've never been to a wedding either."

"Jeez, you've had a pretty sheltered life."

"Well, I wouldn't exactly say that. Let's just say I haven't exactly been exposed to the same cultural experiences you have. Hell, neither of my parents even drink."

I put the cup up to my lips, as I sip the wine, the aroma insinuates itself on my sense of smell. It has a pleasant smell, but a bitter taste. Not that beer or whiskey tastes all that much better, but the taste from the wine seems to linger on my palate.

"Hey, not bad," I'm pleasantly surprised.

We drink wine and eat cheese for a while. It doesn't take long to notice a glum silence has fallen over the barracks. Everyone is lying in their bunk, some writing letters, some reading, but one by one, they fall asleep.

The hooch lights are off and only the soft glow from the string of colored lights on the Christmas tree keep the darkness from seeing the sadness on our faces.

"Merry Fucking Christmas!" Varant says with a tone of resentment, It's Christmas morning. Some of us sit up in our cots and a couple of guys just roll over and go back to sleep.

"Hell, I got to get up to the chapel and go to mass," I say as I grab my towel and shaving gear.

Farmly looks at me and asks, "Why are you going to church?"

I look at him not quite understanding how he can ask the question. "It's Christmas, man, you gotta go to church on Christmas."

"Isn't that being somewhat of a hypocrite? Hell, I haven't seen you go to church since I been here."

I don't know why Farmly has chosen this moment to bust my chops and I really don't give a shit. "So what? What's hypocritical about going to church today? I have no delusions that going to church today is gonna absolve me of any sins, or any nonsense like that. I'm just going because I know if I was home, I'd be going with my family, so this just makes me feel a little bit like being at home...asshole!"

"Oh." Farmly hangs his head ashamed he chastised me.

At church, we receive general absolution and I take communion. It is only the second time I've had communion since the sixth grade. Walking back from mass my thoughts are of home. I wonder what my family is doing. I'm sure my little brothers were up early tearing the wrappings from all the packages under the Christmas tree. We'd always had bountiful Christmas's. I think it was my mother's way of absolving herself from the abuse she gave us the rest of the year. In general, Christmas's have always been the best time of the year in our household. After our Christmas morning, later in the day, we'd visit Grandma Simon and collect even more crap and we'd eat till we were sick.

Back at the hooch I open my footlocker and remove my packages. I hand the largest and heaviest to Jim. "Here, Merry Christmas, prick."

"What's this?" Jim asks as he takes the package. He tears away the newspaper and his face lights up, "Where the hell did you manage to get a grease gun? Hell, man what did you pay for this?"

"Hey, just take it and shut up."

"Here, Merry Christmas." It isn't hard for Varant to tell what is wrapped in the paper but he tears away the paper to reveal a bottle of Southern Comfort, he smiles.

"Hey, this is great! Damn, I don't have anything for you." He says holding out the bottle in front of him with a big smile on his face.

"Just don't drink it all at once and stop your heart again, asshole," I chide as I walk away.

"Here, Lee, Merry Christmas," I hand him the package. It was a last minute change from what I had originally intended to give him.

He takes it and tears away the paper, "A Saturday Evening Post?" He looks bewildered.

"Yeah, here, look." I turn the pages till I find the picture I want. I hand it back to Lee. "That, my friend, is a Norman Rockwell." I point to the Norman Rockwell Christmas picture that covers the page. Lee takes it and sits back on his cot looking at the picture.

"Wait," I say. "There's something else in there."

Lee starts rooting around in the torn newspaper till he finds the packages of condoms and holds them up, "very funny, very funny."

I give Smitty a Hawaiian shirt that he immediately puts on and a small reel-to-reel tape recorder I picked up at the PX for Farmly. Farmly of course feels guilty after busting my chops earlier and for a moment I think he's going to cry.

"Merry Christmas, you black bastard!" I hand Coleman his gift.

He opens the package. It is a silk oriental scarf. I didn't even have to tell him what it was intended for. He carefully folds it into a headband and wraps it around his head takes his Karate stance, makes a couple of hand sweeps, then turns towards me and bows. I pass out a couple of small little gifts and head over to the NCO hooch. Most of them are still sitting around in their underwear drinking wine and singing hillbilly Christmas songs.

"Here ya go, Sarge, Merry Christmas." I hand the package to him.

"What's this?" he asks.

"Sarge, this is the official, U.S. Army 'What a Platoon Leader Should Know About The Enemy's Jungle Tactics' handbook that the Army issues to all infantry platoon leaders."

"Where the hell did you get this?" He seems pleased.

"Well, it occurred to me the infantry aren't the only people out there sluggin' their way around these hills, so they probably should be issuing these to everybody."

"Hey, well Merry Christmas to you too Simon." Fitzpatrick takes the pamphlet and immediately starts reading it.

I give out the last couple of gifts I have and then sit around with everybody trying to make Christmas day as pleasant as possible. Sergeant Pace outdoes himself with Christmas dinner, it's almost as good as the dinner I would be having back home: baked ham, sweet and mashed potatoes, a bean casserole, and either apple or pumpkin pie for desert. Back in the hooch, completely stuffed, I settle into my cot with a paperback book of "Peanuts Cartoons."

"Hey, Simon," Fishe shakes my foot.

"What's up?"

"They need you up at the commo trailer at the switchboard."

"Switchboard! Are you shittin' me? I don't want to be pullin' a shift on the board. Hell, I haven't even had any sleep."

"I don't know, man, but Fitzpatrick says you better haul your ass up there." Jim just turns and walks away.

"Shit! Shit! Shit!" I grumble as I lace up my boots. "Merry Fucking Christmas!"

I walk up the hill, go into the operations bunker and walk back to the commo trailer where the switchboard is set up. When I walk in, I'm surprised to find most of the guys are there..."Merry Christmas!"

I look at them dumbfounded. "What?" Fishe grabs me and sits me down in front of the board, he puts the headset on me and says, "Go ahead."

I'm not sure what's going on, I click the talk button on the headset and say, "Hello?" A voice on the other end says, "Yes, this is the mainland operator at Fort Lewis, number please?"

I look around the room at everybody, unsure of what to do. "Give her your phone number at home, dipshit," Jim says. So I do.

The line isn't great and I have to stick my finger in my other ear to hear, but I hear a phone ringing and then I hear my sister's voice when she picks up the phone.

"Hello?" She answers.

"Mickey? Mickey! This is Billie!" Everyone leaves the trailer. I'm left alone.

"Billie! Hold on." I hear her yell, "It's Billie."

My dad picks up the phone. "Bill, where are you? Is everything okay?"

"Yeah, yeah, everything is great. I have some friends who set up this call; I just want to say Merry Christmas."

I talk with my dad for a couple of minutes, say hello to my mother and all my brothers and sisters. I know I only have about ten minutes. They pass quickly. Talking to my family fills me with a sense of comfort; it's not just pleasing to hear, but comforting. It reminds me once again that I am human, a being filled with emotions, hopes, expectations and aspirations. All the things that are lost when just staying alive is the predominant concern that occupies most of my waking moments.

Walking back to the barracks, I feel like crying, but don't. I know this will be a Christmas I'll remember for the rest of my life and know the best Christmas present I ever got wasn't bought in a store and had no price tag attached to it.

Chapter Eighteen

"All Alone and Feelin' Blue"

"Happy Fucking Birthday," I mumble under my breath. It's a couple of minutes after midnight on January eighteenth. I stare out across the field of elephant grass burned only a week ago that is already several inches high. The moon is high in the sky, a good thing, as it makes identifying silhouettes in the darkness much easier. I look at my watch again even though I checked it just minutes before. *Damn, still two hours to go till I can wake up Fishe.*

We're with Alpha battery, in a valley just south of Ben Het, where we're about seven klicks from Hill 875. The numbering of hills is not the way I would identify them if I were making maps, I'd give the hills more picturesque names. This is probably because I tend to store information better when it is associated with some visual imagery, but I do understand that numbering has tactical advantages. By designating a hill with a number that represents its height in meters it makes it simple to understand how much of an obstacle or hindrance the hill will be when looking at a map, but I still prefer those visual names like *Titty Mountain.* Hill 875 is just thirteen klicks or so from the Cambodian border.

The battery shells the hill constantly, not in support of military operations, just indiscreet bombardment. Every day, all day long, they shell it relentlessly. There doesn't seem to be any pattern to the time or the disbursement. Still, I wondered why we were doing this with 175s seven klicks from the hill, when it could be done fifteen or twenty miles away. I asked Fitzpatrick this very question when we were packing our gear to come out here. He told us the intent was to just shell the living hell out of the hill for a couple of weeks to discourage the NVA from using the hill.

The grapevine chatter has MACV intelligence suspecting a battalion of NVA is busy constructing bunkers and digging tunnels to fortify the hill. Of course, this is of great concern because 875 is so near the Cambodian border. If the VC and NVA are left to develop the hill it could eventually become a very defendable stronghold from which the NVA could launch offensives.

Watching the dozens of rounds pound the hill all day long, I wonder how anything, let alone a battalion of NVA and assorted VC could survive such a bombardment…yet they do. I know because we shell them all day, and they try to mortar us all night or at least they have for the six days we've been out here. We're anxious to get back to our own hill.

For the second successive night Jim, Smitty and I are sitting in foxholes as part of an ambush team. The ambush is set up to intercept any VC patrol unlucky enough to cross our field of fire. Should it be a company, well, we'd be fucked and everyone out here knows it. I don't like it. No one does, even with thirty of us spread around out here. My mind is busy registering complaints no one will ever hear. *Hell,* I think, *this bullshit is for the infantry, I'm just a damn wire stringer!* "Fuck," I mumble.

I pull my poncho over my head and put a Marlboro between my lips. I reach into my pocket and pull out my Zippo...the lighter always feels cool in my hands. I flip the top open and light up. The poncho conceals both the flame and the burning end of the cigarette. The lighter has been with me since boot camp. During its short, but useful life, it's seen a variety of different fuels, lighter fluid, gasoline, fuel oil, JP4 mixed with gasoline, and alcohol. I'm amazed it still works. Who knows what kind of toxic fumes I've sucked into my lungs when using the more exotic fuels. The fuel oil gives off heavy black smoke and the first couple of drags on the cigarette taste just like the fuel smells, but who cares. Would it be any worse than the fumes from the cigarette? No, probably not. Hell, I think the mosquito repellant we bath in will actually burn, how good can that be? I take a couple of quick drags and come out from under the poncho. Funny the kind of crap you think about in the middle of the night while you try to keep awake.

An occasional breeze keeps the elephant grass moving. It moves just enough to make the hair on the back of my neck stand up when it happens. "What's that?" I mumble almost inaudibly as I snap my head around to the left. I catch some motion out of the corner of my eye;

it's accompanied by an unrecognizable noise. I peer out over the grass but see nothing. Still, it is enough to make me pick up the handset on the radio. We try not to talk unless we absolutely have to. We check in once an hour by keying the mike the same number of times as our post designation. The squad leader acknowledges by keying his mike once.

"This is hole four I got some movement sixty yards southwest of my poz.

"Roger, four. Three can you see anything?" Sergeant Leon, the platoon Sergeant, waits for a response.

"Negative, we got nothin'."

"Okay, you guys keep your eyes open out there. Get everybody up, we shouldn't have people sleeping on a damned ambush anyway," Leon checks off.

"Jim, Jim…come on…get up." I shake Jim who's completely submerged himself under his poncho.

"Huh? What? Is it two already? Jesus, I feel like I just fell asleep." He complains groggily. He sits up, puts on his steel pot and looks at his watch. "Hey, what the hell…? What's wrong with you, I still got two hours to go, damn it."

"Hey, Leon says everyone has to get up. Someone called in some movement, so they want everyone up just in case." I keep staring out over the grass and neglect looking in Jim's direction.

"So what was it? Someone get spooked by the wind blowing the grass again?" Jim checks his weapon and shakes out the cobwebs by rotating his head and shrugging his shoulders.

"I'm not sure who it was," I lie, "Someone just called in and said they thought they saw something moving about fifty or sixty yards out there." I point out to my left.

"Well, did anybody else see it?" Jim asks.

"No way, man, no one else saw it."

"Well, what about you? Did you see anything?" Jim's peering out over the grass.

I hesitate just for a second, then respond, "I thought, maybe, I heard something, but can't be sure."

Jim's head turns slowly till he is looking directly at me, his face a scant few inches from the side of my head. "It was you, wasn't it? You called it in didn't you?"

"Yeah, yeah, it was me, but I'm tellin' ya I heard something." I almost feel embarrassed.

"Man, you're lettin' those short timer jitters get to you. You gotta shake that shit off, man, or you'll lose your edge." Jim sort of shakes his head a little. "Look, I know we consider ourselves short, but we got almost three months left, and we ain't gonna be able to dodge assignments for three months. So we gotta be sharper'n ever…it's the only way we're gonna survive, baby."

Once again Jim's logic proves infallible. I don't even have to think very hard, I know he's right. The radio clicks and I realize someone is keying their mike. I'm about to give my keyed response when I hear a whisper on the radio.

"Yeah, this is three; I caught some movement out here. There was a lot of rustling in the grass to the right of my hole."

I furl my brow and scrunch up my face turn and stare out in front of three's position.

Leon asks, "What do you mean rustling?"

"Just what I said, man, it's not the wind, there's something rooting around in the grass. Could be a VC, could be an animal, I can't tell."

"Okay, listen up. Get the Claymores ready, safeties off. Check your field of fire and I want constant reports, if Charlie gets by your holes, we gotta know, got it."

Adrenaline is flowin' now. I check my M-14 to make sure I have a round chambered. I know I do, but check it anyway. Jim checks the belt on the M-60 and cocks the weapon. We have trip flares set up across our field of view and flanking both the left and right of the ambush holes. If Charlie gets within' twenty-five yards, we'll know it. The trip wires are strung taut about six inches above the ground. The only way to get past them is to go over them, which would mean Charlie would have to show himself for a moment. We wait.

The problem with waiting is it nourishes ones level of anxiety, the longer we wait the more trigger-happy everyone gets, I'm no exception. I feel sure there is something out there, I've heard something and hole three just confirmed it. We're supposed to wait till we have verified NVA or VC sightings then try to cut them down before they reach the perimeter of the fire base. A platoon of men is standing-by at the fire base if we need to be reinforced. They'll be deployed to flank the VC once they know how big a force and where they intend to strike.

Standing orders are not to fire unless VC enter the ambush zone. There is some fear if we start popping off rounds every time someone gets an itchy trigger finger our positions will be compromised and the NVA will know exactly where our holes are situated. As simple and uneducated as a lot of us are, none of us remotely entertains the delusion that Charlie doesn't already know the exact position of each one of these holes. The defenses of the battery are set up to make this approach more favorable than any other. The minefields flanking the fire base are heavier with two or three times the mines and much more concertina wire. Hell, we even have motes filled with jet fuel that'll be ignited if they try to breach the perimeter from the flanks. So, in a sense, the VC are being herded right down our throat should they attack. There is no great comfort in knowing this.

"Did you hear that?" I whisper to Jim without turning my head.

"No. What? What did you hear?" We're both staring intently out over the grass. Our heads still, but our eyes scanning back and forth trying to discern the smallest amount of movement or a silhouette that doesn't belong there.

"What the hell is that?" I point.

Jim and I stare at patch of eight-inch grass. It's rustling around back and forth almost like someone is rolling around in it. We stare intently, my finger on the trigger of my weapon, it's taking enormous restraint to keep from pulling the trigger. Then, out of the night, from the vicinity of the moving grass, a high-pitched, bone chilling, hideous-screeching scream.

"Sca...reeeeeeeech!"

As if the screaming had somehow flipped a switch somewhere, it instantly spawns an intensive mass of fire from thirty weapons. The M-60's delivering a symphonic wave of tracers that etch their burning trail through the darkness flowing out of the machine guns like a futuristic kind of laser ray. Jim expends a half a can of ammo before he stops firing. I empty a magazine from my M-14. Then, as if the switch is flipped off, all the weapons stop. We wait for return fire; there is none.

"Fwump... Wham!" Someone pumps an M-79 grenade round to within a couple of feet of the spot. Again, no fire is returned.

Leon is on the radio, "How many, what direction? How come no trip flares have gone off, what the hell is going on?" No one can provide a suitable answer. So, once again, we wait. Nobody bothers suggesting someone crawl out and see what's out there. If someone did, it'd be a very short list of volunteers.

The sun's been up for at least fifteen minutes. Normally, we'd leave our holes in a half-hour or so, but today we're being extra cautious about crawling out of our holes, no one wants a VC sniper blowing off their head.

Jim's found out from Leon that the battery is going to start a barrage in about ten minutes. When the guns start sending their 175mm morning wake up calls to the VC, six of us are supposed to go find out whether or not we scored a kill or just wasted a few hundred rounds of ammo.

When the guns begin their thunderous thumping, we hesitatingly climb out of our holes, crouched, alert, and extremely wary. Jim motions with his head and says, "Okay, let's go."

We spread out, crouch down and begin moving cautiously through the elephant grass. A few moments later, Jim's hand goes up and he stands in a relaxed manner.

"Holy shit, man, that is fucking disgusting!" Lonnie says as we look into the small clearing.

Jim, always looking for an opportunity to use the thirty-eight, unholsters it, takes aim and fires three shots. All three shots thud into the thick heavy flesh of the snake's head, or what appears to be its head. I think it's a python. The damn thing has to be ten or twelve feet long. It's as thick as my thigh and in the process of swallowing what I believe is a little baby pig, at least that's what we think. All we can see are the hind legs and rear end of the animal, the only parts still sticking out of the snake's mouth. It looks like the snake has somehow unconnected its jaw and is stretching it over the baby pig. The snake was still alive till Jim blew the top part of its head off. The snake must have been trying to swallow the pig for a while. *Sheesh, it's ghastly.*

"Christ, that's fucking disgusting!" I just turn away not wanting to look any longer.

"God O' Mighty, that damn snake got its mouth stretched out enough to swallow a damn Virginia smoked ham! Only this ham ain't smoked. Man, what kind of snake is that anyway?"

"I think it's a python," Jim replies. "They squeeze the life out of their prey, then start swallowin' the kill while it's still warm." We grimace at Jim's explanation.

"Geez," I comment, "This is one real big fuckin' snake, man."

I am suddenly struck with a chilling thought. "Man, what a fucking horrible way to die, eaten, slowly." I shudder just thinking about it.

Lindlay notes, "Hey, maybe we should take it back with us. Ain't nobody gonna believe 'dis anyway."

I shake my head, turn and say, "Who the hell cares? Fuck it, let's get out of here, before they stop the barrage and Charlie comes out of their holes and starts takin' pot shots at us." I'm already walking.

We report what we found to Sergeant Leon who seems to digest it without the slightest look of apprehension. We eat, then head for the bunkers and about six hours of sleep.

"What time is it?" I ask, sitting on the edge of the cot inside the bunker.

"About fourteen thirty," Jim is sitting in his cot leaning back against the sandbags reading a book.

"Man, I didn't sleep for shit. Those damn 175s woke me up three times." I stretch and yawn. I look out the doorway and I light up a Marlboro. *Damn, I'm smokin' more and more,* I think to myself. *I must be doin' about three packs a day. How good can that be?*

"So did Fitzpatrick stop by and give us the bad news?"

Jim dog-ears a page and stashes his book, "Yeah, he came by but we lucked out, we don't have to pull ambush duty tonight."

"Thank God! Hell, maybe we can actually get some damn sleep for a change."

"Well, we ought to be able to get some." Jim looks at me and waits for my response.

"Whata'ya mean, *some*?" Suddenly, I'm apprehensive.

"We're goin' out on patrol."

"You got to be shittin' me…fuck!"

We're gonna go on a sweep of the north edge of the valley in about forty-five minutes. When we get back, we're on stand by, but we get to sleep in shifts. If nothing happens, we should log some serious zees tonight."

I want to complain, but what good will it do? Besides, I don't want to turn into a habitual complainer or become a pain in the ass. No one likes listening to someone who bitches constantly. We tend to avoid the bitchers like the plague. They're never happy unless they drag everyone down into their morass of self-pity.

"Okay, what'a we got for eats?"

Jim tosses me a box of C rations which I manage to eat in about ten minutes. I grab the little packet of paper from the rations and head for the latrine.

Thirty-six of us stand around waiting for Sergeant Leon. We're geared up for patrol, lots of ammo, vests, water, smokes, grenades, repellant, a poncho and more ammo. Knowing the weight of all the ammo and crap we carry around, it occurs to me that my M-14, which used to seem incredibly heavy way back when, has become seemingly weightless.

Leon is pretty young for a Staff Sergeant, twenty-two, twenty-three tops. He has very chiseled features and jet-black hair. He reminds me of those guys who model underwear in the Sears Roebuck catalogs. He seems to be okay and doesn't talk down to anybody so most guys have respect for him and respond to his orders readily.

Leon slips on his flak jacket, has his radioman do a commo check, then barks out, "Okay, lock and load, let's move out."

We move out in three squads, moving northwest, avoiding the trip flares and other surprises we've spread around. We work our way towards the edge of the valley, a couple of klicks from the fire base. Our range of operation will fall short of actually patrolling the hills they're meant to discourage the staging of VC patrols or to grab a prisoner if the opportunity arises.

We've almost completed our sweep and are about to begin the return. The second squad moves out of the jungle, lagging behind providing cover for our squad. Leon is just in front of us with the radioman. The point man's arm goes up and his hand clenches into a ball…he gives the signal to take cover. Crouched down, he points to a location in the jungle. Leon signals the other squads and motions for us to move in. We move slowly and cautiously into the jungle, covering just a couple of feet every minute or so. I'm ready to fire, my finger anxiously waiting to squeeze the trigger, beads of sweat rolling down the small of my back.

Come on, come on, where are the little bastards? My eyes are moving around rapidly, stopping for a split second at the slightest movement of every leaf or twig. My heart is pumping so hard I feel my chest heave against the buttons of my shirt with every beat.

With a signal from Leon we shift and move more to the left. We've all been here before, no one makes as much as a rustling sound as we pick our way through the bush.

Leon stops our approach; we wait. Finally, he stands up and signals to withdraw. As we start moving back towards the clearing, a rustling in the bushes makes me snap around and bring up my rifle. *Something is coming... it isn't a person... it's an animal and it's moving fast.* I remember the tiger that Captain Blowhole killed and my heart begins racing even faster.

Jim is a few yards away, his M-16 ready, "What the hell is it?" He yells. I don't turn but keep focused on the jungle, "How the fuck am I supposed to know?" I'm moving backwards now, not fast and not in a panic.

The animal charges out of the brush and ground cover...it's a damned boar! It's coming right at me. I freeze for a second and Jim fires a couple of rounds, both missing. I squeeze the trigger on my M-14, firing from the hip; missing badly. I start to run, immediately I know it's a mistake. The boar overtakes me in mere seconds. It gores me from behind ripping a hole in my left calf. I pitch forward and twist as I fall to land on my back. The Boar is on me like stink on shit, snapping his head all over the place trying to gore me again. I'm whacking at it wildly with the butt of my rifle trying to lunge out of its way. I manage to get the muzzle of my rifle turned towards the boar and start firing wildly. I either graze or scare it, because it screeches and takes off for the bushes. I try like hell to stand up but stumble and fall back down. Again, I try standing, I can hear the mean little bastard making that same hideous noise he made when he first charged and know he's coming again. Jim is next to me trying to help me up. Lindlay and his new pal Lonnie have come over to help. When the boar emerges from the brush again, they all open up with their M-16s, there's a couple of quick squeals and then silence.

"Jesus, can you walk?" Leon asks. My leg is bleeding like a motherfucker and I'm using Jim for support. I try to put weight on my leg and manage to stand, but *god... damn* it hurts like hell.

"Man, look at the size of that pig! Damn things gotta weigh a couple of hundred pounds." Someone says.

"Get Doc Healy up here," Leon calls back to the other squad. Healy, the medic, squats over me and uses his bayonet to split my pant leg up above the knee.

"Any numbness?" he asks as he tears away the pants.

"No, man, it fuckin' hurts like hell," I grimace as he re-positions my leg. He pulls out his canteen and starts washing the wound, looks it over and pulls out a dressing. "Not to wide but deep. Might be able to get by without stitches, but you should probably get 'em." He sprinkles some powder, a disinfectant I guess, and dresses the wound.

"Okay, let's get the hell outta here, *Let's move out.*" Leon motions with his arm as he barks out his command.

Jim and Lindlay act as crutches for me as we make our way back to the fire base. I have an arm behind each one of their necks, and hop along on the one good leg. Darkness is setting in by the time we make it back. The ambush team has already taken their positions.

In the medical bunker, the medic has me face down on a cot. A few electric lights are strung across the top of the bunker, a convenience we do not have in ours, and he's preparing to sew me up.

"You got Novocain?" I ask, hoping to avoid the pain I mentally associate with the sewing job about to take place.

"No, but it won't hurt all that much. They won't evac you for this at night, so you won't get outta here till tomorrow sometime. It'll be better if you let me sew it up.

"Come on, don't be a pussy, let 'em sew it," Jim razzes.

"Yeah, yeah, easy for you to say, you haven't gotten a scratch since we got here. Yeah, go ahead and sew it. Try not to put too many stitches in?"

Doc removes the dressing and looks at it again…it's still bleeding. "Looks like maybe two or three should close it up." He opens his medical pack and pulls out the necessary equipment. He takes some alcohol and wipes the wound.

"*Jee…sus!*" The alcohol burns like hell. He opens a package of what I call thread, but he calls suture. I stiffen when he tears open the little packet that contains the needle. It looks big, real big. It's a big curved needle and he's about to stick it in my leg.

"Man, you ain't sticking that fucking thing in me." I immediately object.

"Come on, it's not going to be that bad, I promise you, Okay? Look, just don't watch. Keep your eyes focused on something else, alright?" He looks at me to make sure I look away. It doesn't relieve my anxiety.

"Yeeeowwww!" I yelp. He pushes the needle through and I can feel the suture pull through the skin on both sides of the wound. He pulls it slowly and it burns, the suture feeling like it is a length of hot wire. He squeezes the wound together with two fingers, ties it off, then sticks the needle through again.

"God damn it! That fucking hurts!"

"Come on, ya pussy, quit whining," Jim jibes.

"It hurts, damn it," I turn to complain to Jim, it distracts me long enough for Doc to finish the third stitch. When I look back, he's tying it off.

"There, ya wimp, I'm done." He pulls out another dressing, cleans off the wound and dresses it. "You won't have to worry about pulling duty for a week or so. It's gonna hurt like hell for a couple of days. Here take these and try to get some sleep."

"What's this, morphine?" I ask as I take the pills.

"Not hardly, just some painkillers with a heavy dose of codeine. When's the last time you got a tetanus shot?" He asks as he packs up his stuff.

"Probably when I got this," I point at the scar over my right eye.

"Well, you better get one when you get back, them pigs are always rootin' around in shit and dirt, so infection is a good possibility. Doc picks up his bag and leaves.

Jim is giggling. "What's so funny?"

"I was just thinking. Ya know they ain't gonna give you a Purple Heart for this, you didn't get it as a result of enemy fire." He laughs even harder. "Damn, that would be a great story for the "Stars and Stripes" 'Short Timer killed by deadly enemy Pig!' " He chuckles some more and gathers up his gear. "See ya in the A.M." Jim leaves the bunker still laughing. Fifteen minutes later the codeine takes effect and I'm out.

"What...? Huh...?" There's automatic weapons fire, explosions, and dirt is falling on me from the top of the bunker.

Wham! Wham! Wham! Three mortar rounds detonate inside the fire base. I grab my M-14 and steel pot and get up, immediately falling to my knees. My leg still hurts like a motherfucker. I get up again and hobble out to one of the perimeter bunkers. There is a tremendous amount of weapons fire, most of it outside the perimeter.

"What's going on?" I ask the guy standing next to me.

"A platoon of VC walked right into the ambush. Trip flares were goin' off all over the damn place, then they started lightin' up the claymores. They've got a good firefight goin on out there. Charlie hasn't gotten past the holes and they sent out the back-up platoon fifteen minutes ago. Looks like they've got Charlie pinned down."

"What about the mortars?" I look around and try to see what kind of damage we've taken, all the 175s are manned and delivering deadly messages to the side of the nearest hill, probably trying randomly to knock out the mortars that are supporting Charlie's retreat. Someone has a field radio nearby and we can hear the chatter from it, but not well enough to determine what's going on. It hasn't occurred to me till this very moment, but I use my lighter to check my watch…It's four-thirty in the morning.

By five-thirty the weapons fire has stopped. The 175s still fire a round every ten minutes or so but everyone else has pulled back inside the perimeter. The wounded are brought back and mop up operations begin. Everything seems to be winding down so I decide to return to the bunker and try to get some more codeine-assisted sleep.

"Simon! Simon! Wake up!" Lindlay is shaking me. I groggily lean up on my right elbow, "Yeah, yeah, I'm awake." I wait for my eyes to focus and my brain to clear a little, then sit up. I'm instantly reminded of the hole in the back of my leg. I sit there grimacing for a few moments till the throbbing subsides.

"Come on, get your gear together, choppers on the way in, they're comin' in to ship you and Fishe to the hospital."

"Fishe?" What do you mean Fishe? I can see Lee's vest is blood stained. "What do you mean Fishe?" I ask again. "What the hell happened?" I'm suddenly oblivious to the pain in my leg and am up on my feet.

"Jimbo took a round in the belly, he's bleedin' bad, it doesn't look like the medics can stop it." There is fear in Lee's eyes; fear is contagious. Staring into his eyes, the fear courses its way through my body and without any further exchange of words, I know it's bad.

Instinctively, I grab my gear and head out the door regardless of the pain. I'm not completely oblivious to it, but don't care. Still, I hobble badly. I can see Jim on a stretcher near the pad with two medics hovering over him. His shirt is torn away and the medics are tending to his dressings. The shirt is completely covered in blood. His face and skin have a hideous pallor obviously from the loss of blood. His eyes are closed and he is unconscious. One of the medics turns to look at me. Looking straight into the medics eyes, hoping to see some glimmer of hope, I ask how bad Jim's injuries are. The encouragement I'm hoping to find is not there.

Still looking me in the eye, he shakes his head and mumbles, "We don't know, we just don't know. He's lost a shithouse of blood. If the chopper don't get here soon, well…"

My stomach retches, I turn away not wanting to look. I don't want this to be my last memory of Jim. Instinctively I begin thinking of him at his best, tears are welling up in my eyes. *"Man, where the fuck is that chopper?"* In the distance, a faint thwack, thwack, thwack, signals the incoming Medivac. Seconds later the Huey noses up and begins lowering itself to the ground. Blinding clouds of red dust swirl around as it touches down. No time is wasted. I'm helped onto the chopper first, then Jim's stretcher is loaded, a medic on the chopper receiving the IV bag, he immediately begins attending to Jim. In a swift smooth action the pilot lifts the Huey off the ground and swings it around a hundred and eighty degrees, then heads for the hospital at Pleiku. I sit with my back against the bulkhead and look at Jim's unconscious body. It occurs to me that when Jim ventured out with the ambush team it was the first time either one of us has been out in the shit without the other.

The Chopper noises are muted. I'm oblivious to the roar and am oblivious to all the vibrations and sensations normally associated with a ride in a Huey. We seem to float across the sky, not quite in slow motion, but not with the thunderous urgency the choppers always seem to emanate. I lean my head back against the bulkhead and close my eyes, I do my best to pray.

The pilot sets his bird down twenty yards from the hospital; they probably do this at least a dozen times a day. The triage team is ready for us; Jim is off the chopper and into surgery in less than two minutes. A nurse attends to my leg and administers a tetanus shot. Someone from the hospital notifies the hill and Farmly is dispatched to pick me up and transport me back to the Hill.

I'm not sure how much time passes, maybe an hour, maybe more, it feels like an eternity. I don't even realize it, but suddenly I'm aware that Farmly is standing next to me asking me if I'm ready to leave.

"You ready?" His tone is one of concern, not the typical sarcasm Farmly is known for.

I look at him and shake my head, "No, I think I'm gonna wait awhile, I gotta know if Jim's gonna make it."

"Hey, sometimes they're in surgery for hours, man, you sure you want to wait around?" He sits down next to me and looks around. "Where do they have him?"

I motion with my head at the hooch across the way. "Over there," I add, "Hey, if you don't want to hang around, just go ahead and go back. I can always catch a ride."

Farmly looks around and halfheartedly says, "Yeah, it's okay with me, but you know they won't let me come back after dark. It could be hours."

"You said that already...I ain't goin' anywhere."

Farmly flops down next to me, I'm sure he's just as anxious to find out if Jim is going to make it. As soon as he sat down I knew he was there for the duration, I knew it without his having to say it…so we wait.

We sit in a blank, a vacuum. Nothing seemingly happening, I'm overwhelmed with a feeling of emptiness that can only be matched by the void of deep space, the limitless hollow, or lack of atmosphere, the blackness. The second hand on my watch moves as though the watch was filled with molasses. Every once in a while I get up and hobble outside the tent to smoke. I lean against the pole staring out over the countryside, unable to focus on anything, then return and sit back down. No conversation is exchanged.

"Hey!" Farmly jabs me with his elbow.

A doctor emerges from the operating hooch. His facemask hanging down on his blood splattered chest. He produces a cigarette, lights it and stands there, contemplating whatever it is that doctors contemplate following a messy surgery. I only hope he's not trying to figure out what he did wrong. Moving towards the doctor, I can see his eyes lock in on us as we approach. He makes no attempt to look away, but just watches as I hobble in his direction with Farmly following. I interpret this as a good sign.

"What can I do for you?" he asks as we draw near. Farmly salutes. I do not.

"We've been waiting, Sir, waiting to find out if our friend is gonna make it?" Farmly points to the tent as he asks.

"Your friend lost a lot of blood and we had to take part of his stomach and small intestines. It's a very serious." He takes another drag from his cigarette.

"Sir, I mean no disrespect but I just want to know if he's gonna fucking make it."

The doctor looks at me. My pant leg is still torn away, my leg is bandaged, both Farmly and I are covered in red dust, we're both carrying weapons and my flak jacket is stained with blood. The doctor realizes we aren't going to leave till we get an answer. He understands we have just come from the shit, probably why he doesn't bust our nuts for being disrespectful.

Tossing his cigarette, he says, "Yeah, I think he's gonna make it. We'll keep him here till he's well enough to transfer then probably fly him to Japan. After he recuperates it'll be back home for him. He won't be returning to your unit. I'd offer to let you see him, but he'll be out of it for hours. Anybody look at that leg?"

"Yes sir, it's been looked at, thank you sir." I salute and turn away.

The ride to the hill is somber. I wonder if I will ever see Jim again. I try to light up, but my Zippo is dry. "Light?"

"Yeah, here," Farmly hands me a book of C ration matches. You know Smitty's orders came through, so did Varant's. They're both out of here day after tomorrow.

The sun is near setting as we pull through the gate of the hill. Driving through the gate doesn't fill me with the sense of security I've become accustomed to since the Hill has become my home. Farmly drops me at the med station where the medics look me over then drive me to the orderly room so I can check in with Neuman. I'll be on light duty for a week or two. I should be relieved I won't be out in the field or have to pull guard duty for those two weeks, but I'm not. In my heart there is a burning urge to kill VC. It isn't a conscious thought, but I feel it and I know what it is.

Inside the hooch I remove my blood soaked boots and fatigues. I can see all of my lower left leg is swollen. The calf is totally black and blue. Farmly got back to the hooch well before I did, so everyone is already talking about Jim. I should feel relieved, the doctor said he was going to make it, but I'm not.

Varant is already packed. His duffel bag is full, all the paraphernalia and pictures he used to have pinned around his bunk is gone. He walks over and sits next to me.

"Normally, I'd have to give you some shit about getting' gored by a goddamn pig, but I guess I should just say goodbye." He extends his hand. I grasp it firmly and shake it.

"Hal, you take care. Man, I'm sure gonna miss ya. We'll never find out anything once you're gone. What the hell are you gonna do when you get back to the States?"

"I'm gonna get shit faced, get a load of pussy, and become a hippie!"

"A hippie, you?"

"Yeah, man, a hippie. All they do is get high, and screw. Hell, I hear sometimes you can get two or three broads in bed with you at the same time!"

"Well don't get too high, man, you can't enjoy all that pussy if you can't remember getting' it."

After Varant ambles off, I lay back on my cot and stare at the black and white pictures stuck to the top inside of my mosquito netting. I reach up and grab the picture of Varant, Jim, and I that was taken just after we got the heater for the shower. I hold it up, look at Varant busying himself around his cot, and then back at the picture. The man in the picture looks much, much younger than the one I see packing his gear. *Christ,* I think, *has this place had that effect on me?* I sit up and wash down a couple of painkillers with a swig of warm beer. I'm asleep before chow time.

Seventy-two and a wake up. Smitty and Varant pile their duffel bags into the back of the Jeep Frenchy will use to get them to PAB. What's left of our platoon is standing in front of the hooch watching them get ready to leave. In a ceremonious fashion, Smitty shakes everybody's hand, then hands me a piece of paper with his address in Oklahoma.

"Here," he says, "look me up when you get back."

Varant shakes a couple of hands, then snaps to attention and makes a half-baked salute. It's the only time I've ever seen him voluntarily follow military decorum; then they're gone. I'm filled with a sense of emptiness.

"Man, I'm right behind 'em." Coleman says as he watches the Jeep drive through the front gate.

"Huh?" I wait for an explanation.

"Man, I'm overdue, my orders should've been here by now. I was supposed to ship out five days ago. Top called over to MACV yesterday to find out what's keepin' 'em." Coleman appears relatively calm, a hell of a lot calmer than I would be.

Back in the hooch I flop back on my cot. *Sheesh! Fishe, gone... Smitty, gone... Varant, gone...Coleman will be gone in a day or two...Shit!* I know Frenchy is shorter than I am, so is Lindlay. Damn, I'm going to be stuck here with Pinetti, and Farmly. *Who the hell we gonna get to replace them?*

These guys have been as close to me as my shadow. Now, I'm overwhelmed with apprehension wondering what the hell I'm gonna do without them.

"Hey, Frenchy," I yell across the room.

"Yeah?"

"How many?"

"Twenty-nine and a wake up baby." He smiles.

"Fuck!"

"Turner, how long you got?"

"Fifty-four and a wake up, Jack!"

I lay in my cot for an hour mentally recapturing all the moments I've shared with these guys. I realize the ten months I've spent with them has bonded us in ways that makes me closer to them than I've ever been to anybody else. I know I'm attached to them for the rest of my life whether I ever see them again or not. I get out of my cot and hobble to the orderly room. Sergeant Neuman is not at his usual place sitting behind the Top's desk. Instead, there is an E-8 named Casey.

Sergeant Casey looks at me and asks, "Can I help you, son?"

"Uh, I was looking for Sergeant Neuman," I almost stutter as I reply.

"Where you been, boy, Sergeant Neuman rotated yesterday. I'm Sergeant Casey the new First Sergeant." He stands up and shakes my hand.

I'm dumbfounded…I stand there with my mouth gaping. I numbly reach out and shake his hand.

"So what was it that you wanted to see Sergeant Neuman about, son?" He sits back down.

"Well, Sarge," I pause for a moment to see if the term Sarge is objectionable, "Well, I've only got a couple of months left, and I'm wondering if I can take my R & R. I'm on light duty so I won't be doing much good around here anyway."

"Where is it you want to go, Simon?" Casey asks.

"Whatever comes up next Sarge."

"You got it. I'll let you know."

"Thanks." I turn and walk out the door.

Jesus, Neuman left and I didn't even know it. I sit down on the sand bag wall that we put up around the barracks and light a cigarette. I shouldn't be surprised everybody's rotating. Most of them came over together as a unit a little over a year ago, so I know I can look forward to a mass exodus and an influx of new faces over the next few weeks. I finish the cigarette and hobble back to my rack.

Chapter Nineteen

"Aloha"

Sixty-seven and a wake up. Coleman is gone, so is Frenchy, only Turner, Lindlay, Pinetti and Farmly make up the remnants of the platoon. Four new guys arrived yesterday and Fitzpatrick has two of them following me around the hill trying to get them up to speed. One of them, a tall skinny guy named Kevin Nelson, is from Chicago. The other guy is from Colorado Springs his name is Robert Nance. It's a good thing he wasn't around when Bennett was here, 'cause I'm sure he'd be calling him Nancy.

The other two guys, Tom Wilcox and John Martin are out with Pinetti troubleshooting a line on the other side of the hill. Wilcox is actually an RTD man who's going to take Varant's place in the crypto trailer. On a run to Pleiku Air Base to pick up some gear I find that Spencer has also rotated back to the State's and his roommate Tech Sergeant Belden has taken over the franchise. My only interest is getting ammo for my thirty-eight's. I have two now, because I inherited Jim's after Ben Het. I'm considering giving it to Fitzpatrick, but haven't made up my mind yet.

We're back at the hill just in time to stand a formation Sgt. Casey is holding.

"Okay, men, Pleiku is off limits. There's been a couple of killings so II Corps is declaring the city closed. Next item, there are four R&R's available: two for Hawaii and two for Bangkok."

I respond immediately, "I'm in, Top!" Turner, Fitzpatrick and Castle lay claim the other three. I'm certain Pinetti would have jumped at the chance, but he's still over on the other side of the hill.

"Okay, Simon, where'd ya want to go, Bangkok or Hawaii?"

Deciding is not easy. The stories guys have brought back from Bangkok are vivid, if you believe them. They always seem to end up being four day fuck-fests. The hotels purportedly have live-in prostitutes that move into the rooms with you when you check in. You can have as many women as you want or feel you can handle. They go everywhere with you and will fuck as often as you want. Hawaii, on the other hand, provides no guarantees. However, it is a major naval seaport, so I'm pretty confident that prostitutes are going to be around, more expensive, but available. Hawaii does have some things that Thailand doesn't: Hawaii is a State... it's America. There will be Americans all over the place. They'll have real American food, there will be people I can talk to who will understand me, and I'm pretty sure, it won't stink. I long ago convinced myself that all these little shit-hole countries, Vietnam, Laos, and Thailand all smell the same way. Another very attractive thing about Hawaii is the R & R is five days plus travel time so I'll be away for eight whole days, that's eight days I won't spend in-country.

"Hawaii for me Sarge."

"Me, too," Turner yells.

"Okay you guys better get your shit together, you ship out tomorrow morning. The Bangkok trip leaves Thursday." Casey relieves us and I make a beeline for the orderly room. I have to get back over to MACV to draw my pay. I've only been drawing about fifty bucks a month and letting the Army roll the rest over from month-to-month so I wouldn't piss it all away. I have over fifteen hundred bucks coming to me; I plan to spend every penny of it.

At seven in the morning Fitzpatrick ferries us over to the terminal at PAB. From there we'll fly to Cam Rahn bay on a military transport. The flight to Hawaii will be aboard a commercial airliner.

"How much dough you got?" I ask turner.

" 'Bout nine hundred...you?"

"Fifteen hundred and I'm blowing every fucking dime, no matter how long it takes."

It's a one-hour flight aboard C-130 to Cam Rahn Bay. Once we're there they herd us through a processing center in typical Army fashion; then we're given a spiel warning us to not catch a flight to the mainland from Hawaii. Special pains are taken to remind us that desertion can be punishable by death – *So can war,* I think.

"Yeah, yeah, come on let's get the show on the road." I mumble under my breath. I'm not in the mood for the normal military hurry up and wait bullshit, the sentiment is shared by everyone in the room.

We line up on the Tarmac as the 707 rolls in - it's nineteen hundred hours. I'm anxious. Most of the day has been spent farting around and I'm not any closer to Hawaii. The hatch opens and a couple of airmen roll a stairway up to the door. A stewardess in a short blue skirt and short sleeve white top waits alluringly in the doorway to greet us. As I ascend the stairway my eyes lock on her nylon covered legs. They're shapely, they're firm, they disappear up into her skirt about mid-thigh...my R&R has officially started.

We're seated five across, three seats on one side, two on the other; I get the window. Five Stewardesses are tending the plane. It's been a long time since I've been around American women…they smell good. I've already started fantasizing about them and know every guy on this plane, is, at this very moment, doing the exact same thing. Every set of eyes on the plane fixates on these women. They go through the safety drill with the oxygen masks and flotation devices, and then, just like that, we're airborne.

I watch the Vietnam coast disappear from the window. I know there are guys down there dying even as I look. I'm glad it isn't me.

"Would you like something to drink?" A stewardess asks. It snaps me out of my morbid train of thought and focuses my attention on my current surroundings.

I look up and her nametag steers my focus to her breasts. They aren't large, but they're big enough so the material stretches away from the buttons when she leans over.

"Do you have American beer?" I ask.

"Budweiser and Old Style." She smiles.

"Old Style for me," I reply. Beer? Am I nuts? That's not what I want.

"Wait!" I call out. The stewardess pauses.

"On second thought, do you have cold milk?"

"You bet, honey." She smiles.

"Then let me have a couple glasses of milk."

Turner looks at me; a look of wonderment washes over his face, he smiles and blurts out, "Yeah, I'll have milk too!"

"Yeah, that's what I'll have," rings out from somewhere behind.

"Me too!"

"Yeah, I'll have milk and beer!"

"Milk here." Everyone wants milk; amazingly they're able to accommodate everyone.

I pick up one of the small cartons. It's cold. Beads of condensation, like ice-cold beads of sweat, wet my fingertips. I pull apart the fold and squeeze it together to make the opening. I can *smell* the milk. I lift the carton to my lips and tilt it up slowly till I feel the cold liquid wash over my tongue and hit the back of my throat. It's good, it's real good. I resist the temptation to down the entire contents in one big swig. Instead, I pour a small amount into my mouth and lower the carton. I close my eyes, lean my head back and let the milk wash around in my mouth. Slowly the milk in my mouth disappears. I know instantly that at this moment in time there is no food I would appreciate more. In Nam, I could get just about anything, anything except fresh milk and hot edible meals. Yes, fresh, whole, homogenized milk, pretty basic stuff, yet we could never get it. Milk is something I've taken for granted for my entire life…I'll never do it again.

I finish one carton and start on the second. A glance at Turner reveals a look of contentment, his big smile an icon of satisfaction. Looking around the cabin I find everyone's face has the same mesmerized look.

"Goddamn, that was good!" Someone yells from a couple of rows in front. "Stewardess, stewardess, can I get more?"

The stewardesses continue serving milk to the delight of everyone on the plane. They serve it till there is none left to be had.

As the plane speeds through the sky on its southeasterly path, weariness overcomes me. Excitement and anticipation have kept me from sleeping for over two days. I tilt back my seat, turn off the little overhead light, close my eyes and drift into a comfortable sleep.

"Simon?" Turner nudges me. I look up and see the stewardess leaning over.

"Would you like a dinner, Hon?"

"No, I think I'll just sleep."

She smiles and says, "If you get hungry later I can get you something for a snack." I smile and drift back to sleep. I spend the next nine hours drifting in and out of sleep, waking only long enough to eat a snack, confirm my whereabouts and then fall back to sleep.

Turner wakes me when the plane starts its final descent to Honolulu Airport. A couple of minutes later the wheels touch the ground and the plane taxis to the terminal.

As we deplane, there are two amazingly beautiful women dressed in tight floral sarongs greeting all the GIs as they deplane. Both women possess shoulder length jet-black hair; amazingly smooth complexions and sexually endearing smiles highlighted by brilliant white teeth. Their sarongs accentuate their figures by stretching the material across their bottoms and wrapping tightly around their waists. The strapless bodices make both of them seem to have overly generous, perfectly shaped breasts.

As we pass, one of the girls Lei's us (I wish) with a sweet smelling floral wreath and follows with a quick smack on the cheek. Though, the kiss is quick and impersonal, I can't help but notice the softness of her lips and the sweetness of her breath.

Walking away, I turn for a final look, as does everybody; like a completely infatuated idiot, I say, "Holy Jamolie! I can't even imagine how it would feel to have a body like that pressed up against mine! Man, oh, man."

Turner replies, "Boy, they don't grow them like that back in the States, do they?"

"This is the States," I quip.

"You know what I mean, asshole."

We board a bus headed for Fort DeRussey. The windows are open and I'm overwhelmed with the sweet smelling brisk air that rushes through the bus. It carries an aroma of freshness and cleanliness so unlike the pungent foul odor of Vietnam. I close my eyes. The air is thick with the smell of Hibiscus, the same flower the Leis are made from. From behind the smile on my face I think Hawaii may be as close to paradise as I will ever get.

Fort DeRussey is a small military post tucked in among the towering hotels and surrounding shops on Ala Moana blvd. In the event that any of us were strapped, we were welcome to use the accommodations available at DeRussey. Hell, they even have their own stretch of beach. It comes as no surprise, but no one opts to enjoy the lovely accommodations at Fort DeRussey. Let's face it, every swingin' dick on R & R wants to live the next five days like it will be our last five days on the face of the earth.

During our short indoctrination we get the dos and don'ts and a quick spiel about the city. Everyone is anxious to get the show on the road; finally, they let us go.

Standing on the sidewalk in our Khakis looking up and down Ala Moana Boulevard, I turn to Turner and ask, "Well, we gonna share a room or what?"

Turner is absorbed with all the activity taking place but stops gawking long enough to reply. "Just for two days. My parents are flying over for my last three days."

"Your parents? Isn't that going to put the whammy on your plans to get some Polynesian poontang?"

Turner replies, "Look, you know and I know what can happen when we get back, I thought it might be the last chance I ever get to see them, but it's more than that, I think it's because I'm afraid I'll forget them, know what I mean?"

It's a sobering thought. I try to remember the faces of my family and immediately know what he's talking about. I wish I had a family picture in my wallet, but don't.

"Hey, I didn't mean to get you all depressed, man." Turner puts his hand on my shoulder and looks at me with a big devilish smile." Hell, we still got two days to tear this place a new asshole."

"You know it, brother. Let's get the show on the road."

Our first stop is the Hilton at the Hawaiian Village, a beautiful hotel not too far from DeRussey; from the looks of it I know it's going to be pricey. We approach the front desk and ask about a room.

The luxuriousness of the surroundings overwhelms me to the point I almost trip over my tongue, "A room...we'd like a room. Uh, how much is it?" It dawns on me I've never actually done this before. I've never ever been in a hotel room, at least not as an adult. Of course I've only been an adult for a couple of years.

The clerk checks his bookings. "Well," he says, "Looks like all we've got is a couple of doubles available. How long will you boys be staying?"

"Depends on how much it is," Turner replies.

"Well the double is eighty-five a night." He patiently waits for our reply.

I instantly realize we're talking about a months pay and comment, "Holy shit! Man, that's way more money than I want to spend on a room."

Turner points out, "Yeah, but if we split it it's only forty a night."

"There's gotta be cheaper places, this is the Hilton, for God's sake." I've never been in a hotel but I know the Hilton has to be one of the more expensive. "Hell, man, I want to blow my money on broads and booze, not on the damn room. How much time we gonna spend in the room anyway?"

Turner begrudgingly agrees. "Okay let's try that one over there." He points to another hotel a couple of blocks west. A large sign on the side of the building proclaims it to be Ilikai. After making the walk, we find to our dismay, the Ilikai is actually more expensive than the Hilton. We agree to spend one night at the Hilton then rent a car and find cheaper accommodations.

We pay in advance and carry our small bags up the elevator to the fourth floor. The room is immaculate.

Turner showers first. When he finishes I enter the bathroom, tear the little paper ring off the toilet seat and take a piss. While pissing, I look around the bathroom, amazed by all the little details. There are several small bars of soap, six bath towels, two shaving towels, four washcloths, a floor mat, water glasses and a small bottle of shampoo. I notice a rheostat switch on the wall and turn it, curious as to its purpose. My head turns up to look at the heat lamp embedded in the ceiling. *Damn,* I think. There is a note on the door requesting that room towels not be taken to the pool because there are towels available at the pool.

After undressing, I climb into the shower. I start with the water warm, but keep adjusting it hotter and hotter till the room is filled with steam. I stand under the flow of hot steaming water letting it run down my face and the front of my body. I slowly lather up with the small bar of soap and washcloth. I move the cloth over my body in small circular motions. The cloth is soft; it doesn't rough itself against my skin. As I rinse out the washcloth I notice that the cloth, once white, is now stained reddish brown. It's just a subtle reminder of the ever-present reddish-brown dust from Nam that has attached itself to us like a parasite. I turn my back to the shower head and lean forward, bracing myself against the wall to let the water flow down my spine for another ten minutes.

"Hey, you gonna spend the whole five days in the damned shower?" Turner yells as he bangs on the door.

I remind myself, the shower will be here tomorrow. *Damn, it's just a shower...and yet, how can it be so pleasurable?* It's almost as if I'm afraid I won't be able to shower again. I dry and re-don my Khakis. I have no other clothes. Turner on the other hand has a Hawaiian shirt and a pair of shorts he picked up at the PX in Cam Rahn Bay. Of course they look pretty stupid with his Army oxfords and black sox. He ditches the socks. Our first order of business is to get some civvies. There are at least twenty or thirty stores in the immediate area that will fulfill this need. Every other store along Ala Moana is either a clothing/souvenir shop or a restaurant.

Exiting the elevator and heading for the entrance, we pass the hotel barbershop. The chairs in the shop are filled with men all seemingly enjoying themselves immensely; it's easy to see why. All the *Barbers* are women, not just any women, but beautiful Hawaiian women. They're dressed in the same type of floral sarongs the girls who greeted us at the airport had worn. All of them have hourglass figures and breasts which seem to be fighting against the confinement of the strapless bodices. We watch as they attend to their customers. There is a lot of stroking, rubbing and touching. It's not sexual, but the idea of having such beautiful women attend to you in such a manner is pure hedonism. I'm mesmerized. The men seated in the chairs make no attempt to divert their eyes from the spectacular view spread out so pleasingly before them as the barbers stand in front of them working on their hair. Without saying a word, Turner and I smile and walk into the barbershop.

We wait anxiously for our turn…my hair has never been cut by a woman. Back in Chicago, all the barbers are men. There are no women barbers, at least none that I know of. As a matter of fact, our little shitty laundry/barbershop/massage parlor in Nam only has men barbers.

One of the barbers approaches me smiling; she, like the girls at the airport, has those pure, milky white, almost perfectly aligned teeth. She bends over, holds her hand out, and says, "You're next, hon." *Damn, I love that.*

Her name is Kerilai, unusual to me, but maybe not in Hawaii, I don't know. I take her hand and she guides me to a chair, sits me down and runs her hands through my hair from back to front with her fingers spread apart. It feels really good. She looks into the mirror at my face and smiles, "How short do you want it, babe?" She asks.

"Just a little trim, I don't want it to look like I'm an *Anchor-Yanker.*" *Anchor-Yanker* is a term of endearment GIs use to describe our comrades from the Navy.

"No sweat." She runs her hands across my unshaven cheeks and asks, "How about a shave?" She looks at me in the mirror still stroking my face. She has total control of the situation and knows it. I don't even ask how much, I just nod like a puppy.

Kerilai tilts the chair into a reclined position and from here I'm looking straight up at her. I do not try to avert my eyes. She folds my collar into my shirt to make it collarless, then walks over to a small stainless steel vessel which resembles a tiny front loading washer. She opens the little door and a cloud of steam signals its purpose. She reaches in and removes a steaming towel with a long pair of tongs. As she walks back towards me she tosses the towel into the air twice, presumably because it is too hot to hold. She leans over me and slowly lays the end of the towel on my face. It's hot! Using a circular motion she winds the towel around my face till my face and neck are covered. Hot damp air fills my lungs as I breathe through the towel. Kerilai's hands gently press the towel against my cheeks testing its temperature. When it starts to cool, she removes it. Next, she takes three fingers and starts spreading a cream on my face in slow gentle motions, leaning over me, smiling. It isn't what I'd call shaving cream, but seems more like hand cream or lotion. From behind, she spreads the cream under my jaw with both hands. *Damn, this is incredible!* When she finishes the application of the cream, she opens up her pearl handled straight razor, pulls a strop out from the chair and runs the razor quickly up and down alternating from one side to the other. She puts two fingers on my chin and tilts my head up. Then with a stroke so gentle I barely feel the razor against my skin, she removes the stubbly hair from my face and neck. Her preparations have prepared my beard for the razor's stroke so well that I feel no resistance to the cutting edge of the blade. Then, just like that, the shave is over. She wipes my face and applies after-shave. It hardly stings at all, evidence that my skin has not been irritated in the least bit.

Kerilai sits me up and wraps my neck with a tissue guard, then tucks in the edge of the apron to protect me from falling hair. She cuts my hair slowly and expertly, alternating between scissors and clippers. The haircut is not quite as exhilarating as the shave had been, but her attention and touching still make it something I will not soon forget. When she finishes she adds some tonic or scented water to my hair and gently rubs it in. After the combing, she works her fingers into my shoulders next to my neck, gently caressing the taught muscles. She moves to the back of the neck and again uses her fingers to expertly stimulate the areas around my head and behind my ears. She takes her fingers and strokes across my face lingering around my eyes. As her fingers stroke ever so softly across my closed eyelids, she applies an ever so light pressure making circles with her fingers. She strokes my face for several more seconds, leans forward, her hair brushing the side of my face and whispers in my ear, "You're all done, Hon."

Yes, I think, *this is Paradise*...the price, twenty bucks and a five-dollar tip.

Turner and I walk up and down Kalakaua Street and hit a couple of shops buying what we feel will be enough clothing to last the five-day stay, three Hawaiian shirts, two pair of shorts and some swimming trunks. I cap it off with a pair of mirrored sunglasses and a pair of sandals.

Back in the hotel room we change into our trunks and head for the beach.

The stretch of beach by the Hawaiian Hilton is filling up fast. We grab a couple of beach chairs and a few towels from a little cabana and park ourselves on the beach. We order beers from a waitress who circulates around the pool and beach.

"Man, look at that." I point out a pair of breasts threatening to escape from a bikini top as an exceptionally well endowed woman walks past.

"Jesus."

"Ya know, at least we don't look like we just got off the boat," I comment as I bring the cold bottle of beer to my lips.

Turner looks at me and asks, "Whata'ya mean?"

"Our tans...we've already got good tans from the Nam. We're not gonna look like we just got off the boat and we probably won't have to worry about getting burned."

"Yeah, except for one thing."

"What's that?"

Turner points at our pasty white legs.

"Oh, yeah, I guess you've got a point." We return to our girl watching.

We leave the beach at five after several beers and about an hour-and-a-half of napping. After a quick supper at a small restaurant we end up at a small bar on Kuhio Street. It's more of a local bar than the touristy lounges found on Kalakaua Street. We notice immediately all the men under the age of forty have hair longer than my last girl friend. In Chicago, long haired hippies were still pretty scarce when I left in November of '65, now they seem to be everywhere.

We're on the prowl. We talked it over and felt we probably would have more luck away from the mainstream tourist joints, so we walked around till we found this place.

The bartender refills our glasses and asks, "You guys in the Navy?"

I lower my glass of beer to the bar. "No, we're army. We just got here for some R & R from Vietnam." Turner just smiles and nods his head in agreement.

"Vietnam, damn, they fly you guys all the way here for a weekend pass?" The bartender seems amazed.

"No, man, we're here for R & R. *Rest and Relaxation,* it's like a five day leave." I try to explain.

"So you guys see any action?"

Turner and I look at each other, then back to the bartender, "Nah."

The bartender walks to the other end of the bar seemingly disappointed we aren't going to be relaying any war stories.

"Over there." Turner nudges me and nods his head in the direction of a small table near the Jukebox. Two girls, neither striking, but neither unattractive appear to be alone sipping on a couple of mixed drinks. Both are well tanned with long straight hair that hangs over the backs of their chairs.

"What-a-ya think? Should we send a drink over?" I'm totally ignorant and have had absolutely no experience in a situation like this. All my experience revolves around asking broads in my high school class if they wanted to go on a date. It is immediately evident that Turner is in the same boat but at least has enough common sense to suggest just going over and saying hi.

The two girls look up, smiling, "Hi," is all we can think to say.

"Well, hi to you. You guys in the Navy?"

"No, we're not in the Navy. Can we sit with you girls?"

"Why sure you can." She smiles.

"My name's Simon and this is Turner." I use last names out of habit, not thinking.

"I thought you weren't in the Navy," one of the girls asks.

Turner protests, "We're not! We're not! We're in the Army. We just got here from Vietnam."

"Ohhhh, so that's why you use last names," The other girl chides. Things aren't going as well as we hoped, but the girls haven't told us to leave either.

"Force of habit. He's…" I turn to look at Turner, realizing I don't know his first name.

"John," he says.

"...and I'm Bill. How about you?"

"I'm Sheila and she's Trish."

Turner asks if they're from the island or from the mainland. Both are from California, here, attending the University. We sit and talk through three beers, several jokes, and some funny stories. I'm thinking things are moving in the right direction when we elicit some genuine laughter out of them. I think the odds of scoring tonight are fifty-fifty at this point and sense we've reached a crossroad that will end the night pleasurably or end up with a trip down the road to disappointment.

The bar is filling up; three guys park themselves at the table next to us. They're in their early twenties, long hair, wearing jean cut-offs; Hawaiian shirts, sandals and all three have attitudes. I sense them staring, but ignore it. One of them, a guy wearing only what I can refer to as weenie glasses and earrings, leans over to Sheila and makes the suggestion to dump the Navy trash and move over to their table.

This compels me to lean over and say, "Hey, why don't you fuck off, Jack?"

"Where's your little white hat, Popeye?" is his response.

Trish blurts out, "Hey, bozo, they're not Navy, they're in the Army, they're here from Vietnam, so why don't you cut 'em some slack."

"Nam! Hey, we got us some genuine baby killers here," the wise ass says to his buddies.

I start to get up, but Turner grabs me. "Hey, fuck 'em, they're just a bunch of faggots whose mothers are probably liberal lesbian homos anyway," Turner says intentionally loud.

The guy with the weenie glasses jumps up, Turner's comment has given him what he was looking for, an excuse to start a fight.

"Hey, why don't you sit back down with your two homo buddies before you get hurt." I snipe.

Another one gets up and starts in my direction, but the bartender has tuned in to the action and yells from behind the bar, "Hold it right there! Either take it outside or sit back down!" They glare momentarily and lower themselves back into their chairs.

This is just a temporary delay. I know we've reached the point of no return. There will be no leaving this place without exchanging blows. The bartender should have thrown one group of us out, but he didn't.

I lean over point at weenie glasses' earring and say, "Hey, Buddy, did you know the custom of men wearing earrings originated on pirate ships?"

"No, I didn't know that, so what?"

"Well," I pause as I turn and look at all three of them, "If you wear an earring in your left ear, it means at one time or another you went down with your ship. If you wear one in your right ear, it means you went down *on your ship!*"

Beer shoots from Turner's mouth as he bursts into laughter. The girls, knowing the situation just escalated beyond control, are already heading for the door as weenie boy jumps from his chair. Turner and I are on our feet as weenie-glasses swings and I turn sideways and avoid his initial blows. I come around with my right arm folded leading with my elbow and catch him squarely in the face, knocking him off his feet. I pounce on him. He's trying to push me off as I pummel him with blows to the face. I know his nose is broken and sense he is no longer a threat, but I keep hitting him. I'm trying to kill him. I know it, but can't stop myself. The third guy who hadn't actively participated in the events leading to the melee is out of his chair. He grabs my hair and pulls me off his friend. A left hand catches me on the side of the face and stuns me. This only boosts my adrenaline; I can feel it surge through my veins. I bend over and lunge at him, grabbing him waist high and driving him back against a table, both of us tumbling to the floor. We swing wildly. I open up my mouth and sink my teeth into his thigh. I feel the skin break and taste the warm blood in my mouth. He screams and tries to pull away. I realize how close I am to his vital organs and instantly realize he is at my mercy so I punch him in the nuts as hard as I can. He doubles over and rolls away. I get to my feet and repeatedly kick at his nuts. Suddenly, from behind, the bartender whacks me across the neck with a club or something. It stuns me; I stumble away. Turner grabs my arm and pulls me towards the door. A large crowd of people has gathered around the melee, but has made no attempt to block our exit.

We run a block or so before we slow to a walk. We turn down a side street and keep walking towards the hotel. We hear police sirens in the background, but have no way of knowing whether they are rolling in response to our fracas. As we walk down Kalakaua towards the hotel we see our faces in the windows of closed stores. We're bloody and look like shit. We stop at a gas station to clean up in the men's room.

"Jesus," Turner says as he rinses his face, "I thought you were gonna kill that fucking guy."

"Yeah, I think you're right. I couldn't help myself. It just didn't seem like it was wrong. "I look in the mirror; no black eyes, a couple of scrapes and some bloody knuckles. A year ago I would have gone out of my way to avoid the fight.

"So what the hell was all that baby killer crap?" I ask Turner as we walk.

"Hell, I don't know, you'd think those assholes who claim they're against the war would be a little more sympathetic. I thought they want to end the war and bring us home, they act like we *want* to be over there fighting, jeez, what the fuck's going on?"

"I think they're all full of shit. They're not trying to get us home. They just want to end the war so they won't have to serve. They're just doing what everybody else is doing like a bunch of fucking lemmings."

We're back in the room by midnight, so much for day one.

Day two we were up at ten and we have to be out of the room by eleven. We take quick showers, have coffee, and check out. We rent a car and drive around looking for another room. We find an inexpensive hotel a few blocks off the beaten path knowing we can always walk or drive to the beach. We discover there are no private beaches in Hawaii, so we can pretty much use the beach anywhere we want. The motel is only thirty-five bucks a night and the car is only twenty bucks a day.

Once we're situated, we decide to drive around the island. Fifteen minutes after I get behind the wheel, I look in the rear view mirror and see the flashing lights of a squad car; ten minutes later I'm looking at a traffic ticket for failing to yield to a pedestrian.

"Are you kidding me? Do you believe this shit? I never heard of any crap like this."

Turner shakes his head, "Sounds bogus to me too." The cop told us in Hawaii, if pedestrian steps off the curb, all traffic stops and allows him to cross. *What a bunch of bullshit.*

Turner is smirking. "So you gonna pay the ticket?"

"Yeah, right. I'm not coughing up twenty-five bucks for no stinking ticket. Shit, who knows when I'll ever be in Hawaii again?" I keep my eyes on the road as I talk, "What do you think, should we go to Pearl and see the memorial?"

Turner says, "Yeah, I guess we can do that, or we could hit the beach again. To tell the truth, I'm horny as hell, if I knew where a whore house was I'd be willing to pay."

Turner is faced with the reality that this is day two and at best, he only has one more day till his parents arrive. After that, his chances for scoring will be zero.

We drive to a place offering a boat tour of Pearl and the memorial. We cruise around Pearl for about thirty minutes and end up at the memorial. A good third of the tourists are Japanese, It seems wrong to me. Japanese visiting the memorial at pearl seems morbid, almost evil in a sense. It's like they've come here to gloat. Maybe I'm oversensitive, but I let myself get aggravated watching them snap their pictures. Perhaps the aggravation is a result of the grins constantly besmirching their faces. I can't convince myself they've come here out of remorse. Hell, it was only twenty-six years ago, for all I know, some of them may have been pilots who flew in the attack. *Damn it! I'm not thinking rationally and I'm over reacting.* I know being in Vietnam is implanting the seeds of prejudice in my veins. *Fuck, I'm starting to think like Pinetti.* I shake it off and try to listen to the tour guide.

"Man, look at that," Turner says, pointing over the side railing at the rainbow stained traces of oil. The tour guide claims the oil is still leaking from the Arizona. I'm overwhelmed with the thought that twenty-six years later, we still are warring. It's like nothing has changed. Like no one ever learns the lessons war is so readily trying to teach.

"Hey, you guys come in on the Missouri?" The guy sitting next to Turner asks, we're sitting in a small bar not far from Pearl.

"No man, we just flew in from Nam, we're Army," I answer. "This here's Turner and I'm Simon." I reach across the front of Turner and shake his hand.

"Hey, no shit. Hell, man, I got back from Nam six months ago. I'm Eastman, Bob Eastman. I was piloting marines up and down the coast, making beach landings for a couple of months. I'm trying to remember what they called that operation." He stares off into oblivion trying to remember. "Yeah, we were landing a couple of companies of marines from the first marine division once a week. I guess they were supposed to be catching Charlie off guard or were trying to get in behind Charlie or something like that. They never really told us shit."

"Hey, man, that makes you part of the brotherhood." Turner tells him.

"Brotherhood?"

"Yeah, of Vietnam Vets." Turner takes a big pull on his beer bottle. The brotherhood thing catches me off guard. It is the first time I've ever heard the phrase. I don't need to ask for an explanation. I knew the minute Turner said it the brotherhood existed and would continue to exist till the last Vietnam Vet is wheeled along some Memorial Day parade when he is ninety-eight years old.

Eastman proves to be a source of some very valuable information. There is indeed a red light district in Honolulu located on Hotel Street. He warns us to stay away from the University pukes who have a real hard-on for service people. I relate our previous night's exploits and assure him we are intimately aware of the potential threat. He tells us scoring with a native Hawaiian is a rarity. Typically, because of tradition, it takes weeks or even months of dating to score. Three or four days just isn't going to cut it. He admits that sometimes you can score with mainlander but they often travel in groups and that makes it complicated. Finally, he gives us the scoop on some good places to eat and a couple of good bars where we won't have to worry about getting our heads kicked in.

The bars on Hotel Street are exactly what you'd expect of a red light district. Seedy smoke filled bars packed to the gills with service men, locals and even some long hairs; everybody is there for the same reason. There are hookers all over the place. Some of them are Polynesian, some black, some white, none of them are striking and a lot of them are plain butt ugly. Many of the girls have arrangements that give them use of the rooms over the bars. Access is usually a door and a small hallway outside next to the bar. So far we've been quoted as little as twenty bucks for a blowjob and as much as seventy-five to get some pussy and twenty minutes in a room upstairs. The varying price ranges are directly proportional to the weight and attractiveness of the hooker. Much as I hate to admit it, the girls in Nam were more attractive and much more accommodating. Turner negotiates a blowjob from a black girl that is administered in the back seat of our rented car. I decide not to indulge. I still have at least three more nights to try and score. I'd actually like a little companionship, some romance, some sensuality. Besides, I can always come back to Hotel Street if all else fails. By the time we make it back to the hotel room we're both shit-faced and we crash for the night.

Days three and four are uneventful. Turner moved out the morning of the third day to join his parents. I called home and talked to my family. My mother was out so I didn't get to talk to her. I got a second traffic ticket for not yielding to a pedestrian, arguing with the cop to no avail. The pedestrian stepped off the curb, but it looked to me like he was waiting for me to pass, evidently the cop didn't see it that way.

I went up to see Diamond Head, then got to see Don Ho, Mr. "Tiny Bubbles," at a club in the International Marketplace. I rented a surfboard but after struggling with it for two hours, and never once being able to stand up, I gave up. A bartender rousted me when I got into a heated exchange because the bastard took a twenty from me and brought me change for a five. He thought I was too drunk to notice, but I wasn't. Didn't matter, they threw me out. I fought the temptation to wait for the prick and went back to my hotel.

Day five I get my third ticket...a damned parking ticket. I throw it in the trash along with the others. I have a light breakfast then hang by the pool talking to a couple from Chicago, the Mazurs. Unbelievably, I find they're from my old neighborhood.

The fifth day is coming to a close. It's been an uneventful day. As evening closes in around me I stand on the beach to watch the sun set on Hawaii one last time. By all rights I should be out tearing up the city with total abandon, instead I'm overwhelmed with a need to be alone. I haven't thought of Vietnam in a couple of days and now face a few mere hours of freedom; I have trouble thinking of anything else.

Someone taps me on the shoulder. I turn to see a Japanese woman standing behind me. The lights from the beach lanterns flicker across her face revealing a strikingly beautiful woman.

"Sorry, it's just that you've been standing in the same spot for over an hour. I couldn't help but notice. Is something wrong?" Her English, though impeccable, has that Polynesian flavor to it.

"An hour, I didn't realize I've been here that long. I guess I was just contemplating what awaits me when I get back." I hadn't even noticed her figure, instead, I peer deep into the black pools of her eyes.

"My, you sound as if you are waiting for the executioner." She smiles.

"It might well be that." This surprises her. "I'm on my way back to Vietnam…noon tomorrow. I've been here for five days of R & R."

"R & R?" Her expression changes to one of inquisitiveness.

"Sorry. It's a five day leave. R & R is Army jargon for "Rest and Relaxation."

"Shouldn't you be out terrorizing the city?"

"You would think, but my heart isn't in it. I was just standing here thinking about how much my life has changed in the last ten months. It's as if I've lived two separate lives. My life before Nam that seems so unreal, as if it had all been part of some elaborate dream; leaving me wonder if life could have ever been so simple. Now my life lacks innocence. I see what my life has become and wonder where it will go or if it will even last much longer. Ten months ago I knew nothing. I had never seen the ocean or a mountain. I had never known a woman intimately or seen death or suffering. I had never done things as simple as being in a hotel room, or for that matter, been away from home. I'd never been on a plane, or rented a car. I never saw hunger or knew fear. I never hated anyone or had taken a life." I pause, turn my face away for a moment then turn back and peer into her eyes with a look of desperation. "That's all changed now. I will never be the same again." My eyes water up a little and I turn away. I feel her hand slide into mine and gently close around my fingers. Without speaking she leads me away.

Chapter Twenty

"Rescued"

"Ssshhh." Wilcox holds his finger up to his lips to stop Nance from talking and Nance nods. Wilcox has the headset from his radio stuck to his left ear and his finger stuck in his right. He scrunches his brow and presses his finger tighter against his ear as if this will somehow make the incoming message clearer.

"It's the FDO, he wants you," he says as he hands the headset to Sgt. Fitzpatrick. Fitz takes the headset, listens for about thirty seconds, then says, "Stand by, Sir," he pulls his map out from inside his shirt, unfolds it, traces around with his finger then reads off our coordinates to the FDO. "Roger, sir, we're about a klick-and-a-half away." A look of consternation washes over his face, his head shakes a little, then he hands the handset back to Wilcox.

"Okay, drop the wiring gear. There's a Huey down about a mile from here. The pilot's dead, the co-pilot's trapped; one of the door gunners is down and the other's been trying to get the co-pilot out. Captain Herber wants us to double time it over there and pull them out."

This is a typical wire-stringing job running connections from Delta battery to a couple of forward observation posts. There are eleven of us...four of whom have never even pulled a trigger. *Fuck,* I think, then we move out smartly.

"Sarge, why the hell are we going? Why don't they just fly in there and get them? Hell, it'll take us the better part of an hour just to find them. It doesn't make any sense." *Well, it doesn't make any sense to me,* I think.

Fitzpatrick doesn't turn to look, but says, "Chopper's down in some pretty heavy jungle, they can't fly in there. Someone's got to go in and pull them out to a clearing. Herber says we're the closest thing to a rescue they've got."

"Sounds like a load of bullshit to me." I shake my head and drop back to my spot at the rear.

Lindlay is behind me mumbling. He's down to ten days and a wake up. He should be back at the hill, not out here in the bush.

It isn't very hot, but sweat rolls off our foreheads as we struggle with the elephant grass. It grabs at our feet and pulls at our legs till our calf muscles burn. Nance trips, pitches forward and disappears in the grass, Lindlay and I help him up, Lee grabbing one shoulder, and I the other. We pull him into a sitting position. He's flushed, out of breath and sweating like a pig. I pull my canteen out and pour water over his face.

"Come on, Nance, get your ass moving, we gotta keep up." I kneel next to him urging him to get back on his feet.

"I gotta rest, I gotta rest."

Fitzpatrick looms over us, his face betraying his lack of patience for Nance. "Nance, get your ass moving. There are people out there waiting for us, they're in trouble, they need us, so get on your feet."

"Sarge, Sarge, I need to rest." Nance is wheezing.

"Okay, Nance, you want to rest? You can wait here; we'll pick you up on the way back...Simon, let's move out."

It's easy to see what Fitz is doing. We're up and moving again. When we've distanced ourselves about forty yards, Nance is on his feet waving and shouting for us to wait. When he catches up, I have him take his ammo out of his pack and put it in the thigh pockets of his pants. I unload everything in the pack but the C rations, tossing the crap over my shoulder as we walk.

We march into the setting sun; darkness will be upon us soon. I believe it might actually be safer out here at night than it is humping around in the daylight. The VC can't see any better at night than we can. The only drawback is it'll make locating the downed chopper that much more difficult.

My calves are killing me and I'm afraid they will start cramping, so I wash two salt pills down with a big swallow of water. An hour passes; were cautiously moving into some pretty heavy jungle.

Fitz raises his arm, "Okay, hold 'em up, let's take five." He unfolds his fire direction map and calls in our position to the fire base. It isn't quite dark yet so I take the opportunity to smoke knowing that no cigarettes will be smoked once darkness sets in.

We move out with Nelson on point. He's new and hasn't popped his cherry. I doubt if he's even fired his weapon yet. Putting a new guy on point always has the potential of ending up with disaster. He could lead us right into an ambush. The rest of us will have to be all that much more alert. It would have made more sense having one of us short timers take point, but Fitzpatrick has to get his new guys experience.

Welcome to the Mechanized Artillery, I think sarcastically.

As the darkness soaks up the remaining daylight, Fitzpatrick stops again. We huddle around him peering at the map he's illuminated with the red lens of his flashlight. He points at the map and says, "Okay, look, according to Herber the Huey went down right here and unless I've totally miscalculated our position, it's gotta be around here some fucking place. It's gonna be hard to find and anybody still alive is gonna be trigger-happy. We all know there is a lot of VC activity around here and you know a chopper going down is bound to draw a lot of interest. We don't want to walk into an ambush, so you guys better keep your eyes and ears open and no fucking noise. Let's close it up, we don't want to get separated." He points at Johnson, Lindlay, Nance and Nelson. "You guys take the rear; we don't want any fucking gooks sneaking up behind us. Got it?" They nod in agreement.

We keep close, only three or four yards apart. I push the leaves quietly out of the way and move three or four steps forward. I pause, then look left and right to make sure I can still see Turner and Prosek. We peer into the darkness trying to recognize the panorama of black silhouettes. The quiet accentuates every little sound made as we creep through the jungle, every blade of grass crushed by one of our boots, every leaf or branch moved by an advancing body, every breath we exhale. The canopy is thick and prevents any celestial light from improving visibility. Perhaps, when the moon is high in the sky it may help, but till that happens it's gonna be pitch black. I once again check my field of vision then wave my arm forward and we move out.

"Pssst." I turn to my right. Prosek has his arm up and points to his ear. We stop, and try to pick up whatever sound he's detected.

What is that? I wonder. I listen more intently. It's moaning, a low anguished moan emerging out of the blackness to our right.

There is temptation to run in the direction of the sound but we hold our ground...this is a very dangerous situation. The goddamn VC may have left the chopper alone just so they could ambush the rescue team...us.

The moaning is like a beacon of light leading us through the darkness. It takes ten minutes of cautiously pushing our way through the bush, but there it is. The Huey is lying on its side. The tail snapped off, the windshield popped out, and only one blade of the rotor still attached to the engine.

Cautiously, we move in. Fitzpatrick and the rest of the squad take cover positions and I creep around to the front of the Huey. I take my flashlight and shine it into the cockpit. *Jesus.* The pilot is in his seat, impaled by a piece of broken rotor. I know without checking he's dead. The co-pilot is the one moaning. I shine my light on him..."What the fuck?" Blood oozes out of his eye sockets down his face and soaks the front of his shirt. One of his legs is broken and bent in an unnatural position.

I lean in, "Can you hear me? Can you hear me?"

"My God!" Fitzpatrick is standing next to me. "What the fuck happened to his eyes?"

"VC, VC," the co-pilot mumbles.

"The VC did this to your eyes?" Fitzpatrick asks.

"VC," is all he says.

"Come on; let's get him out of there." Fitzpatrick crawls through the windshield. He manages to de-skewer the pilot and we pull his body out of the chopper. Prosek and Fitzpatrick unstrap the co-pilot and remove the debris pinning him in. He screams when we straighten his leg. He screams again and again till we have him lying on the ground in front of the chopper...he passes out from the pain. We use the opportunity to splint the leg with a piece of metal debris from the chopper.

One of the door gunners is laying dead in the bushes...his neck broken. This is evident from the way his head hangs limply back between his shoulder blades. He must have been thrown from the chopper.

"Where's the other door gunner?" Lindlay asks.

"I don't know. Maybe he took off when the VC came," Fitzpatrick says.

"Should we spread out and sweep the area?" I wave my arm in the direction of the jungle.

"No, it's too risky." Fitzpatrick takes the headset from Wilcox and radios in. He conveys his report, listens and then replies, "Yeah, I roger that, sir. Just what the hell are we supposed to do?" There's a pause while he listens, then he says, "Yeah, yeah, I roger that." Fitzpatrick tosses the headset back to Wilcox in disgust. "Nobody's comin' till daylight. Herber suggests we start humpin' the co-pilot out and not wait around till the morning. He says, 'It could be dangerous.'" Fitz crawls through the windshield again and roots around the back of the chopper emerging several seconds later with a canvas stretcher.

"Okay, let's get him on this so we can get the hell out of here." It's easy to see he's not happy. We lift the co-pilot and lay him on the stretcher. His voice gurgles and he begins moaning again. Blood is still oozing out of his eye sockets and running down his face into his mouth. None of us have a first aid packet but Lee roots around the chopper till he finds the first aid kit. We bandage up the eyes as best we can.

"They took him…they took Moss," He moans.

Fitzpatrick gets down next to him and talks into his ear. "They took Moss? Is Moss the door gunner? How long ago?"

"Moss, door gunner." He mumbles. "VC took him." Then he lapses back into a pain free state of unconsciousness.

Fitz takes his flashlight and starts walking around, inspecting the ground and jungle. "They went this way." He holds some broken leaves in his hand. He kneels down next to the co-pilot and shakes him. "How many VC? How many VC?"

The co-pilot moves his head towards Fitzpatrick's voice. "VC cut my eyes, they cut my eyes."

"What about Moss? Did they kill him? How many VC?" Fitzpatrick continues shaking him.

"VC, eight, maybe ten, they took Moss." He gurgles and chokes the words out, then again lapses into unconsciousness.

Fitz stands up and turns his head in the direction he believes the VC have gone. He stares thirty or forty seconds, "Okay, we're goin' after him. They can't have more than a half hour or so head start on us and certainly won't be expecting anybody to come after them. Look, you three stay here with the copilot." Fitz points at Turner, Nelson and Nance.

"You gotta be shittin' me," Turner says.

"Hey, the VC were already here, it's unlikely they'll come back." Fitz tries to reassure them. "The VC got what they wanted. You can dig in there behind the chopper and as long as you keep him from moanin' nobody'll know you're here." Fitzpatrick turns to Wilcox, and tells him to give the radio to Turner. If we ain't back by daylight, you call in for extraction. They already know where you are. Then you send them lookin' for us. You got that?" Fitz waits for Turner to nod his head.

"Yeah, I got ya, Sarge." Turner and Nelson immediately start digging a foxhole.

The rest of us huddle around Fitzpatrick. "Okay, I know what you guys are thinking, but there's a good chance we can catch up with these bastards. If they were going to kill the guy, they would have done it here. If we let them make it to daylight, we'll never be able to surprise them and the poor bastard will end up getting tortured to death in some shitty little village somewhere. We ain't gonna let that happen, are we?"

We all mumble, "No, Sarge."

Fitz senses the reluctance, so he tries to encourage us. "Believe me, we've got a lot going for us. The VC aren't going to be travelin' all night, and they might be from a village near here. Hopefully we can catch up with them before they get back to where they came from and they aren't going to be moving very fast draggin' Moss along with 'em. When we catch up with 'em we'll smoke 'em before they know what happened." Fitzpatrick pauses a few seconds, then adds, "What if it was one of you? Okay, let's grease up and move out. Simon take point."

Black and green sticks of camouflage paint cover our faces with patterns that will keep them from reflecting light and break up the outline of our features. We drop all of our unnecessary gear, then reluctantly move out into the dark oblivion of unfamiliar jungle: eight men blinded by darkness, with no way of really knowing whether we are even going in the right direction. I run all of Fitzpatrick's arguments through my mind and conclude he's right. If Moss is ever going to survive, it will depend on our ability to find him this dark night in 1967.

The jungle is heavy, but I've seen worse. The air is thick with mosquitoes. The warm carbon dioxide we exhale attracts them, I only wish I could use repellant to fend them off but know I can't. Our movement is fast, faster than I would have thought. Twice we stop so Fitzpatrick can inspect the area and insure we're still on the trail of the VC. The first time, we found a chewed wad of Beetel nut and footprints from an unknown number of men. The second time because we are overwhelmed by the smell from a fresh pile of crap. It could have been an animal, but Fitz finds it, pokes it a few times and decides it is human… it's still warm.

"How's he know it's still warm?" Wilcox asks.

"I think he can tell by the taste." We smile and take to the jungle.

Wilcox and I hear it at the same time. We signal and drop to the ground. Fitzpatrick moves up between us and we point to our ears, then point in front of us. We hold our breath and listen intently. There...I hear it again... barely audible voices. I crawl to a position behind a tree, lean against the tree and slide up till I am standing. The moon is low in the sky, but the light it provides is unnecessary. Through the bushes and leaves of the jungle I can see small traces of light flickering and darting around in an eerie dance. Peering through the underbrush I realize the light is from the flame of a little stove. A small little device, maybe a little bigger than a canteen. A VC is using it to warm his food or make his coffee. There are a couple of arms, the silhouette of somebody blocking the light as they pass between me and the flame, but I'm unable to discern how many VC there are or if Moss is among them.

I slide back down and whisper in Fitzpatrick's ear, "VC, Sarge. We need to get closer."

Fitz pulls Lindlay close, "We need a better look. Lee, you and Martin get the sixty set up over there." He points to a clump of trees. "When we go you're gonna have to lay down some heavy fire." Then he turns to Wilcox and me, our heads close enough to be kissing. He whispers, "You guys get in there for a closer look. The only sound I want to hear is the moonlight hitting the ground."

Wilcox takes the lead; we edge our way to the right staying crouched. Take a step or two, then pause and wait. We listen for the voices knowing that if they're still talking, we're okay. It's a slow process.

We flank out about ten yards and start to press forward. I stop and drop to one knee. I motion to Wilcox and lower myself to a prone position. Crawling forward inches at a time, keeping my body glued to the ground, almost sliding, propelled by my knees and elbows. I reach a point where a small opening through the bushes gives me a good view of the camp. There are three VC squatting around the little stove, its light casting bizarre shadows across their faces. Two more are lying behind them, maybe asleep, or trying to sleep. To the right I spot our man, he's on his knees, legs bent up behind him, ropes holding his lower body to the tree in such a way that his upper torso leans out away from the tree. His hands are tied behind him and then to the tree. Three VC, two sitting, another standing, are antagonizing him for entertainment. The one standing leans down in his face and says something; the other two laugh, then he slaps him, the little cocksucker. I fight the urge to jump up and blast the little bastard. Ironically, if the little pricks weren't making so much noise we probably would have had a lot more trouble finding them, not to mention being able to get this close...we're only ten yards away.

I back up a little and scrunch around towards Wilcox...I flash four fingers twice. He repeats the signal back to me to confirm the count of eight. I turn my attention back to the VC. I move my finger up to the safety on my M-14 and move it to the off position.

There's a tug on my boot...it's Fitzpatrick. He crawls in next to me and peers through the hole.

No words are spoken. He draws a circle in the dirt with his finger. He makes marks indicating the VC. He points at me, then at Wilcox. Then he points to the marks indicating the VC taunting Moss. I know what he wants. As he disappears into the bushes Wilcox begins the snail's crawl to get up next to me.

We agree on an action plan using hand gestures. It's simple: We wait for Fitzpatrick, and then we go.

Seconds pass...the prospect of charging into a VC camp makes the passage frighteningly slow. The three VC sitting around the stove are sipping some tea. Two of Moss's antagonists have lost interest and appear to be resting on beds of leaves and brush. The other one is still tormenting Moss. I know who my first target is going to be and I know there will be no remorse for this kill.

No telling how much time has passed, I start to worry whether or not my muscles are going to stiffen up. Wilcox has crawled ten feet to my right so we won't be tripping over each other and it separates us as targets.

Come on, let's get this fucking show on the road, I think. Then without warning, *Bratta...brat...bratta...brat!* Martin and Pinetti trace a trail of fire across the sleeping VC. My little antagonist whips around at the sound of the first shot and freezes with a look of disbelief on his face.

Wilcox is on his feet charging through the bushes firing. I stand, bring my rifle to my shoulder and draw a bead on the little cocksucker. He dives for his AK-47; I fire and see the round smack him in his upper right shoulder. The round knocks him back. I squeeze my trigger and see his body jerk three more times as my rounds rip through his flesh. Wilcox has his M-16 three inches from the head of a VC who raises his arms over his head and has a look of terror in his eye. Another made the mistake of going for his gun and now lays dead, blood pouring from two wounds in the chest.

"Cap the little bastard," Pinetti yells.

Martin echoes Pinetti's sentiment. "Go ahead, squeeze the trigger." Instead Wilcox steps back and motions for the VC to stand. The VC stands up, hands locked behind his head.

Fitzpatrick is already at the tree cutting Moss down.

"Get over here and give me a hand," he calls out. Wilcox runs over to help. I take control of the VC and sit him down. Pinetti and Martin are checking bodies.

"Hey, this one's still breathing," Pinetti, says.

"Fuck 'em, just keep your eyes on this prick." Fitzpatrick turns his attention to Moss. He takes out his canteen and pours water over Moss's face, then holds the canteen up to his lips. "How bad are you hurt, can you walk?" Fitz asks.

"I…I...my…shoulder...I think my arm's pulled out of the socket."

Fitz probes, "Can you stand up? We gotta get the fuck outta here. Every VC within two miles is gonna be homing in on us."

He tries to stand, but can't. He falls and cries out in pain. He tries again and fails. Wilcox grabs his arm and helps him stand. Moss, wobbling, reaches out with his left arm to steady himself on Fitzpatrick's shoulder.

"He…he's the one, that's the bastard." Moss points at the VC sitting with his hands locked behind his head.

"Huh? He's the one what?" Fitzpatrick asks.

Moss labors when he speaks, but nods his head in the direction of the VC. "He…he cut Sullivan's eyes."

There's no need for clarification. Sullivan must be the copilot. Fitzpatrick whips around, his eyes pools of hatred, Wilcox slides his arm under Moss's as Fitz releases him. As Fitz advances on the VC, his right hand is busy un-holstering his forty-five. He says nothing, just walks directly up to the VC, sticks the forty-five in his right eye and pulls the trigger. The VC's skull erupts, spewing out bone and brains, leaving a gaping hole big enough to put your fist in. He folds like a wet blanket.

"Holy shit!" Martin exhales. The rest of us turn away matter-of-factly as if nothing has happened, feeling perhaps that Fitz had been too benevolent and castration may have been a more fitting payback.

"Come on, let's dee-dee, we've got to get the fuck out of here." Fitzpatrick is moving and Moss is trying to move his legs. The first few steps are shaky, but he improves after a few strides. Five minutes later we're moving quickly through the bush back towards the downed chopper. Moss is doing okay, but every branch that rubs against his right shoulder makes him wince with pain.

We're not out of shithouse and we know it. If there are any other VC around our gunfire will draw them to the campsite like a magnet. The other problem is navigating through the dark jungle and finding our way back to the downed chopper. The moon is high in the sky now and that helps, but Fitzpatrick will be much more reluctant to light up his flashlight than he was before.

Forty minutes into the withdrawal we stop for a breather. I open a can C rats I have in my pack. Cheese and crackers, hell, I don't have time to fart around with this, so I scoop the entire contents out with one cracker and stuff it in my mouth. I wash it down with the last of the water in my canteen. I use my hand to scoop away some dirt and bury the empty can. We sit for a few more minutes, none of us making a sound. The only sound to be heard is the sound of everyone's labored breathing. There is no other noise.

Fitzpatrick is in the process of standing, when we hear it…movement, heavy movement. We freeze and listen. Undoubtedly, they're VC trying to run us down. Fitzpatrick and Lindlay are frozen; crouched with their weapons ready. In the darkness the VC manage to blow right by us, missing us completely.

"Well, what the hell are we gonna do now?" Prosek asks.

"Looks like we better find our way back to that chopper or Turner, Nance and Nelson are gonna be up shits creek," I answer.

"Simon's right," Fitz says. The gooks are probably following the trail we left comin' from the chopper. We've got two choices: We can move out in a different direction to avoid the gooks, but if they get to the chopper before us...well...our guys are dogshit." Fitzpatrick doesn't say what the other choice is because we already know.

"Okay, then, let's get down there before Turner starts whining about not having any place good to take a shit." I quip. Two of us donate our belts to strap Moss's right arm tight against his body. Fitzpatrick gives Moss his forty-five and three spare magazines and we move out. We jog to the left and fall in behind the VC. They're two or three minutes ahead of us. We have to be careful not to overtake them and turn this into a disaster.

We're moving quickly now, not quite a run, but pretty damn fast. We're making a hell of a lot of noise, more noise than I would want to make moving through here in the daylight. With the moon high in the sky and the canopy thinning a little, vision is improved dramatically. Something inside of me, that little voice, the one that usually tries to warn me that something isn't quite right, is tugging at me. I can see Lindlay up ahead of me start to slow a little then slowly raise his arm. He crouches, turns and looks back at me, listening; I pass the signal along. We listen…the VC column is on our right. They're moving cautiously through the bush...then *they* stop. They've heard us.

We're facing right, our weapons ready, waiting. The sound of a rustle, or leaves being crushed underfoot, the tiniest of sounds, will alert either squad to the others position.

Wait…don't wait? My finger is pressing on the trigger waiting for my mind to make the decision.

Pinetti makes the decision for us. "*Mother…Fuckers!*" He opens up with his M-16. Prosek's M-60 starts strafing the jungle in back and forth movements. I concentrate my fire lower, maybe a foot off the ground, knowing that as soon as the first round was fired the VC dove to the ground - just like we did. It takes about fifteen seconds to empty my magazine. Smoke and chewed up jungle fill the air. There's yelling, cursing and screaming. Fitzpatrick takes a round in his left thigh. Martin screams, but I can't tell how bad he's been hit. I lock in my third magazine when a VC appears out of the jungle in front of me. He doesn't see me, he's looking and firing to the right. I lunge up and jam my M-14 into his side squeezing the trigger. I pump three rounds into him and turn to my left to find Lindlay wrestling with another VC. Lee has both his hands locked around the barrel of the AK-47 pushing it up and out of the way. I swing my rifle around and am about to pull the trigger when they both tumble to the ground. I take two steps toward them, but Lee wrestles the weapon away, twists it around and fires two quick bursts, stands up and empties the rest of the magazine into the darkness of the jungle. He retrieves his M-16 and we turn our attention back to the rest of the squad. Several minutes of intense and close combat pass; Fitzpatrick starts waving his arm frantically, signaling us to stop.

Quiet…it's dead quiet. A cloud of smoke and the smell of cordite fill the air. My eyes keep racing back and forth expecting to see VC charging through the bush. More adrenaline is pumping through our veins than blood. A moan from the jungle breaks the silence.

I look in Fitz's direction. He looks first at Lee, then back at me and signals to move forward. He turns and does the same thing to Prosek and Pinetti. We look back and forth at each other and move ahead slowly. We push our way tentatively through the bush. At my feet lay a dead VC; I'm tempted to turn him face up to see if he's dead, but don't. Lee is only three feet to my left. I snap my fingers and point at the VC. Lee nods. We never roll 'em over or move bodies till they've been checked for booby traps. They haven't exactly had a lot of time in the last two minutes to set traps, but fuck, ya never know. *Doesn't take very long to pull the pin on a grenade and wedge it under a body.*

Fitzpatrick asks, "Well?" is all he says.

I hesitate a little then say, "Sarge, there ain't no point in us rootin' around the jungle checkin' the dead. They have to be gone or they would have popped me."

Doesn't take Fitz long to mull this over, "Yeah, let's just get the fuck out of here."

I try to see if anyone is badly hurt. Martin is bleeding from the left side of his head. A VC round took a big chunk of his ear off. *Bet he won't go out without his steel pot again,* I think. Fitzpatrick's uses his tee shirt to bandage his thigh wound. Everybody else is okay.

"Okay, let's move out." Fitzpatrick is limping badly. Prosek finishes tying his bandana around Martin's wound, grabs the M-60 and we move out.

We limp along for another twenty minutes when Fitzpatrick stops us. He leans back against a tree - he's really in pain - he grimaces a few times, then says, "The chopper should be right around here. Simon, you and Lindlay scout around till you find it. We'll wait here. Watch your ass, those guys are gonna be trigger happy."

The skin on Fitz's face, though still partially painted, is now reflecting moonlight and reveals the expression of pain he is trying to control. He's sweating badly and has wiped most of the grease paint off his face with his shirtsleeve. He points to the right, "My best guess would be over that way. I wouldn't venture more than fifty or sixty yards in any direction. If you don't find it, come back."

Lee and I start creeping through the bush again. We inch along for about thirty yards when I reach out and grab Lee's sleeve to stop him. He looks at me and I point to some debris in the bush at my feet, a piece of panel from the Huey. I point in the direction I want to go.

"Snap!" A branch snaps under my foot.

"Bratta…bratta…brat." Lee and I dive to the ground as the M-16 rounds rip through the bush.

"Check your fire! Check your fire!" I yell, with the side of my head flat against the ground, my free arm trying to cover my head.

Turner yells from his concealed position. *"Simon? Is that you?"*

"Who the fuck you think it is, you dumbass," I yell back. We wait a few seconds and stand up. We hear movement behind us and whip around ready to drop the hammer. It's Fitzpatrick and the rest of the squad.

"I warned ya," Fitzpatrick laughs as he limps past. We move into the partial clearing; as we do, Turner and Nance emerge from their hole, quickly followed by Nelson.

"Man, what the hell happened to you guys?" Turner asks seeing Fitz's bandaged leg and Martin's blood soaked ear patch.

"What the hell do you think happened, dick breath?" I'm a little edgy about Turner opening up on us. "Man, that was a stupid thing to do," I grumble.

"Hey, sorry, but we've heard boucoup movement around here all night. When we heard you guys, we thought it was VC movin' in."

"Shit, shit, shit!" Fitz cranks his head back and forth cursing. "Man, if the gooks didn't know where you were before, they sure do now. Damn it! I was hoping to sit tight till daybreak. We're all fucking drained, damn it. Okay, Turner and Nelson take the first turn at carrying the stretcher we've got to get out of here."

Turner's face goes blank and he looks in Moss's direction. "Sarge, the copilot's dead, he died about an hour ago." We look at Moss, we can tell by the look on his face he wishes he'd been the one to drop the hammer on the VC Fitzpatrick capped.

Wilcox retrieves the radio and Fitz puts in a call to the fire base. Finally he says, "Sir, we're moving out now, we can't wait till daylight." He tosses the handset back to Wilcox.

We march, drudge, through the bush and out into the elephant grass heading east, back towards the fire base. The level of adrenaline in my blood-stream subsides as we move away from the jungle. Weakness starts throbbing through my limbs. I'm overcome with fatigue. I feel as if I will be unable to walk another dozen steps. As light washes across the landscape, illuminating the greased faces of my comrades, it is evident fatigue is overcoming all of us, yet we continue moving, our legs moving automatically, as if driven by a mind of their own.

From out of the sun, now breaching the horizon, we see the silhouettes of three Hueys headed in our direction. I turn and look at Moss, and know whatever life he lives from here on out will be a bonus, the price we paid for it, well, was a bargain, it was a real bargain.

Chapter Twenty-One

"Swan's Song"

March 28th, five days and a wake up. Most of my gear is already packed. For ten straight days, I've managed to avoid any field assignments and have enjoyed the relative safety of the Hill.

A couple of weeks ago I stood on the tarmac at Pleiku Airbase and watched Lindlay and his venereal warts board a plane headed for Cam Rahn Bay, from there he would take a civilian plane back to Washington State and be processed out at Fort Lewis.

Pinetti and I are anxiously awaiting our orders, hoping for once the army will screw up in our favor and we'll get out of here a couple of days early…so far, no such luck.

It's noon; Wilcox and I are hangin' out in the commo bunker, he's tinkering around with some radio equipment and I'm trying to stay awake. I glance at my watch, realize it's lunch time and suggest getting some chow. Wilcox finishes the beer he's drinking, tosses the can in the corner.

He asks matter-of-factly, "Still no orders, huh?"

"Naw, man, we ain't heard nothin'," the disappointment clearly detectable in the tone of my voice.

"Yeah, I can imagine. Farmly bitched about it all day yesterday he came in with you guys, right."

"Yeah, him, Fishe and me, Pinetti was a few days later," I push open the screen door to the mess hall. *Fuck man, I hope these assholes haven't fucked up and forgotten when I got here.*

Later, lying in my cot, one hand behind my head, the other hand toying with my dog tags, I stare at them blankly. I finger them and run my thumb over the embossed writing. I hook my fingernail on the little notch and flick it a couple of times. *These,* I think, *are the true badge of honor.* The simple fact that they still hang around my neck and aren't jammed between my teeth are a measure of success. Hell, depending on your perspective, they're the *only* measure of success. I drop the tags and roll over on my side. Just as I'm about to fall asleep, Fitzpatrick's gravelly voice startles me.

Standing in the middle of the room with one hand on his hip, Fitzpatrick's head sweeps around the room proving to himself that he has everyone's attention.

"Listen Up. We're movin' out at 04:30. We chopper out of Camp Holloway at 05:00 hrs. Get your gear together…then get some sack time."

Wilcox, standing across from my bunk, asks, "What's up, Sarge? Where we headed? What's the detail?"

Fitzpatrick, whose wound turned out to be no more than a deep flesh wound, is still favoring his leg, answers, "Plei Mrong. We're going in to set up a fire base perimeter, it'll be us and the engineers; they'll airlift the big cats in once a perimeter is established."

"Man, what the fuck...are you shittin' me? This is a load of bullshit." I'm on the edge of my cot now, feeling acid drain into my stomach.

Fitzpatrick walks over and looks down at me, then turns to look at everybody else. "Look, the old man says the G-2 report on Plei Mrong is relatively clear. We've done this shit before."

"Yeah, well if there's no VC, what the fuck are they sending Delta battery up there for? Christ, I'm down to five days and a wake up," I complain knowing that nothing is going to change.

"We're goin', maintenance is going, and the support guys from Delta Battery are goin' so there should be about fifty or sixty of us...piece of cake."

His comments carry a tone of finality to them, I know I'm goin'. No amount of bitching is going to change it. *Less than a damn company…Shit, we're always goin' under-fucking- strength.*

Sons-a-bitches! I wad up my fatigue blouse and slam it into the floor. I grab my pack and start rolling my poncho. *Cocksucker!* I jam the poncho into the pack. I pull ten magazines from my footlocker and stuff six of them into the pack. *Man, this is bullshit, just a big load of fucking bullshit.* I sit on the edge of my cot mindlessly disassembling my M-14. *Can you fucking believe this shit?* I pull the crate of grenades out from under my bunk and clip two of them to my harness. *All this time...I'm so close...*

I change my socks, put on my jungle boots and dress. I slip a magazine under the elastic band on my helmet and set it next to my flak jacket. I walk down to the end of the barrack where several cases of C rations are stacked. I pick through them, grab one that appeals to me and walk back to my bunk. *I can't fucking believe this shit, I put in my time, I never fucking bitched, I took my licks, what the fuck do they want from me?* I double check my gear and flop onto my cot; my stomach retches.

Pinetti stops at the foot of my cot and says, "Maybe if we ask Top, he'll keep us back here at the hill, maybe he doesn't know we're down to five days. Whata'ya think?"

"I think this is bullshit, man, just fucking bullshit. They fucking know, they'll just say it ain't like we're shippin out tomorrow."

Pinetti adds his bitching and moaning to my own and goes back to pack his gear.

Acid continues pouring into my stomach. Minutes drag into hours and still I lay staring up at the mosquito netting over my cot. *Just one more time,* I think, *just one more fucking time.* I light a cigarette and watch the glow of the ember intensify as I suck air through the tightly rolled stick of tobacco. The cigarette burns out and I drop the butt into the coffee can of water next to my bunk. I look at my watch; It's almost midnight. I think about getting up to take a piss, but can't bring myself to do it. I light another cigarette; there will be no sleeping tonight. "Fucking bastards," I mumble.

I'm already pulling on my flak jacket when Fitzpatrick comes through the hooch to wake everyone, my eyes burning with the graininess that accompanies a lack of sleep. I walk out of the hooch heading for the mess hall my boots feeling as though the soles are made of lead.

In the chow line I stare at the food, not wanting any of it. I scoop eggs and burnt bacon on the tray, add a couple of pieces of dry toast and a small glass of juice. I'm oblivious to everyone else in the mess hall. I use my fork to push the watery powdered eggs around on the tray; then lay the fork back down without actually using it to put any food in my mouth. I pick up the toast and take a small bite. The bread sits in my mouth un-chewed till my saliva softens it and instinctively I swallow. I down two cups of coffee and go back to the hooch.

On the edge of my cot, in full gear, I wait, my feet sweating inside my boots. *Just one more time...*

We load into the back of the trucks and sit on the little wooden benches on either side of the canvass-covered bed. No one speaks. We sway and bounce as the trucks roll down the road towards the gate, our gear clanging around on the floor. The muscles in the back of my neck stiffen. The front brim of my helmet cuts across my eyes and I look beyond the edge at the faces of everybody in the truck. Exhaust fumes from the vertical exhaust stack permeate through the rear of the truck and make my eyes water.

The ride to Holloway seems excruciatingly long. We dismount just as the faintest amount of light becomes visible on the eastern horizon. I hear the *thwack, thwack, thwack* of rotor blades from the idling choppers. We sit and wait for the signal to load and I use the opportunity to light a cigarette which is smoked in four large drags. Captain Wallace huddles with the NCOs to pass out instructions. When they finish he walks down the Tarmac barking orders.

"Okay, on your feet, let's saddle up." He's waving his arm in the air as he walks by. Begrudgingly, I get to my feet immediately becoming aware of the nausea in the pit of my stomach. As I begin walking towards the choppers, the nausea overwhelms me and I turn to the side and retch, vomit spewing from my mouth. I wipe my mouth and rinse with water from my canteen. I take a few deep breaths, rinse again and then climb into my assigned ship.

The choppers lift off one by one from front to back. They hover a few feet off the ground then slowly tilt forward gaining altitude and speed. They bank into a right hand turn and join up in formation.

The early morning temperature is in the low seventies but sweat rolls down the small of my back. I turn my damp palms up to look at them, and wipe them on the sides of my fatigues. My head falls back against the bulkhead of the chopper. My stomach spasms a few times wanting to retch once again, but I manage to control it. My eyes focus on the door gunner who straps in a belt for his M-60. He pulls the operating rod back and fires a quick burst. My eyes move to the ceiling of the cabin. "Just one more time," I whisper.

We fly into the daylight then turn north. The door gunner leans over and shouts, "Fifteen minutes," then flashes his hand, palm facing us and fingers spread to signal his verbal message making sure we all understand.

As we near our LZ the choppers drop down to tree top level and approach Plei Mrong from the southeast. This time there will be no sudden turns only the back-tilt of the choppers as they brake and plop onto the ground just long enough for us to dismount. I crouch down and quickly move out of range of the rotors, my eyes glued to the jungle that surrounds the clearing. The clearing is almost arena like. I feel like a Christian in the coliseum waiting for the lions to be released.

The choppers are gone and we're standing in the middle of the clearing covered with two-foot high elephant grass. The jungle is three hundred yards in almost every direction. Some of it covers the foothills of some small mountains that rise up a half-mile or so to the west.

We fall in behind Fitzpatrick who has taken control of fifteen men. He is leading us in the direction of the jungle.

"We'll spread out and dig some holes between that clump of trees and those bushes over there." Fitzpatrick points to the landmarks. I momentarily look behind me and find the other groups moving in different directions. An almost indistinguishable sound from off in the distance freezes me. I hear it again and launch myself to the ground. As I hit the ground I hear the first mortar round come whistling in; *"Incoming!"*

"Whump! Whump! Whump! Three mortar rounds detonate twenty or thirty yards behind us. I hear Nelson yell and turn to see him wrenching around trying to grab his back. I grab him by the shoulders and roll him over. I'm surprised to find he has a bullet wound! Suddenly, I realize bullets are zipping all around us. I try to pinpoint the origin of the weapons fire, it only takes a moment to realize an immense amount of small arms fire is raining down on us from the jungle to the north and the jungle to the east putting us in a deadly cross-fire.

Son-of-a-bitch! We've been dropped right in the middle of a fucking hotbed of VC or NVA!

Fitzpatrick yells, "Fall back! Fall back!"

Mortar rounds continue detonating around us. We're out in the open with little or no cover; we're in a crossfire and we're outnumbered by god knows how many.

Once we regroup we try to form a defense using what little cover there is and return fire frantically. Captain Wallace, in a panic, is trying to relate our situation to operations back at the hill, calling desperately for support and evacuation. Prone in the grass, just like everybody else, I see someone lying face down a few feet from me who appears to be dead. The temptation to roll over and use his body for cover runs through my head, but I can't bring myself to do it because I'm not sure he's dead. We have five M-60 machine guns on our side which are trying to lay down a suppressing fire. M-79 grenade launcher rounds are being fired as fast as they can be loaded.

I stare out past the flash suppressor of my rifle; all I can see is jungle. I can't even distinguish muzzle flashes in the bright morning light and it's even worse looking towards the eastern jungle because it's looking directly into the rising sun. *We're fucked.*

"The little pricks couldn't have waited a couple of more days for this shit," I mutter.

Again, Wallace is on the horn trying to get our asses out of here. A minute later a pair of A1E Skyraiders thunder in from the south. Salvos of rockets pound the foothills where we believe the mortars are, then each plane makes several strafing passes over the NVA positions, machine guns blazing.

"You've got to evac us out of here; we have heavy casualties and are under attack!" Wallace listens to the reply, then yells into the handset, "I don't give a fuck what G-2 says, we're getting slaughtered out here, they're cutting us to pieces!"

"The choppers are on their way…maybe twenty minutes," Wallace says.

I come to terms with the inevitability of the situation and realize I am about to die. Fifteen minutes under fire is an eternity, especially when you're surrounded and caught in the open with no cover.

I slap a new magazine into my rifle. I'm down to three. We've fallen back well short of our original LZ. Off in the distance a staccato thwack, thwack, thwack signals incoming choppers...I can see eight or nine inbound Hueys. Two of them split off maneuvering into position to strafe the jungle. The other choppers start setting down forty or fifty yards behind us and instinctively, people begin loading the wounded as fast as humanly possible. The first three choppers lift off with nothing but wounded.

Men pile into the remaining choppers. "Come on, come on," I mumble waiting my turn. Then I'm up, running towards one of the two choppers. *I'm almost there…just a few more strides…come on, come on…*The chopper door is almost within reach, something slams into the back of my leg and I hurtle forward, landing on my face. It feels as if someone took a sledgehammer and pounded a red-hot poker into my calf. The searing pain shoots through my body, bringing the howl of a wounded animal to my lips. I fight the temptation to roll over and grab my leg.

Instead, I keep trying to get to my feet. I can see only one chopper now, I see the men standing in the door screaming and waving at me, the M-60 chattering away, shaking the door gunner's body. I try to stand, lunge forward and fall again. Warm liquid runs down my leg, saturating the inside of my boot. I try to get to my feet using my rifle as a crutch, take a couple of excruciating steps and start to pitch forward. As I fall, hands grab me and arms slide under mine. "Come on, come on, get your ass in gear," someone yells in my ear. Multiple hands yank and grab trying to drag me on the chopper. Even before my body is completely on board, the chopper wrenches hard to the right nearly ejecting me from its safety. It moves away leaving the NVA behind us. When enough altitude is gained and we're out of harms way, the door gunner leans over to me, "You okay? You gonna make it? I look up look...I can't believe it...it's Moss!

He leans forward, grabs my shoulder and says, "We picked up your radio calls and I told the Captain you were the guys that saved my ass. He knows everything so he decided we could make a little detour." He smiles and gives me the thumbs up.

My calf burns like hell; someone is applying a first aid dressing to it. I don't even look to see who it is. I lay back against the cold metal with a single thought going through my mind...*the last time, it was the last time.* Tears run down the sides of my face. I reach into my shirt and clutch my dog tags.

April 3rd, 1967. I watch the Vietnam coast disappear from the window of the 707. The images that flash through my mind will be with me always. Whatever lay ahead for me will forever be influenced by what I'm leaving behind. I wonder, "*What difference had we made?*"